W9-DBN-947

ALMOST 24½ YRS. Love, D. 1/18/68

BPD-F35005   Illustration by George W. Eve (1855–1914)   © 2007 Antioch Publishing

In at the Death

Also by David Wishart

I, Virgil

Ovid

Nero

Germanicus

Sejanus

The Lydian Baker

The Horse Coin

Old Bones

Last Rites

White Murder

A Vote for Murder

Parthian Shot

Food for the Fishes

DAVID WISHART

In at the Death

HODDER &
STOUGHTON

Copyright © 2006 by David Wishart

First published in Great Britain in 2006 by Hodder & Stoughton
A division of Hodder Headline

The right of David Wishart to be identified as the Author
of the Work has been asserted by him in accordance
with the Copyright, Designs and Patents Act 1988.

A Hodder & Stoughton Book

1

All rights reserved. No part of this publication may be reproduced, stored
in a retrieval system, or transmitted, in any form or by any means without
the prior written permission of the publisher, nor be otherwise circulated in
any form of binding or cover other than that in which it is published and
without a similar condition being imposed on the subsequent purchaser.

All characters in this publication are
fictitious and any resemblance to real persons,
living or dead, is purely coincidental.

A CIP catalogue record for this title is available from the British Library

ISBN 978 0 340 84036 8

Typeset in Plantin Light by Hewer Text UK Ltd, Edinburgh
Printed and bound by Clays Ltd, St Ives plc

Hodder Headline's policy is to use papers that are natural, renewable
and recyclable products and made from wood grown in sustainable
forests. The logging and manufacturing processes are expected to
conform to the environmental regulations of the country of origin.

Hodder & Stoughton Ltd
A division of Hodder Headline
338 Euston Road
London NW1 3BH

For the Foxes, Bill, Daphne and Tracy; and also for Canadian fellow-scribbler Al Tassie, whose Macro is different from mine.

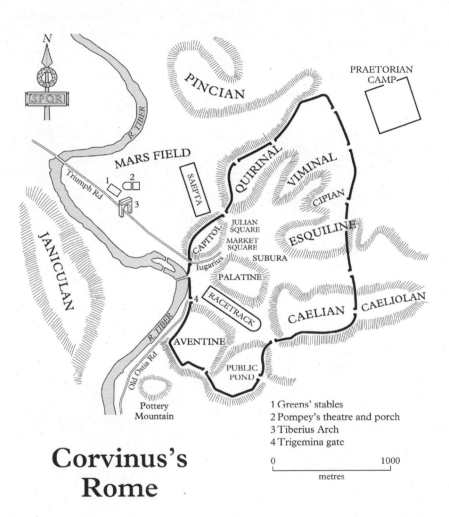

N

SPQR

PINCIAN

PRAETORIAN
CAMP

R. TIBER

MARS FIELD

Triumph Rd

QUIRINAL

VIMINAL

1 2
3

SAEPTA

CIPIAN

JANICULAN

CAPITOL

JULIAN
SQUARE

MARKET
SQUARE

ESQUILINE

Iugarius

SUBURA

PALATINE

4

RACETRACK

CAELIAN

CAELIOLAN

R. TIBER

AVENTINE

Old Ostia Rd

PUBLIC
POND

Pottery
Mountain

1 Greens' stables
2 Pompey's theatre and porch
3 Tiberius Arch
4 Trigemina gate

Corvinus's
Rome

0   1000

metres

DRAMATIS PERSONAE

(Only the names of characters who appear in more than one place are given. The names of historical characters are in upper case.)

CORVINUS'S HOUSEHOLD

Alexis: the gardener
Bathyllus: the major-domo
Meton: the chef
Perilla, Rufia: Corvinus's wife
Placida: a dog. Her owner is **Sestia Calvina**

IMPERIALS, SENATORS AND OTHER HIGH-RANKERS

AHENOBARBUS, GNAEUS DOMITIUS: Tiberius's nephew and the husband of Augustus's granddaughter Agrippina. Co-head of the Aventine fire commission
ALLENIUS, TITUS PAPINIUS: ex-consul. Sextus Papinius's father
ARRUNTIUS, LUCIUS: a leading senator
BALBUS, DECIMUS LAELIUS: aedile (public works officer); Papinius's immediate superior in the Aventine fire commission
CARSIDIUS (SACERDOS), LUCIUS: a senator; owner

of the Aventine tenement. The *cognomen* Sacerdos is not used in the text

FREGELLANUS, PUBLIUS PONTIUS: a senator on Macro's civilian staff

GAIUS CAESAR: Tiberius's appointed successor ('Caligula' – 'Little Army Boot' – was a nickname)

MACRO, NAEVIUS SERTORIUS: commander of the Praetorians, and Gaius's right-hand man

MARSUS, PUBLIUS VIBIUS: a leading senator

TIBERIUS CAESAR ('The Wart'): emperor

OTHERS

ACUTIA: a friend of Albucilla's; widow of Publius Vitellius

ALBUCILLA, LUCIA: widow of Satrius Secundus

Aponius, Sextus: with **Quintus Pettius**, an ostensible stonemason whom Corvinus meets on the Aventine

Atratinus, Marcus Sempronius: Papinius's friend and colleague

Caepio, Lucceius: Carsidius's factor in the Aventine tenement building

Cluvia: Papinius's girlfriend

Crispus, Caelius: an acquaintance of Corvinus's in the foreign judge's office

Lautia: top-floor resident in the Aventine tenement

Lippillus, Decimus Flavonius: a friend of Corvinus's; Watch commander for the Public Pond district. His wife is **Marcina Paullina**

Mescinius, Titus: commander of the Aventine district Watch

Natalis, Titus Minicius: faction-master of the Greens

PAPINIUS, SEXTUS: the dead young man

Rupilia: Papinius's mother

Soranus, Titus Mucius: one of Papinius's set of friends

Vestorius, Publius: a money-lender

I

It'd been three years since I'd last visited the Greens' stables. Nothing had changed. The place still looked like a fortress: high, smooth-faced wall topped with pottery shards set in cement, a gate that would've stopped a charging elephant, and just in case visiting punters still hadn't got the message a door-slave outside with biceps and pectorals that your common-or-garden gorilla would die for.

The scowl wasn't exactly welcoming, either. I should've brought a bunch of bananas with me as a peace-offering, but it was too late now. I stepped up to the guy and gave him my best smile.

'Hi,' I said. 'Remember me, pal?'

The slave stood up, his little piggy eyes under their mat of tangled hair narrowing as he gave me the once-over. It was like watching a Titan off a pediment getting ready for round two of a theomachy. He nodded slowly and spat to one side. I swear the gobbet of phlegm sizzled on the cobbles, and in October that has nothing to do with temperature.

'I don't forget faces, Corvinus,' he said. 'What the fuck do you want?'

Yeah, well. It's nice to be popular. I reached into my tunic and brought out Minicius Natalis's letter.

'I'm here to see the boss,' I said, handing it over. 'Personal invite.'

'That so, now?' He squinted at the seal: pictures he could cope with. Just. 'What about?'

Yeah, I'd been wondering that myself, because the letter didn't say; just that it was important and that Natalis would appreciate a visit as soon as I could manage. 'You have me there, friend. Uh . . . maybe you could sort of take me to him and I could ask? Would that be possible, do you think, or should we give ourselves three guesses?'

That got me a long hard stare. Par for the course: sarcasm's wasted on a racing-faction door-guard. You may as well shoot dried peas at a rhino.

Finally, he spat again, reached up and unbarred the gate.

'Wait here,' he growled.

The bar on the other side clunked into place behind him, leaving me to kick my heels while he consulted higher authority. Not that I was surprised. If Jupiter himself were to come down in all his glory with his eagle on his wrist he still wouldn't get past the front gate unless he was spoken for, and they'd probably frisk the eagle, too. The racing game's a serious business, and faction bosses don't take chances.

Ten minutes later, the troll reappeared.

'Okay, Corvinus,' he said. 'You're cleared. Follow me.'

Inside was a different world. The Greens are Rome's top team, patronised by Gaius Caesar himself – crown prince, soon-to-be emperor (if the news from Capri was anything to go by) and all-round dangerous nut – and so equipped with the best of everything money can buy, plus a few things it can't. There was no sign of the horses, of course – paranoia dictates that these beauties are kept well away from the curious eyes of even legit visitors – but everything else screamed cash and quality, right down to the natty tunics worn by the stable skivvies. Not that it was all surface show, mind: you can't be inside a faction stable for long before you catch the sense of *obsession*. For these guys, anyone from the top man right the way down, the faction comes first, middle and last. And as far as *esprit de corps* goes, if you're looking for the top variety you can forget the legions; they don't even come close.

The admin building was out on its own, set in a snazzy formal garden. It could've doubled for a private house on the Esquiline or the Caelian, even – at a pinch, and barring size – for one on the Palatine itself: PR again, because the faction-master of the Greens is a man with serious clout, and if you have clout in Rome then you're expected to flaunt it. My guide-troll nodded to the door-slave sweeping the porch, crossed the marble-pillared and mosaic-floored entrance hall and knocked on a cedar-panelled door at the opposite end.

'Come in.'

We did. I'd been inside the inner sanctum before, so I wasn't surprised. Forget the snazzy town-house, at least where the interior fittings were concerned: this was a working office, with the back wall lined with cubby-holes for documents, chairs instead of couches and a big desk rear of centre. The furniture was top quality, and the mosaics and murals must've cost an arm and a leg.

'Quality', though, wasn't a word you could apply to the guy sitting behind the desk. Titus Minicius Natalis, the faction-master of the Greens, was a fat, balding, pint-sized runt with a stubbly chin and 'ex-slave' written all over him in block capitals. He wasn't thick, mark you, far from it: you didn't get all the way up from nothing to being the head of Rome's top Colour without brains. Not without a streak of ruthless-ness a yard wide, either. I didn't know if Natalis actually had a white-haired old grandmother squirrelled away somewhere, but if he did I'd bet the old biddy had to check herself regularly for price tags.

'Nice to see you again, Corvinus,' he said. Yeah, well, I couldn't exactly say it was reciprocal, but there you go, you can't have everything. And he was only being polite. 'Sit down, please. That's all, Socrates.'

The troll grunted and exited, closing the door behind him. I pulled up a chair and sat. We stared at each other for a long moment. Then he leaned back, almost disappearing behind the model chariot and horses on his desk.

'So,' he said. 'You got my letter.'

'Sure.' I folded my arms. 'For what it was worth.' We'd never liked one another from the first, and I didn't see any reason not to carry on playing it that way. Still, the bare request to talk to me about something important had had me hooked, and knowing the bastard knew it would do just that irked me. 'What's this about, Natalis? Some more grubby faction business?'

'No,' he said. 'No, it's nothing to do with the faction. Or even with racing.'

'All right.' I leaned back myself, unfolded my arms and crossed my legs while he fiddled with a pen and set it down. The guy was nervous. Odd. 'So what, then?'

'A favour.' He hesitated. 'There's a jug of wine on that table over there. Massic, and good stuff. Pour us both a cup, okay?'

Well, he had his priorities right, anyway, and it'd been a long dry hike from the Caelian. I got up, walked over to the tray and poured. The jug and cups were solid silver, chased with – surprise! – a frieze of running horses. I set a full cup on the desk beside him, sipped at my own, and sat down again.

'I don't think, pal,' I said carefully, 'that I owe you any favours at all. The reverse if anything. Correct me if I'm wrong.'

'You impressed me, Corvinus.' He took a long swallow from his cup and set it down. 'I don't impress easy, and when it happens I don't forget. Oh, sure, I admit it: if there is a debt then it goes the other way, and you got up my nose then just as much as I got up yours, so I can't even claim the benefit of past acquaintance. Truth to tell, you still do.' Well, that was frank, at least. He'd never been one to mince his words, Titus

Natalis. 'Even so, you're a digger with a brain in your head, which is what I need at present, and that's not common.'

'Never mind the smarm, friend,' I said. 'Just tell me what you want, okay? Then I can turn you down flat and we can both get on with our lives.'

Instead of answering, he opened a drawer in the desk, took out a sheet of paper and slid it towards me. I reached over, picked it up and glanced at it.

It was a money order made out in my name. For five thousand silver pieces.

I stared at it, then at him.

'That's just for listening,' he said. He picked up his cup and took another mouthful of the wine. He was looking less nervous now. Maybe it was the wine, but it was probably the money. Guys like Natalis really *believe* in the power of the cheque. 'Fifteen minutes of your time. You want to tell me to get lost at the end of it, that's your privilege. Completely. No reasons from you, no argument from me. Give that to my banker and he'll cash it anyway without a murmur. But if we do end up with a deal, and you deliver the goods – as I'm pretty sure you will – I'll make it up to the round fifty.'

Sweet gods! Fifty thousand silver pieces was a small fortune. Me, I don't do gobsmacked, not all that often, anyway, but I must've gaped. Natalis was watching me closely, half smiling. If you could call an expression that made the guy look like he'd just bitten on a lemon a half-smile.

'Well, Corvinus?' he said. 'What about it? Do I have that fifteen minutes or not?'

I remembered to close my mouth before I answered: we had a certain degree of good old purple-striper *gravitas* to maintain here, and I was buggered if I was going to let him see he'd rocked me. 'You've got the ball, friend,' I said. 'Go ahead.'

'Fine.' He set down the cup. All business now, and not a

trace of nervousness. 'I want you to look into a suicide. A young lad by the name of Sextus Papinius.'

Well, that name rang a bell, at least. And I'd got my mental faculties, such as they were, back into gear. 'Any relation to Papinius Allenius the consular?' I said.

There was the barest hesitation. 'His son. But it's the mother's side of the family I have connections with. If you're wondering, which I suspect you are.'

Yeah. I was, at that. Natalis had started off by saying this had nothing to do with faction business, which meant it had to be private. No one shells out fifty thousand silver pieces unless they have a serious – and personal – vested interest in the matter somewhere along the line. If the lad had been a relative of his I could've understood, but the son of an ex-consul put that right out of court: consular families and those of ex-slaves, even stinking-rich ones like Natalis, don't mix socially, let alone intermarry; not nohow, not never, even in this lax day and age. The obvious alternative explanation I didn't even consider: unless my judgment was way off beam Natalis just wasn't the type to have boyfriends. And that didn't leave much for guesswork.

'The mother's side?' I said.

'Her name's Rupilia. She's from Leontini.' Natalis took another sip of his wine. 'Same as me. *Her* father was Rupilius Hasta, and old Hasta was my first real patron. You getting there?'

Yeah, I was, and it fitted, at least the Sicilian bit did. Something I did know about Natalis from former acquaintance was that he'd started out as a humble driver in Sicily before coming to Rome as third-stringer for the Greens. After which he'd worked – or clawed – his way up the ladder, all the way to the top. And if this Rupilia was the daughter of his first patron then . . .

'The family was the oldest in the region. Big in horse

breeding and racing, always had been. Hasta took an interest in me – I was never his slave, but he liked to help promising drivers – and when I had the chance to move to Rome he lent me the cash.' Natalis got up and moved over to the wine jug. 'Without that money I'd still be in Sicily, probably on the scrapheap by now. And like I told you, Corvinus, I don't forget easy.'

Uh-huh. Check. That's the way Sicilian minds work: you have a debt, either way, then you pay it, QED, end of story. Things were beginning to clear. 'So,' I said, 'when the daughter came to Rome and married Allenius you renewed the link?'

'I'd never broken it. And I kept it up with young Sextus, gladly. The boy was the spit of his grandfather and he'd racing in his bones.' Natalis held up the jug. 'You want a refill?'

'Sure.' I took a long swig and held the cup out for more.

'I don't mean he was a gambler, mind.' He poured carefully. 'Oh, the lad liked to gamble, like any youngster, but he never went overboard, he'd more sense. What he was really interested in was the other side, my side, the cars and the driving. Although *interested*'s not strong enough, not by half: he loved the whole business, loved it as much as I do. He'd've made a driver himself, if things'd been just a bit different. He had the guts for it, certainly, and the heart, easy; he'd guts and heart in spades, Sextus Papinius. But he never had the skill, and knew he never would. Even so, he spent a lot of his free time here, right from when he was knee-high, especially after I became faction-master.'

'So,' I said. 'What happened, exactly?'

'I told you. Two days back he killed himself.' Natalis sank a neat quarter-pint of the Massic at a gulp.

'Killed himself how? Slit wrists? Poison?'

'Neither. He jumped from the top floor of an Aventine tenement.' I must've looked as surprised as I felt, because he shrugged. 'Yeah. The flat was empty at the time, and the tenement was on his visiting list. So that's what he used.'

' "Visiting list"?'

'He was a junior investigation officer. With the claims department of the emperor's new fire commission.'

Right; that made sense. Of a kind, anyway. A few months back there had been a major fire in the Aventine and Racetrack districts. The Wart had appointed a commission headed by his four sons-in-law to assess the damage and arrange compensation and rebuilding. I didn't know yet how old exactly this Sextus Papinius had been, but for a kid from a consular family, age say eighteen or nineteen, which would fit the spirit of things, junior investigation officer would be a logical first rung on the political ladder.

'Why did he do it?' I said.

Natalis gave me a long look. 'That's the point,' he said finally. 'I've no idea. None at all. That's what I'd be paying you to find out.'

'Is the reason so important?'

He shrugged again. 'It is to me. I thought a lot of the kid. And I don't like *not* knowing. If you can understand that.'

'Yeah,' I said. 'Yeah, I can understand that.' I could even sympathise: in his place I'd've wanted to know too, just for my own peace of mind. And I had to admit that he had me hooked. 'Okay. You have your fifteen minutes.'

'Fine.' He leaned back. 'The floor's yours. You got any questions, you ask them and I'll answer if I can.'

'Let's start with the boy himself. He the suicidal type at all? Moody? Get depressed? That sort of thing?'

Natalis shook his head. 'Not so's you'd notice, or not all that often. Certainly no more than any other kid his age.'

'Which was what?'

'Nineteen. He'd just had his nineteenth birthday.'

'What about his character? A loner? Run about with any of the fast crowds?'

'He had his fun. Girls and wine, a bit of wildness here and there, but nothing serious. You know the sort of thing.'

I nodded; yeah, I knew, I'd've been surprised if it'd been otherwise, given the family background. Par for the course. So: your typical rich young lad-about-town, feeling his oats and kicking up his heels before life grabbed him by the balls and turned him into a pillar of society. Only in Sextus Papinius's case it never would, now. 'He get on well with his parents?'

'Parent, singular. Rupilia and Allenius are divorced, have been for years, and Sextus lived with his mother. There's no contact, none, at least as far as I'm aware. I doubt if I've heard the boy mention his father more than two or three times in all the years I've known him. You'll want to talk to Rupilia, no doubt; the house is near the Octavian Porch, one of the old properties on the Marcellus Theatre side. They got along okay in general, as far as I know, although Rupilia' – he hesitated – 'well, bringing up a teenager without a man in the house isn't easy, and Rupilia's not the strong-willed disciplinarian type. You understand me?'

Sure I did. Reading between the lines, I'd guess the kid had been spoiled rotten and grown up a handful. Still, that was nothing unusual in the top bracket, especially these days when single-parent families or parents with their own social lives to think of were the rule rather than the exception. 'So where does the money come from?' I said. Money there would have to be: spoiled-brat, lad-about-town pursuits didn't come cheap.

'Hasta was well off. He settled part of the estate in Leontini on her before he died, plus the income from some property in Capua. Also, of course, when the divorce went through she got part of her dowry back. She's not rich, but she's comfortable enough.'

'And she never thought of remarrying?'

'No.'

Just the bare negative, and Natalis had closed up tighter than a constipated clam. Uh-huh. Well, there could be lots of reasons behind that, and probably none of them was relevant, or my business. I took a swig of the Massic. 'Okay. This tenement. Where was it, exactly?'

'On the river-side slope of the Aventine, near the start of Old Ostia Road. One of the newer blocks. The manager lives on site, which was why Sextus was there that day. Or presumably it was. That's something else I don't know for sure.'

'Name? The manager's, I mean?'

'Caepio. Lucceius Caepio. He's – he was – responsible for two or three other properties that got burned down in the fire.'

'Fine. Last question, pal, for the present at least. Given the kid did actually kill himself, why do you think he did it?' He opened his mouth to answer and I held up a hand. 'Yeah, sure, I know, but you must be able to hazard some sort of a guess. Gut feeling, no comeback.'

'I knew Sextus all his life, Corvinus. And I've already told you. He wasn't the brooding type.'

'But?' There was a *but*: I could see it in his eyes. I waited. 'Natalis. Come on. I'd have to start somewhere, okay?'

He frowned. 'Like I say, he had racing in his bones; maybe one day if things'd turned out different he might've sat in this chair. But this last month – he was round here a lot in that time, more than usual, if anything – I'd the feeling he had something other than the cars and horses on his mind.'

'You're saying he was worried?'

'No. Worried's too strong. Preoccupied, maybe. That the word?' He shook his head. 'Hell, I don't know, not to be sure about, let alone swear to. I could've been imagining things, and if I wasn't it could've been for any of a dozen reasons. You know kids. Certainly he didn't say nothing, which he usually would rather than to his mother if something was biting him. Maybe it was just me; the Plebeian Games're next month, the Blues've been winning lately and the whole place is on edge.' He cleared his throat and suddenly the hard-nosed business-man was back. 'So I can't afford the time to think about it, okay? That's your job, Corvinus. If you want it.'

Despite everything, I was more than half ready to say No: after all, Natalis was no friend of mine, I didn't owe him, and raking through the whys and wherefores of a suicide never does anyone any good. Then I saw the look on his face that maybe he hadn't wanted me to see, and I knew I couldn't.

Besides, I'd got that prickly feeling at the back of my neck. And fifty thousand silver pieces is serious gravy by anyone's reckoning.

'Yeah,' I said. 'I want it.'

'Fine. Then we have a deal?' He stood up and held out a hand.

'Sure,' I said.

We shook.

2

W hen I got back home Bathyllus had the door open and the obligatory wine cup ready poured and waiting. As usual. How he does it Jupiter only knows. Oh, yeah, sure, all good major-domos come equipped with precognition as standard to a certain extent, but Bathyllus's is something else. A couple of years previous as an experiment I'd tried taking off my sandals round the corner and sneaking up on the bugger barefoot, just in case it was something to do with the distinctive sound the leather soles – *my* leather soles – made on the marble steps. I never even got halfway. Getting caught by your major-domo outside your own front door in broad daylight with your footwear in your hands and a good half jug into the game, which I was at the time, doesn't do much for your master-of-the-house *gravitas*, either: you could've heard the bastard's disapproving sniff in Baiae.

I took the offered cup and sank the first restorative mouthful. 'Have a good morning, Bathyllus?'

'Not particularly, sir, no.'

Uh-huh. Now *that* was a sniff. Not to mention a snap, which put things a stage higher. Also, now I came to notice, the little bald-head didn't look too cheerful all round; in fact, on a pissed-off scale of one to ten I'd rate him a good fifteen, and that meant trouble. *Real* trouble.

We were talking seriously peeved here. The military equivalent would be losing Syria.

I set down the wine cup. Carefully, so as not to spill it on the polished tabletop: a seriously peeved Bathyllus can leave you with third-degree sarcasm burns just for provocative breathing.

'Uh . . . everything okay, little guy?' I said. 'I mean, generally speaking, as it were?'

He drew himself up to his full five feet nothing.

'I suggest you judge for yourself, sir,' he said. 'In the atrium.'

You could've used his tone of voice to pickle mummies. Shit; make it Syria *plus* the Rhine-and-Danube. Whatever the trouble was, we'd got it in spades. I left the wine cup where it was, hared off through the lobby and into the atrium . . .

'Oh, hello, Marcus.' Perilla looked up from her chair with a bright smile. 'You're back early.'

I was goggling at the thing lying next to her. 'What the hell is *that?*'

'Don't be silly, dear. What does it look like?' Good question. All I could see was an anonymous mound of greyish-black hair. 'It's a dog, of course.'

'Perilla, where the fuck did you—'

'Don't swear. She's a Gallic boarhound and her name's Placida. We're looking after her for a few days.'

'We are *what?*'

'While Sestia Calvina's in Veii. Didn't I tell you?' Like hell she had. Quite deliberately not. 'Say hello to Marcus, Placida. Nicely, now.'

The mound of hair gave a huge sigh one end and farted at the other. Our atrium, big and open as it was, was suddenly not the place to be.

'Look, lady—' Which was a far as I got before the mound opened a bloodshot eye and erupted to its feet. Paws. Whatever.

'OW-*OO-OO-OO*! OW-OW-OW-OW-*OO-OO-OO*!'

Oh, bugger! I stepped back. Quickly.

'Perilla . . .'

'Placida! *Placida! Nicely*, I said!'

'OW-*OO-OO-OO!*'

I took another step back, but I was running out of atrium. Gods! This was a *dog*?

'*Placida!* Down! Behave yourself!' Perilla had a grip on the brute's collar. Not that it seemed to notice, mind. 'Don't be silly, Marcus, it's only a howl! She's quite harmless.'

'Is that right, now?' Jupiter best and greatest! I had my back to a pillar and I wasn't going nowhere. I'd seen beasts half that size given star billing at the Games and matched against tigers. Winning the match, too, paws down. Standing, its muzzle was above the level of my groin. Not a happy thought, given the distance between us.

The brute shook its head, spattering everything inside three lateral yards with white-foamed drool, farted again and grinned, revealing a mouthful of yellow fangs. My balls shrank.

'There,' Perilla said, letting go. 'That's *much* better. Good dog. *Good* dog, Placida! Who's a clever girl, then?'

Shakeshakeshake. Splattersplattersplatter.

Grin.

Oh, fuck. I stared at the thing in horror. Well, it certainly explained Bathyllus: when you're the sort of guy who tuts over a muddy footprint in the lobby or a smudged mirror, anything that can cover the furniture to a mean depth of two inches in spit and make the place smell like a barnful of incontinent goats all inside ten seconds flat is the stuff of nightmare. What amazed me was that he hadn't gone over the wall already with his buffing rags and polish packed in a carpet-bag.

We'd have to go careful here. Tact, Corvinus, tact. I unpeeled myself from the pillar. 'Ah . . . I'm not criticising, lady,' I said. 'Perish the thought. But if we are really stuck with the thing then wouldn't it be better to keep it outside? In the fresh air, as it were?' Preferably on a barge off Ostia, at the end of a fucking hawser half a mile offshore.

'Oh, no. Calvina was *most* particular about that. And Placida's not an *it*, Marcus, she's a she.' She fondled the beast's long, drooping ears. 'Aren't you, precious?'

Slobberslobberslobber. Grin.

'Uh . . . Perilla,' I said. 'Let's just think about this a minute, shall we? Maybe—'

Which was when Bathyllus came in with the wine cup I'd left.

'OW-*OO-OO-OO!*'

'*Placida!*' Perilla snapped. 'That's enough!'

I had to admire the little bald-head's sangfroid. Not an eyelid did he bat; in fact, the brute could've been invisible.

'Your wine, sir,' he said. 'Lunch will be about ten minutes. Cold pork and vegetable rissoles.'

Shakeshakeshake. Splattersplattersplatter.

Fart.

Oh, hell.

Long, pregnant pause. I'd never actually seen human nostrils flare, but Bathyllus's made a pretty good attempt, although at that point sniffing wasn't a sensible option. He hadn't missed the effects of the multiple spittle fallout, either. You could tell by the way he blanched.

And then it happened. Without any warning Placida ambled across to the square of smooth tiling by the corner of the pool just under our best bronze of Diana tying her hair, spread her back legs and squatted . . .

'*Placida! No!*' Perilla shouted, but the damage was already being done, and spreading. I glanced at Bathyllus . . .

There's a bit in one of these old Greek plays where Atreus, king of Mycenae invites his brother Thyestes to a banquet, serves him up a stew made from Thyestes's chopped-up kids and then at the end of the meal has the severed heads, hands and feet brought in on a platter. The actor playing Thyestes is masked, sure, but if he wasn't the expression on his face at that point would've been a dead ringer for Bathyllus's.

'Oh, *Placida!*' Perilla said.

Grin.

A few days, eh? Life was going to be fun, fun, fun.

We escaped to the dining-room while a tight-lipped Bathyllus organised clean-up operations and Placida was dragged off in ignominy.

'It was an accident,' Perilla said as she lay down on her couch. 'She is house-trained really.' She paused. 'At least, Calvina told me she was.'

Yeah, right; I'd just bet she had. I'd never met Sestia Calvina – she was one of Perilla's poetry set – but she was evidently a smart cookie. 'Listen, lady,' I said. 'Tell someone your canine horror-on-legs is liable to piss on the Carrara and your chances of taking the deal further are zilch. You've been conned.' I threw myself down on the other couch and took an irritated slug of Setinian. 'In any case, what the hell prompted you to take the brute in at all? If Calvina was going off to Veii why couldn't she just have left it at home with her slaves? Why pick on us?'

Perilla straightened a fold in her mantle. 'Marcus, I told you. Placida's a she, not an it. And she's got a lovely nature.'

Right, and I was Queen Semiramis. Nothing that howled, spat, farted and pissed all at complete random and simultaneously could possibly be described as having a lovely nature. Also, I knew prevarication when I heard it. 'Don't faff,' I said. 'Just answer the question.'

'She likes company.'

'*Slaves* are fucking company. And handling the seamier side of the domestic grind's their job.'

'She needs a family atmosphere. A proper family atmosphere, not just—'

'Perilla, that thing creates its own atmosphere, and I don't know about you but I found it fucking unbreathable. If we have to—'

'Stop swearing, dear, it isn't necessary. She hasn't exactly made a good first impression, I admit—'

'*Hah!*'

'. . . but once she's settled in—'

'*Settled in?*' I put down the cup. 'Jupiter bloody God Almighty! Just how long is Sestia Calvina planning to stay in Veii?'

'About a month. But—'

'A *month*? You said a few days!'

'Ah. Yes. Well, actually, it's a month.' She paused and tugged again at the fold in her mantle. 'Or maybe two. Calvina was . . . well, to be honest she was a little vague on that point.'

I groaned. Oh, hell: smart cookie was right. If I ever got within grabbing distance I'd kill the woman with my bare hands. 'Look. Perilla,' I said. 'Two months of that and we'll all be gibbering. Plus being short one major-domo through stroke, seizure, heart failure or desertion. Although the little guy may flip before then and poison the brute. And if so I for one won't blame him.'

'Don't be silly, Marcus.' At least she had the grace to look uncomfortable. 'Bathyllus will come round. Placida's a lovely dog really, very gentle and affectionate. She just happens to have some . . . well, some unfortunate habits.'

'Yeah. Right.' Gods! Thank Jupiter for open-plan architecture and a through draught. 'Why the fuck couldn't Sestia Calvina have a sparrow for a pet like everyone else?'

'Her brother brought Placida back from Gaul. And Calvina always has been rather eccentric.'

'*Eccentric?* Lady, if that's eccentric then I'm a fucking—'

'Marcus! Stop it!'

I subsided. Bathyllus was tooling in with his minions and the lunch trays. If he'd looked any more put-upon he'd've had bow legs and a crouch, and the serving was *pointed*. Which meant plates were put down with a snap like sling-bolts.

'Uh . . . very nice, Bathyllus,' I said. 'The pork looks good. Very . . . ah . . . *porky.*'

'Thank you, sir.' Sniff. Snap. 'Meton will be gratified. Reheating leftovers can be *so* tricky.'

Ouch. Apropos of which . . . 'Has he, ah, met our guest himself yet, little guy? Meton, I mean?'

Snap. 'Oh, yes. They get on very well together.' Snap. 'There is, I think, a great similarity of character.'

I swallowed. Hell. One of life's little constants is that Bathyllus and Meton hate each other's guts because where Bathyllus is the complete control freak Meton is the anarchist's anarchist. If Bathyllus had decided that Placida was our friendly chef's canine soul-mate – and from what I'd seen of her I wouldn't be surprised – then we'd got an uphill struggle on our hands. I'd bet that bastard in the kitchen would play it for all it was worth, too.

Trouble was right.

With a final sniff Bathyllus buggered off.

'Now.' Perilla helped herself to the rissoles. 'Change the subject. You haven't told me how your meeting with Natalis went.'

Shit; in all of this I'd completely forgotten about Natalis and young Papinius's suicide. I filled my wine cup and told her.

When I got to the bit about how much he was prepared to pay she blinked at me.

'But that's ridiculous!' she said. 'Fifty thousand silver pieces is a fortune!'

'Natalis can afford it. With Prince Gaius showering his precious bounty on the team and all set to step into the Wart's clogs when he hangs them up he's seriously rolling.'

'Even so, it's a lot of money just for information.'

'I said: the kid's mother's from Leontini and his grandfather was Natalis's first patron. That'd weigh. Also he seems to've had a genuine affection for the lad himself. Besides' – I reached for the pork – 'reading between the lines I'd guess he has an unrequited crush on Rupilia. At least, I hope for the sake of my imagination that it's unrequited.'

'Hmm.' She reached for the salad bowl. 'So why do you think he did it? Papinius? Commit suicide, I mean.'

'Jupiter knows, Perilla. You know what kids are at that age, they take everything seriously and personal. Oh, sure, from what Natalis told me he seemed a sensible, balanced type overall, but Natalis could be wrong. *Has* to be wrong, because the kid's dead.' I sank a mouthful of wine. 'Nineteen years old. Just getting started. What a fucking waste of a life.'

'So what do you do now?'

I shrugged. 'Talk to people. Rupilia, the factor of the tenement where it happened. Any friends I can get names for. The mother, first. She lives near the Octavian Porch. I'll do that this afternoon.'

'Oh, good.' Perilla gave me a dazzling smile. 'Then you can take Placida.'

I almost swallowed my wine cup. '*What?*'

'She needs to be exercised. She didn't get out this morning, and a walk across the city would be perfect for her.'

Hell's bloody teeth! I had to knock this on the head right now or as sure as eggs was eggs I'd regret it later. 'Now look, lady,' I said. 'You got us into this mess, you can just—'

'Nonsense, dear, she'll be no trouble. And since you're walking anyway . . .'

This was getting silly. 'Perilla, we have a whole houseful of skivvies here! Give her to one of the chair team! These lard-balls could do with walking a bit of the fat off, in fact—'

Perilla set down her spoon. 'Marcus,' she snapped, 'I've already told you! I promised Calvina that we'd do our best to make Placida feel part of the family, and besides, it's a chance for the two of you to get to know each other. Be sensible, please!'

So that was that. Oh, shit. Shit, shit, shit! And I'd've liked to know where that *we* had suddenly appeared from, too.

I was getting very bad vibes about all this; *very* bad.

Ah, well. At least we'd be out in the open air.

3

Trust me: there're more pleasant situations to be in than attached to a hundred-and-twenty-pound Gallic boarhound by three feet of rope and with your major-domo poised to open the door. Especially if the brute knows that in about ten seconds flat it's just you, her and the wide-open spaces and is really, *really* looking forward to it.

'You, uh, absolutely sure about this, Perilla?' I said.

'Of course.' She gave me another dazzling smile. 'You will take care of her, won't you? She's very delicate, and . . . *Down*, Placida! Your Uncle Bathyllus doesn't *want* the top of his head licked!'

Never a truer word was spoken. From the look on his face where the little bald-head's what-I-want-for-the-Winter-Festival list was concerned having his scalp licked by a Gallic boarhound wouldn't make even the top five hundred.

The 'uncle' didn't go down a bomb, either.

'Okay, Bathyllus.' I gave the rope another turn round my wrist. 'Fun's over. Stop messing about.'

Bathyllus glared at me and opened the door.

I'd forgotten about the steps.

'*Oh, shiiiit!*'

'Marcus, *don't* pull on her lead like that! You'll strangle her!'

If only. If only. I tried digging my heels in, but you can't do that on marble, especially if it's been polished by Bathyllus. I hoped the slavering brute had licked his follicles off. We hit the last step at a run and kept going.

'Heel, Placida! *Heel!*'

'OW-*OO-OO-OO!*'

Oh, bugger! *Not* a good start, and the fact that the brute evidently didn't understand Latin didn't help either. Luckily the house next door had a pillared porch at street level. I stretched out an arm and had it nearly wrenched from its socket. We didn't stop exactly, but at least it slowed us down enough for me to get a bit of purchase on the cobbles underfoot and do some hauling of my own. Jupiter! This was worse than driving a four-horse chariot in the Games. At least chariot drivers got fitted with a crash-helmet.

Time to exercise a little authority. I braced myself, pulled back on the rope as hard as I could, wound in another foot or so and gave what was left a firm jerk. 'Okay, sunshine, that's enough!' I said. 'Walk. *Walk!*'

Evidently the concept didn't exist in dogspeak, or maybe the word meant something else in Gallic because she bunched her shoulders and heaved. We compromised on a sprint. Shit; if she kept this up I'd be knackered before we were halfway to the Palatine. Plus being able to tie my sandal-straps without bending down.

Even so, we were doing pretty well until the cat.

'OW-*OOO! OWWOWOW-OOO!*'

'*For fuck's sake!*'

One piece of advice. If you're walking a Gallic boarhound never, *ever* wrap the lead round your wrist. When we hit the woman pastry-seller on the corner I was practically flying. And you ain't never heard language like a pastry-seller's who's just been torpedoed by a hundred and twenty pounds of rampant, howling boarhound plus a hundred and eighty of screaming purple-striper.

'Uh . . . I'm sorry, lady,' I said when we'd picked ourselves up and I could get a word in edgeways. 'Learner dog-walker.'

'*XXXX your "sorry"! Look at my XXXX pastries! All over the*

XXXX *street! Why the* XXXX *don't you* XXXX *look where you're* XXXX *going?'*

Or words to that effect.

Jupiter! 'Ah . . . right. Right,' I said. 'Fair point, sister.' I reached for my purse and took out a gold piece. 'Maybe this'll help.'

She snatched it from my hand, pocketed it, then turned to Placida who was doing her best to gulp down the spoiled stock. Her expression went gooey.

'Ah! XXXX me!' she said. 'Isn't it a XXXX diddums, though! Boy or girl?'

'She's a bitch.'

The woman glared at me. 'Oh, you shouldn't call her that, sir, it's not nice. What's her name?'

'Uh . . . Placida.'

'Is that right, now? Well, you've got to laugh.' She made cooing noises. '*There's* a lovely girl! Come and let me see you, then!' Placida finished off the last pastry and ambled over, grinning. 'My XXXX brother had one of them things. Rest his soul. Lucky, her name was.'

'Ah . . . yeah. Yeah.' Gods! I tugged on the rope. 'Well, it's been nice chatting to you, sister. Sorry about the accident.'

'I remember once she had three of my XXXX chickens in as many XXXX days. And next door's XXXX goat, bless her.'

I gave the rope a second tug, but Placida had found another pastry and it was like trying to shift the Capitol.

'Lovely nature she had, though, and so good with children. My youngest used to swing on her XXXX ears and she never batted a XXXX eyelid.'

'Really? That's . . .' I glanced down again. What the brute was eating wasn't a pastry after all; in fact it looked more like . . .

Like . . .

Oh, gods!

Shlapshlapshlap.

The pastry-seller gave the bent head a final affectionate pat. 'Funny they're such XXXX devils for horse dung, isn't it? Lucky was just the same.'

I made Octavian Porch in good time and – if you didn't count the upset litter and the irate senator with the interesting crotch – relatively unscathed.

Like Natalis had said, Rupilia's house was one of the older properties you get in and around the centre, dating back long before Augustus and Agrippa's public buildings jag and looking as out of place among the surrounding marble as a Samian pot in a Corinthian dinner service: a front door that looked like it hadn't been changed since Cato was in rompers, with a green-grocer's on one side, a cobbler's on the other and a big walled garden attached. There were cypress branches fixed to the pediment and the doorposts, but at least the funeral itself would be over now so I wouldn't be intruding too obviously. I wasn't looking forward to the interview, mind: two days after a death isn't the time for a stranger to come calling, and, like Perilla keeps telling me, tact's not my strongest suit. However, under the circumstances I didn't have much option.

I moored Placida to one of the doorposts, knocked and waited. Finally, the door-slave opened up: a middle-aged guy in a mourning-tunic with his forelock shaved to the scalp. He looked down at Placida, his eyes widened and he stepped back.

'It's okay, pal,' I said quickly. 'No hassle, she's friendly. And if she starts howling just throw her a goat.'

'Yes, sir.' Stiff as hell; but there again I didn't blame him. Opening the door and finding something like Placida sitting grinning at you and breathing horse dung doesn't exactly merit spreading out the welcome mat. 'How can I help you?'

'I was wondering if I could possibly have a word with the mistress.'

'She's in mourning for her son, sir,' he said. 'I don't think—'

'Yeah. Yeah, I know. Look, I'm sorry, friend, but Minicius Natalis up at the Greens' stables sent me round. The name's Corvinus, Valerius Corvinus. If the lady can see me just for a few minutes I'd appreciate it.'

At least the mention of Natalis seemed to register, and it evidently made a difference. The guy stopped frowning and opened the door completely. 'Would you care to come inside, sir? I'll tell the mistress you're here.' He padded off.

'Stay,' I said to Placida. Yeah, well, it was worth a try. On the other hand, you never knew your luck. While I was talking to Rupilia the brute might decide to slip her collar and leg it for the Alps.

The lobby was plain, but it had a good floor mosaic in the old style and a mural that looked like it'd been freshened up recently. I wondered if the place had been in the Papinius family before the divorce, or whether Rupilia had bought it after the split. In any case, it was typical of a lot of top-five-hundred property: no modern flash, old stuff that'd been pricey when it was first bought and was kept up on an income that may've been pretty hefty a hundred years back but hadn't changed much since. Natalis had said that Rupilia was reasonably well off, and that was fair enough; but my guess was that she couldn't afford to splash it around.

The slave came back. 'The mistress will see you, sir. This way, please.'

The atrium matched the lobby: good quality furnishings and fittings, well cared for, but not much that looked like it belonged in the last twenty-odd years. The lady herself was sitting in a chair by the central pool. If Natalis was smitten it didn't surprise me: she must've been a real looker in her time, and she wasn't bad now, even with the mourning-mantle and the puffy eyes; I'd reckon late thirties, very early forties, which given her son's age and the fact that her ex had just had his consulship was about right. And mourning or not, she'd evidently made sure her hair was carefully braided and her make-up well applied.

'Callon says you've come from Titus Natalis,' she said. 'It'll be about Sextus, no doubt.'

Tact, Corvinus. I didn't answer, just nodded.

She looked down at her hands, bunched in the lap of her mantle – she was holding something that I couldn't see – then back up at me. 'Oh, it's all right.' She smiled slightly. 'I was expecting you. Titus said at the funeral that he wanted you to . . . look into the circumstances of my son's death. We discussed the matter, of course, and I finally gave my permission. I don't say that I was totally in favour of the idea, still less that I find the prospect pleasant, but he's absolutely right. Nothing can bring Sextus back, but it would help if I could just understand why he—' She stopped, and her hands clenched on whatever was between them: not a handkerchief, something small and hard. 'Yes. Well, then.' She took a deep breath. 'Now, no doubt you have questions. Please pull up a chair and I'll do my best to answer them.'

I looked around. There was a chair by the wall under a mural of some battle or other; whoever had owned the house before, the Papinii or another family, seemed to have gone in for battles, judging by the rest of the artwork. I lifted it over – it was a real antique, with ivory inlay – set it down and sat.

'I've only one that really matters,' I said gently. 'Do you have any idea – *any* idea – why your son should want to kill himself?'

She shook her head. 'No. No, I don't, none at all.' Her eyes went back to whatever her fingers were clutching. 'Don't misunderstand me, Valerius Corvinus, I'm not pretending everything in Sextus's life was sweetness and light. It wasn't, by any means. We had our disagreements.' She cleared her throat. 'Quite acrimonious ones, especially over money. He was always complaining that I kept him short, that his friends' allowances were much more generous than his was. But he understood that I was doing my best for him and he had all I could afford. Sextus was a good boy at heart. Good and sensible. Spoiled, yes, I admit it – I've no illusions on that score, and the fault is mine – but when all was said and done he accepted things as they were.'

Yeah. Sensible was right; certainly as sensible as you're likely to get at that age. Most nineteen-year-old kids don't think much past their street-cred, and for youngsters like Papinius good street-cred doesn't come cheap.

'Tell me about his friends,' I said.

'He didn't have all that many. Oh, he was very outgoing, he did the things a young man of his station usually does – parties, drinking and so on – but luckily he never got in with any of the really fast sets. Or at least if he did I don't know about it.' She looked down at her hands again. 'In fact I must admit that I don't know much at all about Sextus's private life. Or at least only what he chose to tell me, which wasn't a great deal.'

Yeah, well, par for the course again; show me the parent who ever does. Me, I hadn't told my own parents half of it. 'Could you give me any names?'

'Oh, yes. One, certainly. His best friend was a boy – a young man, rather – called Marcus Atratinus. Marcus Sempronius Atratinus. His father and my ex-husband were close colleagues from the first, and our two families have been on dinner-party terms for years. He and Sextus were the same age. They worked together on the Aventine fire damage commission.'

'You know where I'd find him?'

'At the commission itself, of course; it's attached to the aediles' office. Or if you prefer, at his parents' house on the Quirinal.'

'Your son was a junior investigating officer, right?'

'Yes. He was responsible – with others, naturally – for collecting and validating claims made by property owners who'd suffered losses in the fire.'

'Had he been there long?'

'Since the commission was set up three months ago.'

'How did he get the job, just as a matter of interest? He applied directly?'

For the first time, Rupilia hesitated. Then she said, 'No, actually, he didn't. My ex-husband put his name forward to the senatorial committee responsible for staffing.'

Right. That, of course, was how things usually worked: one of a father's chief responsibilities is to see his son's political career duly launched, and as an ex-consul Papinius Allenius would have serious clout. Still, given what Natalis had said about the family relationships, or lack of them, it was odd. 'Ah . . . I'm sorry, Rupilia, but Natalis told me your husband and Sextus were estranged.'

'Yes. They were. Titus – that's my ex-husband – and I have been divorced since . . . well, for a very long time. We've hardly seen each other in years, not even to talk to. But Titus was never one to shirk his duties. He suggested it himself, and both Sextus and I were very grateful.'

'Your son enjoyed the job?'

She smiled. 'Very much so. He was good at it, too, as far as I know, although again you'd have to ask Marcus Atratinus or Sextus's immediate superior. Once again, I can't provide you with much information. Sextus wasn't very communicative on that subject either.'

'His superior being who?'

'One of the aediles. A man called Laelius Balbus.'

Uh-huh. So at least I'd got a pair of names to follow up: his best friend Atratinus and his boss. They'd do for starters. 'One last thing, Rupilia, and then I'll go. Titus Natalis said he had the impression your son had been . . . he used the word *preoccupied* over the last month. Did you notice anything yourself?'

Again, she took a long time answering. Then she said slowly, 'He was quieter than usual, certainly. But as I told you we didn't talk much; he didn't volunteer information and I'd learned from past experience that any prying on my part was counter-productive. So your answer is yes, although I can't help you with reasons.'

Well, that was about as far as I could manage at present. I got up. 'Thanks for your help, lady. I won't take up any more of your time, and believe me – however this turns out – I'm very sorry.'

'Yes.' Her eyes went down to whatever was in her lap. This time her fingers unclenched, and I could see what it was: one of these small ivory portrait-miniatures. She saw me looking and passed it over. 'That's Sextus there. I had it done for his eighteenth birthday.'

It was good work, obviously taken from life rather than idealised the way these things sometimes are: portrait artists know the importance of flattery, the same as everyone else. Red hair, like his mother's, a nice face, slightly heavy in the jowls; he must've got that from his father, because Rupilia's face narrowed to a sharp chin. And he was smiling, quite content with life.

'He was a lovely boy,' Rupilia said. 'Even now, I can't believe he's dead, and especially that he chose to kill himself. If you can tell me why, Valerius Corvinus, I'll be eternally grateful.'

'Yeah. Right.' I handed the miniature back and stood up. 'I can't promise anything, but I'll do my best.'

Placida was still moored to the doorpost; disappointing, sure, but at least the surrounding countryside seemed intact, apart from a chewed cypress branch, and I actually got a few wags of the tail. Maybe I should push my luck a bit further: there was still a fair chunk of the afternoon in hand, plenty of time to go over to Market Square and see if I could catch young Papinius's best pal Atratinus, talk to his aedile boss if he was available. That, though, I reckoned, would do me for the day. I wasn't feeling too cheerful. Murder's bad enough, but suicide is a real downer, especially where a kid's involved.

On the way Placida discovered a very dead rat in the gutter and rolled on it. Ah, the joys.

4

Like anywhere in the centre of town, the streets between Octavian Porch and Market Square were pretty crowded; not that it mattered, because where clearing a path through crowds is concerned there ain't much to beat a hundred and twenty pounds of single-minded Gallic boarhound. We did the trip in record time, barring the occasional sniff- and widdle-break, then took a sharp left along Iugarius and ploughed through the contraflow in the direction of the Temple of Saturn. I was getting the hang of this dog-walking business now. Half the secret's to keep smiling whatever happens, ignore the screams and curses, and pretend that the brute on the other end of the rope doesn't exist; while the other half's to watch out for incoming problems and avoid ending up a horizontal third in a street chase. By the time we reached the aediles' office at the other end of the square I was getting almost blasé.

'Good dog, Placida,' I said, patting her. '*Good* dog.'

Wagwagwag. Grin.

Yeah, well; we were making progress. Or at least we'd established some sort of dialogue. I left her moored to the statue of a poker-arsed Republican general and happily chewing on something she'd picked up en route, went in and asked the freedman on the desk for Laelius Balbus's department.

'That'll be the Aventine fire damage commission, won't it, sir?' he said.

'Yeah, that's right.'

'Up the stairs and straight ahead of you. It's the third door
on the left.'

'Fine. Thanks, pal.' I paused. 'Actually, I was looking for a
youngster by the name of Sempronius Atratinus. You happen
to know if he's around today?'

'I'm sorry, sir, I—'

'Who wants him?'

I turned. There was a young guy coming down the stairs;
twenty, max, Saepta-bought cloak, sharp Market Square haircut and neatly trimmed lad-about-town beard.

'You Marcus Atratinus?' I said.

'I could be.' He grinned. 'That depends on who you are.'

'The name's Marcus Corvinus. I'm . . . ah . . . looking into
the death of Sextus Papinius.'

'Oh.' The grin faded, and a lot of the lad-about-town
bounce went with it, leaving someone behind who wasn't
much more than a kid. 'Oh, right, then. I'm sorry. How
can I help?'

'You got time to talk? Fifteen, twenty minutes?'

'Certainly. Longer, if you like. I was just going along to
Publius's. First chance I've had all day.'

'Publius's?'

'It's a cookshop on Iugarius. Unless you want to go back
upstairs to the office, but it's pretty crowded up there.'

'No; no, a cookshop's fine.' I wasn't hungry, not this close
to lunch, but after being dragged across half of Rome I could
murder a cup of wine. Personally, if we were going the length
of Iugarius anyway, I'd've preferred Renatius's – it's a lot less
pretentious than most of the places in this part of town – but
it was the kid's shout. 'Uh . . . they allow dogs, do you
know?'

'I beg your pardon?'

'Never mind, pal. Not your problem. Is your boss around
today, incidentally?'

'Balbus? No, he had a Senate meeting. We don't expect him back at the office until tomorrow.'

Damn. Well, there was no great hurry to talk to him anyway, and I'd obviously been lucky to get Atratinus. 'Okay, Publius's it is.'

We went back outside and I unhitched Placida while he stared at her.

'It's a dog,' I said. 'A Gallic boarhound. Her name's Placida.'

'Is that right, now?' He was still staring. 'You, ah, usually bring her with you when you have business in Market Square?'

'Uh-uh. This is the—' Placida's head went up and her ears lifted. 'Oh, *shit*!'

I'd just time to take the strain before we were off, going like the clappers. The gods knew what she'd seen, but a group of what looked like Egyptian tourists clustered in front of the House of the Vestals screamed and scattered in panic while I pulled back frantically on the leash. A gaggle of elderly senators half a dozen yards further on weren't so agile. It gave a whole new meaning to the phrase going through committee.

So much for blasé; well, it'd teach me to be cocky, anyway. Atratinus had been keeping up. Now he grabbed the rope and together we hauled the brute to a tongue-lolling standstill.

'Sorry about that, pal.' I took a firm grip of Placida's collar and held on. 'She almost had me there.'

Atratinus gave me a strange look. We didn't talk much the rest of the way.

Publius's cookshop wasn't far, no more than fifty yards down Iugarius from the start of Capitol Incline. The downside was that there were no mooring posts, no handy statues and no staples in the wall.

Bugger. Ah, well, time for the direct approach, man to . . . whatever. Worth a try, anyway.

I was still holding Placida by the collar. I bent down, lifted her ear and said, 'Listen, sunshine, you're on trust. Any trouble and you've chewed your last bone. Understand?'

Wagwagwag.

I straightened. Atratinus was watching me, fascinated.

'You okay?' he said.

'Yeah. Why shouldn't I be?'

'Right. Right.'

We went in. It was more or less what I'd expected: one of these chichi places you get in the streets and alleyways around the square, with fashionable wines at inflated prices and a menu that strains a gut to make itself look unusual and interesting. This late, it was practically empty, but what customers there were sitting at the tables were around Atratinus's age and obviously, like him, down on their lunch break from the public offices. A few nodded as we passed. A few others – the ones in a direct line between us and the counter – took one look at Placida and pulled their stools in sharply to let us through.

The guy behind the counter was tearing salad leaves into a bowl. He looked at Placida too, then at my purple stripe, and cleared his throat.

'Afternoon, gents,' he said. 'What'll it be?'

'Corvinus?' Atratinus said.

I'd been checking the board. Half the permutations looked dubious as hell and the other half could've been contributed by Mother's whacky chef Phormio. 'You do simple sausages?' I said.

'Donkey, mast-fed wild boar or flamingo with walnuts and Sarsina cheese?'

'*Flamingo?*'

'Very popular, sir. And the walnuts are pickled in balsamic vinegar.'

I glanced down at Placida. What the hell; so far she was

keeping her part of the bargain. And if she chased them then presumably she ate them as well. 'Make it the boar,' I said.

'I'll have the ostrich balls, Publius,' Atratinus said. 'With a rocket and radicchio salad.' He turned to me. 'Fancy the Massic? It's pretty good here.'

'Uh . . . sure. Massic's fine.' Don't ask, Corvinus; just don't . . . bloody . . . *ask*. 'Half a jug, pal.'

The guy behind the counter nodded and gave the grinning Placida – she was sitting nicely, now – another leery look. 'I'll bring the food to your table, sir. Would you like to pay separately or together?'

'That's okay,' I said before Atratinus could answer for us. 'I'll get it.' I owed a bit of philanthropy: Natalis's cheque was burning its way through my belt-pouch. I'd have to lodge it with my banker in Julian Square before I went home.

I paid the tab – pricey, but not as bad as I'd thought it would be – while Atratinus collected the wine and cups and led the way over to the quietest corner.

Curiosity won out. 'Ostrich *balls*?' I said.

'Meatballs made of ostrich meat.' Another sideways look. 'What else would they be?'

'Oh. Right. Right. Placida, settle!' She collapsed on the floor beside my chair with a long-drawn-out sigh. 'Good dog. *Good* dog!' Hey! Success! Maybe we weren't doing so badly here after all. Mind you, we'd been over half of Rome in the past couple of hours and she was probably as knackered as I was.

I turned back to Atratinus, poured wine for both of us and sipped. Not bad; not at all bad. Nowhere near Titus Natalis's Massic earlier on, sure, but definitely no third-rate rotgut. 'Okay,' I said. 'Tell me about Sextus.'

Atratinus took a swallow of his own wine, or more of a gulp than a swallow, like he was steeling himself.

'What do you want to know?' he said.

'Whatever you've got. You were his best friend, weren't you?'

'That's right. Since we were six years old.'

'What was he like? As a person?'

'Quiet. When the company was right he'd join in. Otherwise he'd just smile and keep to the background.'

'And was the company usually right?'

'Most of the time. But like I say, Sextus wasn't the loud type, and he didn't go out of his way to make himself popular. A lot of people found him too serious to be real fun.' He smiled. 'Maybe that's why we got on so well, him and me. Cluvia was always on at him to loosen up more.'

'Who's Cluvia?'

'His girlfriend. Well . . . not exactly a girlfriend, but you know what I mean.' Yeah, I did: for a kid of Papinius's age and background there was bound to be a not-exactly-girlfriend with a no-account name somewhere in the picture. 'You hadn't heard of her?'

'No.' Not that that was surprising, mind, because so far all I knew about the dead kid's friends had come from his mother. And not-exactly-girlfriends are one thing mothers just aren't allowed to know about. Mine certainly hadn't. 'She a cathouse girl?'

'Gods, Corvinus!' Atratinus laughed. 'Don't even suggest that if you meet her! No, Cluvia's respectable. Strictly the independent entrepreneurial type. She's got her own flat on Public Incline near the Temple of the Moon, and when she's not there she manages a perfume shop in the Saepta. That's where she and Sextus met. They've been an item for about six months.'

'She expensive to run?'

For the first time, Atratinus hesitated. 'Pricey, but no more than most. She isn't greedy, certainly. Although Sextus was on a pretty tight budget.'

'Yeah. His mother told me that.'

'You've talked to Rupilia? Oh, yes, I suppose you must've done.'

'They got on all right, Sextus and his mother? From his side?'

'Not bad.' Atratinus took another swallow of his wine; he was looking a lot more relaxed now. 'Better than me and mine, for a start. They lived their separate lives for the most part, and Rupilia wasn't a pryer. So long as he didn't come home drunk too often or get in trouble with the Watch – which he didn't – she left him alone.'

'Money problems?'

Again Atratinus hesitated, but when he did answer it was readily enough. 'Sure. Some, anyway. Like I say, Sextus always was on a tight budget. He paid his share, though, and he was generous when he could afford it. Cluvia didn't have any reason to complain.'

Yeah, well, that was as much as I could've expected. More. I'd've been seriously surprised if he'd said the kid didn't have any problems with cash flow, whatever the situation at home. The phrases *strapped for cash* and *young lad-about-town* go together naturally.

Publius came over with the tray. Not bad portions; that's another thing about these chichi places, they tend to be heavy on the garnish at the expense of what you thought you were paying for.

Placida stood up, sniffing.

'Uh . . . excuse me a minute, pal,' I said. 'Bribery time.' I held the plate of sausages level with the floor. 'Now you just settle, sunshine. *Settle!*'

She glanced at the sausages, then at me, and crouched down. I pushed the plate towards her . . .

Unk. Unk. Unk. Wagwagwag.

Hey again! Barbarian from hell Placida might be, but she

could behave when she wanted to. She wasn't stupid, either. Maybe we could live with each other after all. 'Right,' I said. 'That's your lot. Now let us talk, okay?'

Urp.

'Good dog.' I patted her, then resurfaced and turned back to Atratinus. 'What about the rest of the friends?'

'How do you mean?' Atratinus was tucking into his ostrich balls like he'd been starved for a month.

'There's you and there's Cluvia. Who else?'

'You want particular names? Marcus Selicius. Quintus and Titus Memmius.' He reached for a piece of bread. 'Oh, and the other Titus, Titus Soranus. These're the main ones, anyway.'

The first three didn't ring any bells, but the last one did, very much so; also, Atratinus's eyes had flickered before he'd given me Soranus's name, and he'd slipped it in far too casually for my liking.

Shit.

'Titus *Mucius* Soranus?' I said slowly.

Atratinus took a sip from his wine cup before he answered. 'You know him?' he said. Again, the tone was too casual. A nice kid, Atratinus, but he was no actor.

'Uh-uh. Not personally. But I've heard of him.' Sure I had; nothing good, either. I wondered if the lads' fathers knew that Soranus was one of the gang. 'Isn't he a bit old to be running around with guys your age?'

'He's only twenty-seven.' That was defensive. 'And he's good fun.'

Yeah, right. He would be, at that, and I could see the attraction someone like Mucius Soranus'd have for lads like Atratinus and his mates. It was only when they lost the puppy-fat from between their ears and started counting the coins in their purse, or lack of them, that they might begin to have second thoughts about the bugger's reasons for giving them the time of day. And the difference between twenty-seven and nineteen, in terms of experience, is a lifetime. I let the pause develop before I asked, as casually as I could manage, 'He, ah, get you interested in gambling at all?'

Not casually enough. Atratinus stopped eating and gave me a straight look, his expression definitely sulky. Then he shrugged and picked up his spoon again. 'A little,' he said. 'Where's the harm in that? Like I said, he's good company.'

Yeah, right, sure he was: the way I'd heard it, Soranus made his living out of being good company. If you could call it a living. And I couldn't, under the circumstances, leave things there.

'Did Sextus owe him money?' I said. Silence. Atratinus had put down his spoon again, and I was getting the blank adolescent stare full power now all the way from the other side of the age gap. Shit. 'Come on, pal, this is important! Or it could be.' I waited; nothing. 'Look, I'm not Rupilia and I'm no poker-arsed paterfamilias making silly value judgments, okay? All I want to find out – just like you do – is why your friend killed himself. I can't do that if you hold out on me. So give.'

Atratinus reached for his wine cup, took a long swallow and set the cup down empty.

'Okay,' he snapped. 'Your answer's yes. Satisfied?'

I leaned back. Hell. Still, it had to be something like this. Money or a serious love affair gone sour would've been my two best bets.

'How much?' I said.

'I don't know. Quite a lot. Or quite a lot for Sextus, anyway.'

'He wasn't a gambler. I know that much, at least. Or I thought I did.'

'Soranus has his ways. Oh, he's a friend, I'm not slagging him off, and it was Sextus's business, no one twisted his arm. In any case, everyone gambles in our set. It's expected.'

Gods! Yeah; that was the bottom line, it was *expected*. I

wasn't surprised, not really; I'd been there myself at that age and lost more shirts than you'd see in a Suburan laundry. But there again, with what my grandfather had left me as personal income I was lucky, I could afford it. Sextus Papinius couldn't, and it wasn't his fault: reluctant gambler or not, the lad wouldn't've been human if he'd broken ranks to that degree, and at his age it's easy to get out of your depth before your brain kicks in and stops you. The real responsibility lay with adult bastards like Mucius Soranus who knew full well what was happening and encouraged it. *Lived* off it.

'Was that why Papinius killed himself?' I said gently. 'Because of a gambling debt to Soranus that he couldn't pay?'

Atratinus glared at me for a long time. Then he shook his head. 'I don't know. Maybe. Yes, it's possible. But I don't . . . fucking . . . *know*! All right?'

Uh-oh; sensitive ground. Back off, Corvinus. 'Okay. Okay, pal,' I said. 'No hassle. We'll leave it at that.' In any case, I'd be raising the question with Soranus himself before either of us were much older, and the gods help the bastard if he didn't give me a straight answer first shot. 'Let's change the subject. Tell me about the job aspect of things.' I was making conversation now, going through the motions. As far as the main reason for Sextus Papinius killing himself was concerned, I reckoned I'd cracked it. Not that the answer didn't leave me feeling sick to my stomach.

Atratinus was looking pale, but at least the anger had gone out of his eyes. 'There's not much to tell,' he said. 'We started together, when the commission was first set up three months ago. Sextus was on top of the work, he enjoyed it, he got on well with everyone. No problems there, that I can swear to.'

'He was appointed on his father's recommendation? Papinius Allenius, the ex-consul?'

'That's right. Allenius bypassed the senatorial staffing board and put the request direct to Ahenobarbus himself. Sextus was pretty proud, because he and his father hadn't seen much of each other. You know about that side of things?'

'Yeah. Yeah, I do.' Odd; but then like Rupilia had said her ex was the old-fashioned type who took his responsibilities seriously. Certainly he couldn't've made more effective – or expensive – use of his consular clout, because Domitius Ahenobarbus was one of the commission's four top men, the husband of old Augustus's granddaughter Agrippina and so Prince Gaius's brother-in-law. A five-star imperial, in other words, or four-star anyway. And in the political game you didn't use up an imperial's favours lightly. No wonder Rupilia had said she and Sextus were grateful. 'So what did the work actually entail?'

'We're the commissioners' legs and eyes.' Atratinus had started back in on his meatballs, and he was a lot calmer now. 'There're six of us altogether. It's our job to check out the compensation claims that've been made inside our particular section of the total area. Check them out physically, I mean, as well as on paper. If a property owner claims his property was completely burned down, or damaged beyond repair, we visit the site itself to make sure he's telling the truth. Same with the lesser damage claims. You'd be surprised what some chancers'll try to get away with when there's an imperial-backed compensation scheme up and running, but no cash changes hands until we've authenticated the claim six ways from nothing. You understand?'

'Yeah.' Typical Wart: the old bugger might be ready to peg out at long last – I'd give him six months, max – but he hadn't lost any of his marbles. Tiberius had always been careful with money, the state's especially, and where spending it was concerned – even when his public street-cred demanded that he be generous – he was cannier than a Paduan sheep-farmer. 'So it's a responsible job?'

'Damn right it's responsible.' Atratinus took a swig of his

wine. 'You can't take anything for granted. Like I said, some of
the property owners are bent as hell, and not all of them are
tunics or plain-mantles, either. We don't have the final say, of
course – that's up to the aediles, or the commissioners themselves in the last analysis – but there's so much property
involved that we're given a pretty free hand.'

'And Sextus's patch was where?'

'The south-west corner of the Aventine. Where he—'
Atratinus stopped abruptly.

'Where he died,' I said quietly. 'Right.'

'The tenement where it happened wasn't one of the damaged ones, but the manager had a flat there. He was responsible for two or three burned-out properties further up
the hill.'

'What was his name again? Caepio, wasn't it?'

'That's right. Lucceius Caepio.'

'You happen to know the actual owner?'

Atratinus frowned. 'No. There I can't help you, not offhand, anyway. I could check up, if you like. It'll be on record.'

'No, that's okay. I'll be talking to Caepio shortly myself.'
Going through the motions. I took another gulp of Massic, but
it didn't help. 'Uh . . . one last thing, pal. Did Papinius tell
anyone he was visiting that particular tenement at that particular time?'

I don't know why I asked the question; maybe it was my
suspicious nature, maybe it was because throwing yourself out
of a tenement window wasn't exactly the preferred method of
suicide for someone with Papinius's background. In any case,
although I'd kept my voice neutral the kid was no fool. He
glanced up quickly from his meatballs.

'No one at the office, anyway,' he said. 'Or not unless he
volunteered the information himself. That's not how we work
it.'

'So how do you work it?'

'We've each got our own list, and we take it how we want, when we want. Oh, sure, if Sextus was interviewing Caepio then he'd've arranged the meeting with him in advance. Naturally he would. But only he and Caepio would know.'

'Unless Caepio himself told the owner.'

'Yes. Yes, that's true. But no one else would be involved.'

I topped up both our cups. 'What about the actual, uh, death. You know anything about that?'

He swallowed: a sensitive soul, Marcus Atratinus, despite the haircut and the beard. 'No. Nothing at all. Barring the broad details of where, when and how.'

'Were you expecting it at all?'

'*No!*' That came out so short and sharp that I jumped. I noticed a few heads turn, and Placida shifted against my foot and growled. Atratinus smiled; or almost did. 'I'm sorry, Corvinus,' he said. 'But no, I wasn't expecting it. Why should I? I saw Sextus the morning of the day it happened. We talked about the party that evening, at Vettia Gemella's – she's my fiancée, it was her birthday. He was looking forward to it.'

'Was he bringing Cluvia?'

'No, actually, he wasn't.'

'Any reason?'

'She wasn't well. Or so he said.'

Uh-huh. 'So when did you find out? That he'd killed himself, I mean?'

'The next day. It was all over the office.' He looked at his hands. 'I still can't believe it.'

'That he's dead? Or that he killed himself?'

He looked me straight in the eyes. 'Both,' he said.

Yeah, well, I'd got a lot here to think about, but the kid had done okay and I couldn't complain . . .

Down at my feet there was a *hssss*, and a faint malodorous tendril of something that definitely wasn't scent drifted up from floor level. Oh, bugger. Speaking of complaints, I reckoned we were about due a whole roomful any second now. Time to be going; past time.

I stood up. 'Head for the door, pal. Quick as you can.'

'*What?*' Atratinus was staring. Placida's contribution to the proceedings obviously hadn't reached him yet, but heads at the table behind me had begun to turn. It was all a question, as it were, of the prevailing wind . . .

'Trust me,' I said, lugging Placida to her feet.

A stool at my back shifted. Someone muttered, 'Jupiter bloody hell!'

I turned. 'Ah . . . sorry, pal. It's the dog.' Well, at least I'd already paid the bill, and Atratinus could always come back in after we'd gone. If I hadn't got the poor bastard barred for life, that was. Upmarket chichi places are pretty sensitive about these things.

I dragged the offending brute towards the exit before she could reach second-strike mode.

Once we were out in the open air I turned to Atratinus. 'Thanks, pal. You've been very helpful.'

'Don't mention it.' He was still looking fazed. 'Any time.'

I took a good grip on the leash in case of ballistic cats and . . .

'Uh . . . Corvinus?'

I looked back. 'Yeah?'

'We talked about Sextus's gambling debts. He, uh, took out a loan from a money-lender to clear them. Quite a big one, I think. The man's name was Vestorius, Publius Vestorius. He has an office in Julian Square.'

I nodded; he hadn't been going to tell me that – dealings with money-lenders were another definite no-go subject where lad-about-town solidarity was concerned – but he'd obviously thought better of it. A nice kid, Atratinus. Sextus Papinius had been lucky with one of his friends, anyway.

'Thanks, pal,' I said. 'Much appreciated.'

*   *   *

The rain that had been threatening all day – October's always a very unsettled month – had started down in earnest. I threw the hood of my cloak over my head and let Placida pull me back along Iugarius towards Saturn's temple. Julian Square's just off Market Square itself, and I was going there in any case to lodge Natalis's draft with my banker. I might as well drop in on this Vestorius now, and get it over with.

Shit; a money-lender, eh? And 'quite a big' loan. That gave the affair a pretty ominous slant, as if it hadn't already had one: you don't put yourself in these guys' hands, not if you're a nineteen-year-old kid on a slim allowance, because the interest will be crippling, they collect on the nail every month or add what's missing to the principal, and that's a vicious spiral that only ever gets worse.

If I wanted a reason for young Papinius's suicide, trying to service a sizeable loan from a money-lender would provide it in spades. Bugger. I felt depressed as hell. It looked as though Minicius Natalis wasn't going to have to wait all that long for an answer to his question after all.

5

I was out of luck: when I found it, Vestorius's office was closed. Too early to shut up shop for the afternoon, so this looked bad. Damn. I shoved my head round the door of the silversmith's next booth along where a little bald-headed guy was doing delicate things to a bracelet with a pair of pliers.

'Excuse me, pal,' I said.

The guy glanced up. When he saw Placida the pliers slipped and he winced.

'Uh . . . I was looking for Publius Vestorius,' I said.

He was staring at the dog and sucking the back of his hand where the pliers had caught him. 'Then you've just missed him. He left half an hour ago.'

Bugger. 'You happen to know when he'll be back?'

'Not today. He said he had business in Ostia. You could try again tomorrow, but I can't guarantee it.' He was still staring. 'What *is* that thing?'

'Gallic boarhound.' *Shakeshakeshake. Splattersplattersplatter.* 'Ah . . . sorry, friend. She forgets herself sometimes.'

'That so, now?' He reached for a piece of rag and wiped himself off, glaring. I beat a hasty retreat.

Hell. Well, for what it was worth – not a lot, to tell the truth – I'd got plenty to be going on with, and Vestorius, like Balbus at the aediles' office, could wait for another time. In any case, the rain had slackened off and I might just make it back to the Caelian before Jupiter decided on another cloudburst. I called in at my banker's to lodge Natalis's draft, feeling guilty as hell in the process – the case, if you can call it that, was practically stitched up already, and it had been money for jam – and then headed for home.

Perilla was in her study indexing her book collection, and the place looked like the Pollio Library on a bad hair day. Me, I can't see the point in filling your study up with books – these things only sit there sneering at you – but the lady has some queer ideas about what constitutes comfort and entertainment. Ah, well. It takes all sorts.

'Oh, hello, Marcus,' she said, turning round. 'You're back. Where's Placida?'

'In the garden moored to the fountain. Unless she's halfway to Ostia dragging it behind her.'

'Did you have a nice walk?'

I threw myself on to the couch. 'Lady, watch my lips. That is the last time I take that fucking brute anywhere.'

'Nonsense, dear.' She kissed me, tasting of ink and gum. 'She just needs a little getting used to, that's all.'

'Believe it.' I took a slug of the wine Bathyllus had given me.

She finished tying a tag to a book's roller, made a note on the sheet of paper on the desk, and slipped the book itself into a cubby. 'So. How's the case coming? Do you know yet why Papinius killed himself?'

'No. But I'd guess the usual. Money, or lack of it, rather. Gambling debts. He'd got himself mixed up with Mucius Soranus.'

'Oh, Marcus!' Perilla looked at me with wide eyes. She'd heard of Soranus too: we don't go in for gossip, Perilla and me, but you pick up the occasional nugget here and there, and Mucius Soranus was one of the nastier lumps.

'According to his friend Atratinus he'd borrowed from a loans shark to pay Soranus off.'

'How much?'

I shrugged. 'Exactly, I don't know, but Atratinus said it was a lot. Too much for him, that's for sure.'

'He hadn't told his parents?'

'They're divorced. There's just the mother, practically speaking, and although she seems okay financially I get the impression that actual cash is pretty tight. Certainly she knew nothing about the loan, or she'd've mentioned it when we talked. Natalis neither. My guess is Papinius was too embarrassed to tell anyone at the time and just let the thing get on top of him. You know how kids' minds work at that age.'

Perilla bit her lip. 'The silly, silly boy!' She sat down. 'He didn't leave a note? A suicide note, I mean.'

'No; not that I'm aware of. But again if he had Rupilia – that's the mother – would've mentioned it. Her or Natalis.'

'Don't you think that's strange?'

'Not necessarily. He didn't kill himself at home, so it could've been a snap decision.'

'What was he doing in an Aventine tenement in the first place?'

'Interviewing the factor. At least, I assume that was the reason. He worked with the fire commission investigating damage claims, remember.'

'So he'd probably have had a set of tablets and a stylus with him. To take notes if necessary.'

'Uh . . . yeah.' I hadn't thought of that. 'Yeah, I suppose he would.'

'How about the work aspect of things? As a reason for suicide?'

I shifted on the couch. 'That seems okay. Atratinus was a colleague as well as a friend, and he says Papinius was well up to the job. I've still to talk to the aedile in charge, but there don't seem to be any problems there.'

'So it comes down to money, pure and simple.'

'Uh-huh. He had a girlfriend, too. Not a real gold-digger,

according to Atratinus, but a pretty fast model all the same. Paying her running costs can't've helped.' Shit; this was depressing. I'd seen it before, a thousand times: kid from a good family gets into a fast lifestyle, finds he can't afford to pick up all the tabs and gets into debt, then before he knows where he is he's out of his depth and struggling to keep his head above water. In most cases, when things get really bad he forgets his pride and bawls for help; at which point Daddy steps in, pays the creditors and tears enough strips off the son and heir to make him think twice, if he has any sense, about making the same mistake again. It's a lesson in life nine-tenths of the blue-bloods in Rome go through, and have been doing since Romulus ploughed the first furrow. Only with Papinius it hadn't happened that way, had it?

Bugger!

'So what do you do now?' Perilla said.

'Hmm?' I sank another quarter-pint of wine. 'Go through the motions. I owe Natalis that much, at least. Talk to Lippillus down at Public Pond, clear up that side of things. Have a word with that bastard Soranus, check how much was involved. Not that I'd bet he'll give a toss because if Papinius borrowed the cash from a money-lender the debt'll've been paid already. Cross-reference with the money-lender himself, maybe drop in on Papinius's boss at the aediles' office just for form's sake. Then – well – report back to Rupilia and Natalis. I don't reckon I've earned that fifty thousand, anyway. Natalis can use it to pay back the loan.'

'You're absolutely certain? That it was suicide, and for financial reasons?' Perilla was watching me closely. 'Marcus, you aren't, are you?'

'Sure I am.'

'Then why are you scowling?'

'I'm not. It had to be suicide. I told you.' She was right, though: something was niggling, and in spite of all the facts it wouldn't let go. 'Okay, Aristotle. I won't say they're actually points against – they aren't, because I could explain them away myself – but some things don't add up.'

'Namely?'

'First off, Papinius doesn't sound the suicidal type. Sure, he was moody at times, but show me the teenager who isn't. And Atratinus couldn't believe he'd killed himself when he heard. The last time they saw each other – the morning of the day it happened – Papinius was completely normal and making plans to go to a birthday party.'

'There's the lack of a suicide note, too. I would've expected one, even if it had been unpremeditated. And as I said he probably had a tablet and pen with him.'

'Yeah.' I took a swallow of wine. 'Second, the debt. Natalis said he was no gambler. Add to that, from what Atratinus and his mother told me about him he wasn't your usual fast-set cheese-brained idiot. Oh, sure, Soranus might've rooked him, but I'd bet he was too sensible to lose much more than he could afford. Unless he was drunk, and from what Atratinus said that doesn't seem too likely either.'

'But he did borrow money from that money-lender. What was his name?'

'Vestorius. Yeah.' I sighed. 'Perilla, I *know*, all right? It's stupid. I'm playing devil's advocate here against my own theories. And Atratinus said, quote, that he'd borrowed "quite a lot". If that doesn't square up completely then I'm sorry, it's the best I can do. Besides, I can check with Vestorius himself. In a way, the amount's the clincher. No one from Papinius's bracket commits suicide over a debt of a few thousand silver pieces, unless there're reasons over and above, and if that's all it was then sure, there'd be a chance we might be into a completely different ball-game, but on present evidence that doesn't seem all that likely.'

'Also, if—' Perilla stopped, and shook her head. 'No. I'm

sorry, Marcus; you're quite right, this is pointless. All the same, dear, there's no sense in jumping to a single conclusion this early on, even if it is the obvious one. Get your proof first. You'll feel much better if you can go to Minicius Natalis with your mind completely at rest about things.'

Yeah. I reached over and topped up my wine cup. Putting minds at rest. That was the nub of the business: Natalis's mind, Rupilia's, Atratinus's and now mine. No one was asking for anything more, no one was suggesting anything more, and on the face of it the simplest explanation was also the most likely. Papinius had topped himself. Full stop, end of story, close the book.

So why the niggle? Because – and I had to admit it – niggle there was . . .

Hell. Leave it for now. Tomorrow I'd do the rounds, like Perilla had said drum up the proof that I knew would be there. Sextus Papinius had died because of a gambling debt he couldn't pay and had borrowed over the score to cover. Sure he had.

Maybe.

'So how was your—?' I began.

'OW-*OOO! OWOO-WOO-WOO!*'

'Oh, shit!' I jumped up and ran to the window, spilling my wine. Perilla was about two seconds behind me.

Down below in the garden things were happening, largely involving a ballistic Gallic boarhound, a streak of white fur and what had up until five minutes ago been our gardener Alexis's prized rose-trellis.

'It's next-door's Alcestis!' Perilla screamed. 'Marcus, I thought you told me you'd tied up Placida!'

'I did.' Hell, the knot must've slipped, or maybe she'd broken the rope. In any case it was trailing behind her. As I watched she clambered up the ruins of the trellis ladder and disappeared after the fleeing cat into our neighbour's garden. 'Fuck, she's gone over the wall!'

We raced each other for the stairs. This was serious. We got on okay with old Titus Petillius, sure, but largely because our household and his avoided each other like each had a separate and very contagious disease; a situation that dated back two years or so to when Mrs Petillius had been the guy's house-keeper and – the thought still made me shudder – the love of our Bathyllus's life. Petillius and Tyndaris didn't have kids. What they had was Alcestis: a pure-bred silky-haired green-eyed puffball bought at enormous expense from a Damascene trader and hand-reared to a pampered life of fully indulged luxury.

A situation which, judging by Placida's single-minded pursuit of the beast, was shortly to be revised.

I hit the ground-floor tiles at a run, heading for the front door with Perilla a good second. No sign of Bathyllus, but then this was a job for the master of the house in person: grovelling would be called for, at the very least. I just hoped we weren't too late and Placida had moved Alcestis into the fur mittens category.

We could hear the screaming even before we reached next door's porch. And several loud thumps.

'Oh, bugger!' I turned the door-handle.

'Shouldn't you knock, dear?' Perilla said. 'It isn't very polite just to—'

'Look, lady,' I snapped. 'I'd say the household was pretty preoccupied at the moment, wouldn't you?' Hell. Locked. I'd have to knock after all. I hammered away on Petillius's chichi Egyptian-cat knocker.

Eventually, the door was opened by the major-domo. I didn't know his name – he postdated the wedding – but the guy gave me a stare right off a Riphaean glacier.

'Yes, sir? Madam?'

'Uh . . . can we have our dog back, please?' I said.

'*Marcus!*'

He stepped aside; Bathyllus couldn't've done it better. 'Come in. The mistress is expecting you, she's having hysterics in the atrium. If you'd care to follow me?'

Tyndaris – Mrs Petillius – was lying on one of the atrium couches with her maid trying vainly to bathe her temples with rosewater and getting most of it on the upholstery because the lady was drumming the couch-end with her heels. Hysterics was right. Yeah, well, that explained the screaming, okay. Not the thumping, though: there seemed to be a lot of that, coming from upstairs, like there was some sort of wild-beast hunt going on. Which was probably the case.

A big woman, Tyndaris. Powerful lungs, too. The couch was beginning to buckle.

'Ah . . . hi,' I said.

The screaming stopped like it'd been switched off. Tyndaris hauled herself erect and glared at me like an enraged hippo.

'*Get that . . . that* THING *out of here! This minute! And if it's touched one hair of Alcestis's head my Titus will . . . !*'

'Yeah. Yeah, right. Got you.' I backed away.

'We're terribly sorry,' Perilla said.

'So you bloody well will be!'

'She's, ah, upstairs, is she?' I said. 'Placida, I mean?'

'*Placida?*'

'Yes.' Perilla said brightly. 'That's her name.'

'*Hah!*'

'I'll show you the way, sir,' the major-domo said.

'Don't worry, pal, I think we can manage.' I headed at speed towards the staircase at the far end of the atrium, with Perilla trailing like a pale wraith, and took the steps two at a time.

She was in the main bedroom, on the bed, although there wasn't a lot left of that and what there was looked distinctly chewed. Half a dozen kitchen skivvies with assorted brooms and culinary equipment were cowering in the doorway. There was no sign of the cat, which was probably good news; although on the other hand . . .

'Oh, shit,' I muttered. Obviously the brute had had the time of her life because she was looking as pleased as hell and the room was something out of the stage set for the sack of Corinth. 'Come on, Placida. Home.'

I pushed through the massed minions, grabbed her by the collar and lugged her towards the exit. Halfway there, she pulled away, bent her back, spread her rear paws, squatted and strained . . .

'*Placida!*'

That was Perilla. Too late. Yeah, well, after all the excitement it was only natural, I supposed. Even so, it was the icing on the cake. As it were.

I looked at the goggling skivvies. 'Uh . . . any of you lads have a shovel?'

We went back downstairs and grovelled. You don't want to know the next part. You really don't. Suffice it to say that the upshot was the financial equivalent of Cannae. When the bill hit my banker's desk we'd be living on boiled beets for a month.

'*Just needs a little getting used to*, eh?' I said to Perilla as we walked back with Placida ambling good as gold between us; but the lady didn't answer.

Fun, fun, fun.

6

I was up early the next morning, sneaking out of the bedroom just after first light; not that I needed to bother about waking Perilla, mind, because that lady could sleep through Etna erupting, and she isn't one of nature's early risers. I skipped the shave – I could always have a scrape at one of the booths around the edge of Market Square later if I had time – and went down to the dining-room. No sign of Placida, but then after the previous afternoon's escapade our friendly hellhound was in deep disgrace and relegated to a chained post in the garden. Not that I'd any sympathy, because if the day before had been anything to go by looking after the brute for two months would cost us an arm and a leg. Maybe we'd be glad of Natalis's fifty thousand after all just to pay for the breakages.

I was really, *really* looking forward to going out dogless today.

Bathyllus was doing his pre-breakfast round of the bronzes with the special soft cloth he keeps for raising a shine on the various bums and bosoms. Sometimes I wonder about Bathyllus. All the same, if it keeps the little bald-head happy then who am I to complain?

'Just get Meton to fix me an omelette in a roll this morning, sunshine,' I said. 'I'm off down to Public Pond, and I'll eat it on the way.'

'Yes, sir.' Bathyllus sniffed: eating breakfast on the hoof in a public thoroughfare isn't something the League of Major-domos approves of. 'You'll be back for dinner, of course. I understand Meton is serving fish.'

Oh, gods! I hate fish days. Not the menu, no – what our anarchic chef can do with a few slices of tunny, a bag of clams and a dash or two of fish sauce would have old Lucullus crying his eyes out – but turn up even five minutes late for the off and you find yourself living on boiled cabbage and meatballs for a month. Meton gets very *serious* about fish. 'Yeah. Yeah, I'll be there,' I said. 'Incidentally, you happen to know where Mucius Soranus lives?'

Bathyllus raised an eyebrow, which in Bathyllus-speak is strong stuff, certainly well beyond ordinary sniff-class: just because the guy's a slave doesn't mean he doesn't keep up with the gossip, and where moral rectitude is concerned you could lay him flat and use him to draw lines. Even so, and on his uppers or not, Soranus was one of *the* Mucii who go back to the time when Scaevola played his trick with Porsenna and the brazier, and any prime-class major-domo worth his buffing rag would chew his own leg off before admitting that he didn't know where one of the top five hundred hung out.

'On the Cipian, sir. The big old three-storey property opposite the Porch of Livia.'

Hmm; not all that far away, then. If it didn't risk breaching the three-line fish whip I might be able to take Soranus in last thing. Mind you, a talk with that bastard immediately before dinner could well put me off my feed. I'd have to see how things went. 'Great. Thanks, pal. Now go and organise that roll, okay?'

Bathyllus soft-shoed out and I helped myself to an apple and a few grapes from the table. Early morning, preferably the crack of dawn but I was no masochist, was the best time to catch Decimus Lippillus because he'd be at the Watch-house reading through the reports his deputy on the night shift had left on his desk. Then over to Julian Square to check up if the loan-shark Publius Vestorius was back from Ostia, a talk – if he was available – with Papinius's boss Laelius Balbus, and finally round to Soranus's, ditto. I reckoned that with all these bases successfully covered I'd've done my duty by Natalis, and barring any surprises – which I didn't expect – we could call it a wrap . . .

'I've brought the dog, sir.'

I turned. Bathyllus was standing in the doorway with my portable breakfast in one hand and the other holding Placida's lead. The brute was grinning at me.

Oh, gods. This I did not deserve. 'You have *what*, Bathyllus?'

'For its walk. The mistress was most insistent. She told me last night not to let you leave without it.'

Jupiter sodding best and greatest! 'Listen, little guy,' I said, 'I have about as much intention of spending a second day in that brute's dubious company as I have of tap-dancing naked up the Sacred Way. When Perilla wakes up you can tell her—'

'Tell me what, dear?'

She appeared in the doorway behind Bathyllus and gave me a bright smile. I goggled. Shit, this was a conspiracy: nothing, but *nothing* gets that lady out of bed before the sun's properly up.

'Ah . . .' I said.

'I have explained already, Marcus. Very clearly. I promised Sestia Calvina that we'd look after Placida properly, which means regular walks. And since you're walking anyway then you may as well take her along. I'm sure she's marvellous company, really.'

'Lady, that thing is fucking hell on legs! I'd as soon walk a wolverine!'

'Don't exaggerate.'

'Perilla . . .'

'Besides, after yesterday's little episode with Alcestis we

can't risk leaving her in the garden, can we? She'd have to be chained, which wouldn't be fair. And she *is* getting used to you.'

I opened my mouth, then closed it again: when Perilla's in this mood there's no point in arguing, and where logic's concerned you can forget it. Bugger.

Now I knew how Orestes must've felt when he was stuck with the Furies.

I held out my hand for the lead.

Sure enough, Lippillus was standing at his desk, reading over a wax tablet and chewing on an omelette roll of his own. He looked up when I came in . . .

'What the hell is *that?*'

I sighed. 'Rare Parthian coarse-haired hornless antelope? No. Mutant Numidian hamster? I don't think so. Hyperactive, totally uncivilised Gallic fucking boarhound? Why, I do believe it is.' I pulled up a stool and sat while Placida squatted and lolled her tongue at him. Jupiter, I was knackered. Caelian to Public Pond in just shy of twenty minutes. Someone should explain to canines the meaning of the word 'walk' and how it differed from, say, 'bolt'. 'And don't, *don't* ask about the bag-lady, the cheese-seller, the woman with the poodle or the cat on the flagpole.'

Lippillus was grinning. 'You're tetchy this morning, Corvinus. She yours? You've never exactly struck me as the dog-owning type.'

I shuddered and made the sign against bad omens: with my current run of luck Sestia Calvina over in Veii would be trampled to death by a freak runaway elephant and we'd be stuck with the brute for ever. Not that I'd've thought too badly of the elephant, mind. 'No, we're just looking after her. At least it seems I am. You know the way Perilla's chain of logic works.'

'She's a beauty. Aren't you, girl?' He reached over and ruffled Placida's ears, which put the two of them practically eyeball to eyeball. There isn't much of Flavonius Lippillus in vertical terms, and his no-clout name doesn't do him any favours either with the pukkah Establishment, but you don't get to be Watch commander for one of the toughest districts in Rome without a pretty good reason, and for once the broad-stripers in the City Prefect's office had got it right. What Lippillus didn't know about Watch work you could drop down a hole and forget.

'Yeah,' I said sourly. 'She's got a lovely nature. At least, that's what they keep telling me.'

'So why the visit? Not that you're not always welcome.'

'Do me a favour?'

'Sure.' He laid the tablet on the desk.

'The name Sextus Papinius mean anything to you?'

'Kid who threw himself out of a tenement window two or three days back?'

'That's him. You happen to have the details?'

'Not as such. It's not my patch, Corvinus. The tenement was across the line in Thirteen. Head of Old Ostia Road between the hill and the river.'

'Yeah, I know that.' Bugger. Well, I shouldn't really have expected anything else: these guys don't poach, and they're very careful about treading on each others' toes. 'Still, anything you can give me would be appreciated.'

Lippillus was watching me carefully. 'Why the interest?' he said.

'It's probably nothing. You remember Minicius Natalis, the Greens' boss? He's an ex-client of the boy's grandfather. He asked me to look into the death.'

'Uh-huh.' Lippillus sucked at a tooth, and his eyes didn't waver. Then he said, 'The Thirteenth's Titus Mescinius's patch. If you want to talk to him I can give you an introduction. How would that do?'

'Great!' I didn't know Mescinius, and as a general rule Watch commanders aren't too appreciative of sassy purple-stripers butting in. An introduction from Lippillus would go a long way to pre-emptively smoothing any ruffled feathers. 'He – ah – liable to be informative?'

'He's okay. No ball of fire, mind, but he's straight as a die and he won't hold out on you, so long as you don't get up his nose too much. That I do not advise.' He reached for a clean wax tablet and stylus, scribbled a sentence or two and handed it over. 'There you are. You owe me one.'

'Dinner tomorrow?'

'Make it the day after, with fish. Marcina can't cook fish worth a damn.'

'You've got it. Come on, Placida. Heel.' I stood up and turned to go.

'Oh, and Corvinus?'

I turned back. 'Yeah?'

'Enjoy your walk.'

The Watch-house for the Thirteenth Region was on Old Ostia Road itself, and not far from where the tenement must be. There was a slave outside brushing down the steps.

I hauled on Placida's lead and dug my heels in until she decided to stop. 'Boss around, pal?' I said. The chances were he would be: Decimus Lippillus didn't spend much of his time behind his desk, but then Lippillus was the exception. Most Watch commanders preferred to leave the wearing out of sandal leather to their squaddies.

'Yes, sir. In his office.' The slave pointed through the open door. 'Straight ahead of you.'

'Thanks. Uh . . . you mind looking after this for me?'

Before he could answer I'd slipped him the leash and was past him. I didn't glance back, even when I heard the scream.

The door gave on to a lobby with an unoccupied desk and another door behind it. I went up to it and knocked.

'Come in.'

I did.

'Yes?'

Well, we weren't talking lean and mean here, anyway. He was a big lad, Titus Mescinius, with the proportions – and probably the blubber content – of a beached whale. He'd set down the stylus he was holding and was blinking at me suspiciously.

'The name's Marcus Valerius Corvinus,' I said.

'That so, now?'

Friendly as hell. 'Ah . . . Decimus Lippillus over at Public Pond said you might be willing to talk to me about a suicide a couple of days back.' I handed him Lippillus's note.

He read it in silence. Then he looked up. No smile, but you couldn't expect miracles.

'Papinius, eh?' he said. 'Tragic affair. Tragic. He was only nineteen, you know.'

'Yeah. Yeah, I did.' There was a stool in front of the desk. I pulled it over. 'Mind if I sit down? I've had a busy morning.'

'Suit yourself.' He laid the tablet to one side. 'So you're representing who, Corvinus? Decimus doesn't say. Or are you a relative?'

'Uh-uh. But there's no hassle, I promise. Minicius Natalis, the Greens' faction-master – he's an old friend of the family – and the boy's mother asked me to find out all I could about the death. Why the boy killed himself, I mean. I just wanted to get the facts straight right at the start.'

Mescinius nodded. He didn't look precisely gruntled, but I reckoned that was his normal expression. At least we were over the hump, and Natalis's name seemed to have registered. Maybe the guy was a Greens fan. 'Very commendable. And perfectly reasonable, under the circumstances. I'd be delighted to assist as far as I can. Just let me consult my notes.' He pulled out a drawer in the desk, scrabbled through it and brought out a set of tablets. 'Ah. Here we are.' He untied the laces, opened the tablets and read. 'Yes. Three days ago, two hours or so after noon, at the Carsidius tenement. Several witnesses, particularly the stallkeeper on the opposite side. Death was instantaneous, of course.'

'Carsidius is the tenement owner?'

'That's right. He's a senator; Lucius Carsidius. He has several properties in the area run through a factor by the name of Lucceius Caepio. The man has a flat on the first floor.'

'Papinius was visiting Caepio?'

Mescinius frowned. 'Actually, no, not that day, at least, although he had done on other occasions. Caepio was in at the time – he came downstairs when he heard the shouting – but he'd no idea the young man was in the building.'

'So why *was* he there?'

That got me a look like I was a retarded prawn. 'Surely the reason's obvious from what followed, Corvinus. The boy was mentally disturbed, and he'd decided to kill himself. Under these circumstances I don't think we need look for another explanation, do we?'

Shit. We were only at the information-gathering stage here, and theorising could wait for later. Still, I could feel the tingle of cold at the base of my neck that I always got when things didn't quite add up.

'Okay,' I said. 'So what exactly happened? You said there were witnesses?'

'Certainly. A whole streetful. Although no one saw the actual fall.'

'He didn't cry out? Scream? Anything like that?'

'No. Not as far as anyone reported.'

'And he didn't leave a note?'

'No again. Not in the room, at any rate. He had a tablet and stylus with him when he fell. We found them near the body, but the tablet was blank.'

'The top flat. It was empty?'

'That's right.'

'So how did he get in?'

'He had a key on him. We found that too.'

Jupiter on skates! 'He had a *what*? Where the hell did he get it from?'

Mescinius stiffened. 'I'm afraid I can't say. Presumably from the factor, Caepio, on one of the previous occasions.'

'Why would Caepio give him a key to an empty flat?'

'For the purposes of damage assessment, naturally. You know that Papinius was with the Aventine fire commission?'

'Yeah. Yeah, I knew that.'

'There you are, then. Although the tenement itself wasn't directly affected, the roof would certainly have been exposed to blown embers from properties further up the hill, and of course the top flat lay immediately under the tiles.'

I was staring at him. Sweet immortal gods! This guy was a *Watch commander*? 'But you didn't check,' I said neutrally. 'As to whether Caepio had given him the key or not.'

The drop in temperature was almost physical. Mescinius leaned forward slowly and put his hands flat on the desktop. He wasn't looking friendly at all now. 'Valerius Corvinus,' he said. 'Do you realise just how busy this section of the Watch is? I've two regions under my jurisdiction and precious few men to deal with them, and I can't afford to spend time chasing up every apparent anomaly in an incident, especially where the incident is obviously a suicide and the anomaly will no doubt prove to *be* only apparent. Now. The flat the boy fell from was empty. He had clearly gone there with the intention of killing himself and secured the means of access beforehand. How he did that I don't know, but no doubt there's a perfectly rational explanation. I am very sorry for the lad's family, and I wish you every success in your investigations, but young Papinius's reasons for committing suicide, as such, are not my concern. Under the circumstances I have to regard the matter as closed. You understand me?'

'Yeah. Yeah, I understand.'

'Good.' He reached for a wax tablet. 'Then if you'll excuse me . . .'

Bugger. Well, Lippillus had warned me, and I should've kept a firmer control of my mouth, but all the same . . . Still, there was no use pushing things further. I stood up.

'Thanks for your help,' I said, and exited.

So what now? Obviously, the tenement, and hopefully a word with this Lucceius Caepio. Oh, everything could be above board, like Mescinius assumed, but the way things were developing I didn't like the smell. Not above half, I didn't. Forget about calling the case a wrap: the cold feeling at the back of my neck was telling me it was very much alive and kicking.

So was Placida. The guy I'd left holding her lead didn't look too gruntled, either. Being yanked down a flight of steps and dragged over the cobbles for twenty yards can get some people that way.

7

L ike Natalis had said, the tenement was a fairly new
  property, six storeys high and upmarket compared with
most of the others in the immediate area, which probably
explained why Carsidius's factor had chosen it for his flat.
There was a butcher's shop directly underneath one side of the
entrance door, with a guy looping sausages over a hook, but I
was learning: I didn't even think of approaching him for
information, not while I was attached to Placida. Diagonally
opposite, on the other side of the street, a large-breasted woman
in a bright red tunic and earrings was selling fruit and vegetables
from a stall. Fruit and veg should be safe enough. I took a firm
grip of Placida's collar and manoeuvred her over.

The woman beamed when she saw us coming. I was
beginning to realise that there were basically two reactions
to Placida: one was to coo over her, the other was to look for
the nearest climbable wall. Strangely enough, women seemed
to favour the first option.

'Oooh! Isn't she a pet!' she said. 'What's her name?'

'Uh, Placida.'

'There's a luvvums!' Placida reared, tongue lolling, to put
her paws on the woman's ample chest, but I was ready for that
one and hauled her down before she could cause an embar-
rassing incident. 'Doesn't she have a beautiful face?'

'Yeah. Yeah, she does.' Sure; if you happened to like jaws that
could rip the throat out of a bear and a muzzle permanently
covered in spit. Still, as a conversational icebreaker with strangers

– women especially – I couldn't fault her. I wondered if Perilla's stepdad, the poet, had featured Gallic boarhounds in his book on seduction. The brutes' other, less appealing proclivities would be a bit of a style-cramper at a later stage, mind.

'Now, sir,' the fruit lady said. 'What can I get you?'

'Just an apple, thanks. One of these Matians'll be fine.'

She picked it up, rubbed it off and handed it to me while I took a coin from my belt-pouch.

'I heard there was a suicide here two or three days ago,' I said.

'That's right. Dreadful thing.' She counted out my change. 'He was hardly more than a boy.'

'You see it happen?'

'Couldn't help but, could I? It's the sort of thing gives you nightmares.'

I glanced up at the tenement. Some of these places – the upmarket ones, anyway – have balconies, at least on the first floor, but this one didn't. 'He, uh, jump straight off from the window ledge?' I said.

'Can't tell you that. I wasn't looking. You don't, do you? Not up.'

'He didn't shout first, then, or scream? Give any kind of warning?'

The woman gave me a long stare; the friendliness had gone. 'I'm sorry, sir,' she said finally. 'No disrespect, but I don't hold with ghouls. The poor lad's dead and there's an end of it. That's no one's business but his.' She bent down to rearrange the fruit on her tray. 'Enjoy your apple.'

Yeah, well. That was fair enough; I'd no time for ghouls and rubber-neckers myself. And at least she'd confirmed what Mescinius had said. I put the Matian away for later and crossed the road to the tenement entrance, lugging Placida behind me and steering her away from the butcher's shop.

New was right: the steps were clean, there was no sign of

graffiti on the white-plastered walls inside and no smell of urine on the stairs. Give it time. I tied Placida to the banister, making sure the knot was tight, went up to the first floor and knocked on the door marked 'Lucceius Caepio'.

I thought for a minute there was no one in – tenement dwellers spend most of their time elsewhere – but as I raised my hand for the second knock the door was opened by a thick-set, unshaven guy in his forties wearing a lounging-tunic and chewing on a hunk of bread.

'Lucceius Caepio?' I said.

'Yes.' There was suspicion in his eyes. 'Who're you?'

'Valerius Corvinus. I've just come from Titus Mescinius over at the Watch-house.' No harm in dropping the name, and given he didn't look particularly welcoming I reckoned the ambiguity would get me over the threshold faster. 'You have time for a chat, pal?'

He hesitated, then stepped back, still chewing. The eyes hadn't shifted. 'A little,' he said. 'You'd best come in.'

I followed him, closing the door behind me. There was something badly wrong with the guy's leg, because he held it stiffly and didn't so much move as lurch.

'Sorry about the mess,' he said. 'The wife's at her sister's down in Capua. New baby. You want a bite of breakfast?'

'No thanks. You carry on, though.'

He grunted and sat down at the table. Tenements, even upmarket ones, are pretty basic, and tables don't come as standard, but Caepio seemed to be fitted up quite snugly here. There was even a small dresser with a set of Samian bowls and plates, and a line of the cheap souvenir statuettes they sell outside the Circus. The other thing I noticed was a key-board with numbered hooks fixed to the wall.

'It'll be about that youngster, no doubt,' Caepio said, dipping his crust of bread in a bowl of oil. 'Sextus Papinius.'

'Right.' I pulled up a stool.

'You're no Watchman. Not with that stripe.'

'No. I'm looking into the kid's death. Or the reasons for it, rather. On behalf of the mother and a family friend.'

He gave me a quick, sharp look and bit into the bread. 'That so, now?' he said. 'Sad business. Terrible.'

'He worked for the fire compensation board. I understand you and he had, uh, a professional connection.'

'If you can call it that, sure. I was factor for a couple of other properties further up the hill that got burned down. He came over a couple of times and we talked through the details.'

'But you didn't know he was here the afternoon he died?'

Long silence. Then, finally, Caepio said, 'That's not quite true.'

I frowned. 'I'm sorry?'

'Look.' He took a deep breath. 'I knew he was here, but not that he intended to . . . use the upstairs flat. Okay?'

Shit. 'That's not what you told the Watch, friend,' I said carefully.

'No.'

'All right.' I kept my voice neutral. 'So why the lie? And why bother to tell the truth now?'

'Where lying goes' – Caepio shrugged – 'well, if you think about it you'll understand that yourself. I'd nothing to do with the death, first thing I knew was when I heard the commotion in the street and went down.' He dipped his bread again. 'But the kid had died on my property and I didn't want to get involved, right? Besides, he only called in in passing to confirm some of the figures we'd discussed. At least that's what I thought at the time, because that's what he told me. As far as telling the truth now's concerned' – he got up, hobbled over to the board on the wall and pointed to the last hook – 'there's your answer there.'

The hook, like all the others on the board, was empty.

Uh-huh. 'That's where the flat key was,' I said. Tenement factors use these boards for the keys to the various flats because it keeps everything nice and neat. If a flat's occupied then of course the occupier gets the key, but otherwise it stays on the board. The last two hooks would go with the top floor.'

'Right. I didn't notice it was missing until I got back here after the Watchmen had gone with the body. Didn't know he had it on him, either; still don't, as such, because they haven't been back, but I assume now he must've because it wasn't upstairs when I looked. Did he?' I nodded, and his mouth twisted. 'Right. That solves that one, then. Anyway, it wasn't until later that I put two and two together, and by then I'd told my story. Now I'm just setting the record straight, that's all.'

'You didn't wonder how he'd got into the flat?'

He stared at me, the bread-crust halfway to his lips. 'Jupiter, that's not something you give a thought to! Not when a man's lying there smashed like a doll with his brains . . .' He stopped, looked at the crust and put it down. 'Anyway, the answer's no. No, I didn't wonder, not then.'

'And the Watchman you talked to didn't ask? Where Papinius had got the key from?'

'He hadn't seen it at the time. Or at least he never mentioned it to me, and like I say no one from the Watch office has been here since. I assume it was in the lad's belt-pouch and they found it later.'

Oh, great; score one for the super-efficient Thirteenth District Watch. Gods alive, what a shower! 'So what you're saying – now – is that Papinius dropped in on an excuse and helped himself to the top-floor-flat key?'

'Yes. At least, that's what I'm assuming. The document with the figures he wanted was in my desk in the other room. He'd've known that. He must've taken the key while I was getting it and then gone upstairs when I thought he'd left the building.' Caepio spread his hands. 'Look, I'm sorry I lied, Corvinus. It was stupid, and I've regretted it ever since, but I'm levelling with you now before I get myself into more trouble. After all, what does it matter? And I swear to you the boy didn't get that key from me. Not as such.'

Yeah, well, there was no point in pushing things. And he seemed genuine enough. 'Okay.' I stood up. 'Can I see the flat?'

Caepio was looking relieved. 'Certainly. No problem. It's locked again, of course, because I've got a duplicate. Hold on and I'll fetch it for you.' He got up and lurched into the next room, reappearing almost immediately with a heavy bunch of keys. 'That's the one, the last on the ring. You want me to come up?'

'No, that's okay.' With that leg, climbing five flights of stairs wouldn't be easy. 'I'll drop them back down on the way out.'

'It's the door on the left.' He handed the bunch over. 'Take your time.'

I went up to the sixth. There were two flats opposite each other either side of the landing, and on an impulse I knocked a couple of times at the other door. No answer. Well, like I say that was par for the course: people in tenements are out most of the day, and any top-floor flat will be as basic as you get, with no incentive for staying in.

Once inside the flat itself I opened the shutters to let in the light: tenement windows, especially those on the upper floors, are just holes in the wall, and with the weather we'd been getting Caepio had kept them closed. I'd expected the place to be bare, but there were three or four stools and the framework of a bed, with no mattress. Also, although it smelled stale and unused, it was dry, fairly clean and even clear of dust. Good sign: empty flats, particularly the no-frills variety right under the tiles, tend to get the go-by where everyday maintenance is concerned. Caepio was obviously the conscientious type.

I looked through the window and down. A long way down: six storeys seem more when you're at the top of them. The street below was crowded – it'd been a miracle that Papinius hadn't taken an innocent pedestrian or two with him when he jumped – but all I could see was the tops of heads and my friend the fruit-seller's stall on the opposite pavement. Nothing at eye-level, not for at least a block either side. Good view of the Aventine, if you like that sort of thing. Windowsill chest high, but he could've clambered up easy, or used the stool immediately beneath the ledge to stand on. He'd've had to have climbed, certainly: accident wasn't an option here.

I leaned out and shouted. Two or three heads swivelled upwards briefly.

It all checked; the physical side of things, anyway. I poked around a bit in the room, but there was nothing to see that I wouldn't have expected, and even the bloody Thirteenth District Watch wouldn't't've missed something as obvious as a suicide note that'd got itself mislaid in one of the corners. Bugger. That was that, then.

I took a last look from the window down towards the pavement, feeling my balls shrink: me, if I had to kill myself, I'd do it clean by slitting my wrists in the bath or putting a sword to my ribs and falling on it. Or maybe just lighting a charcoal brazier and shutting all the windows. I sure as hell wouldn't jump from a sixth-floor window in a strange building head-first on to a crowded street. Still, I wasn't Papinius. And he had taken the key. That last I was sure of: Caepio hadn't been lying, I'd bet my last copper penny there, which meant that it was suicide after all, carefully planned and premeditated.

The only question left to answer was the one I'd started with: *why?*

I dropped the keys off with Caepio and went down to collect Placida. Zilch. The banister-holding bracket had been torn clear of the wall, and there was a distinct absence of dog. Which meant . . .

Oh, hell!

Here we went again. I cleared the tenement entrance at a run. Too late, miles too late; I could tell that straight away from the crowd of interested bystanders round the butcher's.

Shit! She'd planned it! She had bloody *planned* it! I'd kill the brute!

I pushed my way through. Placida was up on the counter gulping down the last of the dangling pork links. The butcher himself was standing well clear, cleaver in hand.

Happy, smiling and contented were three things he wasn't.

'That your dog, friend?' he said.

'Uh . . . yeah. In a manner of speaking.'

'Fuck that,' he spat. 'You owe me for' – he counted off on his fingers – 'two pounds of tripe, six chops, three pork knuckles, an ox liver and a bowl of dripping. Plus the sausages, of course.'

'*What? Nothing* can eat . . . !'

'I got witnesses.'

I glanced round. Several of the punters nodded. They were all looking impressed as hell. One old guy with no teeth and a face like a pickled walnut was making a trembling sign against the evil eye.

I sighed and reached for my purse. This was getting monotonous. Maybe we should give the brute an allowance and bill Sestia bloody Calvina when she finally rolled in from Veii.

'You want to look after her better.' The butcher had his hand out. 'Me, I've always said there's no problem dogs, just problem owners.'

'Very profound, pal.' I tipped half of the purse's contents into his palm. 'Have a really, *really* nice day. Come on, Placida.'

I pulled on the dangling lead. She came down, grinning.

Urp.

'Yeah, I'm not surprised.' Well, it might slow her down a bit, at least. It was a long drag from the Aventine to Julian Square, and that was our next stop to see the money-lender Vestorius.

8

Lugging the bloated Placida behind me, I took the hike back to the centre and Julian Square. Bankers and money-lenders tend to keep fairly self-indulgent hours, but the sun was halfway through the morning now and the chances were that if Vestorius was anywhere to be got then I'd get the bastard now.

Sure enough, the Shark was In: a tall, spare, elderly north Italian with a sharp well-starched mantle, a wispy goatee beard and an air that left him somewhere between a professor of rhetoric and any kid's ideal of a cuddly grampa. When I shoved my head round the door of his booth – really, a small room done up like an office – he was slaving over a hot abacus with added ledgers.

'Uh . . . Publius Vestorius?' I said.

'That's right.' I got the full hundred-candelabra smile as he took in the purple stripe on my mantle. Nice teeth, but then loan-sharks, like professional politicians, tend to look after them if they can. A good smile is one of these bastards' most important assets. 'Come in, sir.'

'You mind if I bring my dog with me? Only if I leave her tied up outside she's liable to get bored and eat people.'

The smile wavered. 'I beg your pardon?'

'Joke. In you come, Placida.' I moved aside to let her past, and the smile disappeared altogether. 'Don't worry, pal, she's got a lovely nature.'

'Ah . . . yes.' He rallied visibly. 'Fine animal. Very fine. Do have a seat. You'll find that chair quite comfortable.'

Yeah, I'd bet it was, because the whole room was designed to put the customer at his ease and keep him there while he got rooked. The chair was padded with crimson wool-stuffed cushions. I sat, and sank a good two inches before I stopped. 'The name's Corvinus,' I said. 'Valerius Corvinus. Settle, Placida.'

Amazingly, she did, albeit with a single prolonged belch. I wondered what the odds were in favour of her crapping on the guy's fancy polished wooden floor. Pretty good, I'd imagine, considering how much she'd eaten and her total lack of the social graces. Not that I'd mind, myself. Quite the reverse.

'I'm delighted to meet you.' Vestorius moved the abacus aside. '*Such* unpleasant weather this time of year, isn't it? Still, we can't complain, we had quite a moderate summer. Some wine?'

'Yeah. Yeah, sure.' Me, I never pass up a free cup of wine, and if the bugger wanted to think I was a punter that was his affair.

There was a slave hovering. Vestorius snapped his fingers and the guy oozed across to the wine jug and cups on the small table to one side of his desk. 'Now,' he said, and the smile was back in spades, 'how exactly can I be of help? Presumably you need a loan. I can assure you here and now that there will be no difficulties on that score.'

I waited until the slave had handed me the cup and I'd taken a sip: Alban, and top-of-the-range Alban as well. Profit margins must be pretty generous in the loan-shark market. As if I didn't know.

'Actually no,' I said. 'I wanted to ask you about one of your customers. A young guy by the name of Sextus Papinius. He committed suicide three days ago.'

Vestorius's smile froze. 'I beg your pardon?'

'I'm representing his mother Rupilia and Minicius Natalis, the faction-master of the Greens. They want to know why he did it.' I took another swallow of wine. 'Story I've been told is that he'd taken out a sizeable loan from you some time previous. Can you confirm that? Just for the record.'

The guy was staring at me. He cleared his throat. Finally, he said, 'Yes, of course I can confirm it. The loan was indeed made.'

'And how sizeable was sizeable?'

'You mean you don't already know?' I didn't answer. 'Well, under the circumstances I think I can . . . the sum was fifty thousand silver pieces.'

I blinked: when I'd said to Perilla that Natalis could use my fee to pay back the loan I'd assumed he'd have some change back on the deal. *'How much?'*

Vestorius stroked the emerald ring on his little finger. 'Yes, indeed,' he said. 'A very respectable amount. *Very* respectable. But then the young man seemed reliable, from a good family. And if there is one thing I pride myself on it's my ability to judge people.'

Right. Sure. Only I'd bet, personally, that the smug bugger's assessment of Papinius's risk-rating hadn't stopped him from adding a fairly swingeing interest clause to the contract. Quite the reverse. 'When exactly did he borrow the money?' I said. 'If you don't mind telling me?'

'Not at all. It was just under a month ago.'

'Did he happen to say what he needed it for?'

'Valerius Corvinus, it is not my practice to discuss—'

'Come on, pal! I told you, the kid's dead and his family and friends want to know why he killed himself. This is no time for professional ethics. If that's the phrase here.'

That got me a long cool look, but finally Vestorius said, 'Very well. The answer to your question is no. Papinius didn't volunteer the information, nor did I enquire. Why should I? It was none of my business.'

'Did he offer any security?'

The guy hesitated. 'As I said, and as you know, he came from a good family – a consular family, on his father's side – and he'd just embarked on what would no doubt have been a long and successful political career. Under these circumstances, a security pledge is a mere formality.'

Uh-huh; in other words, for swingeing interest read gutting: the kid must've been desperate. But fifty thousand! That was serious gravy for a nineteen-year-old's gambling debts. 'He was over the legal age, his mother didn't know anything about the transaction, and as far as I know he'd no private source of income,' I said carefully. 'So now he's dead how do you reclaim the principal?'

Vestorius looked fazed for a moment, then he smiled. Now we were face to face at close range I noticed that two of his front teeth were wired-in gold, and I wondered if some customer in the past had knocked out the originals for him. If so I wouldn't't've blamed them. 'Oh, that isn't a problem,' he said.

'Is that so, now? And why not?'

'Because the loan was repaid four days ago.'

I stared at him, wine forgotten. 'It was *what*?'

'Yes, indeed.'

'Who the hell by?'

'By young Papinius himself, of course. In cash.'

'The whole boiling? All fifty thousand?'

'Plus the interest. Sixty thousand in total.' Vestorius was still smiling. 'I was as surprised as you seem to be, naturally – I'd understood it was to be a long-term arrangement – but that was his decision. And quite acceptable on my part.'

'Where the fuck did a kid like that get sixty thousand silver pieces cash in hand?'

He shrugged. 'Again, I didn't ask. It—'

'Was none of your business. Got it.' I'd had enough of this bastard. I stood up; Placida, too. 'Thanks for your time, pal. Have a nice day.'

'You also, Valerius Corvinus. And I'm sorry to hear about young Papinius's death.' He reached for the abacus.

'Yeah. Sure you are,' I said. *Sixty thousand* silver pieces. This was getting complicated. 'Come on, Placida. Heel.'

But she'd ambled off into the far corner and was arching her back and straining. Vestorius's eyes widened in disbelief as she deposited the evil-smelling remains of two pounds of tripe, six chops, three pork knuckles, the ox liver and a bowl of dripping. Plus the sausages . . .

Oh, joy!

I grinned and left Vestorius to his cleaning up. Maybe I could warm to Placida after all.

Okay; so what next? I might as well follow the original plan and drop in on Papinius's boss, the aedile Laelius Balbus. If he was in. In any case, the aediles' office wasn't far, just the other side of Market Square.

Where the fuck did an impecunious teenager like Sextus Papinius get his hands on sixty thousand silver pieces? In cash and at short notice, too. Not from his mother, that was clear: even if she'd been covering up for some reason and lying six ways from nothing I'd bet the lady didn't have that sort of loose change. The same went for Natalis as a source: he'd have the cash to hand, sure, no problem there, but he would've told me if he'd given it to Papinius, because money wasn't something Natalis was coy about. The father Allenius was an obvious possibility, at least on the face of it, but I'd reckon from his past track record paying off an estranged son's debts to that tune just wasn't on; getting him his job with the fire commission had been favour enough.

Getting him his job with the . . .

I slowed down. Oh, shit. Oh, no.

You'd be surprised what some chancers'll try to get away with when there's an imperial-backed compensation scheme up and running.

Atratinus had said that. But surely Papinius wouldn't've been such a bloody fool. And he just wasn't the type.

Or was he? It would explain how he came by the sixty thousand, certainly. And, given certain circumstances, it would explain the suicide, too.

Bugger. Still, theorising could wait until I'd talked to Balbus. Not that I'd take Placida in with me this time: public officials get very *intense* about boarhounds crapping on the government's tiling.

One curious thing. As I left Julian Square I had the distinct feeling that I was being followed; nothing definite, and the few times I turned round didn't provide any evidence for it. Even so, the feeling was there, and it wouldn't go away.

I was lucky: the aedile was in and free to see me. He was a big man my age, with heavy eyebrows and an even heavier gut that projected well over the desk as he stood up to shake hands.

'I've been expecting you, Corvinus,' he said. 'Atratinus said you'd had a chat with him over lunch yesterday, and I thought I might be next. Have a seat.'

The visitor's chair had ivory inlay and small golden birds on the pillars of the backpiece. It went well with the rest of the office's furnishings, which were a lot more upmarket than you usually find in a public-sector room. Still, with four deputy imperials fronting the commission that wasn't surprising.

'Now.' Balbus settled into his own chair. 'What can I tell you about young Papinius? Not much more than you've already heard, probably. He was with us practically from the start, he was good at his job and seemed to enjoy it, got on well with his colleagues and his superiors. A very, very likeable and promising young man.' He spread his hands. 'That's about all, I'm afraid. His death – and especially the fact that it was self-inflicted – was a tragedy.'

'You've no idea why he should want to kill himself?' I said.

'None.'

'Because I was wondering – seriously wondering – if the kid wasn't on the make.'

Balbus . . . froze. There's no other word for it. The guy simply went rigid, every muscle, like concrete setting.

'I beg your pardon?' he said at last.

'Taking back-handers. Bribes. From the claimants he was responsible for interviewing.'

We stared at each other, the silence lengthening. Finally Balbus said, quietly, 'How did you know?'

Bugger. Well, the odds that I was wrong hadn't been all that good to start with. Even so . . . 'I didn't,' I said. 'Not as such. But making the connection doesn't exactly take a huge leap of intuitive genius, pal. He was in debt to a money-lender up to his eyeballs, with no way out. Then suddenly he's in the position to buy himself off. The job he's in, the chances he has, the money had to come from bribes.'

Balbus cleared his throat. He looked sick. 'I had no proof,' he said. 'No real proof, that is. Not that it matters now, of course. The boy's dead and there's an end of it. Practically speaking, it makes no difference; we'll double-check his as-sessments and if there are discrepancies they'll be rectified. As far as the people who slipped him the cash are concerned . . . well, I don't think we'll be hearing any complaints from them.'

'So,' I said, leaning back in my chair. 'How did *you* know?'

'I told you. I didn't either, not for certain. I still don't. All my evidence was circumstantial and cumulative: a claim passed that seemed on the high side, but not suspicious enough to merit further investigation, a hint from one or two honest quarters that Papinius seemed to be angling for a back-hander – again, in a way that was ambiguous enough for him to deny convincingly. That sort of thing. I didn't, of course, know anything about the debt aspect or I might've felt justified in taking more direct action.'

'So how were you handling it?'

'With very soft gloves. Like I said, he was a nice lad in himself, serious-minded, an ex-consul's son and with a good, caring mother. Efficient and conscientious, too, prime future senior administrator material. If I'd reported the matter his career would've been finished, at the very least. Possibly he'd've been exiled, certainly he'd be disgraced for the rest of his days. I didn't want to do that, Corvinus, especially since as I've said I'd no actual proof. One mistake and the boy's whole life is ruined, and I wasn't even certain he'd made the mistake. You understand me?'

'Yeah,' I said. 'Yeah, I understand.' Hell!

'So I had a quiet word with him. Unofficially, off the record, in private. No one knew anything about it, about any of it. Not even my suspicions. I'd been careful over that from the start, and I told him I had. I didn't make any accusations, just presented him with the facts. Such facts as I had. He . . . well, I think it registered. In fact, I'm sure it did.'

'When was this?'

'Three days ago. The, ah, morning of the day he died.'

'Uh-huh.' Shit. Well, then; that was that. A combination of guilt and the prospect of public disgrace and a ruined career, with no realistic way out. No wonder the poor sap had killed himself. Case solved, close the lid. What the hell I was going to tell Natalis, mind – let alone his mother – I didn't know. Not the truth, certainly: it might not actually kill Rupilia but a truth like that she could do without. Still, that was my problem. I stood up. 'Thanks, Balbus. You've been very helpful.'

'Yes . . . well . . .'

I turned to go. My hand was on the door-handle when he called out: 'Corvinus!'

I looked back. 'Yeah?'

Balbus must've read my mind. 'Don't tell Rupilia,' he said. 'She's a good woman, and she loved her son. Like I say, it doesn't matter any more. As far as Rome's concerned, the thing's over and done with.'

I nodded, and left. Over and done with. Right. What I needed now was a drink.

The fool! The bloody young fool!

Only . . .

On the way down the steps of the building to pick up Placida from where I'd left her tied to the general's statue I met Marcus Atratinus coming up. I still felt sick, but when I saw him the niggle came back with a vengeance. Hell, I couldn't just ignore it: I owed myself, and the dead kid, that much at least before we finally put the cap on things.

'Hey, Atratinus,' I said. 'One question. Straight answer, under oath, no faffing. You up for that?'

He gave me an uncertain grin. 'Of course. Whatever you like.'

'Was Sextus Papinius an honest man? Yes or no, no half measures. Go for it.'

The grin faded and he looked at me like I'd grown an extra head. The look wasn't too friendly, either. 'Sextus Papinius,' he said carefully, 'never did a dishonest or a mean thing in his life.' Then, turning towards the Temple of Jupiter Stayer of the Host next door, he raised his hand. 'You want your oath then you've got it: So help me, Jupiter.'

I frowned: the niggle was there, full strength now. Hell. 'Yeah,' I said. 'Yeah, thanks, pal. That was what I was afraid you'd say.'

I left him staring, hand still raised. Complicated was right.

9

I found a wineshop off the Sacred Way that didn't mind dogs and settled down with a half jug to think.

Oh, sure, the solution all made sense, every bit of it, and if Papinius hadn't got his sixty thousand from bribes then where the hell had he got it from? I didn't have an answer to that; I didn't even have the ghost of an answer. Besides, if he was crooked and he knew he'd been rumbled then suicide was a logical way out. Not the only way, but an obvious one to a guy with Papinius's background and character. No problems there. Everything fitted together like the stones of a good mosaic.

Only . . .

Only there was the niggle that just wouldn't go away. I kept sticking on two things. One was Atratinus's insistence – backed up by my own gut feeling – that Papinius was as straight as they come; the second was how the kid had died. Razor, knife, sword, poison even at a pinch, fair enough; but no aristocratic Roman, if he's got a choice in how he's going to kill himself, chooses to jump from a tenement window. That's just not the way we do things. It's just too bloody infra dig.

Besides, from what Atratinus had told me Papinius hadn't signalled it. And although I hadn't asked Caepio direct, he hadn't implied that the kid was unduly upset or preoccupied immediately beforehand, either. That wasn't natural. Plus there was the absence of a suicide note . . .

That Papinius had committed suicide out of guilt and the

fear of exposure made sense, complete sense, sure, no argument. But it just didn't . . . fucking . . . *fit*!

I took a long swallow of wine. I hadn't been in this place before, and I doubted that I'd bother to repeat the experience because the wine was over-priced and second-rate. No wonder the guy behind the bar hadn't objected to a flatulent Gallic boarhound on his premises. Lucky for me, really, but then I was getting used to breathing through my mouth.

Right. So let's assume that the perfect, logical solution was a load of balls. Start with the assumption that Papinius wasn't crooked, he wasn't taking bribes, and – most important of all – he didn't kill himself. Also, shelve the problem of the sixty thousand for the moment, plus the whole question of what *did* happen in that Aventine tenement.

Where did that leave us?

Either with Balbus lying through his teeth for reasons of his own, or with the whole business being a set-up. That was where.

The first scenario was about as likely as a flying pig. I didn't know Balbus personally, but I knew him by reputation and the guy was lily white: good at his job, honest, trustworthy – as far as any career politician can be honest and trustworthy – and with no dirty laundry in the basket, at least any that gossip could pull out. And Roman gossip is pretty thorough. Besides, what would he gain by fingering young Papinius? He couldn't be on the fiddle himself and trying, somehow, to cover his tracks through a subordinate; the commission had been set up by the Wart in person, Tiberius was no fool where sniffing out peculation was concerned, and he got very *serious* about crooked government officials. The game just wasn't worth the candle, and if Balbus was bucking for consul in a few years – which he would be, as aedile – then he'd be a fool to put his reputation on the line for a few thousand silver pieces, even if we did have a change of emperor by that time.

So scratch that. Balbus wasn't lying, at least not intentionally; he'd told me the truth as he saw it. Which meant we were left with the set-up theory . . .

Only that was flying-pigs country as well. If Papinius had been set up then why and for what? Who the hell would bother fitting a no-account, nineteen-year-old kid into a frame and then – presumably – faking his suicide?

Shit; the whole boiling was one endless frustration: look at it one way and it made sense, only it didn't; turn it round and the same thing happened. The hell with it. I took a deep breath, then another slug of wine, and tried to calm down . . .

Okay. So forget logical theorising. We play it both ends against the middle, dig into the laundry basket at random and see what crawls out.

I'd still got two names to talk to, Mucius Soranus and Papinius's girlfriend Cluvia. It was still early, the Saepta wasn't too far off and the Cipian Mount was on the way home. Sod the wine; if I hurried, and Placida co-operated, I could manage both and still be back in time for Meton's fish.

I reanimated the petomaniac dog and left.

I hadn't gone two hundred yards before I knew – for definite this time – that I was being followed. Oh, sure, Perilla would've pooh-poohed the feeling, because it wasn't logical, but even with all the little practical distractions like discouraging Placida from mugging passing bag-ladies for their shopping, cleaning up after donkeys and shoving her nose against slow-moving strangers' bottoms the back of my neck was prickling all the way, and that's something I've learned not to ignore. Who was tailing me exactly I didn't know; the area round the square and the Sacred Way is one of the busiest in Rome, the narrow streets don't help matters, and taking your eyes off an over-enthusiastic boarhound even long enough to glance over your shoulder is not a good idea. Still, I'd've bet every coin I'd got left in my belt-pouch that someone was there. Which was strange. Who the hell would bother, and why?

Not that it'd be difficult, mind. Street life in Rome may be pretty eclectic, but you don't see many purple-stripers being dragged along behind Gallic boarhounds. I'd be a hard mark to lose. They'd only have to follow the cursing.

Ah, well; I'd enough on my plate at present to worry about. Whoever they were, so long as they behaved themselves they could do as they liked. I shoved the problem to the back of my mind and pressed on towards the Saepta.

Atratinus had said that Cluvia managed a perfume shop. Pretty useful. For somewhere like the Saepta, that's like saying someone runs a philosophy school in Athens or a fish restaurant in Massilia: close your eyes and heft a brick in any direction you like up the Saepta Julia and chances are you'll hit either a perfumier or an haute-couture mantle-maker. Me, I'd call that a public service, myself, but then I'm prejudiced.

So finding Cluvia wasn't easy, especially with Placida on the team: like I say, the Saepta caters to a pretty upmarket clientele, and slavering Gallic boarhounds straining at the ends of leashes aren't too popular with the well-dressed and pristine. Once I'd dragged her out of a litter she fancied sharing with a screaming dowager and persuaded her that the little yapping brute belonging to the spangle-haired young gentleman having hysterics in the nail-bar didn't want to play chase-your-tail up and down the concourse, she wasn't too popular with me, either.

Gods!

I finally tracked Cluvia down to a little corner booth off the main drag. There was a window-shopper hanging about – she could've been sister to the woman in the litter – but she took one look at Placida coming panting towards her, screamed and bolted. So much for customer relations. I grabbed the beast's collar and pulled her to a slavering halt.

The woman behind the counter was a looker, but most of it was artificial and if she was a day under thirty I'd eat my sandals.

'Ah . . . excuse me,' I said. 'Is—'

'We don't sell flea powder.' She was staring at Placida with a sort of fascinated horror. 'Try Constantinos's next to the baths.'

'Uh . . . no, actually, I wanted to talk to you about—' I stopped, because she was pointing and the horror in her face had gone up a notch. I glanced down. Placida was dragging her backside along the ground with an expression of intense and ecstatic concentration. 'Oh, that's okay. She's been doing it on and off since Julian Square. Itchy anal glands, I think. Or maybe she just wants your attention.'

'Really? Then she's got it. That is totally *gross!*'

'I'm sorry,' I said quickly. 'I'm not a customer. My name's Marcus Corvinus and I just wanted to ask you a few questions about your boyfriend.'

Pause. This time it was me who got the stare, straight off a glacier. Eventually she said, and you could practically count the icicles, 'Did you, indeed? And which boyfriend would that be, now?'

Oh, great. 'Uh . . . Papinius?' Then, when the death-stare didn't shift: '*Sextus* Papinius? Your name is Cluvia, isn't it? Or have I got the wrong shop?'

She turned round to the marble shelf behind the counter and began straightening the display phials with little jerks of her fingers. If ever a back radiated anger then Cluvia's was the one. 'No,' she said, and I could almost *hear* her teeth clench. 'I know perfectly well who you mean. But boyfriend's the wrong word because we're not an item any more. I suggest that if you want to know anything concerning Sextus Papinius you ask him yourself.'

'Yeah, well, that's . . .' I began, and then my brain caught up with my ears. Fuck. 'You, ah, didn't know, then?'

'I didn't know what?'

There wasn't any way out of this. 'That he's, uh, dead. Look, lady, I'm sorry, I thought—'

The fingers had stopped. One of the phials tipped over, rolled off the shelf and smashed on the shop floor. Cluvia collapsed like a string-cut puppet, and I was just in time to get my hands beneath her armpits before she hit the floor herself.

Oh, shit. Nice one, Corvinus. Very tactful.

At which point: '*OW-OOO-OWOWOW-OOO!*'

Bugger. That we could do without.

'Shut up, Placida!' I snapped, giving her a back-heel kick. '*Settle!*'

The woman in the trinkets shop next door – she'd been taking an obvious interest right through the conversation – had moved like greased lightning out from behind her own counter and round the back of Cluvia's. I felt the dead weight lift. Jupiter, the woman was strong!

'Thanks, sister,' I said.

That got me another glare, hundred-candelabra strength, delivered at point-blank range. By this time women – customers and stallholders – were flocking in from all directions like hens to a spilled bucket of barley. Let's hear it for female solidarity. Speaking of which: 'OW-*OOO-OOO-OOO!*'

Oh, shit. '*Not* you, sunshine!' I hauled Placida clear and backed off while the ladies formed a protective screen as effective as a legionary shield-wall and did whatever the hell women do under these circumstances.

There was a clothes booth further along where a male shopkeeper was goggling at the scrum from above his racks. 'I'll . . . ah . . . just wait over there, shall I?' I said.

'You do that, chummy!' the first woman snapped over her shoulder. 'And take that bloody Cerberus look-alike with you!'

I beat a retreat across to the clothes booth, dragging the

howling, hysterical Placida behind. The guy stepped back quickly.

'What the hell happened there?' he said.

I grabbed Placida's muzzle and forced it closed while she grizzled her way into silence. 'I told her her boyfriend had just died. Ex-boyfriend, rather.'

'Oh, bugger.' The guy was small, dapper and unassuming, with the nervous-eyed, hunted look that I supposed went with the job surroundings: as far as I could tell where male stallholders were concerned he was in a minority of one. 'I'd keep well clear for a bit, then, mate.'

'Yeah. Yeah, right.'

'Nice dog. It is a dog, isn't it?'

'That depends on the time of the month.'

He gave a nervous giggle and backed away a bit more.

Over by the perfume counter the scrum was already beginning to break up. From its centre came Cluvia, walking towards me. She didn't look too hot, but at least she was mobile. Wrestles-With-Bears gave me a final glare and went back to her bangles. I took a firm grip of Placida's collar and forced her down.

'What did you say your name was?' Cluvia said. She sounded a bit distant, like she was taking trouble over the words.

'Corvinus. Marcus Corvinus. I'm . . . ah . . . a friend of Sextus's mother.'

'Really. So how did it happen? How did Sextus die? An accident?'

'Uh-uh.' I swallowed. 'He killed himself.'

'Oh.' She frowned and made a jerky movement with her hand. The bracelets – she was wearing at least three of them – jangled on her wrist. 'Can we go elsewhere, do you think?'

'No problem.' I was watching her carefully. It'd hit her hard, sure, but she had herself under control now. More or less. A tough lady, Cluvia. 'Look, I'm sorry if I—'

'Forget it. It doesn't matter.'

We left the main precinct in silence, the now-placid Placida walking between us, and found a bench against the wall of the Agrippan Baths. She sat down and I waited while she took a few deep breaths.

'All right,' she said finally. 'Tell me.'

I told her, while she looked down at her hands. The fingers were covered with rings and the nails were well manicured. Thirty-something she might be, but the lady took good care of herself. I'd noticed that the female-solidarity pack had freshened up her hair and make-up, too.

'Why did he do it?' she said when I'd finished.

'I don't know. Not exactly.'

'Could the reason have had anything to do with Mucius Soranus?'

The question came straight out, like she'd been meaning to ask it from the very first and had just been waiting her chance. I glanced at her sharply. 'What makes you think that?' I said.

'Because he's a bastard. And there was something between him and Sextus.'

'How do you mean, "something"?'

'I don't know. But Sextus hated him for it.' She frowned. 'No. Hate's the wrong word. So's frightened. Something between the two, maybe.'

'Why should he be frightened of Soranus?'

'He wasn't. I told you, it's the wrong word, and Sextus wasn't frightened of anyone. He didn't hate anyone, either. Sextus was a lovely boy. You don't meet—' She stopped, pulled a handkerchief from her tunic sleeve and dabbed at her eyes. 'I'm sorry.'

'He owed Soranus money. From gambling debts.'

'Yes. That's right.'

'A lot?'

'I don't know. A few thousand, maybe.'

'As much as fifty?'

She looked up, startled. '*What?* No!'

'He borrowed fifty thousand silver pieces about a month ago from a money-lender in Julian Square. You didn't know?'

'That's ridiculous! Sextus wasn't a gambler! Not that much of one!'

Yeah. Check. 'Odd thing was, he paid it back just before he died. Plus ten thousand interest.'

She was staring at me now. 'Corvinus, what is all this?' she said. 'Did you come just to break the news to me that Sextus was dead – though why a friend of his mother's would bother to do that I don't know – or was there another reason?'

'You know Minicius Natalis?'

'The faction-master of the Greens? Yes, of course. Not personally, but Sextus used to talk about him. He spent a lot of his time at the Greens' stables.'

'Natalis wants to know why the boy did it. He's asked me to find out.'

'Oh. I see.' She looked down at her hands again. 'I'm afraid you've had a wasted journey, then. I don't know anything about his reasons. As you'll no doubt have noticed, I didn't even know he was dead.'

'You, uh, said you weren't seeing each other any more.' Jupiter, I hated this tactful stuff, but it was a question that had to be asked. 'Was that your doing or his?'

'His.'

Yeah, well, I'd sort of got that impression from the whole conversation, but it was good to have it confirmed. 'Care to tell me why?'

'You could've guessed that yourself.' Her voice had toughened, but she still didn't look up. 'He'd found someone else. A *lady*' – she stressed the word, but there were other harmonics there – 'by the name of Albucilla. She's a friend of Soranus's.'

The eyes lifted. 'That's another reason I don't like the man, if you're interested.'

'Uh-huh.' Another name. Well, I needed all the leads I could get. 'You know anything about her?'

'No. I don't particularly want to, either.'

'Fine, fine.' The tone would've had Cleopatra's asp handing in its poison sacs. Not that it mattered: the name was enough at present. Back off, Corvinus. 'No problem. So, uh, tell me more about Sextus.'

'Like what?'

I shrugged. 'Lady, I'm at sea here. I'm just taking what I can get and hoping somewhere it'll make sense.'

'I said. He was a lovely boy, the kind you don't meet very often, almost like someone from a story-book. A thinker, not just a pair of hands.' She sniffed again. 'Generous, and I don't mean only with money. Good fun, when he wanted to be. He had a strong sense of justice. And he was very proud of his family.'

'His family?'

'His father, especially. Sextus wanted to be worthy of him. That's why he took his job on the fire commission so ser-iously.'

Shit. Well, score another point against the corruption angle. Still, Rupilia had told me at the start that he'd been grateful, and like I said Allenius had come through in spades where using up valuable clout was concerned. It was a pity the kid had died when he did. Me, I knew from personal experience how looking at relationships through adult eyes can change things.

Maybe I'd have to have a talk with Allenius after all.

'Get back to Soranus,' I said. 'I thought they were friends.'

Cluvia stood up. 'I'm sorry,' she said. 'I've told you all I can. As far as Mucius Soranus is concerned, I've nothing definite to give you. Sextus was . . . very secretive. Even with me. I don't like Soranus, I never have; he's a manipulator, a parasite, and Sextus would've been much happier staying clear of him. But then he always did have a mind of his own, and maybe it's just my prejudice talking. Now, if you'll excuse me, I've a shop to look after.'

She left, and I watched her go. Well, that was that; certainly food for thought. *Someone from a story-book*, eh? High praise, indeed.

Okay. Last trip of the day, through the Subura to the Cipian and your all-round-popular slug Mucius Soranus.

IO

After that chat with Cluvia, I had some ideas of my own re
Soranus's relationship with young Papinius and the reasons for it. Trouble was, like most of the evidence I'd collected so
far, they didn't square with the picture I'd built up of the kid,
either. Bugger. Triple bugger. But then, maybe I was completely wrong about him after all – maybe everyone else was – and
the squeaky-clean nice-lad image was a total con.

The weather had changed again, and we'd got one of these
beautiful, cool, autumn days when walking in Rome's a
pleasure, even through the narrow crowded streets at the
centre where the sky's just a ribbon of blue that starts six
floors above your head. Yeah, well, I'm city-bred, me, and
although open spaces, greenery and the scent of pines and
cypress are nice in their way give me a pavement or cobbles
under my sandals, the smell of cookshops overlaid with
donkey-droppings and the merry cries of street-hawkers going
about their lawful business of ripping off the punters and I
know where I am. These pastoral-poet guys with their bleating
goats and oaten pipes can stuff their phalaecean hendecasyl-
labics where the sun don't shine.

Placida seemed more co-operative, too. Or maybe she was
just storing it up and waiting her chance. I was beginning to
have a healthy respect for that brute's intelligence.

There were a few big old properties opposite Livia Porch
but I asked a kitchen-slave shelling peas outside one of them
for directions. Soranus's place was a corner building that from

the looks of things had seen better days but was still hanging in. The door was open and the door-slave was sitting on the threshold, eyes closed and communing with nature . . .

At least this was the case until Placida licked his face. He woke with a scream of horror and levered himself upright.

'Sorry about that, pal,' I said, pulling her back. 'Lapse in concentration. Is the master at home?'

'He's in the garden, sir.' He glared at Placida and mopped the drool off with his tunic sleeve. 'Who shall I say?'

'The name's Valerius Corvinus. He doesn't know me, but I'm here on business.' I wasn't going to give Soranus any prior idea why I'd called. I wanted to do this cold.

'Very well, sir. If you'd like to leave your, uh, your . . .' – another glare – 'tied to the railings and wait in the atrium I'll see if he's receiving.'

Now *that* I didn't like the sound of. I wasn't risking a brush-off, especially if Soranus found out later through the grapevine what I'd wanted, in which case I was as likely to get a second chance to talk to him as Placida was to win the Year's Sweetest Pet award. 'Tell you what, pal,' I said. 'The dog's highly strung, she likes company and she doesn't take to being tied up and ignored. Now I *could* get you to walk her round the block a few times while I'm having this long business conversation with your master. You'd be safe enough. Probably. On the other hand, I'm sure Soranus wouldn't mind if you showed us both through straight off. I'm easy, the decision's all yours. What do you think?'

Down at his groin level Placida yawned, showing a set of teeth like you'd get on a marble-saw, and the door-slave flinched. 'Ah . . . it's this way, sir,' he said quickly. 'If you'd care to follow me?'

'Sure. No problem.'

We went through the lobby and across the atrium to the garden opening at the far end. Hanging in was right; like

Rupilia's place, most of the furniture and the decor had been good in its day but was looking a bit past it now. Two or three nice bronzes, either originals or good copies: Soranus couldn't've been badly on his uppers, but then if I was right about the major source of his income and he made a habit of it then that was to be expected. A masculine room, too; no feminine touches. I didn't know whether the guy was married, but I'd imagine not. A wife in the background wouldn't fit in with the lifestyle.

He was sitting in a folding chair under a pear tree with a pile of wax tablets and a wine jug and cup on a table beside him. He looked up when we came through the portico, closed the tablet he'd been studying and laid it on the pile. Late twenties, good-looking, sharp tunic and haircut. From what I could see, he'd kept himself in shape: well muscled and no sign of a paunch. Grade A blade-about-town material, in other words. Yeah, right; I could see how he'd impress wannabe-sophisticated kids like Papinius and his friends. Women too; women would really go for Mucius Soranus. They might regret it later, mind.

'Who's this?' he said to the slave. 'And what the hell is *that*?'

Not exactly full of welcoming good cheer. Well, that made things easier. 'My name's Marcus Corvinus,' I said. 'I'm here about a young friend of yours, Sextus Papinius.'

I'd been looking for it, and it came: a flicker of the eyelids and a slight turn of the head. 'What about him?' he said. Then, to the slave, 'You can go, Scorpus. I'll talk to you later.' The guy left at a run.

'You know he killed himself three days back?' I said.

'Yes, I know that. I was sorry to hear it. Papinius was a nice kid.'

'So everyone tells me.' No offer of a chair, so I sat on the corner of a handy stone flower-chest. Placida was making use of the outdoor toilet facilities. 'He owed you money, I understand. A gambling debt.'

'That's right.' The tone was cool, but I could feel that beneath his patrician shell the guy was nervous as a cat: he hadn't moved a muscle since he'd dismissed the slave, and his eyes hadn't left my face. 'Or partly right.'

' "Partly right"?'

'He paid it. Oh, it must be a month since or near about.'

'Care to tell me how much was involved?'

'That's none of your business.' I waited, and he shrugged. 'Very well. It's not important anyway. Two thousand, silver.'

'That so, now?' I said. 'So what was the other forty-eight thousand for?'

His jaw dropped. 'What?'

'About a month back, the same time you say he paid you off, Papinius took out a loan from a money-lender for fifty thousand. Coincidences like that just don't happen, pal, or if they do they stink like ten-day-old fish.'

'I don't know anything about—'

'Come on, Soranus!' I was on my feet. Placida looked up from where she was doing a bit of impromptu topiary and growled. 'Two thousand for a gambling debt, sure, I could believe that; any lackbrain kid can lose that much with a little encouragement from bastards like you. But fifty thousand, now, fifty thousand's pushing it, especially where Papinius is concerned, and that's what you got from him. So what were you soaking him for? Taking back-handers from property owners who reckoned they were owed more than their fair share of the Aventine fire fund? Or was it something else?'

He'd gone grey. He stood up himself, raised a trembling arm and pointed. 'You get out,' he said quietly. 'You get the hell out. And if you repeat one word of these lies in public you'll find yourself sued from one end of the civil courts to the other. Is that clear?'

Placida was really growling now, and her hackles were rising. I reached out to grip her collar and felt her muscles tense. Soranus flashed her a look and swallowed. 'Yeah. Yeah, that's clear,' I said. 'No problems on that score, pal. I just wanted to tell you that I knew, that's all. To make you sweat. Because when I have got the proof – and believe me I'll get it – I'm going to take it round to the city judge's office myself and then watch them nail your fucking hide to the Julian Hall floor.' I turned to go, pulling the still-growling Placida with me, and then another thought struck me and I turned back. 'Oh, by the way, who's Albucilla?'

If he'd been grey before he'd've doubled now for week-old uncooked pastry dough. I thought for a moment that he was going to do a Cluvia into the ornamental flower-bed, but he pulled himself together.

'Get out of my house!' he shouted.

'*OW-OOO-OOO-OOO!*' Placida launched herself forward, almost dragging me with her. Soranus half screamed and took a step back against the chair, arm raised. For two pins I'd've let go the collar, but then the authorities might object to one of the top five hundred having his throat torn out in his own garden. Besides, she'd probably have got food poisoning.

'Pleasure's all mine, friend,' I said. 'I'll see you around.'

We left.

Well, that'd been fun. Maybe not exactly politic, but the bastard would only have lied anyway, and as far as cage-rattling went I didn't think I could've done better. Soranus had been frightened; that much was obvious, and it had nothing to do with Placida. Also, it was all to the good, because when I'd threatened him with the city judge I'd been bluffing. With Papinius dead, there wasn't a hope of proving he'd paid Soranus hush-money. At least, not much of a hope. At least . . .

Hell. We'd just have to see. It would give me a great deal of personal satisfaction to nail the slimy bugger, and he'd find himself hard put to try any more blackmail when he was twiddling his thumbs out in Lusitania or living on frozen beets somewhere north of the Hellespont.

His reaction to Albucilla's name had been interesting, too, whoever the lady was; which last was something I'd have to chase up before I was much older. Food for thought again.

And speaking of food I'd done enough for one day. We both had. Home, for Meton's fish.

II

It turned out I had plenty of time. Meton (I got this from Bathyllus, when he handed me the usual belt of Setinian at the door) had had a slight contretemps with the guy down at the fish market who was standing in for his usual supplier over the quality of the sea-urchins, which resulted in said guy almost having to have the offending crustacea surgically removed and Meton being forcibly restrained by five of the fish-seller's mates and a handy tunny. The result was fish was off the menu, Meton was nursing a glorious shiner plus a sulk at the market officer who had taken the fish-seller's side, and we were having slow-marinated lamb's liver and long-cooked pork. Eventually.

Yeah, well; it's all part of life's rich tapestry.

'Where's the mistress, little guy?' I said, sinking the first welcome mouthful of Setinian.

'In the bath suite, sir.' Bathyllus was eyeing Placida with a look that was so jaundiced it was practically the colour of his snazzy yellow tunic. Evidently I'd walked our barbarian house-guest off her paws because as soon as we'd cleared the lobby she'd sprawled out full-length on the atrium floor. 'Apropos of which . . .' He sniffed, pointedly, and gave the dog another sizzling glare.

Yeah, I'd noticed the smell myself. It would've been hard not to at any distance of less than ten yards. *Penetrating* is the word; or maybe *corrosive* is better. 'She, uh, rolled on something,' I said. 'In the gutter outside that new butcher's shop halfway down Head of Africa. My guess would be past-its-sell-by-date tripe, but it was too far gone to judge.'

'Indeed, sir?'

'Still, no problem, sunshine.' I was taking off my sweaty tunic. 'You can heat up a couple of buckets of water, take her out into the garden and sluice her down.'

Heh-heh!

Not an eyelid did Bathyllus bat. 'Actually, sir,' he said, 'the mistress left strict instructions in that regard. To apply if you came home in time, sir.'

I paused re the tunic. Oh, hell! I was beginning to get a bad, bad feeling about the way things were going here. There were too many 'sirs' for a start, and the little bugger was wearing a smug expression which I didn't like the look of by half.

'Cut the faffing, Bathyllus,' I said. 'Just tell me.'

'Well, sir, we've put a tub in the bath suite and—'

Jupiter bloody Almighty! I held up my hands, palm out. 'Oh, no,' I said. 'No way! Look, pal. I have had sole and total charge of that brute ever since breakfast and I reckon I've done my whack. All I want now is a quiet bath, a few cups of wine and dinner. I am *not* playing bathtime games with a fucking Gallic boarhound, especially one that's been rolling in decomposed pig offal. All right?'

'Perhaps you'd like to tell the mistress that yourself, sir.' Smirk.

Hell. Fuck. Double fuck. I finished removing the tunic and pitched it into a corner.

'Come on, Placida,' I said.

She was waiting for us, sitting on the bench.

'Oh, hello, dear.' She brushed a damp strand of hair out of her eyes and gave me a welcome-home kiss. 'Good, you've brought her. Everything's ready, and the water shouldn't be too hot now, it's been standing for half an hour.'

'Perilla . . .'

'The sponge is over there with another two bucketfuls for the rinse, and I've put some perfumed oil in. Down, Placida, no, I don't want licked, thank you very much. My goodness, she does smell a bit, doesn't she, Marcus? What've you been doing with her?'

'Lady . . .'

'Never mind, we'd best start. Get her into the tub.'

I goggled. '*Me* get her . . . ?'

'Oh, really, dear! It can't be all that difficult!'

Hell. I took hold of Placida's collar and pulled in the required direction. The first two or three feet were okay, but the last bit, when she caught sight of the water and realised what was happening, was something else . . .

'Uh, I don't think she wants to go,' I said. Understatement: it was like trying to haul the Temple of Saturn up Capitol Incline.

'Nonsense. She loves being bathed. Calvina told me.'

'Really? Is that so, now?' I was beginning to develop a real respect for that woman's powers of falsehood and duplicity. 'You care to pass the message on to the dog, lady?'

'All right. Then you'll just have to lift her in.'

Oh, Jupiter! 'Yeah, and add a slipped disc and double hernia to all my other problems. Perilla, come *on*! You know how much that fucking beast weighs?'

'Marcus!'

Shit; I didn't deserve this. I took a firm grip on the collar and *pulled*. Placida crouched down and pulled back. Her claws scrabbled on the marble and she held her ground.

Stalemate.

'Perhaps you'd care to help, lady,' I grunted.

'Oh, *really*!' Perilla got up and joined me . . .

'She is strong, isn't she?' she said after a bit. 'And very determined.'

'Yeah,' I gasped. 'Yeah, you could say that.'

'I think she might be moving. One more pull.'

Scrabblescrabblescrabblescra-a-a-pe . . .

Yes! Well, at least we were within striking distance now. I let go the collar, lifted the brute's front paws over the edge of the tub, went round to her rear end and *heaved* . . .

SPLASH!

'*There's* a good girl!' Perilla stepped back. 'Stay there, now. Marcus, don't let her climb out. *Marcus!*'

Hell and bloody damnation! I hung on, spat a mouthful of perfumed water over my shoulder and said, 'Lady, I could do with just a little more help here, if you know what I mean.'

'*OW-OOO-OOO! OWOWOW-OOO-OOO!*'

'*Ouch!*'

'Placida, be quiet! Don't be silly, it's only a bath, we're not killing you.'

'*OOO-OOO-OOO!*'

Threshthreshthreshthreshthresh . . .

Jupiter bloody best and greatest! I'd never actually mud-wrestled a manic hippo before, but this must've come pretty near, and the banshee howling in the enclosed space wasn't doing my eardrums any favours, either. I gritted my teeth and held on for dear life . . .

'Get me the sponge!'

'What?'

'*OOO-OOO-OOO!*'

'The *sponge!*'

'*What?* Marcus, I can't hear what you're—'

'*OOO-OOO-OOO! OWOO-OOO-OOO!*'

'*For the gods' sake, woman, get me the fucking sponge!*'

She sniffed. 'Very well, dear. There's no need to swear. There, now. You hold her down and I'll sponge her. Good dog, Placida, *good* dog! No need for all this fuss, is there?'

'*OOO-OOO-OOO-OOO!*'

'*Shit!*'

'*Marcus!*'

'Yeah, well.'

'Just hold her down and let me do the work. She is really being very good. Underneath it all, I mean.'

'*WHAT?*'

'Well, she hasn't actually bitten you, has she?'

I clenched my teeth. There are times when words just aren't adequate.

Eventually . . .

'Now. That should do it. Just the rinse and we're done. *There's* a clever girl, Placida! One more bucketful. Mind your head, Marcus. I said, mind your—'

'*Ouch!*'

'Well, I did warn you.' She put down the empty bucket. 'Good. You can let her go now, dear. Placida, *careful*!'

Placida emerged from the bath, not *quite* like Aphrodite from the foam off Paphos.

Shakeshakeshake. Splattersplattersplatter.

'Oh, bugger!' Still, I was soaked anyway. Another few gallons of tripe-and-perfume-flavoured water wouldn't make all that much difference.

'Well,' Perilla said as we dried ourselves. 'I think on the whole that was quite successful, don't you?'

'Ah, there you are, sir. Dinner is almost ready. Did you enjoy your bath?'

'Fuck off, Bathyllus.'

12

Dinner, when it finally came, was worth waiting for. Meton may've been sulking, but the guy is a professional to his gorilla-sized fingertips, and the long-cooked pork in cumin and aniseed was a dream.

No dog, either. I insisted on that, and for once Perilla didn't object; maybe our bathtime romp had soured her, too, just a little. Where the brute was exactly at that precise moment in time and what she was doing I didn't know, and cared less. The screams weren't reaching us here in the dining-room, anyway, and that was the main thing.

Bliss.

'So.' Perilla dipped a crust of poppy-seed roll into her sauce. 'Did you find why the boy killed himself?'

'I don't know,' I said.

'How do you mean, you don't know?'

I reached for the puréed lentils that had come with the pork and helped myself to more. 'According to Laelius Balbus, he was on the take and knew he'd been caught out.'

She put down the crust. 'Oh, Marcus!'

'Yeah, well. He wouldn't be the first to go that road. Kid in need of money finds himself in a job where there're plenty of rich punters who want to get richer. They suggest that if he turns a blind eye to certain inflated figures on their claims sheets a few gold pieces might find their way into his purse. Where's the harm? The only party to lose out is the state, and the state can afford it. So long as he's careful and no one gets too greedy it wouldn't be noticed.'

'And you think Papinius wasn't careful.'

'No. Or that's the theory to go with the scenario, anyway. In the event, he was doubly unlucky. First, his boss wasn't the type who just signs things unread; which wouldn't necessarily have been fatal, mind, because Balbus is a nice guy, he knew what the result would be if he blew the whistle, and he didn't want things to go that far unless they had to. Second, though, there was his pal – his so-called pal – Mucius Soranus. And *he* was another thing altogether.'

'Soranus found out somehow that the boy was taking bribes and decided to blackmail him.'

'Yeah. Again, that's the theory. Soranus is no Balbus. He's greedy and he's ruthless. One word in the wrong ear – like to Domitius Ahenobarbus, say, or one of the other commission bosses – and Papinius would be finished. Career over, next stop exile. So in exchange for not telling Soranus wants serious gravy: fifty thousand silver pieces. The only way Papinius can get that kind of money is to go to a loans shark, which he does and pays off Soranus. Only a month down the line he finds out from Balbus that he's been sussed in any case.'

'And so he kills himself. Marcus, that's dreadful! The poor boy.'

'Right. Problem is' – I hesitated – 'as a scenario, it stinks.'

Perilla had been helping herself to the stew. She put down her spoon.

'I beg your pardon?'

'It doesn't work, lady. No *way* does it work. Or if it does I'm a blue-rinsed monkey.'

'But surely—'

'Papinius was no crook, I'd bet my last copper on that. And if he was honest then there was no kickbacks scam and the whole scenario collapses. A priori, a fortiori, QED.'

She was staring at me. 'Marcus, be reasonable! You can't just dismiss the bribery aspect out of hand, because from what you say it's central to all the facts. Without it Soranus had no grounds for blackmailing the boy, and if he wasn't then why the money-lender? Not to mention that your Laelius Balbus confirmed it. Or do you think he's lying? And if so then why on earth should he be?'

I sighed. 'Look, I've been through all this myself, right? Sure, it all adds up, right down the line, no arguments. For everything to make sense Papinius had to be bent. Only, believe me, he wasn't, and if he wasn't on the fiddle then why should hc kill himself?'

'Very well. What proof do you have that he *wasn't* crooked? Real proof, I mean.'

'He's just not the type.'

'Oh, *Marcus*! Very objective! I'm afraid that's not an answer, dear.'

'Okay.' I leaned back and pushed my plate away. 'He's got glowing character references all round. Titus Natalis, his mother, bribery accusation apart even Balbus. Young Marcus Atratinus practically threw me down the aediles' office steps for suggesting hc might be dishonest, his ex-girlfriend went all dewy-eyed when she talked about him and even that shit Soranus called him a nice kid.'

'You don't think they might all be rather biased as character witnesses? Soranus aside? After all—'

'Jupiter, Perilla! We're talking unanimous here, and that doesn't happen often, not to that degree, certainly. If it was all a front then as a con artist the guy must've been bloody brilliant. Besides, there're other things that don't fit either.'

'Namely?'

'How and where he died. By rights the kid should've slit his wrists in comfort at home. Diving from an Aventine tenement just doesn't make sense. And you can add the fact that he'd just paid off the loan, as well.'

She sat up. 'He had *what*?'

'Yeah. Right, that's what I thought. Vestorius told me himself, the loans shark. Principal and interest, sixty thousand in silver. Where the hell did the money come from?'

'The bribes. Naturally.' A fighter, Perilla.

'Sixty thousand silver pieces? That's some whack, lady. And if he was raking it in to that extent he wouldn't've needed a loan in the first place, would he?'

'Hmm. You're right, it is rather strange.' She went quiet for a moment. 'Then . . . Marcus . . .'

'Yeah?'

'What you're actually saying is that you don't think Sextus Papinius committed suicide after all. That he was murdered.'

Well, it was nice to hear it first from someone else. It didn't sound so stupid that way.

'Yeah,' I said. 'Yeah, I suppose I am.'

Bathyllus came in with the skivvies. 'Have you finished, sir?'

'Clear away, Bathyllus, but give us ten minutes before the dessert. And tell Meton that was excellent. As usual.' Nothing wrong with a bit of unsolicited smarm when you have a sulking chef to contend with.

'Yes, sir.' He lifted plates. 'He'll be extremely gratified.'

Which reminded me. 'Oh, Bathyllus. Incidentally, before I forget. Decimus Lippillus and his wife are coming round for dinner the day after tomorrow.'

'Very well, sir. I'll pass on the message.'

'Lippillus asked if we could have fish.'

'Ah.'

'Right. Tell the stroppy bugger from me it's non-negotiable. If he wants to brawl with half the fish market and get himself slugged with a tunny that's his concern.'

'I'll . . . work on it, sir. Perhaps a little more tact and some rephrasing would be in order.'

I grinned and reached for my wine cup. Bathyllus buttled out.

'So,' Perilla said. 'If it was murder then *why* was it murder?'

'I haven't a fucking clue.'

'*Marcus!*'

'Yeah, well. Look, lady, you said it yourself: all the hard evidence points to suicide. All I've got on the murder front is a half-baked gut feeling.'

'Don't mix your metaphors. Or whatever that was.'

'Okay, Aristotle. You want to indulge in a bit of unscientific theorising yourself, then?'

'Certainly not. Even so, you need to start somewhere. A list of questions would help.'

I lifted the wine jug and refilled the cup. The lady was right, and if I put the googlies into words maybe something would suggest itself. 'Okay,' I said. 'First question: why choose the tenement as a place to kill himself?'

'It could have been a spur-of-the-moment decision. And if he was visiting it in any case as part of his job—'

'No.' I shook my head. 'He wasn't, or not by prearrangement. Not according to Caepio the factor, anyway. Caepio said he'd only called in on spec to check on a couple of figures, and it turned out that that was only an excuse to get the top-flat key. Whatever his reasons for going up there the kid had everything planned beforehand.'

'This is assuming, of course, that the factor is telling the truth.'

'Perilla, look, I know that, okay? We're drawing in crayons here. Just keep things simple at this point, fine?'

'If you say so.'

Shit; I *hated* it when she put on that demure look. She was right, sure; dead right: Caepio could be lying through his ears, especially since he hadn't mentioned the missing key until circumstances forced him to. But like I said we were on the nursery slopes. 'Connected with that,' I said. 'Why the window? If he was planning on suicide from the start and just wanted a quiet place to do it, then why the hell didn't he bring a knife or a razor with him and go out like a proper Roman gentleman? Why choose to take a nose-dive into a fucking crowded street?'

'Marcus, if you're going to swear then—'

'Yeah, yeah, right. Sorry. The answer's obvious, anyway, given the murder option. He didn't, he was pushed; probably knocked unconscious first, because he didn't shout or scream. Only then we're into a whole new can of worms. Who killed him and why? How did they know he'd be there? *Why* was he there? A dozen new questions and then some. Make them up for yourself, lady, but if you can give me a hard answer to any of them I'll eat this fucking napkin.'

'There's no point in getting annoyed, Marcus. I can actually see the problem. What's your second question?'

'The bribes. If Papinius wasn't taking bribes then why was Laelius Balbus so sure that he was?'

'Discounting completely the possibility that Balbus might be lying?'

'Come on, Perilla! Crayons, remember?'

'Very well. *Was* he sure?'

'He said he didn't have definite proof, but yeah, I'd say so. And Balbus is a smart cookie.'

'Did he talk to the boy about it?'

'Yeah. Yeah, he did.'

'And Papinius admitted it?'

I opened my mouth to answer, then stopped. Shit; I hadn't thought of that. 'I . . . don't know,' I said. 'Not for certain. Balbus didn't say; he only said it had registered.'

' "Registered"? Isn't that an odd word to use? I would have

expected either an admission or a denial.' She shook her head. 'Never mind. Leave it for now. Carry on.'

'Fine.' I took another swallow of the Setinian. 'Three: if Papinius wasn't taking bribes then why the loan? No bribes, no blackmail, right?'

'Unless – as you say – the suspicion, and the proof, of guilt were strong enough to justify it, true or not. Or perhaps Soranus was blackmailing him for something else.'

'Gods alive, he was an ordinary nineteen-year-old kid! What else could he put his hand up to that was worth fifty thousand silver pieces to keep under wraps?'

'Hmm.' She was twisting a lock of her hair. 'You're certain he *did* pay the money to Soranus?'

'Lady, I told you. I'm not certain of anything. Soranus denied it, but then he would, wouldn't he? And if it didn't go to him then who did it go to?'

'All right,' Perilla said. 'Fourth question.'

'Four's just that: the sixty thousand payback. Where would a kid like Papinius get that sort of cash?'

'Strictly speaking, Marcus, he wouldn't have to. Given certain circumstances.'

I stared at her. '*What?* But—'

'If we're being absolutely accurate, he'd only have to find the ten thousand interest. That is, if he still had the principal intact.'

I let that sink in, at least, as far as it went, which wasn't saying much at this point. Bugger, she was right; technically, at least. Although then we'd be left with the problem of why he'd needed the fifty thousand in the first place, and why he *hadn't* paid it over.

'Question five,' Perilla said.

'Five is—' I started, but then I stopped as the yawn hit me. 'Look, lady, I don't know about you, but I'm whacked and my brain's beginning to hurt. Let's call it a night, shall we?'

'If you insist.'

I kissed her. 'Come on, Aristotle. Bed. Tomorrow's another day.'

'Mmm.'

There was a cough behind me. Bathyllus had oozed in on my blind side. Impeccably timed, as always. 'Will you be wanting the dessert now, sir?' he said.

'No, I think we'll skip it after all, sunshine.' I took a last swallow of wine, just to empty the cup. 'Oh, Bathyllus. One thing, little guy. Before we pack in.'

'Yes, sir?'

'A lady by the name of Albucilla. Ring any bells?'

'No, sir. I'm afraid not.'

'*Lucia* Albucilla?' Perilla said. 'Satrius Secundus's widow?'

I turned back. 'You know her?'

'Not personally. But I have heard the name, and I've seen her about once or twice. She uses the Apollo Library.'

Hey! 'You know where she lives?'

'No. Why would you be interested in Lucia Albucilla?'

'Papinius's ex-girlfriend mentioned her as the reason why she *is* an ex. And Albucilla, seemingly, is a pal of Soranus's.'

'Ah.' Perilla was frowning. 'I'd've thought she would be a little old for Papinius, myself. She must be in her thirties. Early thirties, at least.'

'That so, now?' The library came as a surprise, too: Albucilla could be no society bubblehead, which was what I'd thought originally. But then Cluvia hadn't been that type either, she was about the same age, and from all accounts Papinius wasn't your lack-brained young Market Square dandy. 'She have a reputation as a cradle-snatcher at all?'

'Albucilla? I've no idea. But then as I say I don't know the woman personally.'

Hmm; well, I'd just have to add a chat with her to my things-to-do list. If she frequented the Apollo Library on a regular basis then they should be able to help me with an address. But that was for tomorrow, and I felt another yawn coming. I took Perilla's elbow and eased her off the couch.

'Let's hit the stairs, lady,' I said, 'before my head opens up round the ears. Goodnight, Bathyllus.'

'Goodnight, sir. Pleasant dreams.'

Frustrations or not, I still felt happier. Suicide's tricky, but you know where you are with a murder.

Apropos of which, I hadn't mentioned the feeling that I was being followed; but then Perilla wouldn't've understood that.

13

I must've been seriously whacked, because the sun was already streaming through the cracks in the shutters when I woke up. Perilla was still flat out. Good: just before I'd dropped off I'd had a stroke of pure genius re the dog-walking problem, and putting it into operation required that the lady should be firmly unconscious.

I slipped out of bed, got dressed, then went downstairs and through the peristyle into the garden. Placida was tied to one of the pillars, flat out as well and snoring. I sneaked past, carried on to the shed at the bottom and knocked.

'Yes?'

Great; he was in. I opened the door.

Okay, we were rolling. Dogless for sure this time.

Let's hear it for subterfuge.

While I was eating breakfast I thought about the day ahead. I'd have to revisit the Aventine tenement, for a start, talk to the tenants, because if Papinius had been murdered there was an outside chance that whoever did it had been spotted. Not much of one, because tenements are usually empty in daylight hours, but a chance none the less. Of course, our murderer could've been the factor, Caepio. Take Papinius up to the top floor on some pretext or other, knock him senseless while his back's turned, push him out the window and the job's done. As far as motive was concerned – well, turn the bribery business around, have Papinius discover that Caepio was fiddling the damage claims and threaten to report it, and you'd be talking a valid scenario, especially if the order to kill him came from someone who really had a vested interest. Someone like Caepio's boss, the tenement owner. Carsidius was another possibility I'd have to look into.

So pencil the tenement into the day's programme. It'd mean an after-sunset visit, but I could cut a deal with Meton re missing dinner and have lunch in a cookshop somewhere instead.

Second was the Apollo Library on the Palatine, to see if they could give me an address for Lucia Albucilla. Papinius taking up with her could be sheer coincidence, sure, but it was worth checking. Albucilla was a friend of Soranus's, after all, and if that bastard wasn't involved somewhere along the line I'd eat my sandals.

Third . . .

Third was Papinius's father, the consular. It wasn't all that likely, given their relationship, or lack of one, that he'd paid the kid's debt for him, but—

'Everything all right, sir?'

'Hmm?' I looked up. 'Yeah. Yeah, thanks, Bathyllus. Oh, by the way. Papinius Allenius. Any idea where he lives?'

'On the Pincian, sir. But the Senate's in session today. If you wanted to talk to him you might catch him after the meeting.'

Good thinking. And if I was going over to the Palatine in any case Market Square wouldn't be much out of my way. Things were shaping up nicely. There was only one potential glitch. 'Uh, how's Meton this morning?' I said.

'Still not quite himself, I'm afraid.'

Shit. Bad news; bad, bad news. Well, it couldn't be helped. If I missed dinner without giving him prior warning we'd be eating turnip for the next month. Not a thing you'd like to risk. 'Ask him if he'd care to have a word, would you?' I said.

'You want to talk to him in person, sir? *Meton?*' Bathyllus doesn't blanch easy, but he came pretty close. The Elder Cato might've looked the same way if someone had suggested inviting Hannibal and the Carthaginian Senate round for drinks and nibbles.

'Yeah. Yeah, that was the general idea.'

'*Now?*'

'As ever is.'

He swallowed. 'Very well. If you're sure.'

'Just do it, Bathyllus.'

'Yes, sir.' He exited.

The breakfast wine was well watered. Even so, I swallowed two full cups of it while I was waiting. When you're interviewing Meton, total sobriety is a complete bummer.

'What is it, Corvinus? Only I've got stock on the boil and it wants skimming.'

I looked up. Hell. Being belted in the eye with a tunny by an enraged fishmonger hadn't improved the guy's physiognomy any. 'Meton!' I said. 'How's it going, pal?' He didn't answer, just glared at me with one good eye and the other looking like it'd collided with a paintbox. Fuck. 'I was wondering about the menu for tonight. You got anything special planned?'

'Hare stuffed with liver and sausage. Flavoured with oregano and cumin.'

'Great. Great. That sounds marvellous. The sort of thing that you could, er, easily reheat, right?'

He gave me a look. *Baleful* comes to mind: Meton has bale by the bucketload, even without a black eye. 'You kidding?' he said. '*No one* reheats hare with liver and sausage!'

'Is that so, now?' No answer. Not that I expected one, of course: it'd been the equivalent of saying 'Pardon?' to the Delphic Pythoness. 'It's, ah, just that I'd kind of planned to give dinner the go-by tonight. As such. In effect, as it were.'

Meton scowled. 'You're eating out?' He made it sound like I

was intending to screw a sheep *coram populo* on the Speakers' Platform.

'No. *No!* But . . .'

He was flexing his fingers, the way he did when he got agitated. Hell. 'Listen, Corvinus. Ariston, down the game market, you know how often he gets a really good hare? We're talking quality free-range here, none of your hutch-bred tat. Same goes for the liver. Prime milk-fed calf's, marinated for two days in wine must. *And* I made the sausage myself. Old Patavinian recipe, beats Lucanian into a cocked hat. With the hare and liver, it'll be a dream. And you are asking me to fucking *reheat*?'

He hawked and spat on the tiles.

Gods! This could get nasty. 'Meton, pal,' I said. 'Look. Let's be reasonable about this, okay? It's no big thing. All I'm trying to tell you is that I've got to go down to the Aventine tonight. Unavoidable business. So I'll miss dinner.' I paused for this to register. Nothing; not a flicker. I might as well've been talking Babylonian. Ah, well; press on. 'There's, uh, there's this thing called a compromise. It means that if you—'

'The Aventine? You're going over to the Aventine?'

'Yeah.'

'Okay. Cardoons.'

I blinked. 'What?'

'Cardoons.'

'What's "cardoons"? Some sort of *recherché* swear-word?'

'What's "*recherché*"?'

We stared at each other. Impasse. Or whatever. I cracked first. 'Ah . . . *recherché* means that I don't know what "cardoons" means, sunshine.'

Pause. Then: 'It's, like, your compromise.'

He'd lost me. Not that that was difficult in Meton's case, mind. His way of thinking wasn't just lateral, Archimedes could've used it for lifting water. 'Uh . . . "cardoons" means "compromise"?' I said. 'Like "pax" or "feins" or "barleys" or whatever the hell kids say when they want time out in a game?'

'Nah. A cardoon is a kind of fucking artichoke. *Everyone* knows that.'

'But artichokes don't—' I stopped. Bugger; I was losing the plot completely here. Start again. 'Meton. Pal. Hold it there, okay? Just pretend I'm stupid, right? For purposes of argument.'

He grinned, revealing a set of teeth like the tombs on the Appian Road. 'Easy. Done it.'

'Great. Now, could you maybe just extrapolate a little?' Then, when the scowl came back: 'Explain, sort of?'

'If you're going to the Aventine you'll pass the vegetable market.'

'Uh . . . yeah. Yeah, I suppose so. If I went out of my way a bit.' Like straight past it and right down all the way to the Tiber, for example. Hell!

'There's a stall there, south-west corner. Belongs to a woman called Flavilla Nepia. She sells the best cardoons in Rome.'

Click. Finally. 'Got it,' I said.

'Buy the small ones, okay? As many as you can get. The big ones can be stringy.'

'And that's your compromise? A bag of this Flavilla Nepia's cardoons?'

'Yeah. I'd go over there myself, but I'm pretty busy at the moment so you can do it for me.'

'Right. You've got a deal. Now—'

'You soak them in water and vinegar before you cook them, you know. Otherwise they go dark.'

'Is that so? Well, well, that is fascinating. Now I'm sorry, but I've got—'

'And when you *do* cook them, you have to remember to add some flour to the water to keep them nice and white.'

'Really? Well, thank you, Meton. Always an instructive

pleasure talking to you, and as ever I have really enjoyed our conversation. Only now I'm a bit pushed for time, so—'

'They're rubbish cold. You got to eat them hot, with some cheese grated on top. Some prefer Bithynian, but me, I find it too salty, and anyways since they started using them linen wrappings you can't find good Bithynian in Rome worth a fuck. Vestinian's not bad at a pinch, sure, and it's easy come by, but we're definitely talking second-rate there. A good Sarsinan, now, that's another matter, you can't beat Sarsinan on cardoons. Only trouble with Sarsinan is if you use too fine a grater the—'

'Right. *Right!*' Jupiter! 'So the bottom line is, Meton, that I can look forward to really yummy reheated hare with liver and sausage tonight, can I?'

He sniffed. 'Bugger that, Corvinus. I'll do you meatballs.'

I watched the guy lumber off to skim his stock, then left the table and went through to the peristyle. Time to put Operation Ditch Placida into action.

She was up and waiting for me, tongue lolling. Yeah, well, she wasn't a bad dog really, not considering the fact that she was a total barbarian with as much of the social graces as would fit on a pinhead, but letting myself be dragged across Rome for a third day in succession just wasn't on.

I unhitched her and fixed the lead on to her collar. Great joy and excitement.

'Come on, Placida,' I said. 'Walkies.'

We headed across the atrium at speed. Bathyllus was buffing bronzes.

'You're off, then, sir?' he said.

'Yeah.' I tugged Placida into the closest I could get to a standstill. 'Tell Perilla I'll be skipping dinner but that I've cleared it with Meton. Oh, and by the way, he's gobbed on the dining-room floor again.'

Bathyllus's eyes closed briefly. 'Thank you for that infor-mation, sir,' he said. 'Shall I open the front door for you?'

'Yeah. Yeah, that might be an idea.'

We scrabbled through the lobby, through the open door and down the steps. I let Placida pull me the length of our garden wall plus next door's house, paused to make sure that no one was watching, then took the sharp left down the alley and another left at the end, back parallel to the way I'd come.

Outside our garden gate, Alexis was waiting as per instruc-tions. Alexis is our gardener, and the smartest cookie on the staff.

'There you go, pal.' I transferred the lead. 'Take her down the Appian Road, turn her loose, let her chase a few rabbits and piss on a tomb or two. Stay out as long as you like, the longer the better. I'll be out until this evening, after dinner, but if you keep her in your shed when you get back I can pick her up from there. Okay?'

Alexis grinned. 'If the mistress finds out, sir, she'll kill us both.'

'True. But then what can go wrong? Thanks, pal. I won't forget this. Ever.'

Free!

Okay. The Senate meeting wouldn't be out for a good three hours yet, minimum: the gods knew what these broad-striper buggers talked about in the Curia Julia, but they took their time over it. My best plan was to start off over at Apollo's temple on the Palatine, where the library was.

Gods, it was great to be dogless!

The good weather was holding as I took the road that led from Head of Africa towards the Scaurian Incline, up the eastern slope of the Palatine and across the top of the hill to its western edge. Libraries always make me nervous. It isn't just the books – I've never been partial to that musty smell of old papyrus and glue – but raise your voice above a whisper in these places and you're liable to have your balls frozen off by glares from half a dozen different directions at once. Get caught chewing on a takeaway pastry while you're browsing and it's a nails-and-hammer offence with no appeal. The Apollo Library serves a purpose, sure, but you wouldn't like to spend time there when you didn't have to. Give me a wineshop any day of the month.

I found the guy in charge and introduced myself.

'Ah, the Lady Rufia Perilla's husband?' He was a dry old stick who looked like he'd been put together with papyrus and glue himself. Probably around the time of Alexander. 'Charming woman. And a real pleasure to meet you, sir. How can I help? A book, perhaps? We have several of these.' He chuckled. Yeah, well: librarian humour is pretty basic.

'Actually,' I said, 'I was hoping you might help me trace one of your regular clients. A lady by the name of Lucia Albucilla.'

'*Really?*' His eyebrows rose. 'Well, well. We're not the, aha, the Danaid Porch here, you know. That's further along. I don't think I could actually—'

I sighed. 'Look, I don't want to chat her up, pal, I just want the answers to a few questions, right?'

He beamed. 'Of course. Of course. Forgive me. Not that I'd disapprove of a little dalliance, far from it. No harm in that. Why, in my younger days—' He stopped. 'Well, that's beside the point. Lucia Albucilla, you say? Splendid woman. Superb *carriage*. She reminds me very strongly of—'

'Pal.' I laid a hand on his arm. 'Just an address. Please? If you've got it?'

'Certainly. Certainly. A moment, Valerius Corvinus, while I check the records. We keep very thorough records, you know. You'd be surprised how many people accidentally leave the building with a book caught up in their mantle. Women especially. I have been advocating body searches for years, but—'

'Ah . . . the *address*, pal? Please?' Before we all dropped dead of advanced age. Gods!

'Yes. Yes, of course.' He went over to the desk. 'The filing system is my own. Alphabetical, and thoroughly cross-referenced. Albucilla will be under A, naturally, or I could find her under L for Lucia. I always cross-reference, you see. It does obviate a certain amount of confusion. Then she has another entry under M, because—'

'Great. Very ingenious. Very thorough.'

'Oh. Yes, yes, of course. Well, no doubt you're a busy man, Valerius Corvinus. I'll just . . . yes.'

I twiddled my thumbs while he looked through the cards.

'Here we are.' He pulled one out. 'The Caeliolan, near the Temple of Ancient Hope. Will that suffice?'

'Marvellous. Thanks a lot, friend. I'm—'

'Of course, she *is* on the premises at the moment.'

'She is *what*?'

'Here, sir. In the reading-room. She came in about an hour ago.'

Jupiter in a bloody pushchair! 'Then why the fuck didn't you tell me at the start?' I said.

He blinked. 'Because you asked me for her address, sir. And, Valerius Corvinus, I have never in my thirty years of—'

'Where is the sodding reading-room? Or do you fucking have to look that up alphabetically as well?'

He drew himself up, bristling. 'Over there. Past the statues of the Graces. Let me say, however, that never in all my thirty years as senior librarian have I been exposed to such—'

'Right. Right. Thanks, pal. Much obliged.'

I left him to his card index.

Albucilla was easy to spot, because while the place was pretty full of punters she was the only woman. She was sitting near one of the windows with a book-roll open on her lap, although she didn't seem to be reading it, just staring into space. *Splendid carriage* was right: I was getting the full profile with the sun behind it, and unless a lot of the top half was mantle I could understand how she'd have my pal the librarian dribbling into his gruel. Strong jawline, too.

I walked over. 'Uh . . . Lucia Albucilla?' I said. Her head whipped round; I doubt if she'd even heard me coming. 'I'm sorry. I didn't mean to startle you.'

'That's all right. I was miles away.' She smiled, or tried to. The face matched the jawline: *handsome* rather than beautiful, with the features looking like they'd been hacked out of marble. She was the colour of marble, too; a dead, pasty white that together with her make-up left her looking like a doll. I reckoned Perilla's estimate of early thirties for her age was well on the low side. By present showing she could've been forty, easy.

'My name's Valerius Corvinus,' I said. 'I was wondering if I could talk to you about Sextus Papinius.'

There it was again: the same flicker of the eyes I'd got with Soranus. She turned her head away. 'I don't think I know a—' she began.

'Come on, lady!' We were getting Looks now from the other punters, and I lowered my voice. 'Of course you do! The kid who killed himself five days back.'

'Oh, *that*—' She stopped and took a deep breath, then turned back to face me. The smile hadn't shifted, but it looked ghastly. 'Yes. Sextus. I'm sorry, how silly of me. Forgive me, Corvinus. It is a little close in here, isn't it?'

It wasn't, particularly, that I'd noticed: this was October, after all, and the window was open. Still, I wasn't going to argue: the punters' Looks had moved up a notch to Glares, and the next thing that'd happen would be a visit from the library's tame satyr. That I could really do without, especially in the guy's present mood. 'You want to talk outside?' I said.

'Yes. Yes, perhaps it would be better.' She rolled up the book, fastened its laces – I noticed that her hands were shaking – laid it on the table beside her and stood up. 'We can go into the garden.'

She led the way and I followed her in silence. The garden was through the portico that led off the entrance hall, in an angle between the library building and the temple itself: a careful arrangement of formal walks and flower-beds with more statuary than you could shake a stick at. Apart from an old guy fast asleep – or possibly dead – on a bench in the corner it was empty. We found another bench under a plane tree and sat down. The lady was a better colour now, but she was still nervous as a cat.

'I was so sorry to hear about Sextus,' she said. 'He was a lovely boy.'

'Yeah. So everyone tells me.' I wasn't quite sure how to play this. From what Cluvia had said, and from the fact that she was a friend of Mucius Soranus's, I'd been expecting a sort of femme fatale. I could still have got one, mind, because in her own way the lady was a looker, but if so she was the well-groomed polished kind that you see at all the best dinner parties.

'You didn't know him, then?' she said.

'No. I'm just . . . looking into his death. As a favour to his mother and Titus Natalis of the Greens.'

That got me another flicker, but she'd obviously got herself in hand and if I hadn't been looking for it I might not've noticed. 'Really?' she said. 'I wouldn't have thought that there was anything to—'

'His ex-girlfriend Cluvia said that you, uh, knew him pretty well latterly. Through a mutual friend, Mucius Soranus.'

Her hand was resting on the arm of the bench. The fingers tightened momentarily. 'Cluvia is a—' She bit back on the word, but not soon enough for me to miss the sudden hardness

of tone that suggested there was steel under the polish. Then it
was gone and she tried another smile. 'I think as an informant
Cluvia may have given you completely the wrong impression
about our relationship, Valerius Corvinus. I liked Sextus, but
he was an acquaintance rather than a friend, and he was
certainly not – as your tone seems to imply – a lover. Not even
in the most minor sense. If you want an explanation for her
attitude, I can only suggest jealousy.'

'Is that so, now?' I kept my voice non-committal.

'Yes, it is. Sextus, I know from certain remarks he made,
was becoming tired of her, and obviously she was looking for a
scapegoat. I happened to be the one she chose. As far as
Soranus is concerned, the situation is similar. He's quite
definitely an acquaintance, not a friend.' She stood up.
'Now, if that's clear I'm afraid I can't help you any further.'

I didn't move. 'So if Papinius was an acquaintance,' I said,
'what sort of acquaintance was he?'

'I'm sorry. I don't understand.'

The hell with tact. 'He was a nineteen-year-old kid, lady,
and you're old enough to be his mother. What did you have in
common? There must've been something.'

Silence. Then she said, 'I . . . really, Corvinus, I see no point
in continuing this conversation. I'm sorry you've had a wasted
journey, but I honestly can't help you further.' She turned
away, just as another woman came hurrying through the
portico.

'Lucia!' Raised voice; obviously agitated. 'Thank Juno I've
caught you! Have you—?'

Then the woman saw me, and she stopped dead. Her hand
flew to her mouth, covering it, and her eyes widened in a shock
that was almost comic. I glanced back at Albucilla. I couldn't
see her face – it was turned towards the new arrival – but her
whole body froze. The woman came towards us, more slowly
now; she'd almost been running to begin with. There was

something familiar about her, but I couldn't recall a name offhand.

Albucilla turned back to me. 'It was nice meeting you, Valerius Corvinus,' she said quickly. 'Do tell Sextus's mother how sorry I am about her son's death.'

'Uh . . . yeah,' I said. 'Yeah, I'll do that.'

I nodded to the second woman – Jupiter, what *was* her name again? – and walked across to the portico. Just before I went inside, I looked back. The two were standing side by side, staring at me.

The librarian was at his desk, talking to a late-middle-aged purple-striper with an obvious toupé. I went over.

'Ah . . . excuse me,' I said.

'Yes?' The satyr wasn't exactly friendly. To put it mildly. Nor, by some sort of osmosis, was the other guy. The two of them were glaring like I'd just propositioned them.

'That lady who's just gone out into the garden. You mind telling me her name?'

'Acutia. Although, my dear sir, I can't see that it's any business of yours.'

Acutia! Yeah, of course she was. I remembered her now; it'd been years and she'd aged, but she still had that mousy look about her. 'Did you tell her I was there?'

'Certainly not! Why should I? She asked to speak to the Lady Albucilla and I so directed her.' He drew himself up again. 'And now perhaps you'll have the grace to explain why—'

But I was already heading for the exit.

Shit. What was going on?

14

I had a good hour to kill, maybe two, before the Senate meeting finished. That suited me fine, because I had a lot of hard thinking to do. Over to Renatius's on Iugarius, then, for a seat and a half jug of wine.

Early as it was, there were two or three punters at the bar, but I didn't know any of them, so I just nodded.

'Haven't seen you for a while, Corvinus.' Renatius was cutting up greens for the lunchtime salad option. 'The usual, is it?'

'Yeah.' I took the coins from my purse and laid them on the counter while he filled the half jug with Spoletan. I eyed the greens. 'Uh . . . incidentally. You ever hear of a thing called a cardoon?'

'Course I have. It's a kind of artichoke.'

'Right. Right. Just checking.'

He brought the jug over and pulled a cup down from the rack. 'You want anything with that? Cheese? Olives? Sausage?'

'No, I had a late breakfast. Cheers, pal.' I picked up the wine and the cup, took them over to a corner table, sat down and poured.

So. That little meeting had been interesting. Whatever was going on – and something was, that was clear, although I hadn't a clue what it could be – Lucia Albucilla was in it up to her carefully crimped fringe. More, she was running scared: the way, when I'd come in, that she'd been sitting staring at nothing, inside her own head, how she'd jumped when I'd first spoken to her and the expression on her face before she had herself under control all showed that the lady had private problems and was living on her nerves. Above all, to claim that she'd never even heard of Sextus Papinius when Cluvia was under the impression they were already an item was a sign of sheer bloody panic. As far as the question of whether the two actually *were* an item was concerned, I'd keep an open mind. There was the age difference for a start. Sure, granted, there are any number of society ladies who run a toyboy, in some circles he's practically a fashion accessory, but usually these women are fifty plus, dress like twenty and act like fifteen. From what I'd seen of her Albucilla just didn't fit the mould. On the other hand, why Papinius should be attracted to Albucilla made more sense, especially since I already knew he went for older women. The kid was mature for his age, he was an idealist-cum-wannabe sophisticate, and he'd been brought up by his mother. Yeah, I could see Papinius making the first approach. In which case Albucilla might just be flattered enough to play along.

I took a swallow of the Spoletan. It's good stuff, or Renatius's is, anyway; not nearly up to Latian standards, but a good swigging wine perfect for getting the brain cells working. Over at the bar, two of the punters had started up a dice game: strictly illegal in a public place and where money's involved, but that's a technicality that no one pays any attention to. Renatius wasn't even making a token gesture to stop it.

Albucilla had been pretty cagey over her friendship with Soranus as well. That was more understandable. If the bastard was bent – which he was – she wouldn't want that connection pointed up. Especially if, somewhere along the line, blackmail was involved . . .

Shit! I needed more facts!

Then there was Acutia. I'd met the lady years back, when

we were in Antioch chasing up the Germanicus connection. She'd been a local-poetry-klatsch pal of Perilla's, married to Publius Vitellius on the governor's staff, and even allowing for her literary interests she was your total archetypal bubblehead. She'd be a widow now, of course, unless she'd remarried, because Vitellius had slit his wrists at the time of the witch-hunt after Sejanus fell, and good riddance to the bastard. Acutia puzzled me seriously. Oh, sure, given she was in Rome there was no reason why she and Albucilla shouldn't be friends or meet at the Apollo Library, particularly if Acutia was still on her poetry jag. No problem there, none whatsoever. But why, when she caught sight of me and Albucilla together, should she act like she'd just strolled out on to the sand in the arena and found that the cats were loose?

Odd, right? And suspicious as hell.

She'd wanted to talk to Albucilla about something important, that had been clear enough. Oh, yeah, there was the slight possibility that I might be overdramatising: like I said, when I first met her in Syria the lady had been a complete bubble-head, and to a woman like Acutia something important could cover anything down to an invitation to a honey-wine party or the latest snippet of society gossip. I knew that, I'd been around bubbleheads most of my adult life, both the male and female varieties. Still, taken together with her reaction when she spotted me I couldn't help wondering if there wasn't a lot more to it. There had been genuine panic in her voice. Panic and fear, which chimed with the way Albucilla had reacted to me.

So let's go the whole bean-bag and assume that whatever she wanted to talk about had something to do with Sextus Papinius . . .

I took another swig of wine. It didn't help.

Shit. I was building sandcastles here, and I knew it. Come to that, I was building sandcastles without any fucking sand.

Sure, Albucilla and Papinius were connected, because she'd been the kid's ladyfriend, or whatever. Also, she had links with Soranus who was definitely in the frame. Albucilla I could see working out somewhere along the line, no problem. But *Acutia*? Where did she fit in? If she fitted in at all. Or maybe I was just letting my suspicious nature lead me by the ears . . .

Bugger; all I had was questions where what I needed was facts. The case just didn't make sense.

Leave it for now, Corvinus. Give your head a rest. At least I wasn't being dragged through the streets of Rome at the end of a boarhound.

I stood up, hefted the jug and wine cup, and went over to the bar to shoot the breeze with Renatius and the punters.

The sun was well past the halfway point and almost into its third quarter when I left the wineshop and walked up Iugarius towards Market Square. The Senate meeting might not've broken up yet, but I could sit on the steps of the Julian Hall across the road from the Curia and watch for the doors to open. It beat a hike to the Pincian, anyway, and I didn't know Allenius's address. I just hoped that he wasn't still in mourning – if he ever had been – and had skipped the session.

In the event, I'd cut it fine. I was just passing the Temple of Saturn when I saw the first broad-striper heading towards me through the crowd. Shit. I pushed through and stopped him.

'Uh . . . excuse me, sir,' I said. 'Was Papinius Allenius at the meeting?'

He gave me a pop-eyed stare. 'Yes. Yes, I believe he was.'

'You happen to know if he's gone yet?'

The guy turned, scanned the crowd for a moment and then pointed. 'There he is,' he said. 'You'll have to be quick if you want to talk to him, though. He's on the grain surplus commission and they've got a meeting this afternoon.'

'Fine. Fine, thanks.' I slipped between a couple of narrow-stripers haggling over a shipment of roofing-tiles, trod on the toes of a plain-mantle who'd decided he needed some valuable time out and was standing staring at the sky and finally ran the guy down just short of Vesta's temple.

He wasn't all that pleased about it, mind.

'Papinius Allenius?' I said.

'Yes,' he snapped. 'What do you want?' He was a tall, thin-faced guy in his mid-to late-forties who looked like he lived on a diet of bread, lemon juice and rectitude. He reminded me a lot of my own father: Dad had had that same look of pokered-rectum respectability. In fact – although I'd never met the man before to my knowledge – twenty years back they'd probably been bosom chums. I noticed he wasn't wearing a mourning-mantle, and he was freshly shaven.

'My name's Valerius Corvinus, sir,' I said. 'I, uh, was hoping to have a word with you about your son.'

He stared at me for a moment. Then he nodded. 'Your name has been mentioned to me, Corvinus. I have a meeting shortly, but I can spare a very few minutes if that will suffice. We'll adjourn to the Temple of the Twin Gods, if you don't mind. It'll be quieter.'

'Sure. No problem.'

We left the main drag and headed down Vestals' Alley. Twin Gods wasn't exactly private – nowhere in Market Square is private, that time of day – but at least we'd be out of the crowd. He went up the steps and stopped beside a pillar.

'Now,' he said, 'before we go any further let me say that I viewed Sextus as no son of mine. I had very little contact with him after the divorce, nor with his mother, except what duty compelled, and I can tell you absolutely nothing about the reasons for his suicide. Is that clear?'

I blinked. 'Uh . . . right. Right.'

'It's as well for you to understand my position right from the start.'

'Sure.' Jupiter! 'But you, ah, did get him his job? With the Aventine fire commission?'

He looked at me down his nose and took his time answering. Finally, he said, 'I know my duty, Corvinus, and I have never in my life shirked it. Sextus's post was part of that duty. It was a completely separate issue and has nothing to do with anything else. Now if you'll excuse me—'

'Did you give him – lend him, whatever – sixty thousand silver pieces?'

He'd been turning away. Now he turned back, mouth hanging. 'Did I do *what*?' he said.

'The kid borrowed fifty thousand from a money-lender about a month ago. Just before he died, he paid it back, plus the interest. You've no idea where that came from?'

'None whatsoever,' he snapped. 'Certainly not from me. It's the first I've heard of it.'

He wasn't lying. I suspected that, like Dad, Allenius didn't believe in telling lies, except as a last resort, when he'd do it with style. Twisting the truth and slithering out from under, that's something else again; any career politician manages that easy as breathing, and Dad – and, I'd suspect, Allenius – did it all the time. But the denial came out too flat to be ambiguous, and the shock on Allenius's face was too real to be fake.

'Fine,' I said. 'Just asking.'

'Very well.' He glanced up the alley, towards the Sacred Way. 'Now if you'll excuse me I really must—'

'One last thing,' I said. I hadn't intended to ask the question, but Papinius Allenius was as good a source for the answer as any. 'You know a senator by the name of Carsidius?'

'Yes. Of course I do.'

'He, uh, "reputable", if you know what I mean?'

I knew it was a mistake before the words were out of my mouth. Allenius drew himself up straight and gave me the full, arrogant broad-striper glare, point-blank range: the look that for centuries has had foreigners from Britain to Parthia wondering if their underwear is showing. 'Reputable?' he snapped. '*Reputable?* How dare you, Corvinus! Lucius Carsidius is a close and deeply respected friend not only of mine but of the most honourable lights of the Senate. And if you imagine for one moment that men of unimpeachable honour and integrity such as Vibius Marsus or Lucius Arruntius would associate with someone whose morals were less than the very strictest, then—'

'Uh, right. Right,' I said quickly, backing off: the guy was working himself up into full Ciceronian denunciatory mode, and heads were beginning to turn fifteen yards off. 'I understand.'

'And so you should!' He was glaring at me. ' "Reputable", indeed! Now if you've finished with your questions I have a meeting to go to. Good-day to you!'

Before I could answer, he set off down the portico steps, and this time he didn't look back.

Shit. I grinned and shook my head: yeah, Dad to a fault. And Arruntius and Marsus, eh? Now, *there* were another two names from the past!

Funnily enough, from the same bit of the past as Acutia . . .

Hell. Coincidence, it had to be. When he'd chosen them as examples Allenius had been right: the pair of them *were* the Roman Senate, or at least between them they led the most reputable bit of it. If Carsidius was part of their gang then he was Respectable with a capital 'R', and you couldn't say that about every broad-striper by any means. Some of these bums on the Curia Julia's benches belonged to crooks and swindlers who'd leave the worst the Subura or Ostia could produce looking like eight-year-old apple-scrumpers. Just because your family name's Cornelius or Junius doesn't mean you're not as bent as a Corinthian whore's hairpin; quite the reverse, because most of the time that's how your ancestors made their pile in the first place and feathering your own nest at other people's expense is practically a family duty.

At least Carsidius had his vote of confidence. Whether the bugger deserved it or not was another matter.

Well, so much for that little interview. I'd never met young Papinius, but I could see why the two hadn't got on: the parallels with me and my own father were too close for comfort. All the same, Dad and I had made it up before he died, and although we were always chalk and cheese we'd at least reached a modus vivendi. Papinius and his father evidently hadn't been so lucky. Sad, sure, desperately sad, but that's how things go. It wasn't too uncommon, either.

Still, there were a few things that didn't quite gel there. As I followed Allenius down the steps and rejoined the crowd I was thinking hard.

15

So. What now? I'd got plenty of time in hand before there'd be any point in heading down to the Aventine, but I'd better go over to the vegetable market south of Cattlemarket Square to fulfil my part of the deal with Meton. If he was so picky about the size and quality of his fucking cardoons then leaving things too late, when all the best ones might've gone, was not a good idea. Mind you, I reckoned I deserved better from his side of the deal when I did finally get back home than meatballs. That was pure sadism.

Speaking of which, lunch. I'd left that pretty late as well, but there're some good cookshops around the square that do all-day specials of tripe, liver and kidneys. Now that breakfast had worn off, I could combine the cardoon hunt with a mid-afternoon meal.

Duty first. Vegetable market, south-west corner, stallkeeper by the name of Flavilla Nepia. Check. I took the series of alleys that link the south side of Market Square with Tuscan Street and headed for the river.

I got the cardoons no bother. In fact, it was a positive pleasure, because Meton's Flavilla Nepia turned out to be a big-boned stunner from Sicily, and a very switched-on lady indeed. So much for names, although what parents would call their kid Dumb Blonde to begin with I just couldn't imagine. The stall was pretty quiet – most of Rome's bag-ladies and kitchen slaves do their shopping early morning – and after she'd helped me load a string bag bought from one of the nearby stalls with half her remaining stock we got chatting about the empire's biggest island. She didn't like Etna, either, so we had a lot in common.

By the time I'd found a cookshop and eaten a leisurely couple of skewerfuls of kidneys with a plate of bean stew and a hunk of barley bread the sun was only a handspan above the Janiculan rise. Perfect. Rome's tenement population would be getting ready to call it a day and head back for the evening soup-pot. I finished the last of my quarter jug of Florentian – you don't see that one often in the city, but the cookshop owner was from the region, and it wasn't a bad choice – and headed in the direction of Old Ostia Road. The narrow streets were full of home-going Aventine tunics, but if a purple stripe don't get you much extra consideration in a crowd a large string bag of very prickly cardoons does, especially if you're prepared to use it.

Not a patch on a Gallic boarhound, mind. I wondered how Alexis was getting on with her. Or not, as it may be. Still, he could look after himself.

I reached the tenement while there was still some light in the sky. It was a beautiful evening: cool, clear, with not a hint of rain. Cooking's frowned on in these places, for obvious reasons – a spilled brazier can send the whole place up like a torch in minutes, and the bad ventilation can kill you before you even notice – so in good weather the locals tend to use the street as a dining-cum-sitting-room until it's time to pack in and go to bed. It's more sociable, too, and tenement punters tend to be a sociable lot, as a rule. There were a good few families outside round folding tables, sitting chatting while Ma or Grandma stirred the bean-pot on the portable stove and laid out the bread and greens.

I stepped on to the pavement to avoid a trio of charging, shrieking kids playing catch-as-catch-can on the road and went up to the nearest brazier.

'Uh . . . excuse me, sister,' I said.

'Yeah?' The woman beside it was cutting sausages from a string and laying them on the grill. She looked up, saw the purple stripe and her eyes widened: you don't get many purple-stripers round the tenements, especially at dinner-time. 'You lost, sir?'

'No. I was hoping someone could help me with the answers to a few questions.'

She frowned: the combination of a purple stripe and questions isn't too popular in places like the Aventine. Then she turned and yelled, '*Quintus!*'

A big guy who looked like he unloaded barges for a living detached himself from a gaggle of male punters shooting the breeze a few yards away and sauntered over, flexing his muscles.

'Yeah?' he said, looking at me. Friendly as a bear with boils. 'Problems, my love?'

'Gentleman says he's got some questions.'

'That so, now?' The friendliness wound down another notch. A bear with boils plus a bad case of haemorrhoids.

I put down the bag of cardoons and held my hands out, palms first. 'No hassle, pal. I'm looking into that suicide a few days back. The young guy who threw himself from the top-floor flat.'

'You with the Watch?'

'No, I'm a . . . friend of the family.'

'Then you can tell them it was no suicide.' The woman sniffed. 'The Watch need their fucking heads examined.'

My stomach went cold. 'You, uh, got a particular reason for thinking that, sister?' I said.

'Now, now, Aristoboulê, dear,' her husband grunted un-easily. 'Don't you go spreading rumours.'

She ignored him. 'The boy had a mother and she's got the right to know,' she snapped. 'What sort of thing is that to tell a woman, that her son's killed himself when he didn't? It's a shame and a slander.' She folded her arms across her very considerable bosom and glared at me. 'You talk to Lautia, sir. She'll put you right. She heard the buggers moving about in there before the lad even arrived.'

Everything went very still, the cold feeling in my stomach dropped a few degrees, and something with lots of legs began a march up my spine. 'There was someone in the flat already?' I said.

'Aristoboulê . . .'

'Course there was. You talk to Lautia about it, sir. She lives just across the landing. Lautia'll tell you.'

Damn right I'd talk to Lautia! I looked round. 'Ah . . . which one is she?'

'The thin girl with a nose like a parrot.' Aristoboulê jerked her head towards the edge of the group. 'And you can just stop looking at me like that, Quintus Maecilius! How would you feel if the boy'd been one of ours? Suicide! It's a shame and a slander, and that's the gods' honest truth!' She hacked off another sausage. 'Fucking Watch!'

I edged round the jutting breasts. So might Ulysses have skirted Charybdis. 'Right. Right,' I said. 'Thanks, sister, much appreciated.'

She turned back to her sausages, muttering darkly, while Quintus shot me a look and slunk off to rejoin his mates. I squeezed between the tables – I was getting quite a few looks now, but curious rather than hostile – and went up to the young parrot-nosed woman who was busy feeding an equally parrot-nosed infant spoonfuls of mashed beans from a dish.

'Lautia?' I said.

'Yeah?' She scooped a stray bit of mash from the kid's chin and popped it into the open mouth, then glanced sideways at me. Like the sausage-woman's, when she saw the purple stripe her eyes widened. Apart from the nose, she was quite a looker, and no more than eighteen.

'The name's Corvinus,' I said. 'Marcus Corvinus. The, uh, lady over there with the sausages said you might be able to help me.'

'What with?' She set the bowl down, her eyes still on the purple stripe. The kid grabbed the spoon and banged it hard on the table. 'Decimus! You stop that right now!'

'Just some information. No hassle, I promise.'

'Information about what?'

'You live on the top floor, in the flat opposite, right?' She nodded. 'According to, ah, Aristoboulê there you were at home when Sextus Papinius killed himself. Died. Whatever.'

She'd been listening wide-eyed. 'That was his name?' she said. 'Papinius? I didn't know.' She swallowed. 'Look, if you're from the Watch I'm sorry I didn't—'

'Uh-uh, this is strictly unofficial. I'm a friend of the family. His mother asked me to find out how he died.' Not exactly true, but on the Aventine family'll outrank Watch any day of the month. 'Like I said, sister, no hassle. I give you my word.'

'All right,' she said. 'Yes. I was in. I'm not usually, but Decimus had a touch of fever, it was raining and I didn't want to take him outside.' The spoon came down again and she turned away. 'Decimus! Behave yourself, I'm trying to bloody talk! Gemella, will you take him for a minute?'

A teenager at the next table smiled at me shyly, got up and lifted the now-squalling kid away to sit on her lap. Better her than me: young Decimus had a great future as a blacksmith. Lautia nodded her thanks.

'Okay,' I said. 'You want to tell me the whole story? From the beginning?'

'Not much to tell.' She pushed a strand of hair out of her eyes. 'It must've been about halfway through the afternoon. I was changing Decimus's nappy and I'd opened the door because he'd got the runs and—'

'Yeah, yeah, okay.' Gods! Some details I *didn't* want to know! 'Got you. And you saw . . . ?'

'No. I didn't actually see anything because I was busy with Decimus. But I heard someone unlock the flat door opposite, go in and close it behind them.'

'Hang on, sister.' I held up a hand. 'You sure about this? Especially the unlocking?'

'Course I am. There's a sort of "clunk" when the key turns. My lock's the same.'

'One person or more?'

'I can't tell you that. I just heard the sound of the lock and the footsteps.'

'Okay,' I said. 'Go on.'

'That's it. At least, that was all until about ten minutes later when the young gentleman arrived. Your Papinius.'

'*You saw Papinius?*'

'Oh, yeah. I'd put Decimus down for his nap and I went to close the door again. He was just putting the key in opposite.'

'Did he say anything?'

'"Don't worry. I'm just inspecting the property." Something like that, anyway.'

'Uh-huh. How did he look? Normal? Nervous? Guilty, even?'

'He was a bit flustered. Like I'd caught him doing something wrong. If he'd been an ordinary working man I'd've thought he was up to no good, but being a purple-striper and nicely spoken and all . . . well, that's a different thing, isn't it?'

'You're sure he had a key?'

'Certain. Like I said, he was fitting it in the lock when I came out.'

'Did he use it? I mean, was the door locked again after the first time?'

'I don't know about that. Decimus started crying again so I went straight back inside and left him to it. Then, it must've been, oh, about five minutes later I heard people shouting in the street. I looked out of the window and saw . . .' She stopped. 'Well, you know the rest, sir. I knew it was him. I could . . . I could see the purple stripe.'

'You didn't go down yourself?'

'No. I'd Decimus to think of.'

'Did you hear anything else? Afterwards? From the flat opposite?'

She was quiet for a long time. Then she said, hardly loud enough for me to hear, 'Yes. Yes, I did.'

Shit. 'Come on, sister. Tell me. No comeback, I swear it.'

'About two minutes later I heard the door open and close. Very quiet. Then someone went down the stairs.'

I didn't ask if she'd opened her own door to look. She wouldn't have done, no way: Lautia wasn't stupid, she could put two and two together and she'd know a lone woman in an empty tenement who'd just for all practical purposes witnessed a murder wouldn't stand a snowball's chance in hell if the killer knew she'd done it. Besides, she'd had the kid with her.

'You didn't tell the Watch?' I said gently.

'No. They never asked me. They never even talked to me. Besides, they're the Watch, aren't they?'

Bugger. There you had it, the Aventine in one. Not just the Aventine, but any of the other tenement districts in Rome: they kept themselves to themselves, and they left the Watch strictly alone. And score another for fucking Mescinius, the Thirteenth District so-called Watch commander. That inefficient bastard couldn't find his arse with both hands and a map.

One thing was sure, though: forget suicide, totally. What we had was definitely a murder. Plus there was something else. I could count up to two, and two keys figuring in Lautia's story was one too many in this business. Lucceius Caepio, our forgetful property factor, had serious questions to answer. Apropos of which . . .

I glanced up at the first-floor window. Factors, unlike run-of-the-mill tenement punters, can afford to bring in takeaways from cookshops and burn lamp-oil in the evenings, and the light showed through the chink in the shutters. The guy was at home. No time like the present.

I turned back to Lautia, reached into my purse and took out a half gold piece. 'Here, sister,' I said, laying it on the table. 'Thanks for your help. Buy the kid a sledgehammer.'

Her jaw dropped. 'But you don't have to—' she said.

'Sure I do. Thanks again. You've been really, *really* helpful.' I was picking up my bag of cardoons when I had another thought. 'Uh . . . by the way. How long's the flat been empty? You know?'

'No. I only moved in last month.'

'You ever see anyone else there?'

'No. But then I'm out all day, usually, like I said. I help out on a clothes stall in the market.'

'Fine. Thanks again. Enjoy your dinner.'

Right. Time for explanations, and a certain amount of buttock-prodding. I went upstairs to talk to Caepio.

16

Caepio didn't exactly seem delighted to see me. Not that I'd been expecting otherwise.

'Valerius Corvinus?' he said when I pushed past him into the living-room. 'What're you doing here at this time of night?'

'Sextus Papinius was murdered,' I said. 'And you know it.'

He went grey. 'But that's—' he began.

I stepped within grabbing range. He flinched. 'Look,' I said, 'there was someone in the flat upstairs when he arrived, okay? I know that for a fact. They didn't leave until after he was fucking dead, and then they slipped out quietly while everyone else was rubber-necking at the body. Now put these three items together and tell me I'm jumping to unwarranted assumptions. *Pal!*'

'Who've you been talking to?' he whispered. 'Holy gods!'

'Never mind that! They were there, right? So who were they?'

'Corvinus, I swear to you—'

The hell with this. I reached over, gripped the tunic under his throat and pulled him almost off his feet. He went rigid. 'Papinius had a key. Maybe he took it for himself like you said, or maybe you gave it to him; the jury's still out on that one, and it doesn't matter anyway. What does matter is whoever went into the flat before he did had a key of their own. So where did that one come from? Maybe they borrowed your bunch of duplicates while you were standing with your eyes conveniently closed? In which case, friend, even if you didn't do the actual killing yourself you're well and truly screwed.'

'Corvinus, please . . .' The guy was white and shaking.

I let go of him. He pulled up a stool and sat.

'Okay,' I said. 'Now talk.'

He swallowed and rubbed his throat. 'I swear to you. Please! Any god you like, on my grandmother's grave I swear it, I don't *know*! I don't know who the killer was, I don't know where he got the key. It wasn't mine. I was here all the time and the bunch never left my desk. Corvinus, you've got to believe me! The first I knew Papinius was dead was when I saw his body in the street, and that's the holy truth!'

He wasn't lying, not in his state. If he hadn't pissed his pants it was probably because his bladder was already empty. And he couldn't've been the murderer: Lautia had said Papinius had been on his own, and if Caepio had decoyed him into the flat to kill him they would've been together. Besides, with his gammy leg he'd never have got down five sets of stairs in time to pretend he'd only come from the first floor. So scratch Caepio's duplicate set. What did that leave us with?

'Carsidius,' I said.

Caepio's head snapped up. '*What?*'

'Your boss. The owner. He got a set of keys too?'

'Yes, of course he's . . .' Then his brain must've caught up with his mouth because his jaw dropped open. 'Holy gods, no! No, never! Carsidius wouldn't . . . he's got no reason to!'

'Okay. So you tell me, sunshine. Where did the key come from?'

'I don't *know*! It could've been a copy, an illegal copy, I mean. Or the killer could've picked the lock.'

'Fine. So how did he get his hands on an original long enough to get the copy made, and why should he bother on the fucking off-chance that Papinius might choose to go up there some day to be murdered? And picking the lock's out. Lau—'

I stopped myself. 'The person who told me said they'd heard the key used.'

'You don't want to believe Lautia, Corvinus. That little slut's—'

I reached out and grabbed him again; maybe harder than I'd meant, because he gave a terrified gasp. 'Listen to me, pal,' I said softly. 'Listen very carefully indeed. If I find that the lady's been hassled by you or by anyone else just because she had the decency to tell the truth then by every god in the pantheon I swear you'll wish you'd never been born. Clear?'

'I wouldn't—'

'Then just make very, *very* sure you don't. Right.' I let him go and pulled up a spare stool. 'So. Personally, since we've got a murder here, I'd say your Lucius Carsidius has just shot up into the number one suspect slot. If you're not happy with that then you go ahead and convince me I'm wrong.'

He was the colour now of an old dishrag. He took a deep breath. 'Corvinus, believe me, Carsidius would be the last person to kill Papinius. Or have him killed.'

'Yeah? And why's that?'

'Have you ever met the man?'

'What does that have to do with it?'

'You wait until you do, then you can accuse him to his face and see what he says. He wouldn't, in the gods' name he wouldn't! That's all I'm saying.'

Bugger. He meant it, too. 'I'll ask you again, friend,' I said. 'You want to give me a why? A real one?' But Caepio's lips were tight shut. 'Come on! Carsidius has the only other key!' His eyes shifted. 'Or has he? Caepio!' I thought of grabbing him by the throat again, but the guy clearly wasn't talking and there was no point to gratuitous violence. Shit; what was going on here? I took a deep breath. 'Okay. Okay. If it wasn't Carsidius had the boy killed then who was it? You know, you bastard, or if you don't you can make a pretty good guess. So spill!'

The look he gave me would've frozen a basilisk, but behind the eyes there was pure terror.

'I can't,' he whispered. 'Jupiter, Apollo and all the gods help me but I can't! It's more than my life's worth. Just leave me alone, all right?'

We stared at each other. He was breathing hard, but his jaw was clenched. Impasse. Well, short of beating the bastard to a pulp or lugging him down to the Watch-house where Mescinius would probably have me for assault and battery myself there wasn't anything more I could do. I left him to his unfinished supper – it was laid out on the table – and let myself out.

Home.

It was dark when I left the tenement, the party was over downstairs and the street was deserted. Bugger; I should've thought of that: walking in Rome after dark, even in the centre, where I wasn't, isn't a healthy occupation, and the purple stripe didn't help any, either. Quite the reverse. Still, it was too late for grief now.

I shouldn't've ditched Placida after all. Nice timing, Corvinus.

The best way to the Caelian was to follow the western slope of the Aventine and then cut to the right through Circus Valley. Not exactly a salubrious area, any of it, and there was certainly no street lighting: you got torches at the doors of upper-class houses, sure, but not outside tenements, and tenements, in this part of Rome, were all there were. Well, I could pick up a litter or a couple of torch-boys at the junction with Public Incline.

I hefted the bag of cardoons, cursing Meton for not asking for a pound of chitterlings instead, and set out, keeping my eyes skinned for footpads. I'd given up carrying the knife strapped to my wrist years ago. That's what age does to you.

They hit me halfway to the junction, two of them, coming from behind. I was lucky: I heard the slap of their sandals on the cobbles, and I turned as the first of them reached me. I'd just time to get the bag between me and him, chest height, before he got the stab in, and the cardoons took its whole length. I grabbed him, pulled him towards me and kneed him hard in the balls. He doubled up with a grunt. One down, or at least out of it temporarily. That only left the second . . .

I pulled the bag free and shoved it into his face. One thing you can say for cardoons, the buggers in their natural state are spiky as hell, and a faceful of them judiciously applied is no joke. He cursed and lashed out. The knife he was holding sliced through my tunic, cutting my upper arm. Out of the corner of my eye, I saw his mate stagger to his feet and come at me from the side, knife held level, swearing blue murder . . .

Oh, shit.

Someone shouted. The first guy stopped and looked round. Then he was reeling backwards holding his head while whoever had hit him went in to finish the job with a vicious swipe of his stick to the ribs. There was a dull *thunk*, and I thought I heard bones crack. The guy screamed and staggered away at a run, clutching his side.

Meanwhile, his pal was having serious problems of his own. There were two newcomers, and the second had gripped his arm, spun him round, grabbed him by the belt and thrown him hard against the streetside wall. He hit it head-first with a sickening crack, dropped his knife and collapsed in a huddle on the pavement. It was suddenly very quiet.

I straightened. Yeah, well, maybe someone up there did have time for half-assed purple-stripers after all. It'd been a close thing, though.

'You okay, friend?' The first guy – the guy with the stick – was coming over.

'Yeah,' I said. 'Yeah, I'm fine. More or less.'

'Let's look at that arm.' Before I could say anything, he'd pulled back the tunic sleeve and was examining the cut. It hurt like hell and there was a lot of blood, but even I could see that it was only a flesh wound. 'Just a scratch. Caught you with the edge on the upswing. You'll live.'

'Seems like it, thanks to you, pal,' I said. 'Good thing you came along. They had me cold there.'

'You're welcome.' He was a big lad, late thirties, with arms like a blacksmith's. The first mugger had been lucky to get off with a busted rib and a cracked skull. 'Any time.'

'This one's had it, Sextus.'

I glanced across. His mate was kneeling beside the second knifeman. Right: I could see that for myself. The chances of anyone with a head that shape still being a viable commodity were zilch.

The first guy grunted. 'See me weep,' he said. 'Leave the bastard for the Watch.' He turned back to me. 'Bloody stupid, that, wasn't it, sir? You often do your shopping after dark?'

I grinned. 'No. And you're right, it was bloody stupid.'

'So long as we're agreed.' There was no answering grin. 'Don't do it again's my advice. You be more careful next time. Now, Quintus and me'll see you as far as the chair rank at Public Incline. You won't have no more trouble, I'll guarantee that.'

'Fine by me.'

'Let's be going, then.' He turned and walked off.

'Sextus and Quintus, eh?' I said, falling in beside him while his mate brought up the rear. 'Anything tacked on to the blunt ends?'

The pause was hardly noticeable, but it was there. 'Sextus Aponius and Quintus Pettius,' he said.

'Pleased to meet you. Marcus Corvinus. It was lucky you came along when you did. You live locally?'

'More or less. Near Pottery Mountain. We were on our way home. Got a stonemason's yard up by the Trigemina Gate.'

Well, that explained the muscles. The other guy wasn't any midget, either. 'You work late. Not that I'm complaining, mind.'

'Had to wait for a delivery. How's that arm?'

'It'll do.' I'd been pressing my hand over it to keep the cut closed, and if the bleeding hadn't actually stopped I wasn't in danger of draining away any more. 'So I'm taking you back in the wrong direction?'

'Look, sir, I told you, no problem, right? Quintus and me, we enjoyed the workout. That right, Quintus?' He glanced back.

'Yeah.' Obviously a man of few words, Aponius's mate, but with biceps like these he was doing okay. When he'd hit the wall that second mugger had been flying. No wonder his skull had smashed like an eggshell.

We walked on in silence. Finally I could see the torches ahead that marked the small square where the litter rank was. Journey's end. I reached into my purse. 'Thanks a lot, friends. Have a drink on me, next time you're out. And if you let me know more exactly where this yard of yours is—'

'Nah. Keep your money for the chair,' Aponius said. 'Our pleasure. Just be more careful next time, like I said. See you around, Corvinus.'

And they nodded and walked off, back the way we'd come.

I took the first litter, gave the guys the address, and settled back, trying not to bleed on the cushions.

Interesting, that. One or two aspects of it in particular . . .

Theorising and contemplation, though, could wait. First I'd have to think what I was going to tell Perilla, because when she saw the state I was in the lady would hit the roof.

17

I got the litter guys to drop me at the back gate, paid them off and went inside and through the garden to Alexis's hut. He was still up and waiting: I could see the line of lamplight under the door. I pushed it open.

'Hey, Alexis!' I said. 'Sorry I took . . . *For shit's sake, you stupid dog, it's me!*'

'*OWOO-OO-OO! OWOWOW-OO-OO-OO!*'

All I had time for was one fast backward step. Not fast enough. Both paws got me square in the chest and I went arse over tip into the rhododendrons.

'*Leave*, Placida!' Alexis pulled at her collar while I tried to fend off the slobbering muzzle. 'I'm sorry, sir, she's just saying hello. Are you all right?'

'Yeah. Yeah, I'm fine.' Well, I would be if my cut arm wasn't screaming in agony. Still, there was no point in complicating matters. I picked myself up while Alexis held the brute clear. 'How was your day?'

'Not bad, sir. We had a lovely walk, didn't we, Placida?'

'*What?*'

'No problems at all. She was as good as gold all the way. I took her as far as the third milestone, let her chase some rabbits among the tombs, like you said. Then when we got home I smuggled her in and fed her and she's been flat out on the floor ever since.'

'Ah . . . Well done, Alexis,' I said weakly. 'I knew I could depend on you.'

'You're welcome, sir. Same thing tomorrow?'

'Sure. If you don't mind.'

'Oh, I don't mind at all.' He scratched Placida's head. 'She has a lovely nature.'

'Yeah. Yeah, right. Uh . . . goodnight, pal.'

'Goodnight, sir.'

Bloody hell! Even so, it looked like Operation Ditch Placida had been a resounding success. I fastened on her lead, let her drag me to the garden gate then doubled back round to the front door. Bathyllus was still up, not that I'd expected otherwise, and I sank the first cup of Setinian gratefully while Placida nosed around checking whether our lobby had been invaded by any strange canines in her absence.

Bathyllus must've noticed the state of my tunic – there were half a dozen lamps burning in the lobby – but he didn't comment.

'Meton's left a plate of cold meatballs for you on the dining-room table, sir,' he said. 'And the mistress is waiting for you in the atrium.'

Oh, shit. I swallowed: this was going to be tricky. 'Okay, little guy,' I said, handing him the bag of cardoons. 'Pass these on for me, would you?'

'Yes, sir.'

I filled the cup, took another fortifying gulp, and went through to the atrium.

'Hi, Perilla,' I said. 'Nice evening?'

She looked up from her book. Hell: four large candelabra fully equipped with lamps. No chance; *no* chance. Bathyllus had followed me in, too, and he was hovering at the edge of the lamplight like a third actor who's hoping he's in the wrong play.

Perilla set down the book-roll. 'Oh, good, you're back,' she said. 'Now you can tell me why you—' which was when she saw the bloodstain on my tunic sleeve, plus the rest of the extensive collateral damage, and her eyes widened. '*Marcus!* What on earth!'

'It's just a cut,' I said hurriedly. 'It looks a lot worse than it is.'

She was already halfway across the room. 'Bathyllus, get Sarpedon!'

'Yes, madam.' He turned.

'Hang on, Bathyllus,' I said. Sarpedon was our family doctor, one of the best in Rome. He wouldn't take kindly to being hauled out of bed for what was basically a minor clean-up job. Besides, he charged a fortune. 'I'm okay, lady, honestly. All it needs is a bit of vinegar and water.'

'Oh, for heaven's sake!' She reached over. 'Take your hand away! Let me look!'

'Uh-uh. I'll do it,' I said quickly: concerned Perilla might be, but she's no gentle-handed nurse. I peeled back the tunic sleeve. Luckily, although thanks to Placida the cut had started bleeding again, it didn't look too bad.

Perilla examined it. 'That's a knife wound!' she said.

'Possibly. Possibly. But—'

'Bathyllus! Fetch a basin, a sponge, vinegar, linen dressing and a bandage!' The little bald-head shot off like he'd been greased. 'Now, Marcus. You are going to sit down and explain. And this had better be good.'

Here we went. I stripped off what was left of the tunic and sat down on the couch. 'It's no big deal. I got mugged. Or at least partly mugged. On the Old Ostia Road.'

'*Partly* mugged?'

'We were interrupted by a couple of stonemasons. At least they said they were stonemasons.'

'What do you mean, "said"?'

'They weren't. They were army.'

'Oh, come on!'

'Lady, I *know*, right?'

'And where was Placida in all this?'

Hell. 'Ah . . .'

'Marcus, you may be silly enough to go walking on the Aventine after dark; in fact, having lived with you for almost twenty years I know you are. But I would've expected even an Aventine mugger to hesitate before getting involved with a dog of that size—'

'Yeah, well, she—'

'. . . unless, of course, you'd also been silly enough to leave her behind this morning with Alexis.'

Shit. 'You knew?'

'No. At least, not until ten minutes ago when I heard her howling at the bottom of the garden and watched you sneak her out the side gate. That made the inference fairly obvious. Marcus, how could you have been so *stupid*?'

'Okay.' I grinned. 'It's a fair cop, lady. But she had a good run with Alexis out the Appian Road. Better than she'd've had with me.'

'That's not the point, and you know it. Well, it serves you right, that's all I can say.' Bathyllus came in with the basin and the fixings and put them down on the table beside me. 'Thank you, Bathyllus. Arm out.'

I held it over the basin while she sponged the cut clean . . . '*Ouch!*'

She sniffed. 'Marcus, if you won't have Sarpedon then don't complain. I'm doing my best. Also, I'm not feeling particularly sympathetic at present.'

Gods! 'Look, lady,' I said, 'I've been mugged once already this evening. Once is enough.'

'Partly mugged. And as I say it serves you right.' She put on the dressing, held the end of the bandage up for Bathyllus to slit and then tied the two ribbons together. 'Comfortable?'

'No.'

'Good.'

I leaned forward and kissed her. She was shaking.

'Wine, Bathyllus,' I said. 'Unwatered, and another cup. No arguments, lady, it's medicinal.'

He buttled off.

When he'd gone, Perilla sat back against me and closed her eyes. 'You could have been killed,' she said quietly.

'Yeah. Right,' I said. 'But I wasn't.'

'Not this time. Next time you may not be so lucky.'

'If I have Placida with me?'

'It's not the dog, Marcus. You know it isn't.'

'Yeah,' I said, and kissed her again. 'Yeah, I know.'

We sat for a while. Then she opened her eyes and said in a more normal voice, 'Why are you so sure that your two stonemasons were army?'

'Because they were too good. Trained professionals. They went through the muggers like a dose of salts. Also, one of the bastards died and they didn't even bat an eyelid, and with your ordinary tunics that isn't natural.'

'Hmm. How old were they?'

'About the same age as me. Mid- to late-thirties.'

'Very well. There's your answer: old enough to have got their discharge. There's no reason why they *shouldn't* be ex-army and stonemasons as well, is there? Did you ask them?'

'Uh, no, but—'

'Then don't look for unnecessary complications.'

'Discharged soldiers get their severance pay in land.'

'Which they can then sell. Just because they're veterans doesn't mean to say they're natural farmers. And soldiers are trained to work with stone. It might even be a family business one of them's gone back to.'

I frowned. She was right, sure. And I hadn't asked. Even so . . .

'You think it was just an ordinary mugging?' She was

twisting her hair. 'Or had it something to do with the Papinius business?'

I'd been wondering that myself. 'I don't know,' I said. 'It could've been coincidence, sure. Like you say, the Aventine's no place to be alone after dark. All the same, now that I know for certain that the kid was murdered I wouldn't like to lay odds.'

She sat up. 'You're sure about that?'

'Oh, yeah. No doubts now whatsoever.' I told her what Lautia had told me, plus highlights of the Caepio interview. Halfway through, Bathyllus came back with the wine, plus a half jug of ready-watered stuff on the side. Perilla sipped at hers while I took a gulp before topping up the cup from the jug.

'Then who was responsible?' Perilla said.

'Jupiter knows. Maybe this Carsidius, for all Caepio says. He's the most likely bet.' I took another swallow. 'That was odd. The guy was adamant Carsidius wouldn't've done it, but he wouldn't tell me why. And he's got beans to spill himself, that's definite.'

'But why should Lucius Carsidius kill the boy? Marcus, his factor's right, Carsidius is a well-respected senator, even I know that. He is *not* the sort of man to go around killing people. Or having them killed.'

'Turn the bribery on its head: Carsidius was fiddling his damage claim, Papinius found out and told him he intended to report it. The well-respected senator angle's no barrier, lady, not where peculation and rooking the government's concerned. Broad-stripers've always looked on that as a traditional right, not a crime. And if Carsidius had a reputation to consider it would've made the threat of exposure even worse.'

'Bad enough to go the length of murder?'

'Why not? They're all callous bastards at root, especially the so-called respectable ones. Remember Lamia?'

Perilla closed her eyes briefly. 'Yes, Marcus,' she said quietly. 'Oh, yes.' Aelius Lamia and his senatorial sidekick Arruntius had been instrumental, when Sejanus fell, in having the guy's children executed. One of them was a twelve-year-old girl, and since executing an under-age virgin is against the law Bastard Lamia together with oh-so-honourable pride-of-the-fucking-Senate Arruntius had told the public strangler to remove the latter half of the legal stumbling-block before he carried out the order. It was the reason – then – that we'd left Rome, and I'd sworn I'd never come back. The lady still had nightmares, off and on. Lamia himself was long dead, but Allenius had told me that Carsidius and Arruntius were friends and soul-mates. He'd meant it as a character reference. Me – well, it just made my gorge rise.

'But Balbus said Papinius was taking bribes,' Perilla said. 'Or do you think he was lying after all?'

'I don't *know*.' I took an irritable swig of wine. 'Maybe. It's a possibility. Maybe it's a cover-up and Balbus is in it too. I wouldn't put anything past these senatorial bastards. One sniff of scandal and they close ranks and lock shields like a fucking legionary tortoise.'

'A cover-up for what?'

'The gods know. I'm talking through my ears here. The only thing I'm absolutely certain of at this point is that the kid's death was no suicide.'

'Marcus, be careful. I have a bad feeling about this. I don't think your muggers were ordinary Aventine knifemen.'

'No, lady. Neither do I.' Well, it'd explain my own gut feeling that someone had been tailing me for the last couple of days. Mind you, I didn't believe in my altruistic stonemasons' deus-ex-machina act either; that was just too neat to be coincidence. I finished the wine at a swig. 'The hell with it for now, anyway. I'm starving, it's been a long time since lunch and Bathyllus mentioned something about meatballs.'

'Oh. Oh, yes, they're on the dining-room table.' Perilla got up. 'By the way, where's Placida?'

I looked round. 'She was right behind me, but I haven't seen her since . . . *Shit!*'

I leaped off the couch and ran through to the dining-room.

No meatballs. No dog, either, just an empty plate licked clean and a few breadcrumbs. Hell. The end of a perfect day. I went back to the atrium, stomach rumbling.

'Have they gone?' Perilla said.

'Like the snowfall on the river. Bugger!'

'Never mind, dear. A heavy meal last thing at night isn't good for you anyway.'

'A plateful of meatballs isn't a heavy meal, lady. And I'd've liked to've been given the option. I hope the brute has heartburn.' Ah, well. The joy of pets. And I had had my dog-free day; I couldn't grudge her half a dozen of Meton's meatballs in return. 'Bed?'

'Bed.'

Tomorrow I would track down Carsidius.

18

It was pretty late when we woke the next morning, but then I reckoned I was owed a bit of a lie-in, not to mention a substantial breakfast. Besides, I'd got quite a strenuous day ahead of me, beginning with a hike over to the Trigemina Gate to check on the bona fides or otherwise of my stonemason chums. In the unlikely event that they did turn out to be pukkah then fine; once I had an address I could thank them by sending a couple of jars of Caecuban. If not . . . well, we'd have to think about that.

'You'll be taking Placida, naturally,' Perilla said as Bathyllus poured her breakfast fruit juice.

She'd caught me in mid-bite of my honeyed roll. I almost choked.

'Jupiter, lady, I've got a job to do!'

She sighed. 'Marcus, we talked about this last night. Oh, I quite agree, she'd be far better off with Alexis. He's much more reliable, and at least he can be trusted to look after her properly, but—'

'*What?*' I set down the roll.

'Well, you haven't exactly been a good influence so far, have you? She was a perfect angel when she came, and look at her now.' I was staring open-mouthed. She reached for the grapes. 'Oh, I'm not blaming you, dear, it's not completely your fault: animals are very sensitive to these things. But even so, after the events of yesterday evening I'd be happier knowing you have her with you.'

There ain't no justice. Bugger. Trapped again. Not that I would've minded all that much about that – she was right; if someone *had* set these two muggers on me then having Placida on the team would be a serious disincentive for a second attempt – but being accused of corrupting the brute's morals *really* hurt. I hoped I never met the sainted Sestia Calvina because unless somebody restrained me I'd vivisect the lady with a rusty sawblade.

Yeah, well. Like the Stoics say, when Fate frowns on you all you can do is give her the finger and grin back. Besides, Alexis had said that Placida had been good as gold yesterday. Maybe she was settling down.

And maybe we'd be hit from above by a shower of pigshit.

Bathyllus oozed over. 'Would you like some more rolls, sir?' he said. 'Madam?'

'Uh-uh. Not for me, anyway, little guy,' I said, standing up. 'I'd better be going. Oh. One thing. You have an address for Lucius Carsidius? The senator?'

He hardly blinked. 'Yes, of course. He has a house on the Esquiline, overlooking Patrician Street.'

'Could you send a skivvy round? Ask if it'd be convenient to call on him some time this afternoon.'

'Yes, sir.'

'Fine. I should be back here in time for lunch and you can give me his answer then. Where's Placida?'

'With Meton in the kitchen, sir. She spends a lot of her time down there. As I said, they've become quite friendly.'

Gods! Put these two together and you had the potential for a partnership made in hell. Still, that was Meton's business. Or at least I hoped it'd stay that way.

'Wheel her up, then, pal,' I said. 'Let's get this over with.'

'Don't forget Lippillus and Marcina are coming to dinner tonight,' Perilla said. Damn; I had. Never mind, the Esquiline wasn't too far away and an afternoon appointment with

Carsidius would get me back in plenty of time. 'Oh, and Marcus?'

'Yeah?'

'Be careful.'

Although *good as gold* didn't exactly describe Placida's behaviour on the walk – there was a minor incident involving a pie-seller near the Racetrack, but the guy had snapped his fingers at her and it was his own fault – we made it without too much trouble. Maybe sending her out with Alexis hadn't been such a bad move after all, and she'd decided to turn over a new leaf.

Maybe.

The Trigemina Gate's on the river side of the city, beyond Circus Valley and opposite the north-west corner of the Aventine. That stretch, following the river and all the way south to Pottery Mountain, is definitely industrial area, mostly the heavy or bulk variety because the raw material can come up or down the Tiber by barge and doesn't have to be transported overland all that far. So we weren't exactly short of stonemasons' yards here. Accordingly, I gave it a fair crack of the whip; I asked at every yard and every wineshop from the Sublician down to Drusus and Germanicus Arch.

No one had heard of either Sextus Aponius or Quintus Pettius.

Okay, so check. So much for the accidental stonemasons; the buggers had been tailing me right enough. The question was why? And who had sent them? Not that I wasn't grateful, mark you.

Well, at least I'd done my duty by Perilla. What with the trip over to the gate and subsequent detours up and down the river bank, Placida couldn't complain that she wasn't getting her share of exercise. I wasn't going to do an Alexis and risk letting her off the lead, though, even in the comparatively open ground near Pottery Mountain. Chasing rampant Gallic boar-

hounds over half the Thirteenth Region was a pleasure I could
do without.

I got back home in time for a quick lunch before my
arranged appointment with Lucius Carsidius. Perilla wasn't
in, so I left Placida sleeping it off in Alexis's shed and headed
up to the Esquiline.

Carsidius was everything I'd expected: a handsome, upright,
silver-haired senator who just radiated respectability, honesty,
trustworthiness, love of honour and the embodiment of everything that has made Rome great. Dad would've loved him.
More, he'd chosen to see me in his private study, where the
eyes of a dozen generations of his family in the form of portrait
busts glared down at me as if I'd just pissed under their noses
on the fancy mosaic floor.

He was also, very plainly although he tried to hide it,
nervous. And . . . *angry*. There was no other word for it.

Odd.

'Valerius Corvinus,' he said, rising. 'Do come in, please.'
Then, to the slave who'd brought me in: 'Bring us some wine,
Flavius. Corvinus, you'll find that chair most comfortable if
you'd care to sit.'

I sat. He did the same, behind his desk. We looked at each
other.

'I'm—' I began.

He held up a hand. 'I know why you're here,' he said. 'To
ask me about the death of young Sextus Papinius. But first I'm
afraid that I have a confession to make. Rather a serious one,
as it happens.'

'Uh . . . you have?' I said.

'Yes. You see, I bribed him.'

This wasn't how it was supposed to go. I stared at the guy.

'You did *what*?' I said.

'I gave Sextus Papinius twenty thousand silver pieces. In

exchange for his accepting some false information regarding the damage to several pieces of property I have on the Aventine.'

My brain had gone numb. 'Uh . . . run that past me again, pal,' I said. 'You're telling me, free, gratis and for nothing, under no compulsion or threat whatsoever, that you slipped the boy a back-hander?'

'Yes.' His face was unreadable, although I thought I detected a slight hint of distaste. 'I'm not proud of myself, not in the least. Quite the reverse. And I've already confessed to Laelius Balbus, in exchange, of course, for an assurance that the matter ends here and there will be no prosecution. Under the circumstances that would be in no one's interests.' The door behind me opened and he glanced over my shoulder. 'Ah. Here's the wine. Just pour it and go, Flavius, we're discussing business.'

He did. I looked at Carsidius over the wine cup. 'How much did you say you'd given him?' I said.

'Twenty thousand silver pieces.'

'You're sure it wasn't fifty?'

'Fifty? Why fifty?'

'Fifty seems a nice round number. Although sixty would be even better.'

'No. It was twenty thousand, and it represented a . . . shall we call it a ten per cent commission on what I personally would make from the deal.' His lips twisted. 'No doubt he made similar arrangements with other customers but I know nothing of them.'

'But now you've lost the lot, so you're twenty thousand down.'

'Yes. Do try the wine, by the way.'

I did. It was Falernian. Proper Falernian, which is saying something. More, I took a proper gulp, because any minute now I'd be out on my ear, and good Falernian you don't waste. Ah, well: it had to be done.

'I'm sorry, sir,' I said, 'but you're lying.'

He blinked, as if I'd hit him. 'I beg your pardon?'

'You didn't bribe Papinius at all. The kid was straight, I'd bet my back teeth on it. So the question is, why are you saying that you did?'

'I . . . I've never . . . never been . . .' He was red-faced and spluttering. I'd done it deliberately, of course: broad-stripers like Carsidius aren't used to being called liars to their faces. There're so many lies spouted in the Senate-house that call someone a liar one minute and five minutes later you're leaving yourself wide open to the counter-charge; with the consequence that no one uses the word at all, however deserved it is. Work out the cumulative effect on truth, justice, honesty and fair-mindedness in your average senatorial debate over the centuries and you'll realise just why Rome is the caring, sharing mistress of the world that she is, loved and revered throughout her empire. And why all senators, silver-haired or not, friends of Arruntius and Marsus or not, are total bastards at heart.

'One reason I can think of,' I went on, since I obviously wasn't going to get an answer to the question anyway, 'was that you had Papinius killed yourself and bribery's the lesser of the two crimes. Admit to the second and ipso facto you can't be guilty of the first. Why the hell you'd want him dead, mind—'

Suddenly, Carsidius stood up. I had to admit it was pretty impressive. He was a tall guy, ramrod-straight, and like I say he looked the part. There was no spluttering now, either. He glared at me, walked over to the shrine in the corner and laid his hand on top of it.

'Listen, Corvinus,' he said. 'Listen very carefully. I swear by all the gods of my family, by Jupiter, Mars and the pantheon, that I had no part, active or passive, in the killing of Sextus Papinius. Now, will that satisfy you?'

'Fine.' I was impressed, despite myself, but I wasn't going to show this bastard that. No way. 'You want to swear now that you *did* bribe him?'

He took his hand from the shrine like it was red-hot. 'You insult me!'

'Damn right I do, pal!' I was on my feet and angry myself now. 'It seems that's the only way I'm going to get any truth here! Now what the fuck's going on?'

'*Leave my house!*'

'When I'm good and ready. Let's talk keys.'

The guy was red enough for an apoplexy. 'Valerius Corvinus, unless you leave now, I'll—'

'That flat had three keys that I know about. One went to the tenant, and if the place was empty it was kept on the board in Caepio's living-room. That was the one – according to Caepio – that Papinius took the day he died and which was found on his body. The second was on Caepio's duplicate bunch, and he swears it never went out of his hands. The third was yours, and *that* one, pal, I know nothing about. But whoever killed Papinius had a key, and yours is my best bet. So if you didn't have the kid murdered then you tell me about that key. Or was there a fourth?'

He was visibly shaking: with anger, mostly, but there was something else. 'There was no fourth!' he snapped. 'If it was my key – and I take your word that another key was used – then I know nothing of the whys and wherefores involved. Why should I? Holy immortal gods, Corvinus, do you know how much property I own in Rome and elsewhere? Yes, I've got keys, any number of them, but I don't keep them myself any more than I personally collect the rents!'

Bugger. Now *that* was something I hadn't considered, and I should've done. He was right, of course: no property owner of Carsidius's class dirties his hands with the everyday, mundane processes that net him his yearly income. 'Okay,' I said. 'So who does keep them?'

'My bailiff, naturally!'

'Yeah, I'd sort of assumed that. He got a name?'

'The . . .' Carsidius sat down and took a deep breath. 'His name was Faustus.'

'"Was"?' My guts went cold. 'You mean he's dead?'

'Certainly not! At least, as far as I'm aware. If you must know, I discharged him three days ago. For reasons that have no bearing on the matter and which don't concern you.'

Uh-huh. And my name was Cleopatra. 'So where is he now?' I said.

'Neapolis. Brindisi. Capua, perhaps. He may even have taken a ship from Ostia or Puteoli and gone abroad. In any event he told me at our last . . . meeting that he was leaving Rome. Where he chose to go when he left my employ was none of my concern, and I certainly didn't bother to ask.' Carsidius had picked up a stylus from the desk. 'Now. This interview is at an end. I would ask you not to trouble me again.'

I stood up and set the wine cup down carefully. 'Fair enough, pal,' I said. 'Thanks for your time.'

I was heading for the door when he said, 'Corvinus!'

I turned. 'Yeah?'

He was sitting with a face like one of the portrait busts. 'I've always been a faithful servant of the emperor. I've done my duty, however unpleasant I've found it personally. I want you to remember that.'

'Bully for you,' I said.

I opened the door, and left.

One minor point, and it didn't strike me until I was out in the street and beginning to cool down. When Carsidius had taken his oath, he'd used the word 'killing' apropos of Sextus Papinius; not 'death' but 'killing'. Yeah, sure, I'd introduced the idea of murder myself, but only as a theory, and it wasn't a theory that Carsidius – ipso facto – would be exactly ready to entertain. So why had he done it?

Shit, it was probably nothing, just my hypertrophied imagination kicking in again. All the same, it was interesting.

So what did I make of that?

I thought it over as I walked back down towards the Caelian. The guy had played absolutely true to form. I'd rubbed shoulders – reluctantly for the most part – with broad-stripers all my life, and Carsidius was right-down-the-middle typical: ego the size of the Capitol, touchy as hell where his honour was concerned – at least, as far as the part of it other people saw went – and fully prepared to lie through his teeth while at the same time damning your eyes for daring to question his veracity. The smart-as-paint Greeks, who can be cynically accurate buggers when they like, take their word for reputation – *doxa* – from the verb 'to seem', which is spot-on. With these bastards, appearances are everything, and to hell with the muckier reality. Papinius Allenius had been dead right when he'd bracketed Carsidius with Arruntius: they were a pair and no mistake, both in the bad and the good. Ignore the veneer of Roman *honestas*, which is a con in any case, think in terms of Greek *doxa* and you won't go far wrong. For all Carsidius's air of outraged rectitude I wouldn't trust the guy an inch.

Not over the killing, mind. The broad-striper code may be elastic, but it only stretches certain ways: in some directions it's rigid and unbreakable. Like taking unforced oaths. Carsidius hadn't had to do that business with the altar, especially there in the study with his ancestors looking on. No, I was with Caepio there: whoever had had the kid murdered, it wasn't our poker-backed senator pal. Or at least – thinking of the actual wording of the oath I stopped and rephrased that – at the time when the murder was being planned and committed Carsidius hadn't known about it. *That* would've been a typical bit of senatorial wriggling . . .

So why had he compromised his reputation by lying about the bribes? Lied he definitely had, the business with the altar – again – proved that beyond a doubt. But if he was lying, then . . .

I slowed. Okay, Corvinus. Think it through, boy.

Reputation. *Doxa*. Carsidius had admitted bribery to me, sure, but that was in a one-to-one situation, with no witnesses. His reputation – as far as the rest of the world was concerned – was safe. Oh, yeah, he claimed he'd also told Balbus, but then Balbus was in the same boat. When we'd met I'd been the one to suggest that Papinius had been taking bribes. All Balbus had done was confirm it; but – and this was the point – he'd made it clear that apart from talking to the boy himself he hadn't taken the matter any further. So again we had the one-to-one, no witnesses scenario, because Papinius was long past confirming or denying anything. Okay. So what we had here was a closed circle. I start the bribery rumour myself, Balbus picks it up like the gift it is and passes it to Carsidius, who feeds it back to me, while telling me he's already made his own confession to the aedile, who's had the business shelved. Result – or this is the plan, anyway – dumb-head Corvinus goes off whistling into the sunset believing that Papinius was on the make, his boss had caught him at it and as a consequence the kid had committed suicide. End of case, end of investigation, pull down the blinds and go home . . .

It worked. Sure it did. The big question was why? Why should two prestigious, well-respected senators get together to produce a cover-up for a murder?

It didn't make sense; none of it. Nor did the business with the keys. That had been another lie on Carsidius's part, and not a very good one, either. Sure, he might well have had a bailiff called Faustus, but trying to shift the blame on to him and then telling me in the next breath that the guy had just been coincidentally sacked and had left Rome for parts unknown was in the tap-dancing oyster bracket. Keys were important, I knew it in my water. Carsidius knew it too, which was why the bastard had practically fallen over himself to fob me off. The question – again – was *why*?

It was starting to rain: big drops from a blackening sky. I covered my head with my cloak and picked up speed.

One last, *last* thing. That 'something else' besides anger in Carsidius's look, when I'd asked him about the key.

It had been fear.

19

Well, that'd been short and sweet. I got home in plenty of time for a leisurely bath, a second-of-the-day shave and a less-than-hurried change into a decent lounging-tunic. Lippillus wouldn't've minded if I'd got in on two wheels as usual, and neither would Marcina, who was a very nice lady indeed, but Perilla would've had my guts for sandal-straps. They arrived just short of sunset: bang on time, in other words, but then Lippillus knew and loved our Meton. Fifteen pre-dinner-drink minutes before zero hour was allowed; give it twenty and you were pushing things. Once, we'd had a couple of Perilla's poetry-klatch cronies over for a meal and they were an hour late. We were having soles, and soles were what we got. In a way. How the surly bugger managed it I've no idea, but you could've walked on them to Puteoli.

'Hey, pal!' I said as the door-slave brought them through the peristyle into the garden; luckily, the rain had passed off and we had a fine evening. 'Bathyllus, a drink for the Watch commander.' I'd got in a jar of Signinan, special: Signinan's mostly medicinal, but the top vintage – and this one was *top*, ten years old if it was a day – was something else, dry as a bone and when it was chilled sheer perfection. Lippillus was no wine expert, but he knew good stuff when he tasted it, and on a Watch commander's pay that didn't happen all that often. 'Marcina. You want wine or are you having one of Perilla's fruit juices?'

'Wine, please, Marcus.'

No ordinary Roman matron, Marcina Paullina. She's
North African, a good foot taller than Lippillus, and a total
stunner.

'Do it, little guy,' I said. Bathyllus soft-shoed off.

'How's the dog?' Lippillus said.

'Oh, Placida's settling in very well.' Perilla smiled. 'Isn't she,
Marcus?'

'Uh . . . yeah. Yeah, she is. In a manner of speaking.'

Lippillus was grinning. 'You're lucky, then,' he said. 'I was
talking to Quintus Pilius earlier. He's Watch commander for
the Fifth and Sixth, says there's this thing up on the Viminal
belonging to a woman called Sestia Calvina, and you would
not *believe* . . .' He stopped. 'Have I said something wrong?'

I was grinning too. Perilla had coloured up to her earlobes.
'No, pal, not at all,' I said. 'We're fascinated. Carry on.'

'Ah . . . there's not much to tell, really.' Lippillus shot
Perilla a nervous sideways glance. You could've used the
set of her lips to draw lines. 'Pilius was probably exaggerating.'

'That so, now?'

'I mean, *nothing* could possibly—'

'Wine, sir.' Bathyllus had come up with the tray. Saved by
the butler. Never mind, I'd get the whole story later.

Lippillus took a cup, and while Perilla's and Marcina's
attention was on their own drinks he turned away and said
quietly, 'You got a moment, Marcus? In private, before we
start?'

Uh-oh. He might be wearing his best party mantle, but
currently the guy had his Watch commander's face on. Also, I
hadn't missed the fact that Marcina had taken Perilla's arm
and was leading her out of earshot like she and Lippillus had
arranged things in advance. Which, I would bet, they had.

So. Business.

'Yeah,' I said. 'Yeah, of course I have.'

'Lucceius Caepio hanged himself last night.'

Oh, shit. 'He did *what*?'

'Titus Mescinius sent to tell me just before we left. He thought you might be interested.'

I glanced over at Perilla. Her head was turned in our direction, but Marcina was keeping her busy. So; arrangement was right, and very sensible: to Perilla, a dinner party was a dinner party, and if she caught us talking murder there'd be hell to pay later. 'You have any details, pal?'

'Not many. His wife found him when she came home this morning. You know she was in Capua, visiting her sister?'

'Yeah. Yeah, Caepio told me.' My brain had gone numb. Bugger, what a mess! 'Was the suicide genuine?'

Lippillus gave me a sharp look. 'As far as I know. Or at least, as far as Mescinius does. There any reason why it shouldn't be?'

I was thinking back to how the guy had looked and acted the day before. It was possible, sure. Caepio had been desperate enough, and frightened enough – the gods knew why, or what of – to have taken his own life, but another suicide was too coincidental for comfort. 'No,' I said slowly. 'Or at least nothing definite. Even so—'

'There were no suspicious circumstances. At least that's what Mescinius says.' *Hah!* 'Suicide note, the lot.'

'Did Caepio's wife identify the handwriting?'

That got me another sharp look. 'Not as such. When she talked to Mescinius the lady wasn't in any fit state to swear to her own name, and anyway he didn't think to—'

'—ask.' I banged the flat of my hand against the portico pillar. '*Right*, par for the fucking course! Jupiter bloody God Almighty!'

Lippillus shrugged. 'Mescinius may not be the greatest brain in the world, Marcus, but he's a good Watchman. And at least he let me know. He didn't have to do that.'

'No. I suppose not.' I took a swallow of the Signinan. Hell!

'Besides, I haven't finished. One thing he did do, with you in mind, was have a quick poke around. He found this in Caepio's desk. Just the one, which was why he noticed it.' He reached into a fold in his mantle and brought out a key.

I took it, and the hairs stirred on the back of my neck: keys; this whole thing came down to keys. 'It fits the top flat, right?' I said.

'Right. It didn't come from Caepio's bunch of duplicates, either, that was one thing Mescinius did check. And it isn't the one the kid had on him when he died, because Mescinius never got round to sending that back. Interesting again?'

'Yeah.' I was still staring at the key. 'Very.'

'Want to tell me why?'

'You really want to know?'

He grinned and shook his head. 'No,' he said. 'Perhaps I don't, at that. I told you at the start, the Thirteenth's not my patch. Now. Duty done.' We'd been speaking almost in whispers. He raised his voice. 'What's for dinner?'

'Meton's been slaving his little socks off. Listen and drool. Poached eels in a nut and onion sauce, baked bluegill with quinces and a shellfish ragoût. Plus – *ta-daaa!* – a small sturgeon slow-cooked in saffron and wine must. That do you?'

'Great! Let's—'

At which point Perilla screamed, '*Placida!*'

I whipped round, just in time to see a familiar grey-black figure streak towards me through the peristyle with what looked like an oversize book-roll in its mouth. Close behind was Meton, armed with a cleaver, and three or four assorted kitchen skivvies . . .

Oh, fuck! The sturgeon!

I grabbed Meton by the scruff of the tunic as he passed. Stopping him wasn't easy – me, I'd back a chef who's just lost a sturgeon slow-cooked with saffron and wine must against a *qef*-stoned German berserker any day of the month – but I managed it somehow. Then I spun him round and kneed him hard in the balls.

'*Marcus!*' Perilla put hand to mouth in horror as our prize chef sank groaning on to the path.

'Shock tactics, lady,' I said. If he'd caught up with Placida she'd definitely have rustled her last larder, and total fucking menace though she was I didn't want that on my conscience.

Besides, sinking Meton was worth a sturgeon any day of the year.

The skivvies were milling. 'It's okay, lads,' I said. 'We'll take it from here. Anyone see where she went?'

'Ah . . . that was the dog, wasn't it?' Lippillus said.

'Yeah.' I was scanning the garden. No sign: she'd gone to ground with the sturgeon attached. Bugger. Double bugger. Well, that was that, then. It'd be inedible now in any case.

'Sestia Calvina's dog?' Lippillus said.

'That's the bunny.' I told you he was quick. 'We'll just have to make do with the sundries. Sorry about this, pal.'

'Don't be. Best dinner party I've been to in years.'

'I thought Meton took it very well, all things considered,' Perilla said as we were getting ready for bed.

'Yeah, well, after I explained to him that he'd run into the stone Priapus by the flower-bed—'

'Marcus, you didn't!' She was laughing.

'The guy was completely out of it, lady. He'd've believed anything I told him. And anyway the whole thing was his fault: she'd been planning it from the start, and if he hadn't en-couraged her she'd never have been near the kitchen.' I stripped off my tunic. 'He was just grateful that when he hit the statue he was facing forwards.'

She pulled back the blanket. 'What was Lippillus talking to you about?'

'Hmm?'

'Oh, come on, Marcus! You managed that very well between you, not to mention Marcina, but I'm not entirely gormless. It had to do with Papinius's murder, didn't it?'

I grinned and moved across to the bed: gormless she mightn't be, but the lady had a streak of curiosity a yard wide, and I knew she'd been itching to ask me all evening. 'Yeah. Lucceius Caepio hanged himself yesterday.'

'Oh, no!' She frowned. Then she said, hesitantly; 'I suppose he genuinely *did* hang himself? I mean—'

'Yeah. Yeah, that's what I thought.' I blew out the lamp and got in beside her. 'Jury's still out. Not that it matters all that much in the long run. The *really* odd thing was that Mescinius found a key in the guy's desk that fits the lock of the top-floor flat.'

Perilla sat up. 'But that's—'

'Really odd. Right. I just said so.'

'Marcus, there *wasn't* another key to the flat! Not one that Caepio should've had, anyway.'

'Check. Even slow-as-paint-drying Mescinius noticed that. There was the one on the board, that Papinius took, that was found on the body and that Mescinius still has, and a second that was on Caepio's duplicate bunch; I know that for a fact, because I used it myself when I was inspecting the flat. So where did the third come from? And why did Caepio have it?'

Long silence. Then she said slowly, 'Of course, if it was the one the murderers used to get in—'

'Then Caepio must've given them it. In which case he knew who they were, and he was involved after all up to his eyeballs. Yeah, I'd got that far myself. But it doesn't make sense. Caepio wasn't lying; no *way* was he lying! So why did he have that extra key?'

'Unless he didn't. The same people who killed Papinius could've murdered Caepio and put it in the desk themselves.'

'Why the hell would they do that?'

'To implicate Caepio? I mean, if a third key were found—'

I punched the mattress. 'Perilla, that is *crazy*! It'd be a wasted effort! Caepio was no killer, not even by proxy! I'd swear to that myself!'

'All right. Then where did the key come from? Look, what are the options? Either Caepio had the key originally and gave it to the murderers who gave it back when they were finished, or they had their own key and slipped it into the desk when they faked Caepio's suicide. There isn't any other explanation.'

'Fine. So let's take them one at a time.' I leaned back on the pillow and closed my eyes. 'Scenario one. It assumes pre-meditation on the part of Caepio and/or his boss Carsidius. Right?'

'Why?'

'Perilla, it's a third key. Tenement flats only have two on-site, one for the tenant and one for the factor, and where the top flat's concerned they're accounted for. Either Caepio had to have it specially made, or he had to get the already existing third from Carsidius's bailiff on some pretext or other, or *Carsidius* had to get it from his bailiff himself. Which means that either one or both of them decoyed Papinius to the tenement, which means that they're individually or jointly the murderers, or at least they instigated the killing. You follow?'

'Of course I follow. I told you, I'm not gormless.'

'Good. Don't sniff. Motive's fine, or possibly fine: Carsidius was working some scam to do with compensation for property lost or damaged in the Aventine fire, the kid found out and threatened to report it. Opportunity, too: it was Carsidius's tenement, and getting Papinius there at a suitable time would've been easy-peasy. There're only two flies in the ointment, but they're biggies. One, both Caepio and Carsidius swore they'd nothing to do with Papinius's death, and for different reasons I believe them. Two, why should the actual killers return the key at all? It's served its purpose. Why not chuck it in the Tiber or something similar and get rid of the incriminating evidence?'

'So you think the second theory's the more likely? That the murderers – double murderers – planted it to implicate Caepio, and through him Carsidius?'

'Gods, lady, I don't know! If they weren't in Carsidius's pay then how did they get their hands on a key in the first place? Whose pay *were* they in, if anyone's? And why target a respectable senator and his factor? Besides, there was no guarantee lame-brain Mescinius would even find it, quite the reverse. The second scenario's just too fucking complicated.'

'Marcus—'

'Yeah. Yeah, I know. But I just feel where this case is concerned that I'm bashing my head against a brick wall.' I put an arm round her. 'Whichever way you turn it, it doesn't make any sense. One thing, though. Caepio had beans to spill, and so does his boss. Carsidius may be no killer, or not of Papinius anyway, but he's in something, somewhere, up to his neck, and he's covering like crazy.'

She snuggled against me. 'Don't worry. It'll work out eventually.'

Yeah. Right. When pigs sprouted wings and looped the loop above Capitol Hill.

20

I woke up the next morning no further forrard. Okay; so what now?

I'd tried things head-on and got nowhere; it'd been like looking at one of these Parthian rugs proper-side-up, at the pattern the weaver wants you to see. Fine. So let's do it another way: turn the rug over on its front and look at the underside. Lucius Carsidius might be squeaky-clean and one of the doyens of the Senate, but like I'd said to Perilla the guy was covering something; that I'd bet my back teeth on. I hadn't forgotten Mucius Soranus and his good friend – however much she denied it – Lucia Albucilla, either. Plus various odds and sundries that I'd think up as matters progressed.

All of which meant I needed to talk to one guy: Caelius Crispus.

We went back a long way, Crispus and me; certainly further than he'd like to recall sober. Not that it made for a good relationship, because the bugger would cheerfully have eaten my liver raw. So. Not exactly a friend. None the less, if the three-faced, immoral, slimy, blackmailing bastard *did* happen to be run down by a cart as he was crossing the road or – more likely – was pulled out of the Tiber wearing concrete boots something precious would go out of the world. The air would smell cleaner, mind, but in his own sweet way Crispus was unique, a professional dirt-digger to his carefully manicured fingernails who took an honest pride in his work and a craftsman's delight in thoroughness and attention to detail.

As a result, what he didn't know about the top five hundred's dirty linen just wasn't worth the effort.

Well, the good thing about last night was that Placida was firmly grounded. After Lippillus and Marcina had gone, I'd sent in the heavy squad, they'd dragged her out from the bush she was lying under in a sturgeon-induced stupor, and we'd shackled her in ignominy to one of the peristyle pillars. Not even Perilla objected. And if Sestia Calvina had turned up unexpectedly the lady would probably have punched her lights out. Perilla can get very *serious* about some things, like sturgeon cooked in saffron wine must, for example. And she has a vicious left hook.

So no walkies today. I ate a quick breakfast and set out for Market Square. If he hadn't been poisoned, knifed, strangled or more legitimately disposed of by one of his erstwhile victims, Crispus would be over at the praetors' offices on the Capitol where he was one of the foreign judges' reps. With any luck I could catch him and make his day while the bastard was still fresh enough to enjoy it.

Market Square, as it usually is that time of the morning, was already heaving. There must've been another Senate session pending, because the area between the Senate-house and the Julian Hall was packed with broad-stripers in groups of two or three, engaged in the quaint time-honoured Roman custom of pre-session wheeling and dealing, backbiting and general character assassination. I noticed, over by the Senate-house door, Lucius Carsidius in deep conversation with a couple of other senior broad-stripers, one of whom was my old pal Lucius Arruntius. Carsidius glanced up as I passed, then turned his back when I gave him a cheery wave. Arruntius ignored me, too. Yeah, well; it's nice to be popular.

I checked with the guy at the desk that Crispus was still infesting the building, found his office, knocked on the door – he'd moved up another notch, seemingly, to walnut panelling and ivory scratch-boards above the brass handle – and went in.

'Hey, Crispus,' I said. 'How's the lad?'

He'd been eyes-down at his desk taking notes on to a wax tablet from a paper roll. His head came up looking like Pompey's when the Egyptian vizier pulled it from the pickle jar.

'Oh, shit,' he said.

I walked across the polished wood floor, pulled up a chair and sat down. 'So how are they treating you these days?' I said. 'Not overworked? Bright-eyed, bushy-tailed and getting your regular eight hours?'

'What is it this time, Corvinus? As if I didn't know.'

'Perilla sends her regards.'

'Stuff Perilla. Look, I'm busy.' He held up the wax tablet. 'The senior praetor wants this digest for the Nucerian committee meeting this afternoon and he isn't a patient man. Plus I've got a dozen reports to read.'

I grinned. 'You turned respectable, pal? Conscientious, even? Well, now, there's a thing!'

'Fuck off. Please.'

'Come on, Crispus! I need your expertise, and it won't take long. Just a bit of information, okay?'

He sighed and put down the tablet. 'Maybe. Depending what it is. Fifteen minutes, no more. And that's only because calling the slaves and having you thrown out on your ear would be more trouble than it's worth.'

'There's my boy!' Jupiter, this was *Crispus*? Respectable was right. Still, the bugger was getting older, like the rest of us. Maturing, like a cheese. He was even sporting a natty middle-management bald patch that he'd carefully combed the hair over. With his background he'd never make praetor, sure – the good old Roman political network had some standards – but he wasn't doing too badly on the sidelines. Maybe he'd just finally decided to cash in his winnings and quit while he was ahead of the game. Pity, really; I'd quite enjoyed my occasional bouts of Crispus-baiting, and the guy had had a horrible fascination about him.

'So,' he said. 'Get it over with. What do you want to know?'

'Lucius Carsidius. He as squeaky-clean as he's made out to be?'

His eyes widened. 'Carsidius the senator?'

'Is there another one?'

'What's your interest in him?'

'That's my business, pal. He above board, or what?'

'Of course he is. He's one of the straightest men in Rome.'

Bugger. One thing about Crispus – and I couldn't see it having changed, even in his new-model, born-again, conscientious civil servant persona – was that he genuinely loved gossip for its own sake. Oh, sure, he could be duplicitous as hell when he liked, he could lie through his teeth when it suited him, but when he said a guy was straight in that disappointed tone there wasn't any room for manoeuvre and you might as well put up the shutters and go home. Still, I owed it my best shot. 'Crispus,' I said. '*No one* is absolutely straight, especially if he's a fucking senator. So give.'

He spread his hands. 'You want the worst? Okay. Fourteen years back, the time of the Numidian war, he was on the North African staff. He was prosecuted before the Senate for selling corn to the enemy. The case collapsed for want of evidence and he was acquitted nem con. That do you?'

I sat back. 'That's it? That's the *worst*?'

'You asked for it, you've got it. Nothing else, public or private. To my certain knowledge.' He sniggered; a flash of the old Crispus. 'And believe me, Corvinus, I would *know*.'

'Jupiter, pal, that's impossible! There must be something!'

'You want a potted biography? Because that's all I can give you. His father served with Germanicus on the Rhine, and Carsidius grew up hero-worshipping him. When Germanicus died he kept up with the family, Agrippina and young Nero especially. Eight years back, when Nero was exiled, he was one of the few senators who spoke up for him against the emperor, which didn't do him much good politically but earned him a lot of brownie points with the more responsible broad-striper elements who he is now very much in with. He's not ambitious – never made consul, stuck at praetor – but word is he did any job he had well and came out the other end smelling of roses. End of lecture.'

'Crispus, you are not helping here.'

Crispus shrugged. 'I'm telling it like it is. They don't come cleaner than Carsidius. He's no time-server, never has been. Since the business with Nero he's made his peace with the Wart and supported him right down the line, sure, but in the process he made no secret of his friendship with the Julians, especially when they started . . . dying off. That didn't do him any harm. Quite the reverse. Tiberius might've hated Agrippina's guts, but he never was one to hold a grudge, and Carsidius didn't suffer.'

'So he gets on well with Crown Prince Gaius?'

That got me a long look. 'No,' Crispus said slowly. 'No, I can't say that he does. Possibly for reasons that . . . well, you know as well as me. But then he's not alone there, and like I said he's no time-server. Stupid, in my view. Nothing wrong with a bit of judicious arse-licking, especially these days.'

Yeah; right. In a few months' time – it couldn't be longer – the Wart would be dead and Gaius would be emperor. Everyone knew that: the bugger might be twiddling his thumbs on Capri waiting to step into the imperial sandals, but in effect, through his sidekick Sertorius Macro, he already controlled Rome for definite and the empire by extension. 'Crispus,' I said. 'If I told you that Carsidius had admitted bribing a junior city officer to accept a beefed-up property damage claim, what would you say?'

Crispus gave a bark of laughter. 'I'd say you were talking through your ears, boy. Carsidius wouldn't stoop to bribery if his life depended on it.'

Uh-huh. So much for that, then. Clear and unequivocal.

'Okay,' I said. 'Leave Carsidius. Let's move on to Mucius Soranus.'

'Ah.' Crispus smacked his lips. 'Now *that's* more like it! What do you want to know?'

'Whatever you've got.'

'We're dragging the sewers here. That bastard's crooked as a snake's backbone.'

I grinned: definite pleasure, there, and relief. Also perhaps just a touch of respect: one professional talking about another. Maybe the new Crispus was only skin-deep after all. 'Yeah. I already knew that, as it happens,' I said. 'Any details? Current, as it were?'

'You kidding, Corvinus? How long've you got? Me, I've a report to write.'

'Fine. Just to go with one name, then. Sextus Papinius. Papinius Allenius the consular's son.'

'Allenius's son.' Crispus shot me a look and sniggered. 'Oh, yes. Right. You mean the kid who threw himself out of a tenement window a few days back. That what all this is about?'

'Could be.'

'Soranus was bleeding him, sure. What for I don't know, but he'd got his hooks in good and proper. You have any idea yourself? I mean, one good turn deserves another.'

'Uh-uh.' We'd got the old Crispus back in spades: the guy lived from information, the grubbier the better, and black-mailing blackmailers was a nifty little earner. 'Sorry, pal. I was hoping you might be able to tell me.'

'Damn. You levelling?'

'I'm levelling.' I was, too: I didn't owe Soranus any favours, and handing the bastard over to Crispus's not-so-tender mercies would've been poetic justice. 'Never mind. What's his connection with Lucia Albucilla? You heard of her?'

'Sure. Satrius Secundus's widow. She and Soranus are an item, or they were until recently. Wild lady. She took up with him right after her husband died. Some say she gave Secundus the push herself to open up a little space. Some say she and Soranus were screwing already long-term, but' – and he winked – 'if they were then given her other long-term attachment it was three in a bed. Me, I have my doubts. Soranus wouldn't've minded, but Sejanus was another matter, he was strictly hetero. Weird, but there you are. It takes all sorts.'

Bells were going off all over my brain. Shit! Perilla had told me who Albucilla was, but at the time it hadn't registered: the widow of one of Aelius Sejanus's closest supporters who'd turned informer to save his skin when the bastard fell but had died himself the following year. Now Crispus was telling me that she'd been a lot more at the time than just the surviving relict; and *that*, given certain much more recent events, was interesting. Oh, sure, we were talking old history – Sejanus had been dead for five years – and it could be pure coincidence. None the less, it gave us a link. 'You're telling me that Albucilla was Sejanus's mistress?' I said.

'*A* mistress. *A* mistress, Corvinus. One of several. That bastard got around, and being the charismatic guy he was he had more than one outwardly respectable matron willing to drop her pants for him. If you ask me, Lucia Albucilla was the real Sejanan of the partnership. Certainly she'd more guts than Secundus had.'

'You said she and Soranus were an item, a long-standing item.' Hell. So much for the lady's calling him an acquaintance; but then my guess was that at the time she'd been running scared and just wanted rid of me. 'Any idea why they broke up?'

'Uh-uh. She didn't say, he didn't say. Not to anyone. But whatever it was, it was sudden.'

'She do much in the way of cradle-snatching?'

He gave me a sharp look. 'What?'

'Papinius's ex-girlfriend seemed to think Albucilla had seduced him. That likely, do you suppose? She go for youngsters as a rule?'

'It's been known. Not that the lady's unduly particular where the age of her menfriends is concerned. *Eclectic*'s the word I'd use.' He beamed. 'That's Greek, Corvinus, as I hope you noticed. As was *charismatic*.'

'Yeah, it did register.'

'I'm teaching myself Greek in my free time.'

'Oh, whoopee.' *Definitely* a new model Crispus. The old type wouldn't've recognised the aorist of *pherein* if it'd jumped up and bitten him. 'You know whether there might've been any other reason for Albucilla to have taken Papinius on? Besides the sexual?'

'No.'

'And you don't know either why he killed himself?' I wasn't going to suggest murder to Crispus. No way. The bugger would've used the information somehow, and I didn't want the trail muddied at this stage.

'I told you. Soranus was soaking him. That's reason enough for me.'

Yeah, well, he'd done his best and I couldn't complain. I stood up. 'Okay,' I said. 'Thanks, Crispus, I owe you one. I'll see you around.'

I was just leaving, my hand on the door-knob, when he said, 'Corvinus?'

'Yeah?' I turned.

'Wait a minute. A freebie. No skin off my nose, but you might be interested.'

'What in?'

'You called the kid Papinius Allenius's son.'

'So?'

'Rumour is he wasn't. Old rumour, nineteen years old. His natural father was Domitius Ahenobarbus.'

I stared at him.

Shit!

21

'It explains a lot of things, lady,' I said when I'd finished telling Perilla about the subsequent gossip with Crispus. 'Why the divorce. Why Allenius never took any interest in him. Why the consular's so bitter against his ex-wife. Allenius and Ahenobarbus were of an age, they were colleagues. Only thing was, Ahenobarbus was related to the imperial family. There wasn't much a career politician like Allenius could do about it.'

'You think he knew?' Perilla said. We were in the garden, me with a half jug of Setinian, Perilla with a chilled fruit juice. No Placida: the lady had relented and let Alexis take her out rabbit-chasing. 'The boy, I mean.'

'Sure he did. Cluvia told me: he was proud of his family, his father especially. I thought that was odd at the time; the Papinii are no great shakes, and although Allenius had made consul he was no ball of fire personally. Besides, he and young Sextus had hardly ever spoken. Change Ahenobarbus for Allenius and the Domitii for the Papinii and you've got a pretty good pedigree. In social terms anyway, because the gods know who'd want that bastard Ahenobarbus for a father.'

'But why didn't Ahenobarbus acknowledge him?'

'Gods, Perilla! For any number of reasons. One, whatever his own private life was like, Tiberius was a moralist in public. How do you think he'd've reacted if it came out that one of the imperial family had got a colleague's wife pregnant? Two, the pressure would've been on – if Allenius had blown the whistle and subsequently divorced Rupilia, which he would've done –

for Ahenobarbus to marry her, and Ahenobarbus had much bigger fish to fry than a hick provincial from Leontini. She'd been an amusement, nothing more, and young Sextus had been an accident. Three, on Allenius's side – Rupilia's, too – where was the benefit? Rupilia would be disgraced, Allenius laughed at, and with Ahenobarbus as an enemy his career would be down the tubes before it'd even started. As it was, if he kept schtum, at least officially, he was owed.' *Doxa*; it all came down to *doxa*.

'But he still divorced Rupilia.'

'Sure he did. As soon as he could, right after the birth. I never said he didn't have a concern for his honour, and raising another man's child by his wife while having to pretend it was his own just wouldn't sit with a guy like that. Only thing was, he didn't give out the reason.'

'Hmm.' Perilla was twisting her lock of hair. 'So what has this to do with the murder?'

'Fuck knows.'

'*Marcus!*'

'Yeah, well. Maybe nothing. Probably nothing. Still, it opens up another angle. And I'll have to have a word with Ahenobarbus.'

'Why should you do that?'

'Lady, he was the kid's real father. He knew, young Papinius knew. The chances are Papinius got his job with the fire commission directly through Ahenobarbus, not via Allenius. That means Ahenobarbus had a personal, vested interest in him. And I'll bet you a jar of Caecuban to a pickled anchovy that the solution to all this has something to do with the kid's job. Good enough?'

'Not really.'

'Stick, then.' I leaned over and kissed her. 'Also, apropos of nothing whatsoever, I've got a link between Albucilla and Acutia.'

'Between Albucilla and who?'

I did a double-take. Oh, yeah: the day I'd talked to Albucilla at the Apollo Library had ended with me being mugged, and subsequent events had pushed that little interview into the background. Perilla didn't know about her, because I'd never mentioned the lady. 'You remember Acutia in Antioch?' I said. 'Publius Vitellius's wife?'

'Oh, *that* Acutia! Yes, of course I remember her; mousy little thing. And I did know she was in Rome, it's only that our paths don't cross nowadays.'

'That so, now? Anyway, I bumped into her at the Apollo Library. She and Albucilla seem to be good mates.'

'Really? So?'

'You don't think that's strange?'

'No, Marcus, of course not. Why should I? And what has Acutia to do with Sextus Papinius in any case?'

I ignored the last bit; yeah, I was wondering about that myself. 'Or that both of them should just happen to have had connections with Aelius Sejanus?'

'Marcus—'

'Albucilla's husband was one of his pals before he betrayed him, and according to Crispus Albucilla was his mistress. And that bastard Vitellius – well, you know all about him.'

Perilla sighed. 'Marcus, dear, I'm sorry, but so what? Half of Rome had connections with Sejanus, one way or the other. And if he was a . . . common interest between the two women then it's perfectly natural that they should be friends. However, Sejanus is dead, and if not exactly forgotten then the next thing to it. Support for him – if that's what you're accusing the two of them of, and the gods know in what sense – is no longer an issue. Besides, why on earth should it be relevant? From what I remember of Acutia and know of Lucia Albucilla they may not be particularly similar in character, but that's no bar to friendship. They obviously share literary tastes, for a start.'

'Yeah. Yeah, I realise all that.' I took a morose swig of the Setinian. Perilla might be right, sure, but I'd seen what I'd seen: those ladies had had something cooking together besides a common interest in lyric poetry, I'd bet my sandals on that. And although the Sejanus link was probably completely incidental I still couldn't get it out of my head. 'Still . . .'

'What did Crispus have to say about Carsidius?'

'Hmm? The bastard's pure as the driven snow. Any more perfect and they'd deify him.'

'That doesn't sound very promising.'

'Too right it isn't.' I took another pull at my wine cup. 'One thing, though. You can forget the bribery aspect. When I suggested it Crispus laughed in my face, and Crispus can scent a crook like a dog scents vomit.'

'Marcus, please—'

'So Carsidius lied. *Why* did he lie? Someone put him up to it, but who?'

'Balbus, perhaps.'

'Or Ahenobarbus. He's part of the equation now, remember, and he's Balbus's – and Papinius's – ultimate boss. It all comes down to the fucking fire commission. There's a cover-up involved there, and it's a top-level one; for Balbus and Carsidius to be involved at the least it has to be.' I poured myself more wine from the jug. 'Jupiter and all the ever-loving gods!'

'Don't get annoyed, dear.'

'I'm not annoyed, I'm frustrated. There's something we're missing, something big. Until we know that nothing makes sense.'

'All right. Say there *is* a connection with the commission. What could it be?'

'Peculation on a major scale. Creaming the top off the Treasury allocation. That much is obvious.'

'How would it work?'

'How should I know, Perilla? It wouldn't be easy, that's for sure. The Wart set the commission up himself, and the Wart's no fool. Four men at the top – *four* – all on a level, all imperials by marriage. Domitius Ahenobarbus, sure, he's as crooked and ruthless and self-serving as they come, but he's got colleagues who'll be watching him like hawks. Watching each other, too, because they're no saints either, and you can bet that each of them would just love to see one of the others step out of line so they could yank the rug from under. Come down a step and it's the same: checks and double-checks all the way down the line, the Wart's seen to that. And to round things off, we've got to believe that someone like Lucius bloody Carsidius, who never bent a rule in his life, will tie himself in knots and lie like hell to cover for whoever *is* milking the scheme and is a murderer into the bargain. Fuck!' I banged the table and the wine jug jumped. 'The whole thing's impossible!'

'Marcus, dear, don't lose your temper.'

'Yeah, well. It is.'

'So assume that it isn't. How would Papinius fit in?'

I took a deep breath. The lady was right: losing my temper didn't help. We had to look at this thing dispassionately. 'Not as a major player,' I said. 'Maybe he saw something he shouldn't've seen, heard something, read something . . . Perilla, this is sheer fantasising!'

'He was Ahenobarbus's son. You know that now. If you think Ahenobarbus is the most likely villain – and I'd agree – then that fact might be relevant to his involvement. At least it puts it within the bounds of possibility.'

'Sweet immortal gods, lady! He was a nineteen-year-old kid on the bottom rung of the ladder! What chance would he have to be privy to any sort of secret?'

'I don't know. Of course I don't. But he was murdered, after all, and his death disguised as suicide. Surely that counts for something?'

That stopped me. Yeah, right; that was the absolute bottom line, and there was no escaping it. Someone had decided that the kid was too dangerous to live, and had enough clout to cover his tracks by putting pressure on some of Rome's top men. We weren't playing games here.

I would definitely have to talk to Domitius Ahenobarbus.

At the end of the garden, the side gate opened: Alexis back with Placida. She looked up and saw me . . .

'*OW-OOO! OW-OOO-OOO-OOO!*'

Oh, hell.

Now I knew what a Gallic boar felt like when it saw a hundred and twenty pounds of boarhound racing towards it. I just had time to get up and put both my hands out before she hit.

'You have to forgive her really,' Perilla said as I picked myself out of the flower-bed and fended off the brute. 'With all her faults she *is* very affectionate. And she's definitely beginning to take to you, Marcus.'

'Yeah. Yeah, right.'

Problem was, she still smelled of fish.

22

Arranging an interview with Domitius Ahenobarbus was easier said than done.

You don't just drop in uninvited on someone who's nephew to the Wart and the husband of Augustus's granddaughter, and who knows exactly where that puts him on the social ladder. I'd never met the guy personally, which suited me just fine because in addition to being a four-star imperial he was a five-star bastard: short-tempered as a rhino with a migraine, arrogant as hell and with a streak of malicious cruelty a yard wide. The story went, he'd once driven over a kid on Appian Road just for the fun of hearing him scream. He'd've had the mother, too – so he told his pals later over dinner – but she moved at the last minute and he had to choose between them.

Not a nice man, Domitius Ahenobarbus.

So I did things properly. I had Bathyllus put on his best tunic and hernia support and sent the little bald-head over to the Palatine with strict instructions to impress. I'd wondered what to use as an excuse for the meeting and decided in the end not to bother: if the bastard was as aware of who I was and what I wanted to talk about as I thought he'd be then I'd be wasting my time wrapping things up in fancy language. Besides, whether he was a four-star imperial or not, in terms of family history the Valerii Messallae were as good as the Domitii Ahenobarbi any day of the month, so bugger him sideways and twice on the kalends.

All of which was why, next day, I found myself outside the

main gate of the emperor's palace. The Wart hadn't lived there for years, mind, let alone stuck his boil-encrusted face inside the city's sacred boundary-line, but Ahenobarbus and young Agrippina – there were no kids, yet – had taken over one of the wings and were doing a pretty good job of acting as stand-ins. Rumour was, the two were well matched. By all accounts Germanicus's daughter was as cold and calculating as her mother, with all the qualities of a first-class bitch in the making.

'Marcus Valerius Messalla Corvinus to see Gnaeus Domitius Ahenobarbus,' I said to the door-slave.

The guy looked at me like I'd turned up selling brooms. 'Do you have an appointment, sir?'

'Of course I've got a fucking—' I caught myself. Steady, Corvinus! *Gravitas, gravitas!* 'Ah . . . yeah. Yes, of course I have.'

He checked a wax tablet and made a tick with his stylus. 'Ah. There you are. Very well, that seems to be in order. If you'll come this way.'

I followed him, hitching up my formal mantle. Gods, I hate these things! Yeah, sure, they're impressive, especially out in provinces where most of the locals make do with a loincloth or animal skins turned inside-out, depending on climate, but they impress because they're totally impractical. Anyone who's had to move any distance wound up in twelve feet of carefully choreographed woollen blanket, and who isn't a complete mental cheesecake, will agree with me. Still, you had to make sacrifices.

We went through what seemed miles of rooms and out into a central garden loud with peacocks and the sound of water from the ornamental fountain. Ahenobarbus was sitting under a trellised vine dictating to a secretary. No mantle for that guy: he was wearing a simple lounging-tunic. He looked up and frowned. He was big, red-haired – the family hadn't got the surname Bronzebeard for nothing – and built like a bull.

Red-haired. I remembered the miniature that Rupilia had shown me. Yeah; that's where the kid had got it from. Not from his mother at all, or not completely. And the shape of the face made sense too.

'That's all right, Callistus, you can go,' Ahenobarbus said. The secretary closed the roll, tucked his pen and ink-bottle into a pouch at his belt, bowed and left. 'Have a seat, Corvinus. Ruber, a chair.'

There was a wicker chair at the end of the loggia. The door-slave pulled it up, saw me settled and then moved off.

'Now.' Ahenobarbus was still frowning. 'What can I do for you? According to your major-domo you wanted to talk about young Sextus Papinius.'

'Yeah. That's right.'

'Then I'm afraid you've had a wasted journey. I knew the boy by sight but—'

'He was your son.'

Silence; *long* silence. The frown deepened to a scowl. 'You know, I find that rather insulting,' he said carefully. 'Sextus Papinius's father was Papinius Allenius, the ex-consul. If you've been listening to any *other* rumours then I strongly recommend in your own interests that you discount them for what they are. Complete and utter nonsense.'

'That so, now?' I said. 'Me . . . well, I didn't know the kid when he was alive, but I've seen his portrait. He had red hair and a full jaw. Sound familiar?'

'His mother has red hair.'

'Sure. But not the jaw. Nor does Allenius. You've got both.'

He stared at me like I'd crawled out from under a stone: evidently, the guy wasn't used to being contradicted. Tough. I stared back; like I say, a Valerius Messalla's got his own pride, and I wasn't here for fun.

'What do you want, exactly?' he said. 'Just out of interest, you understand.'

'To know why the kid was murdered.'

His eyes flickered. 'Papinius committed suicide.'

'No, he didn't. Someone decoyed him to the top floor of the tenement, probably slugged him from behind and then pitched him through the window. You know anything about that?'

He stood up quickly. 'Now you really are being insulting. I'll ask you to leave, please.'

'Not yet. Not until I'm done. Two questions. First: if the kid wasn't your son then why did you have Allenius put him forward as a junior officer on the fire compensation commission?'

For a moment I didn't think he'd answer. Then he said, through tight lips, 'I didn't. The suggestion – the request – was Allenius's, I only approved the appointment. We're old colleagues and I was happy to help his son begin his political career.'

'Come on, pal! Allenius hadn't had anything to do with the boy since he was born and wanted nothing to do with him then. So why should he bother calling in a valuable favour?'

'Are you accusing me of lying? Because if so—'

'Okay,' I said. 'Second question, two parts. Young Papinius was being blackmailed by a guy called Mucius Soranus to the tune of fifty thousand silver pieces. He borrowed the cash from a money-lender by the name of Vestorius. Just before he died he repaid the loan in full, plus the interest, sixty thousand in all. He had to get the money from somewhere. My guess is that it came from you. Right or wrong, and if right then why should you pay? And what the hell did Soranus have on him to merit that much bread?'

'Sextus Papinius' – Ahenobarbus's face had gone as red as his beard, and I could see his fists flexing and unflexing – 'was taking bribes. According to Laelius Balbus—'

'Wrong, pal. Wrong, wrong, wrong. Also, a mistake. First

off, Papinius was straight as a rule. He wouldn't've taken a bribe from anyone. Second, according to Balbus he kept the bribery issue a secret between the kid and himself. So how the hell do you come to know about it?'

I thought he'd hit me – he was within spitting distance of it, and from the expression on his face hitting me was the least he'd've liked to do – but he turned away.

'*Ruber!*' he shouted. Then he turned back to me. 'Get out,' he said softly. 'Get out now, while you can still walk, or I'll have my slaves break your legs, arms and ribs and throw you out. And if I find that you've dared to make these disgusting accusations public, Valerius Corvinus, then believe me you will be very, very sorry indeed. Do I make myself clear?'

'Yeah,' I said, standing. 'That's clear enough. You've been very informative. Thanks for your time, pal.'

He didn't answer, just glared. I followed the silent slave to the exit.

I'd come by litter, naturally: a walk halfway across Rome swathed in a formal mantle just isn't on, especially when you have to arrive fresh, clean and sweet-smelling at the end of it. All the same, I'd done my duty now by the conventions and it was a lovely morning, far too good to be carried through the crowded streets in a curtained box. So once I was clear of the palace I told the litter-guys to stop, got out, stripped off the mantle and continued down the incline on foot.

Well, that'd been interesting. I'd made myself a serious enemy, mind, and no doubt when the blood stopped pounding in my temples I'd regret it, but all the same I wasn't too unhappy. I'd rattled the bastard's cage good and proper, and to good purpose: whatever Ahenobarbus's involvement was in all this, I'd bet my last copper penny he wasn't innocent. And I hadn't missed the implications of that threat, either.

Ahenobarbus wanted things buried, which meant there *was* something to bury.

So what was it? The smart money was on some sort of scam, current or previous, involving the fire commission. What it was, and how it worked, like I'd told Perilla, I hadn't a clue, but it had to be possible. Given that, everything slipped into place, and it explained why Ahenobarbus had been nervous as a cat in an oven. Every one of my shots had gone home, that I'd swear to. Imperial the guy might be, but as long as the Wart was still on his perch getting caught with your hand seriously in the till was not a good idea whoever you were, because if there was one thing Tiberius *really* took exception to it was high officials on the make. And if the old emperor did hand in his feed-bowl shortly, that wouldn't do Ahenobarbus any favours either. Brothers-in-law or not, he and Gaius were far from being bosom buddies, and that went for Rome's next emperor and his sister, too. In spades. If rumour was to be believed, Agrippina hated Gaius's guts, and it was mutual. Not that I blamed the lady there: family loyalty wasn't exactly one of our crown prince's leading features, however much he might pretend to the contrary, and cuddly and likeable were two things that the bastard wasn't.

So no wonder Ahenobarbus was nervous. And if he was responsible for this whole boiling then it would explain a lot. Certainly he'd have the clout to put pressure on Balbus, no argument there; he'd even manage, if push came to shove, to make up a convincing case that proved young Papinius was taking bribes. Also if he'd known that a top-notcher like Domitius Ahenobarbus was behind Papinius's death then it was no wonder that Caepio had been shitting bricks about pointing the finger.

Carsidius, mind . . . Carsidius was something else. He was the one bit of the puzzle that wouldn't fit, whichever way you turned it. Carsidius worried me.

I was heading towards the Caelian and home, down Scaurus Incline. What made me look back, I don't know – maybe just instinct – but just at that moment the crowd parted and I saw a couple of familiar faces. My stonemason chums Aponius and Pettius.

Uh-huh. Check.

I turned quickly and carried on walking. They might've noticed they'd been spotted, sure, but I'd managed not to make a big thing of it so maybe I was lucky. Okay, Corvinus, so let's play this nice and gently; these were two bastards I really needed to talk to, but if it was mutual I'd be very surprised indeed. Ahead, where the incline met the flat of Caelian Valley, was a seriously built-up area, with lots of tenements, shops and side alleyways. I slowed to make sure they didn't lose me – not that I reckoned there was much chance of that – ignored the first two openings on the right then turned the corner of the third, between a high-rise and a butcher's shop. Then I ducked into a handy doorway and waited.

Aponius passed me first, eyes front scanning the pavement ahead. I stepped out and grabbed him.

'Just a minute, pal,' I said. 'I'd like—'

Which was as far as I got before Pettius's shoulder slammed into my back, pitching me into one of the city's ubiquitous bag-ladies coming the other way loaded down with half the vegetable market. She went down with a thump and a scream, scattering onions and turnips. Meanwhile, Aponius had twisted like an eel to one side and planted a fist in my ribs. It was like being slugged with a rock. I collapsed against the tenement wall, gasping.

Aponius chuckled. 'Sorry about that, Corvinus. No hard feelings, eh?'

And then he was gone. Both of them were gone, pushing their way through the gathering crowd and into the next alley.

Shit!

I started after them. A hand caught my ankle and I went arse-over-tip to the ground, landing on my sore arm. Pain lanced up.

'What the hell d'you think you're doing, sonny?' the bag-lady snapped, letting the ankle go. 'You think you own the fucking street?'

'Uh . . . I'm sorry, grandma.' I stood up, trying to hug my arm and my ribs at the same time. 'Accident.'

'Holy Mother, I'll give you accident!' She glared up at me like Allecto on a bad day. 'That's my Quintus's dinner there, all over the fucking road!'

'Ah . . . yeah. Yeah.' I fumbled my belt-pouch open and took out a couple of silver pieces. 'Look, buy him a chicken, okay?'

'Chicken brings him out in a fucking rash!'

I pressed the money into her hand, shoved through a knot of supportive and very vociferous tunics and headed for the alleyway.

Too late. Miles too late.

Bugger.

Nothing else for it. I went home.

23

Perilla was in the atrium, having her hair done.
'Oh, hello, dear,' she said. 'How did your talk with—' At
which point she saw the state of my tunic. The streets of Rome
might be okay to walk along, most of them, but rolling about in
them is a bad, bad idea. 'Marcus! Not *again*!'

I held up both hands. 'Yeah, yeah, I know. But no damage
this time, lady, it's just dirt. I, uh, took a bit of a tumble.'

'We'll finish later, Chloë,' she said to the maid. The girl
nodded and scurried out, taking her curling-tongs with her
and giving me a scared glance over her shoulder. New staff.
She'd get used to it. 'Marcus, you do *not* take a tumble in a
litter! What happened, and where's your mantle?'

'That's okay. I left it with the lardballs. They not back yet?'

'No. Or not to my knowledge. And don't change the
subject.'

The buggers had probably stopped off at a wineshop to
refuel. I didn't use them often, and they took every chance
they could get to jump the wall. Well, I didn't blame them. It
was a nice day.

'Look, I just banged into a bag-lady on Staurus Incline, all
right?' I said, and took a swig from the wine cup Bathyllus had
provided me with. 'I wasn't looking where I was going. It's
easy enough done.'

'Marcus Valerius Corvinus!'

Ah, well, it was a fair cop. 'Remember the two fake stonemasons?' I said.

'Yes, of course I do.'

I gave her the basic outline. When I'd finished, she said, 'They were following you? Why? Who sent them?'

'Jupiter, I don't know! But I'd give it good odds, lady. And they're not interested in conversation. Unfortunately, I had my chance and I blew it all over the shop. No bones broken, though. Seriously.'

She sniffed. 'All right. What happened with Domitius Ahenobarbus?'

I told her the details. Such as they were. 'He's covering. The gods know for what, but he's covering, and he's scared.'

'*Ahenobarbus* is *scared*? Be serious, Marcus! He's one of the most powerful men in Rome!'

'Even so.' I took another sip of wine. 'It's a scam. It has to be. And in that case, of course he's scared. Imperial or not, if he's stepped out of line the Wart'll nail his skin to the Senate-house door if he has to get off his deathbed to do it. And if *he* doesn't then Gaius'll do it for him.'

She was quiet for a long time. Then she said, 'Marcus, I don't like this. I don't like it at all. It's beginning to turn very nasty.'

I knew what she meant; to be honest, I didn't like it either. I've said it before, I'll say it again: you don't mess with imperials, even when they're second-rank ones, and if someone of the calibre of Domitius Ahenobarbus had something private cooking then lifting the lid of the pot and dipping your spoon in was a bad, bad idea. Still, the job had to be done, and I had enough problems without worrying about Perilla worrying, as it were. I put down the wine cup, went over and kissed her.

'Look, lady,' I said. 'I've got a charmed life, all right? And I'm on the right side of the fence. The guys who should be sweating blood – and I'll bet they are – are the ones who had young Papinius thrown through a window. Who they are, and why they did it, I don't know, but I have to find out, okay?'

She rested her forehead against my chest for a moment. 'Yes. Yes, I suppose you do,' she said. 'I'm sorry, dear. I won't mention it again.' A pause; then, like she was asking a doctor for a verdict that she knew already: 'Do you think there's any possibility that Ahenobarbus could have been involved? Directly involved, I mean? In Papinius's death?'

I went back to my couch, taking my time doing it. That was a question I'd been trying not to ask myself. Still, it had to be faced. 'It's possible,' I said carefully. 'In theory, anyway. Leaving out the whys and the wherefores.'

'His own *son*?'

'That wouldn't count much with him, Perilla. He's a callous bastard, Ahenobarbus. Papinius was nothing to him but a by-blow and I doubt if he'd think twice about having him killed. If it became necessary, if he had a good enough reason.'

'And you think that he might have had?'

I took another gulp of the Setinian. 'Maybe. You could argue for it, anyway. Certainly he got the kid his job on the commission; *he* did, not Allenius, although Ahenobarbus fixed things publicly so it'd appear otherwise. There must've been a reason for that besides paternal affection, which like I say just isn't that bastard's bag. Six gets you ten having Papinius to hand on the staff was an essential part of the scam.'

'But, Marcus, you said it yourself. Papinius was nineteen years old, hardly more than a boy. What use could he be to someone like Ahenobarbus?'

'I don't *know*! Jupiter, lady, if I'd got that far I'd have the whole thing!' I swallowed another mouthful of wine. 'In any case, whatever it was it went wrong. Badly so, and my bet is that it was the kid's fault. Maybe he got cold feet, maybe he blabbed to someone out of turn, maybe he just made a mistake. Whatever happened, he became the weak link. Which is where Mucius Soranus comes in.'

'There is one major problem, of course,' Perilla said.

'Yeah? What's that?'

'Whatever Papinius was involved in would be illegal, wouldn't it? Certainly dishonest.'

'Naturally it would. That's the whole point.'

'But if Papinius knew that – well, surely you've been insisting all along that he was fundamentally an honest young man? I thought that was axiomatic.'

'No problem there, lady. In fact, things make more sense that way. Okay. Scenario. Imagine you're the kid, right? You've just landed your first responsible public post and you're on the ladder a good step higher than you'd expected to be. How do you feel?'

'Very proud. Over the moon. And desperate to do well.'

'Fine. At that point, completely out of the blue, one of your top bosses – your *top* bosses, the emperor's own nephew – calls you into his office or wherever and tells you you're his son. How does that grab you?'

Perilla was looking thoughtful. 'I suppose I'd be totally dumbfounded. Unless I'd suspected it already, naturally.'

'Yeah, right. Still, the qualification doesn't signify. Young Papinius was no bonehead, and he hadn't led a sheltered life, either. He must've heard rumours, and what with the timing of the divorce and his legal father's attitude to him and his mother over the years he'd have to've been thick not to put two and two together. But he couldn't've been *sure*. Now he was. We know he was, because Cluvia told us he was really proud of his family, and of his father in particular. That'd make no sense where Allenius was concerned – up to that point Papinius had scarcely even mentioned him – but if he meant Ahenobarbus it makes sense in spades. Okay?'

'Yes. Go on.'

'So.' I refilled my wine cup. 'Ahenobarbus calls you in and hits you with the whammy. He also tells you that he's directly responsible for getting you the post. Like you say, you're totally gobsmacked. Then – this is the clincher – he says he's got a very special job for you within the commission. Very important, very hush-hush. How do you react?'

Perilla smiled. 'Again, I'd feel proud and privileged; too much so – which is clearly where you're leading, Marcus – to ask any questions.'

'Right. Only, like I say, you're no bonehead. You've got stars in your eyes at present, sure, but over time when the glitter begins to wear off your brain kicks into gear and you begin to think about what you're doing.'

'And it doesn't seem so innocent any more.'

'Right. So what happens then?'

'I . . . begin to have second thoughts.'

'Fine. Only problem is, you're in the scam – you know by now that it's a scam – up to your neck. You want out but you've nowhere to go. You can't blow the whistle on Ahenobarbus, because you're a no-account nineteen-year-old kid, and who would believe you against him? Added to which, he's your father. Your real father. Maybe you even think of what it'd do to your future political career. You're honest in yourself, sure, but for someone like you a career is your life. Balancing honesty now against your whole future is a tough decision for a nineteen-year-old to make. So what do you do?'

'I confide in someone. Someone older, someone neutral.'

'Yeah. Not your mother, because you don't talk, and what could she do anyway? Not Allenius; *definitely* not Allenius. Not Minicius Natalis either, because he's in thick with Prince Gaius, and Gaius for all his faults is Official with a capital O. So who?'

She was twisting the lock of hair beside her ear. 'Lucia Albucilla,' she said.

'Bang on the button. Albucilla's perfect. She's a woman, so she wouldn't matter—'

'Thank you, dear.'

'. . . she's been around, she's experienced, smart. She'd know what to do. Best of all, you're in love with her.'

'Marcus, you do not know that!'

'It's a fair assumption.' I took another mouthful of wine. 'So you tell Albucilla the whole story. Only then—'

'Albucilla takes it directly to her friend Soranus.' Perilla frowned. 'You're right. It works.'

'Whereupon Soranus zaps you with a demand for fifty thousand silver pieces or he does his duty as a responsible citizen and peaches to the Wart and you're up shit creek without a paddle. Without a fucking *boat*.'

'Of course, there is still one more problem.'

'Yeah? What's that?'

'You're going to tell me that Papinius went to Ahenobarbus and made a clean breast of things, after which Ahenobarbus paid off the loan he took out from Vestorius. Aren't you?'

I blinked. 'Uh . . . yeah. Yeah, more or less. Or that Ahenobarbus found out some other way. It comes to the same thing.'

'Very well. In effect, then, Soranus had already been paid off. So why should Ahenobarbus subsequently kill Papinius? What reason would he have?'

'Perilla, the kid had become a liability! He'd blabbed once, he obviously wasn't happy about what he was involved in, and he could well blab again, to someone higher up the ladder this time who might just believe him. Ahenobarbus couldn't risk that. He had to cut his losses.'

'Then if he didn't balk at murder, why not kill all three of them together – Papinius, Soranus and Albucilla – and solve the whole problem at a stroke? Plus save himself a considerable amount of money.'

'Lady, that's silly! Ahenobarbus might be an imperial, he's certainly ruthless enough, but he's no fool. Three suspicious deaths at once? All of bona fide aristocrats? You think that wouldn't get noticed, maybe even on Capri?'

'There would be nothing to link them to him, not directly. And surely it would depend on how important whatever he wanted to cover up was. Also – well – why should the deaths be suspicious? If he could successfully disguise Papinius's murder as a suicide – which he would have done if you hadn't become involved – what was to stop him doing the same for the others?'

'Same answer. Three suicides at once would get noticed.'

'Accidents, then. A mixture. Anything. And don't quibble, you know I'm right.'

I sighed. Yeah, well, she had a point, and as far as Soranus was concerned if that bastard hung up his clogs I doubted if there'd be many tears shed, quite the reverse. Maybe the same went for Albucilla: from what I'd heard of her the lady wasn't exactly a universally popular and respected pillar of society. And certainly it would explain why, when I'd talked to them, they'd both given the impression of pissing their pants about something. Knowing you'd made a guy like Domitius Ahenobarbus seriously peeved wouldn't be exactly conducive to peace of mind and a good night's sleep. 'Okay,' I said. 'Point taken.'

'Another thing it doesn't explain is the peripheral detail.'

'Uh . . . come again?'

'Balbus and Carsidius, for a start. Marcus, they're honourable men! Oh, yes, perhaps honourable only in senatorial terms, but that's amply sufficient here. For your theory to work, they'd both have to be hand-in-glove with Ahenobarbus, and if he were engaged in some sort of illegal activity then that doesn't make sense. Not to me, at any rate. Both of them lied to you over the bribery issue, and in neither case – unless they *were* involved with Ahenobarbus in a cover-up – was it necessary.' She straightened a fold in her mantle. 'I'm sorry, but if that's your theory then it has too many holes.'

Bugger. Right again, and I couldn't even put hand on heart and say there *was* a scam to cover up in the first place. Stymied. I sank the last of the wine in my cup. 'Okay,' I said. 'Let's leave that aspect of things for now. Where do I go next?'

She sniffed. 'I would've thought it was obvious.'

'Really?' I reached for the jug. 'Where's that?'

'Acutia.'

I paused. Hell, right; I'd forgotten about her. Still . . . 'Okay. Although on present showing I can't exactly see the lady being willing to spill any beans. If she is involved somewhere along the line, then—'

'Marcus, why must you always be so *direct*?'

'Fine, Aristotle. You tell me, then.'

'You've got your Caelius Crispus. I've got Sergia Plauta.'

'Who?'

'Your mother's friend. The dowager; remember?'

'Oh, yeah.' I'd never actually met Plauta myself – Mother's pals can be pretty wearing at close range – but I'd heard both Mother and Perilla talking about her. Sergia Plauta was your *echt* blue-blood society matron, six steps to the right of Sulla and a force to be reckoned with in the honey-wine-klatsch set. 'You reckon she can help?'

'I'll be very surprised if she can't. Plauta's the biggest source of female gossip in Rome. She's also – and I don't often use the term, Marcus – a complete cat. Yes, I think she could help a great deal. If properly approached.'

'Not directly?'

Perilla smiled. '*Not* directly. Leave it to me, dear. I'll invite myself round tomorrow.'

'Hey, that's great!' I refilled my cup and took a slug of the Setinian: the world was suddenly a brighter place. 'See if you can find out—'

'Excuse me, sir.'

I turned round. Bathyllus had oozed in on my blind side. 'Yes, little guy, what is it?'

'A slave has just come with a message. From Mucius Soranus.' That with a slight sniff: like I said, Bathyllus has standards. He'd probably had the poor bugger disinfected at the door.

I set down the wine cup. 'Is that so, now?' I said carefully.

'Yes, sir. The gentleman wants to meet you. Tomorrow morning at dawn. In Pompey's theatre.'

'He *what*?' I goggled. Perilla was staring.

'That's what the man said. I did think myself it was a little odd, but—'

'Jupiter's bloody immortal balls! At *dawn*? He say what it was about?'

'No, sir. I asked, of course, but he didn't know. He'd only been told to take the verbal message.'

'Don't go, Marcus!' Perilla said.

Yeah, that was my first reaction too. A dawn meeting at Pompey's theatre just didn't make sense. If everything was on the level then the bastard could've asked me round to his house at a civilised hour, although given how we'd parted on the last occasion I couldn't think what the hell he'd have to say to me. Something stank like a week-old codfish.

'The guy's still here? The slave, I mean?' I said.

'No, sir. He delivered the message and left. I said you'd want to speak to him personally, but—'

'Okay. Okay, Bathyllus.' I waved him away. 'You did your best. Go and polish your spoons.' He exited. 'Gods!' I reached for the wine cup.

'Marcus, you *aren't* going to go, are you?' Perilla said.

'Sure I am. What choice do I have?'

'For heaven's sake!'

I was thinking. I'd go, sure – I had to, it might be important – but I wouldn't go alone. No *way* would I go alone, not the way things were shaping. Forget Placida this time, she was too unreliable. Half a dozen of my biggest lads with weighted sticks were another matter; and Soranus's message – if it was Soranus's – hadn't mentioned anything about a solo interview.

If the meeting was above-board, though – and I'd put that in the flying pigs category – then it was going to be interesting.

24

I was up in good time, two hours before dawn at least; to tell the truth, I hadn't slept all that much. Perilla was awake and around too. She hadn't slept much either.

'Be careful,' she said as she kissed me goodbye.

'You've got it, lady.' I checked the knife taped to my forearm – carrying a sword inside the city limits is strictly illegal, and I was in enough trouble already – and whistled up the Wrecking Crew. They were the biggest, meanest half-dozen Bathyllus's team of skivvies could provide, built like the doors on the State Treasury and more than twice as thick. Mind you, I wasn't taking them for their powers of conversation. Apropos of which: 'Okay, boys? All got your sticks?'

'Yeah, boss.' The leader grinned. He'd lost a few teeth here and there, but the effect was balanced by his broken nose and shaved head.

'Fine. So let's go walkies.'

Pompey's theatre is the other side of the Capitol, in Mars Field near Tiberius Arch; in other words, a long hike from the Caelian. We weren't bothering with torches: there was a full moon, no footpad in his right mind was going to cross six very hefty buggers just begging for the chance to try out their new toys, and in any case in the lead-up to dawn the streets were full of wheeled carts making their deliveries and plain-tunics en route to work. We got some strange looks on the way over – you don't see purple-stripers out and about much before the

second hour – but again because of the Wrecking Crew most
punters gave us the pavement to ourselves. The sky was just
beginning to lighten when we reached the Temple of Hercules
and the Muses just shy of the theatre complex.

The doors of the theatre were open. That was my first
surprise. The second, when I went inside, was that there were
no slaves about. That was weird. An open door in a public
building first thing in the morning means the bought help are
up and around polishing the floors or sweeping the steps and
generally making sure that the place is respectable and heart-
of-the-empire standard. Not a soul. Zero. Zilch.

I checked that my knife was loose in its sheath, motioned
the Wrecking Crew to stick close behind, and climbed the
stairs to the auditorium. The sun was up now, although it
was hidden by the Capitol rise, and when I got out into the
open air I could see clearly along the ranks of seats. No one.
Nothing.

Shit.

Fair enough. There was no point in skulking around. I put
my hands round my mouth and shouted: '*Soranus!*'

A flock of sparrows flew out of the cavea to one side of the
stage far below me. Nothing else moved. Bugger; it had been a
wasted journey.

Or had it?

I looked down at the stretch of paving that separated the
stage proper from the lowest half-circle of seats. In front of the
raised stage platform, at ground level, there was a line of
statues. Propped against one of them was . . .

The hairs on the back of my neck rose.

'Fuck!'

'Trouble, boss?' That was the head slave of the Wrecking
Crew. He sounded pleased.

'Down we go, lads,' I said. 'Keep your eyes skinned.'

Yeah, sure; it could've been one of the theatre skivvies

sleeping on the job: he was too far away for me to see his face clearly. And pigs might fly.

I went down the gangway to the senatorial seats, lowered myself carefully over the barrier on to the orchestra floor, and crossed towards the stage platform. The Wrecking Crew followed.

Yeah, that was Soranus all right, and he was definitely an ex-blackmailer: his throat had been cut ear to ear. No blood, though, on the paving-stones at least, barring a couple of smears. This corpse had been dumped. Well, I couldn't say it was altogether unexpected; the whole set-up had stunk from the beginning, and a corpse at the end of it had been one of the possibilities.

It's funny how your mind registers little things at a time like this. For me, then, it was the bare knees of the statue above him: Diana the Huntress, in her short dress and wreath, poised and about to throw her javelin. The statue looked quite new, the bronze hardly tarnished. Soranus's head was propped against the goddess's legs.

Then I noticed something odd. Yeah, well, you know what I mean.

The guy's right arm was stretched out straight in front of him and to one side, the hand clenched into a fist and resting knuckles-down on the orchestra floor, like he was holding something out towards me. I reached down and prised the fingers apart: either he hadn't begun to stiffen properly yet or he'd been killed quite a while ago, because they opened fairly easily.

Soranus was holding a silver piece.

I sat back on my heels to think. Bugger; what was going on here? It got weirder by the minute. If the body had been dumped, as it had, then why—

'Sir! Sir!'

I looked round. An old guy – obviously a slave, from his

tunic – was hobbling towards me along the line of the platform. I reached down and took the coin from Soranus's hand,
then stood up to wait for him.

'You're Valerius Corvinus, sir?' he said.

'Uh . . . yeah. Yeah, that's me.' Jupiter! Weird was right!
'How the hell—'

'I was told to wait for you, sir.' The guy was white and
shaking, and it wasn't just old age, either. 'Until you'd found
the . . .' His eyes slid to what was left of Soranus, then back to
my face. Whatever he saw there can't exactly have been
reassuring, because he took a step back. 'Believe me, sir, I
didn't . . . I had nothing to do with . . .'

'You want us to beat him up, boss?' The head of the
Wrecking Crew again. I had to hand it to these guys. They'd
taken finding a dead man with his throat slit in their stride like
it happened every day of the month. Not a grunt from any of
them. Phlegmatic isn't the word. Maybe 'bovine' covered it.

'No. No, that's okay,' I said. Then, to the slave: 'Tell me.'

'They brought the body in a cart, sir, about an hour ago. I
was . . . I sleep in one of the booths beside the entrance. They
must've known that, sir, because they woke me up and told me
to open the door.' His teeth were chattering. The fact that the
Wrecking Crew to a troll were standing close beside him
fondling their sticks can't've helped his confidence that he'd
come out the other side of this intact much either.

'You're the caretaker?'

'Yes, sir. Almost all my life, ever since the Divine Augustus
rebuilt the theatre, sir.' His hand pawed at my tunic. 'Sir, I've
told you the gods' truth! Don't let me be tortured! I didn't kill
him!'

Shit. 'Look, no one's going to torture you, pal, okay?' I said.
'Right. So who were "they"?'

'Two men, sir. Big-built, about your age, sir, or a bit older.
One called the other Quintus. They said if I called the Watch

before you came, or if I warned you, they'd come back and . . .
Sir, I don't know any more! Please!'

No, he probably didn't, and he was obviously close to
wetting himself as it was. No point in terrorising the guy
further. Besides, I knew who the killers were: they hadn't made
any secret of it, quite the reverse. Which was weird in itself.
'It's okay, pal,' I said. 'You're off the hook. Go and call the
Watch now. Oh, and they'll want to know the dead man's
name. Tell them Mucius Soranus. He lives – lived – over on
the Cipian near Livia Porch.'

'And . . . I know your name, sir, but you live . . . ?'

'On the Caelian, foot of Head of Africa. They can find me if
they want to. I doubt they'll bother, though.' Not if the head of
the Ninth Region Watch was anything like Titus bloody
Mescinius, that was. Gods! What a mess!

Well, there wasn't much more I could do here, was there?
Home.

Perilla was waiting. She ran across the atrium floor and
hugged me tightly. She was white as an unused dishrag.

'You're all right?' she said.

'Yeah. Yeah, I'm fine. No problems.'

'What happened? Did you see Soranus?'

I unpeeled her. 'Yes and no.'

'Yes and no?'

I told her.

'It was your stonemasons?' she said when I'd finished.
'You're certain?'

'Couldn't be anyone else. The whole thing was a set-up.
Surprise surprise.' I stretched out on the couch and poured
a cup of Setinian from the jug Bathyllus had handed me at
the door. 'Never mind. At least I didn't get killed or beaten
up.'

'Marcus, don't joke! Please!'

'Well, it was always a possibility. Still, that wasn't the purpose of the exercise, was it?'

She gave a little shiver and sat down on the couch opposite, hands clenched. 'So what was, do you think?'

'Search me. Some sort of message, sure, that much is obvious. But what kind? A warning? "Lay off or you'll be next"?'

'*Marcus!*'

'Yeah, well.'

The lady had got a bit of her colour back, although she still didn't look exactly happy and her fingers were still wound together. 'Your pseudo-stonemasons,' she said. 'What were their names again?'

'Aponius and Pettius. At least, those were the names they gave me.'

'Yes. They did *save* your life last time. That doesn't fit with a warning, does it?'

'Nothing about this case fucking fits!'

'Gently, dear. There's no point in getting angry.' She took a deep breath and let it out. 'Or upset.' Her fingers untwined themselves. 'Let's be logical. If it wasn't a warning, then what kind of message was it?'

'Jupiter, Perilla, I already said, I don't know! Anyway, what kind of sick brain sends messages using a corpse?'

'It isn't just that. The whole situation is . . . odd.'

'You're telling me.' I took a swallow of wine. Nectar! All the way to Mars Field and back in a morning had left me with a throat dry as a leather strap.

Perilla was looking pensive and twisting at her hair. Good sign; a *thinking* Perilla I can cope with. The other kind makes me nervous.

'To begin with, why Pompey's theatre?' she said. 'Soranus was practically a neighbour of ours. They could have left his body anywhere. Why choose the other side of Rome, especially if the whole point was simply to have you find it?'

'Yeah. Yeah, I was wondering that myself. Maybe it was just a quiet, out-of-the-way place.'

'There are quiet, out-of-the-way places far closer to the Caelian than Mars Field, Marcus, especially at that time of the morning. Besides, Pompey's theatre isn't exactly isolated.'

'Okay. Then maybe he was killed close by. Decoyed to somewhere in the neighbourhood some time yesterday, bumped off and shelved for delivery first thing. Certainly that explains the dawn meeting. They'd have to use a cart to transport the body, and that means a dusk-to-dawn time-slot.'

'It's possible. But still, the distance wouldn't matter. They'd have all night to do it, and it's unlikely they'd be stopped by the Watch because from sunset to first light the streets are full of carts. Besides, if the murder was committed nearby they wouldn't want to advertise the fact.'

'Okay, Aristotle.' I took another sip of the wine. 'I'm open to suggestions.'

She took a long time answering. Then she said slowly, 'I think it's more complicated than that. It's more of a code. Or a puzzle.'

'Jupiter's holy balls, lady! Why should guys like Aponius and Pettius set me a puzzle? They're fucking—'

'Marcus. Stop it, please. I don't mean the actual killers, of course I don't. I mean whoever sent them, whoever was behind the murder. Mind you, to be honest I don't see why they should bother either. This isn't a game.'

'Too right it isn't! Bloody hell!' I reached for the jug.

'Nevertheless.' Perilla's hand went back to her curl. 'Just calm down and let's think. Pompey's theatre. What's special about Pompey's theatre?'

I grinned. 'You're on your own there, sunshine.'

'Very well. It's the oldest stone theatre in Rome, originally built by Pompey on the model of the theatre at Mytilene and renovated by Augustus. Anything else?'

'Perilla—'

'All right. Perhaps not that, then. Theatres in general. What do they call to mind?'

'Actors? Acting? Plays?' I frowned. 'Tragedies. Comedies. Masks.'

'Fine. That's better. Masks. People pretending to be some-one they're not. Acting out a play that isn't real. Possible? Anything suggest itself?'

'Uh-uh. Besides, the body wasn't on the stage.'

'Ah. Good point.'

'I'm sorry, but this isn't helping, lady.'

'No. No, perhaps it isn't.' The curl knotted, and she began prising the hairs apart with her fingernails. 'But there must be something.'

'He was leaning against a statue.' The fingernails stopped. Her mouth opened, then closed. 'Perilla?'

'No. It was just a . . .' She shook her head. 'Never mind, it'll come again if it's important. What kind of statue? Who to?'

'Diana. Diana as Huntress.'

'So a woman's statue?'

'Of course a fucking—'

'Marcus! Hunting. Women.' The tangle came free. 'Any-thing significant there, do you think?'

'How the hell should I know?'

'Think metaphorically, dear. This is a puzzle, remember. Soranus was a blackmailer, women are a natural target – *quarry* – for blackmailers. And Diana doesn't have a good reputation where men trespassing on her private affairs is concerned. The hunting goes both ways. Remember Actaeon?'

'Who?'

'Oh, *Marcus!*'

'Yeah, well, I think we're maybe getting just a little over-subtle here.'

'I disagree. The puzzle element – if this is a puzzle – fits in better with how a woman's brain works than a man's. Diana engineered Actaeon's death because he'd . . . transgressed. Offended. Crossed the line. However you want to put it. That much fits, at least.'

'Jupiter, lady! You're saying the person behind Papinius's murder was a *woman*?'

'We're talking about Soranus, not Papinius. And no, of course I'm not. Or . . . not necessarily so.'

'Okay. We've got two women in this case. One's Albucilla, the other's bubblehead Acutia who wouldn't recognise a puzzle if it bit her in the bum. You like to choose, maybe?'

'Three.'

'Three what?'

'Women in the case. You've forgotten one.'

'*Cluvia?*' I goggled. 'Oh, come on! She was just the kid's girlfriend!'

'She was very fond of him, and after what you told her she probably blamed Soranus for his death. Do you know anything about her, anything at all barring her connection with Papinius and where she works?'

'Uh, no, but—'

'From what you do know, would you say she was capable of planning a murder? Not of committing it herself, but arranging to have it done, given that was possible?'

I thought back to my talk with Cluvia. Yeah, that had been one very feisty, intelligent lady; and Perilla was right, she did seem very stuck on young Papinius. Still, none of that, even put all together, was enough to qualify her as a murderess. 'She's a viable option, sure,' I said cautiously, 'but I wouldn't rate her all that high. Besides, how would you explain the fact that her pals Aponius and Pettius – and they must've been her pals, ipso facto – were tailing me?'

Perilla sighed. 'Ah. I'd forgotten that. Perhaps not Cluvia, then. Never mind, it was only an idea. Get back to Soranus's body. The silver piece.'

'That part's clear enough. It's the reason for the murder. Soranus was a blackmailer. He was taking money, specifically from Papinius.'

'Hmm,' Perilla said.

'What do you mean, "hmm", lady?'

'Oh, I don't know. It's just that—'

'Just that what?'

She frowned. 'No. You're right, of course. I'm being silly. And it does make perfect sense.'

'So.' I took another mouthful of wine. 'We know why Soranus was killed, we know who did it, at least as far as the actual killers are concerned. Why drag me into it?'

'Marcus, I don't know. No more than you do. Leave it for the present.' She got up. 'Meanwhile, I'm sorry, but I'd really best be going.'

'Yeah? Where to?'

'Sergia Plauta's. You remember, I said I'd invite myself round this morning?' Ah. Right. Re the not-so-sharp Acutia. 'She doesn't live far away, on the slope facing the Palatine. I thought I might call in in passing on the way to the Apollo Library and allow myself to be sidetracked into honey wine and gossip.'

'You sure she'll be there?'

'Oh, yes. It takes her the whole morning to have her hair done and her make-up applied. But I'd better go now, in case she's going out afterwards. I was only waiting in until I knew you were back safely.'

'Fine. Good luck, lady.' I grinned. 'Oh, and by the way, speaking of the Apollo I'd watch that chief librarian if I were you.'

'Drepanius? He's a sweetie!'

'He's a randy old bugger.'

She kissed me. 'Yes. That too. I'll see you later, Marcus. Incidentally, Placida hasn't had her walk yet and Alexis has some winter digging to do. If you're at a loose end this morning then perhaps you could take her.'

Hell.

One thing, though. Why should I keep thinking about pastry-sellers?

25

Yeah, well; needs must. I collected a delighted Placida and we set off at speed down Head of Africa. I wasn't bound for Appian Road and the open country, though. Oh, sure, when the weather's good Perilla and me'll take an occasional stroll through one of the public gardens, but when I wear out sandal leather on my own I like it to be for a reason. If the case was on hold for the day – as it was – then we'd take time out to go to Scylax's gym near the Racetrack.

I still called it that, although Scylax himself had been dead for years. The gym was one of the oldest properties I owned, and was currently run by Daphnis, Scylax's erstwhile sand-sweeper turned businessman extraordinaire. Daphnis was okay at root, but you had to keep an eye on him and I hadn't been down there in months. Too many months for safety. Now would be the perfect opportunity.

Besides, that abortive brush with my stonemason pals had shown me that I could do with a decent workout. A massage'd be good, too.

We reached the gym. I let Placida drag me across the crowded training-ground and push open the door of the office, where Daphnis was sitting at a desk to one side flicking beads on an abacus and making notes on a wax tablet.

'Hi, Daphnis,' I said. 'How's the lad?'

He looked round and did a double-take. 'Corvinus! What—'

Which was all he had time for before Placida hit with both

front paws and a tongue. Daphnis screamed and the abacus and tablets went flying.

'She's a big softie, really,' I said.

'*Corvinus, you bastard! Get it off me!*'

Fun was fun, but enough was enough. I pulled the slobbering dog away and took a firm grip of her collar. Daphnis picked himself up, dusted himself off and sat back down on his bench.

'Where the *hell* did you get that thing?' he said.

'She's on loan from a friend of Perilla's.'

'A *friend*? Jupiter!' He retrieved the abacus and tablets. Yeah, well: Daphnis never had been one for the old client-to-patron respectful approach. That, together with the per-manent designer stubble and his habit of picking his nose when he was in a particularly thoughtful mood was part of the guy's unique charm. 'Now. You here to look over the accounts? Because I'm up to the eyeballs in work at present so you can bloody well forget it.'

'In that case, purely pleasure, sunshine.' I forced Placida down into crouch position. 'Just a workout and a massage.'

He sniggered evilly. 'The massage won't be no pleasure, Corvinus. We've got a new guy on the staff with hands like fucking rooftiles. Good masseur, mind.'

'That's okay,' I said. 'I'll risk it.' There wasn't no way I was going to back down in front of Daphnis. *No* way. And his technique couldn't be any worse than Scylax's had been. Ten minutes with Scylax and they'd had to peel me off the ceiling.

'Great. Don't say I didn't warn you.'

'I won't. Promise. Is Publius around?' Publius Avillius was the head trainer, an ex-legionary centurion who'd been taken on after Scylax died. He'd had a drink problem until his daughter locked up the wine jars, but he was firmly on the wagon now, and although he wasn't in Scylax's league where teaching fighting dirty was concerned there wasn't a better man with the short sword in Rome.

'Yeah. He's on his break in the privy, communing with nature. Give him ten minutes.'

'Fine. I'm in no hurry.' I leaned over and moved a couple of abacus balls along their wires. He pulled the machine out of reach. 'So how are things? In general, that is?'

'You must've seen for yourself when you came in. We're bursting at the seams. Apropos of which, old Fannius in the potter's shop next door is giving up business and moving to his daughter's in Capua. I thought we might take over his yard and knock a hole through the wall if you're agreeable. Expand into the women's market.'

'The *women's* market?'

'Yeah.' Another evil grin. 'Don't tell me it's never been done, I know that. Still, it might be interesting. Get a few retired female gladiators in as trainers, modify the programme a bit, target a young age-group. Lots of feisty girls out there who want more out of life than sitting at home doing crochet. As an idea, it could be a winner.' He winked. 'Especially since it's a low wall.'

'You pulling my string?'

'Could be. You decide.'

I stood up; a little of Daphnis went a long way. Besides, he'd already picked up the stylus again in a not-so-gentle hint that I'd used enough of his valuable time. 'Yes to buying the Fannius place,' I said, 'but as far as Amazon Annexe is concerned I don't think Rome's quite ready for female body-building classes, pal. You'd have both of us pegged out for the crows by irate male relatives inside of a month.'

He shrugged and reached for the wax tablet. 'Suit yourself. But you're passing up on a real goldmine.'

'I'll take that risk. Watch you don't sprain your fingers on that abacus, Daphnis.' I moved towards the door.

He set the tablet down. 'Hey. What about the dog?'

'Oh, she'll be no trouble. She's settled now.' She was flat

out, doing her random-pile-of-hair impression. 'I'll pick her up when I leave.'

'Like hell you will! Corvinus! *Corvinus!*'

I went back out into the sunshine: the weather had cleared, and it was a beautiful October day, not too hot but without a cloud in the sky. There was a stone bench to one side, and I sat on it to watch the punters while I waited for Publius to come out of the latrine. Daphnis was right, the place was full: there were a good dozen of various ages and conditions hammering away at each other with wooden swords, some of them with assistant trainers looking on or giving one-to-one lessons. Daphnis got them from the gladiatorial schools – retired gladiators are fairly common in Rome; the ones who come out intact the other end have to be *good* to do it, and the sand's in their blood – or from among the number of ex-squaddies who'd blown their discharge grant and needed a steady job to pay for the pulse porridge and sour wine. I watched as one of them, a single-lessoner, ducked under a roundhouse swipe from an obvious complete tyro and prodded him in the ribs with the tip of his dummy sword.

'*Not* the bloody edge, sir,' he said wearily. 'You're a swordsman, not a fucking lumberjack. How many times do I have to tell you? Use the point!'

I grinned to myself as he took the abashed kid – he can't've been more than fourteen and looked a complete penpusher in embryo – through the motions of the legionary punching stab. Yeah, well, at least we were providing a valuable service here. The boy had a purple stripe on his tunic, and in two or three years' time he could be out on the fringes of the empire doing this for real. I'd never been in that position, sure, but the lessons with Scylax had saved my life a dozen times. Especially the lessons they don't teach you in the army. Knifemen in Rome are simple, direct souls; not a lot of them have read the military manual or even looked at the pictures, and when push comes to shove knowing when to plant a judicious knee in the balls or a fist in the throat can come in very handy.

I'd been sitting there for a good ten minutes when Publius limped out of the privy. He'd taken a German spear in the right leg nine years before, in the Frisian revolt, and it'd severed a tendon so he couldn't bend the leg at the knee; which was why he'd been invalided out before his time and, incidentally, explained the drinking. Not that it cramped his style as a swordsman any. I'd made the mistake, the first time I fought him, of allowing for it and got a jab in the ribs that still gave me a twinge months afterwards.

He saw me, and came over, throwing a perfect military salute on the way.

'Good to see you again, sir,' he said. 'You fighting today, or just visiting?'

'Fighting,' I said. 'If you've got the time.'

'Always got the time for you, sir.' Yeah, well, it made a change from Daphnis. And the guy was no arselicker, either: when he said 'fighting' he meant it. Witness that first stab. 'There's a clear space over there.'

We walked over to the edge of the group, picking up a couple of wooden swords from the pile on the way. He stopped and came on guard.

'Any time you're ready, sir.'

I took it nice and slow to start with. I needed to warm up, if he didn't, and besides, wading straight in with Publius was a bad, bad idea: it just meant you got clobbered barely a dozen moves into the bout, or he let you wear yourself out trying to get through his guard and *then* clobbered you. As it was, he didn't even have to shift his feet: every stab of mine was deflected past his body with a wrench of the wrist that had me moving back and on guard again quickly before the point of his sword caught my ribs on the riposte. Five minutes later I was sweating, and Publius's breathing hadn't even quickened.

'Not bad, sir,' he said after a particularly savage parry-and-twist had almost taken the sword from my hand and he'd waved a pause. 'You could do with coming down here a bit more often, though. You're signalling far too much and your guard's downright sloppy in places. I could've had you a dozen times over.'

I grinned and wiped the sweat from my eyes. 'Yeah,' I gasped. 'Yeah, no argument, pal. Sorry. Want to try again? I'll try to concentrate more.'

He came on guard, but this time he made the first move. The stab came quick as a striking snake, and I just managed to catch the edge of his sword between my blade and hilt and turn it away from my exposed side. He stepped back, changed the angle and lunged again: all far too fast for me to bring the sword round to block the thrust, but I somehow managed to swerve and the point just brushed my tunic. Then I lunged in my turn at his exposed armpit, but there, suddenly, where it shouldn't have been, was his hilt between us. The jar and wrench as the blades met threw me to one side and his sword was coming straight for my unguarded chest. I leaped away so the wooden tip barely touched me. Not that I had any illusions on that score: he'd pulled the punch, and if it'd been a real fight he'd've skewered me.

'Much better,' he said. 'You're thinking ahead now and you're moving faster. Still, not good enough yet. On your guard again, please.'

We kept it up for another half-hour or so with breaks for me to get my breath back. By the end I was sweating like a pig, Publius was looking as cool as when we'd started and my ribs were sore from half a dozen thrusts I hadn't managed to block. I'd touched him once, more by luck than design, or maybe he'd just felt sorry for me: but it was on the arm, not in the chest, and I'd left myself open when I did it so if he'd wanted to he could've given me a real stinger. I stepped back and held up my sword.

'That'll do me for today, pal,' I said when I had enough breath to speak. 'Thanks a lot.'

'Any time, sir.' He grounded his own sword. 'Like I said, not bad. But watch your point and be a lot faster on the return.'

I gave him the usual salute at the end of a bout, sword to chin, nose and forehead, then handed the blade over and walked back towards the admin buildings. Time for the massage part of the proceedings, if the new masseur wasn't occupied, before I stiffened up completely. I wasn't totally displeased by the way the workout had gone. Even on my best day I'd never been able to give Publius a real match, but like I say there wasn't a swordsman in Rome to touch him. If you can last half an hour with Publius Avillius and walk away with only half a dozen bruises you're doing pretty well.

There was no sound from the massage-room. Yeah, well, that was all to the good, anyway: when Scylax had done the slapping and rolling you could hear the screams halfway to the Racetrack. I pushed open the door and went in. It took a moment for my eyes to accustom themselves to the dimness, and in that moment, at the back of the room beyond the massage table, something *loomed*.

'Afternoon, sir,' it growled.

My eyes had adjusted now. They went up . . . and up . . .

Oh, bugger.

Daphnis hadn't been kidding. The guy was the size of a small house, and he had to hold his arms out at an angle to give the muscles room to fit in. His hands, knuckle to knuckle, must've been nine inches across, at least. This was not going to be fun. Still, it was too late to back out now, and after my bout with Publius I could do with loosening up if I didn't want to crawl home to the Caelian.

Mind you, that might be preferable to doing the trip on a stretcher.

'Uh . . . What's your name, pal?' I said.

'Orestes.'

'That so?' I started removing my tunic. 'I'm Valerius Corvinus.'

'The owner?'

'Yeah, that's right.'

He grinned and reached for a towel. 'Pleased to meet you, sir. Mister Daphnis has told me a lot about you. A very nice guy, Mister Daphnis.'

Oh, shit.

'Just lie flat on the table and we'll have these muscles purring in no time at all.'

He cracked his knuckles and picked up the oil jar.

It wasn't as bad as I thought it would be. It was worse.

I staggered out of the massage-room half an hour later feeling like I'd been mugged by a sadistic gorilla. Constructively mugged, though, if you know what I mean: Big Orestes might be a complete sadist – ninety-nine out of a hundred masseurs are – but he knew his job, and like he'd said my muscles were purring. Taken together with the workout, I reckoned I couldn't've spent a more profitable hour and a half.

In more ways than one. In between the screams, and to take my mind off the bastard's knuckles forcing their sadistic way between the plates of muscle in my back, I'd been running over certain aspects of the case. And I'd had an idea. It was an outside chance, of course, but not one to pass up on just for that reason. They're a close family, the military.

'Hey, Publius!' I shouted. The ex-centurion was busy with a middle-aged purple-striper with a gut like an amphora. He turned round, said something to the guy and then limped over.

'Yes, sir,' he said.

'Just a thought. You ever come across a couple of ex-army men by the names of Aponius and Pettius?'

'Sextus Aponius?'

I blinked. Shit. 'Uh . . . yeah. Yeah, that's him.'

'Yes, sir. Knew him well. He was a centurion in the First Germanica, time I got this leg of mine. He's no ex, though, or he wasn't last I heard.'

'But if he's still with the First he'd be on the Rhine, right?'

'No, sir. At least, what I mean to say is he's not with the First any more. After the Frisian business he got transferred to the Praetorians.' He grinned. 'Lucky bugger. Those sods have it cushy, pardon my Greek, sir.'

My brain was whirling. 'The guy's a *Praetorian*?'

'Far as I know, sir, unless you know different or it's a different man altogether. I haven't seen him in quite a while. I can't help you with the second name, mind.' He looked over his shoulder at the fat purple-striper. 'Was that all, sir? Because Tattius Geminus can be a bit stroppy if he doesn't get his full time.'

'Yeah. Yeah, that's all.' Jupiter bloody best and greatest! 'Thanks, Publius.'

'You're very welcome, sir. I'll see you again soon, I hope.'

'Ah . . . yeah. Yeah, right.'

He gave me a funny look – I must've looked as out of things as I felt – and went back to his pupil.

I shook my head to clear it. Shit. Okay: collect the dog, go home, talk to Perilla. I walked across to the office and opened the door.

Placida was sitting just inside the threshold. Daphnis was on his feet, back pressed hard against the far wall. He couldn't've got any closer if he'd been a coat of paint.

'Having fun, pal?' I said.

'*You bastard, Corvinus!*'

Placida growled a warning, and Daphnis tried to squirm his way up the wall.

'She's been there practically since you left,' he whispered. 'She wouldn't let me near the door and I didn't even dare fucking *scream*.'

'Must be your breath-freshener. She's never done that with anyone else.'

'*And* she's eaten the abacus!'

I looked down. Sure enough, there it was, reduced to a tangle of wires and vulgar fractions. 'Placida's very, uh, tactile. If that's the word. Or do I mean oral? Can you say that?'

'Just get her out of here, okay?'

'You sure?'

'*Corvinus!*'

I grinned. 'Yeah, okay, pal. Come on, Placida. Home.'

I set off back to the Caelian, brain buzzing. So. At least one of my fake stonemasons was a Praetorian, eh? Oh, sure: it made finding the guy easy-peasy, because the Praetorian camp was slap-bang next to the city boundaries, just beyond the Viminal Gate; but at the same time it left me with two major questions and a bigger-than-major worry. First question was what the hell was a serving Praetorian – possibly two – doing mixed up in this business? Second, if they were moonlighting or doing a favour for a pal then what had made them confident enough to give me their real names?

The worry was that slice it how you would Praetorians were Praetorians, and some of these pals were very important men. A couple even had names ending with 'Caesar'.

I didn't like the smell this case was beginning to give off; I didn't like it at all.

26

P erilla wasn't back when I got in, but then I hadn't really
expected her to be: we weren't halfway through the
afternoon yet, and unless Sergia Plauta had had a prior early
engagement they'd probably have a fair amount of character
assassination to get through. I'd thought about dumping
Placida and going straight up to the Praetorian camp, but
I'd decided against it. First of all, it was quite a hike, and I'd
had my whack of exercise for one day; second, I wanted to see
Perilla first. You didn't just walk into the camp of the emper-
or's personal guard and accuse two of the city's best and finest
– assuming Pettius was a guardsman too – of murdering a
Roman noble and using the corpse as a messenger-boy. Not if
you wanted to walk out again. Sertorius Macro, the Praetorian
commander and – in Tiberius's and Prince Gaius's absence –
the de facto most powerful man in Rome, would get pretty
intense about having two of his men accused of murder. And
Macro was someone I definitely didn't want to cross.

Oh, and yeah, sure, it had also occurred to me – I'm not
stupid – that he might be involved directly himself, either off
his own bat or in his official capacity. How or why that might
be I hadn't the slightest idea, but I really, *really* hoped that he
wasn't because it was a nightmare scenario. I'd had enough
grief and heartache bucking his predecessor Sejanus, and I'd
seen enough of the guy five years back on the journey from
Capri to know that he was a seriously mean bastard in his own
right. Certainly not the kind to welcome me with open arms

and split a jug while we swapped jolly reminiscences about pulling Sejanus's plug for him.

So I didn't do anything or go anywhere, just lay around in the atrium with half a jug of Setinian, twiddling my thumbs and worrying, until the lady chose to reel home full of honey wine and salacious gossip. Which she did, about an hour later.

'Hello, Marcus,' she said. 'Have a nice walk?'

'Yeah, we went to Scylax's gym. Tell you about it afterwards.' I gave her the welcome-home kiss: honey wine on the breath, sure, but she was still mobile and coherent.

'How's Placida?'

'Lying knackered in the garden. She had a hard morning intimidating Daphnis. So: was Sergia Plauta on form?'

'Very much so.' She collapsed on to the couch just as Bathyllus drifted in touting for drinks orders. 'Placida isn't the only one. That woman is *exhausting*. Some fruit juice, please, Bathyllus. Or better still a plain tisane, unsweetened. I've had enough honey to last me a month.'

'Okay,' I said as he soft-shoed out. 'Let's have the gory details. Unload.'

'Acutia is having an affair with a man called Pontius Fregellanus.'

'Yeah? And who's he?'

'A middle-aged noble. He's on the staff of Sertorius Macro.'

My head came up so fast I nearly dislocated my neck. '*Shit!*'

Perilla gave me a sharp look. 'Marcus, what's wrong?'

'Nothing.' Oh, sweet immortal gods! Please, *please* let it not be Macro! 'You've got the ball, lady. He's a Praetorian officer?'

'No. He's a civilian, in charge of the camp's clerical division.' I was still getting the suspicious stare. 'Are you sure there's nothing wrong?'

'Positive. What sort of guy is he?'

'Stolid, worthy and serious, from what Plauta says, and she wasn't being complimentary. His main interests, apart from his work, seem to be old Republican history and collecting rock samples. But he is – or he appears to be – totally captivated by Acutia. There's even talk of a marriage.'

Jupiter in a wheelbarrow! *Captivated*, eh? Well, there was no accounting for taste. The woman was still good-looking enough in her mousy way, sure, but she was no Cleopatra, and from what I remembered of her she'd as much character as a polyp. Still, a boyfriend on Macro's staff . . . That couldn't be coincidence; no *way* could it be coincidence. The ice was already forming on my spine.

'Anything else?' I said.

'That's the gist of it. I'm omitting the finer details of how they met – Acutia seems to have been the motive force there – and the blow-by-blow account of the affair so far. Plauta gave me that in graphic detail, although after her summation of Fregellanus's character and from my own knowledge of Acutia's I suspect that most of it was her own invention.' Perilla grinned. 'She does have a very *vivid* imagination, Sergia Plauta. Either that, or a great deal of very questionable past experience.'

'When did it start? The affair, I mean?'

'Comparatively recently. Three months ago, according to Plauta.'

About the time when Papinius landed his job at the commission. Well, again that could be coincidence, but still . . . 'And you say Acutia made the running? That not a bit out of character for the lady?'

'A little. But she is older than I am, Marcus. Time's running out for her. And she's been widowed for five years.'

Yeah. Since her husband Vitellius topped himself at the emperor's request over the Sejanus business. Sejanus. Shit, now that *had* to be a coincidence! Sejanus was dead and burned, he couldn't be a factor. And, like Perilla had said before, there couldn't be very many people in Rome from the top families who hadn't had dealings of one kind or another with him. Even so . . .

'This Fregellanus,' I said. 'He political, at all, now or ever?'

'No, not in the least. Not in the way you mean it, anyway. He's technically a senator but he rarely attends meetings and he's never been on any important committee. "A nondescript", Plauta called him, and I think she's probably right.' Bathyllus buttled in with the tisane. 'Ah, thank you, Bathyllus. Just set it on the table, please.'

'He's never married?' I said when the little bald-head had gone.

'Again, no. Why, I don't know, and nor, more to the point, did Plauta. There was nothing . . . well, there was no *sexual* reason why not. Perhaps he was just shy around women. Some perfectly normal men are.'

Yeah; and it would explain why Acutia had to make the running, too. Bugger; I was spinning cobwebs here, and I knew it. From an everyday, innocent point of view it all made perfect sense. Like Perilla had said, Acutia wasn't getting any younger, and knowing a woman's husband had been deeply involved with Sejanus, especially in the immediate aftermath of his fall, would be a powerful disincentive for potential suitors. Fregellanus might be no ball of fire, but he was a senator and so a social equal, and Acutia was lucky to get him. Besides, by the sound of it the two were just made for each other: solid bachelor with an interest in historical writing meets bubblehead widow with a penchant for poetry. It was a marriage made in heaven. Bring on the bluebirds and the slave with the nuts.

Still. Soranus, Albucilla, Acutia, Fregellanus, the Praetorians. The chain couldn't be a coincidence; not with Aponius tying in from the other side to complete the circle . . .

Ah, well. Leave it for the moment. Certainly Fregellanus was another reason for going up to the Praetorian camp. Not that I particularly wanted a reason.

'Your pet scandalmonger give you anything more on Albucilla?' I said.

'No, not really. Just more or less what we had already: that she is, or she was, now, Mucius Soranus's long-time lover. Neither of them was particularly faithful to the relationship, mark you, and it always was a rather loose one.' Perilla sipped her tisane. 'What was interesting, though, was that Plauta said there'd been a coolness on both sides just before Soranus's death. More than a coolness, a separation. The two seemed to be avoiding each other altogether.'

'Yeah, that's what Crispus told me. How long before?'

'Only a matter of days. And yes, Marcus, I do see the implications. Since Papinius's murder, probably.'

'Or just before it, when they found out – as I'd bet they did – that Ahenobarbus had paid the kid's debt to Vestorius. If my theory's right then by that time the two of them must've been shitting bricks.' I reached for my wine cup. 'Did Plauta have anything to say about Albucilla's relationship with Papinius?'

'Oh, yes. Quite a lot, in fact. They were certainly lovers in the physical sense; I was treated to a good half-hour's worth of juicy circumstantial evidence to that effect. Probably not an invention in this case, because Plauta's maid is Albucilla's maid's cousin.'

'And that affair had been going on how long?'

'Again, two or three months. Possibly not the sexual side of things, but certainly the attachment.'

I took a mouthful of wine. 'And Albucilla engineered it, right?'

'Oh, yes. I was wrong about her cradle-snatching tendencies, or lack of them. Seemingly she quite often used Soranus as a means to pick up young men, and as I say they had quite an open relationship. She was very discreet, though, and the affairs never lasted long.'

Yeah, well, I'd got that already from Crispus, too, or some of it. I should've made the obvious inference, though. 'Long enough to get her into their confidence, maybe,' I said. 'Winkle out any little secret they had that she could pass on.'

'Mmm.' Perilla sipped her tisane. 'Yes. That's what I thought.'

'No wonder the bastard was so accommodating. The two of them had a nice steady racket going. Soranus gets in with the young lads-about-town set, then when he finds a likely mark Albucilla seduces the kid and gets him to tell her bedtime stories. Whereupon Soranus puts the bite on.' I swallowed another gulp of Setinian. 'Neat.'

'Neat and very nasty. Yes.'

'Only with Papinius they bit off more than they could chew. They found they were tangling with Ahenobarbus.'

Perilla frowned. 'Yes, but Marcus, they must've known that at the outset. I mean, the secret they were blackmailing Papinius over involved Ahenobarbus from the very beginning.'

'Yeah. Shit.' I shrugged. 'Well, maybe they got greedy. Thought the returns were worth the risk. Or Soranus did. That'd explain why they quarrelled, wouldn't it? Albucilla wasn't keen on things from the start and Soranus persuaded her. Then when everything went pear-shaped the lady wanted out, only it was too late; she was already in shtuck up to her ears.'

'Yes.' Perilla was still looking thoughtful. 'Yes, that would fit.'

'In which case now Soranus is dead – murdered – she'll be really panicking.' I finished off the wine in my cup. 'Maybe I should have another talk with Albucilla.'

'Mmm.' She looked up. 'Well, that's about all I have. Now tell me about your day.'

Here we went. I took a deep breath. 'Aponius and Pettius are Praetorians. At least, Aponius is.'

She almost spilled her tisane. '*What?*'

'Yeah. He served on the Rhine with Publius, the head trainer down at Scylax's, nine years back. Publius said he'd been transferred to the Praetorian Guard.'

Her eyes were wide. 'Oh, *Marcus*! That's why you were so shocked when I told you about Fregellanus!'

' "Shocked" doesn't cover it, lady,' I said grimly. 'There has to be a link.'

'Sertorius Macro?'

No fool, Perilla. Still, there was no point in both of us worrying. 'Not necessarily,' I said. 'After all, why should Macro involve himself in anything shady? It'd do him far more harm than good. He's a big man these days, bigger than anyone in Rome, and when Tiberius pops his clogs and Gaius is emperor he'll be even bigger. He's got other fish to fry than settling the hash of some cheap blackmailer, and all he has to do is sit pretty, keep his nose clean and wait. Plus, where the hell he'd fit in with young Sextus Papinius's death Jupiter only knows.' I refilled my wine cup. 'Uh-uh. Don't look for bogeymen under the bed before we have to. Fregellanus is link enough for the present.'

She was quiet for a good half-minute, sipping her tisane. Then she said, 'You're going to the Praetorian camp tomorrow, aren't you?'

I hadn't missed the overtones. 'Uh . . . yeah,' I said casually. 'Yeah, that would seem the logical next step.'

'And you'll be seeing Macro?'

'If he's around, sure. After all, it's only polite. He is the boss, and—'

'Marcus, be careful! I know you have to do it, but *please* be careful! No accusations, no heavy-handed questions. Macro's far too powerful to offend, and if he is involved then letting him know you think he is would be very dangerous indeed.' She paused. 'Besides. I've got a feeling about all this, and it isn't a pleasant one.'

I got up, went over and kissed her. 'We've been through this before,' I said. 'Yeah, I'll be careful. No sass, I promise.'

Definitely no sass. Especially since I'd got a nasty feeling about all this, too.

27

The Praetorian barracks are to the north-east of the city, between Viminal Field and Nomentan Road. They're pretty new, only about fifteen years old: before Sejanus persuaded the Wart to bring them all together the nine Praetorian cohorts – with extras, just short of five thousand men – were spread through Italy, with only a single cohort stationed in Rome itself. Yeah, sure, having what amounts almost to a full legion, and that made up of the best troops in the empire, free, ready and waiting to send off to a sudden trouble spot at a moment's notice makes sense, but it's a double-edged sword: whoever commands the Praetorians effectively controls the city, or could do if push came to serious shove. Which was why, of course, Sejanus had suggested the amalgamation in the first place; why the Wart, when he sent Macro to pull Sejanus's plug, gave him a letter appointing him as the guy's replacement; and why, currently, the said Macro was de facto the most powerful, most dangerous bugger in Rome.

I was doing this properly. Oh, yeah, although the barracks weren't exactly next door it would've been an easy hour and a half's stroll, quite pleasant in good weather, which that morning it was; and although I'd pass by the Caeliolan, where according to Perilla's satyric librarian pal Albucilla hung out, this early in the day was too soon for a social call. I could have my second talk with the lady on the way back. If there was an 'on the way back'. On the other hand, arriving at Macro's front door on foot and in a travel-stained tunic wouldn't do much for my personal street-cred.

So I put on my best mantle and took the litter again. Apart from anything else, the long run would do our lardballs good: Perilla did use them whenever she went out, sure, but that didn't happen too often and litter-slaves need to be constantly exercised if you don't want a team bulging with unsightly fat and panting at the slightest incline. I also took four of the Wrecking Crew along, this time in their best tunics. Mostly for the show when I reached the barracks: if things got sticky, as they might, even four extra-large trolls on the staff wouldn't be much help against nine cohorts of Praetorians. I didn't even *think* of taking Placida. Praetorians aren't exactly noted for their sunny, easy-going natures, and just one anarchic paw out of line in the wrong company could have us both in shtuck.

We processed up to the gate in fine style, and the squaddies on guard even came to attention when I got out of the litter. I gave my name to the duty officer, twiddled my thumbs in the guard-house for ten minutes while he checked with higher authority and was then escorted up the Headquarters Road towards the headquarters building itself.

When he'd had the place built, Sejanus had done himself and his men proud. There weren't any fripperies, sure, visible ones anyway – this was a working army camp, after all – but the barrack blocks were solid, concrete-built with heavy tile roofs. They all had verandas, too, and there were quite a few squaddies lounging about them in tunics or leathers shooting the after-breakfast breeze. I remembered what Publius had said about the Praetorians being a cushy posting. Yeah, that squared. As the empire's elite, they'd be fairly certain of staying put for the duration of their service unless something drastic went wrong on one of the frontiers that the local troops couldn't handle, they had Rome on their doorstep when they were off duty and, best of all, they were paid at three times the rate of the ordinary legionary squaddie. If the buggers weren't exactly laughing, they could at least raise a chuckle.

Outside the headquarters, my escort handed me over to the officer on duty – you could've used the guy's breastplate as a shaving-mirror – and went back to guarding the empire's heartland against any band of marauding barbarians that might've slipped across the border and crossed five hundred miles or so of Roman territory without being noticed.

'The commander's in here, sir,' the duty officer said. 'If you'd care to follow me.'

Two minutes later I was face to face with Sertorius Macro, for the first time in five years.

He hadn't changed much; still the hard, bulldog face with the chiselled features and eyes like chips of marble, although his close-cropped hair was greying at the temples. And he'd kept himself in shape. I couldn't tell whether he had a paunch under the leathers and breastplate, sure, but when he got up and came round the desk with his hand held out to shake he moved easily, like a fit man ten years younger.

His grip was powerful, too.

'Valerius Corvinus,' he said. 'A pleasure to see you again. Come and sit down.'

There was a chair in front of the desk: plain oak, but good quality. I pulled it up and sat while he went back to his own chair. An orderly had followed me in and was standing at attention.

'Some wine, Titus,' Macro said to him. Then, to me: 'Not too early for you, Corvinus?'

'Uh-uh. A cup of wine would be great, thanks.'

The orderly gave a crisp salute, right-about-turned and exited.

'How's your wife?' Macro said. 'Ah . . . Rufia Perilla, isn't it?'

'Yeah. Yeah, Perilla's fine.' I was feeling pretty gobsmacked. I couldn't complain of the reception, anyway. The guy couldn't've been more affable if I'd been a long-lost brother, and that was weird, because when we'd seen each other last he'd hardly spoken half a dozen words to me. Mind you, then he'd had other things to think about. Like killing Sejanus.

'Ennia and I must have the pair of you round for dinner some evening. I'm sorry we seem to've lost touch over the years. Perhaps we can do better in future. After all, in a way I do have you to thank for the fact that I'm sitting here today.' Jupiter! 'Now.' Macro smiled and steepled his fingers. 'How can I help you?'

'Ah . . .' I was trying to keep my jaw from sagging. This wasn't how I'd envisaged things happening at all; or maybe it was, in my dreams. Not that I was complaining, mind. 'Actually, I was hoping to talk to someone on your staff. Pontius Fregellanus.'

I was watching his eyes when I said the name, and there was nothing. No reaction. Zero. Zilch.

'Fregellanus? Why would you want to talk to him?' The orderly came in with a wine jug and two cups. 'That's fine, Titus. Just put them on the desk, pour and go.'

I waited until he'd done all of that, with due military precision. The guy probably went to the toilet by numbers. Then I said, 'I thought, maybe, that he might have something to tell me about the death of Sextus Papinius.'

I was watching closely. Zilch again.

Macro picked up one of the wine cups. 'That the youngster who threw himself out of a tenement window ten days or so ago?' he said.

'Yeah. I'm . . . looking into the circumstances. As a favour to Natalis of the Greens and the kid's mother.'

'So how do you think Fregellanus can help?' There was nothing in Macro's voice beyond polite interest.

I shrugged; this, at least, I'd been ready for. Not that I had a proper answer; not even a *genuine* proper answer. 'Maybe he can't,' I said. 'In fact, probably he can't. But I'm just checking round the lad's friends and acquaintances to see if they can shed any light on why he might've done it.'

That, at least, got me a sharp look. 'I didn't know Fregellanus even knew young Papinius, let alone that he was a friend,' Macro said. 'And frankly, Corvinus, I can't see that being very likely. Fregellanus is as old as I am, and, to tell you the truth, the man's a monumental bore. What would he have in common with a . . . How old was Papinius?'

'Nineteen. But—'

'With a nineteen-year-old lad-about-town?' He shrugged. 'Still, you know best, I suppose.'

'He's only a friend of a friend. But I'm trying to cover every angle. They may've been at the same party and he may've noticed something.'

'Sounds pretty tenuous to me.' The grey eyes rested on mine for a moment. It was like being raked by a fusillade of stones from an *onager*. Then he shrugged again and sipped his wine. 'Well, as I say, you know your own business. If you want to talk to Fregellanus then go ahead. He should be around at present. I'll get my orderly to show you to his office.'

I picked up my own wine cup and took a swallow of the wine: Faustinian, and bloody good. I was seriously puzzled: puzzled and relieved. Relieved that Macro wasn't showing any signs at all of being mixed up in this business, puzzled because the guy was so matey. Dinner invitations, indeed! Just wait until that one hit the mat. Perilla would have a fit.

Against all expectations, we were doing okay here. Time, maybe, to push my luck a little.

'Ah . . . there was something else,' I said. 'I was looking for a couple of men, centurions possibly. Sextus Aponius and Quintus Pettius.'

Was that a flicker? It was there and gone before I could be sure, but I'd lay good odds that it'd been there. Still, that was all I got. When he spoke, his tone of voice hadn't changed.

'The names ring a bell,' he said, 'although I couldn't swear to them. I'm afraid I don't know half my centurions except by sight. A terrible admission for a commander to make, but there you are, I've always been bad with names. They were friends of young Papinius as well?'

'Uh, no, not exactly. Or not as far as I know, anyway.' Even with this new super-friendly version of Macro I was treading carefully; keeping as close as possible to the truth without risking setting the guy's back up. 'I thought they might have some connection with a guy called Mucius Soranus.'

For the first time, Macro frowned. 'Oh, I know Soranus. By name, at least. What does he have to do with it?'

'Papinius owed him some money. A large gambling debt, so his friend said.'

'That certainly makes sense.' Macro drank some of his wine, a proper swallow this time. 'He's a bad one, that, Soranus. As far as any of my lads being tied up with him goes . . . well, they're no paragons, but I'd be sorry to hear it. You've met him yourself?'

'Yeah. Yeah, twice.' I judged the risk and decided to push things a little more. 'In a manner of speaking. The second time was pretty much one-way. When I got to where we'd arranged to meet he was dead with his throat cut.'

Macro set the cup down slowly. 'That so, now?' he said.

'I . . . ah . . . thought Aponius and Pettius might have something to do with it.'

'Did you, indeed?' His voice was neutral. 'Excuse me.' He stood up, went to the door and opened it. 'Titus!'

The orderly came in and snapped to attention. 'Yes, sir!'

'Sextus Aponius and Quintus Pettius. Centurions, I don't

know the cohort or cohorts. Find out if they're on base. If they are, I want to see them here as of five minutes ago.'

'Yes, sir.' The guy saluted and left. Macro closed the door.

'Let's have the details,' he said.

With that tone you didn't argue. I told him – not the whole thing, of course, just the circumstances of the rendezvous and what I'd found.

'Pompey's theatre?' he said when I'd finished. 'Why should he want to meet you at Pompey's theatre?'

I shrugged. 'That's a mystery to me too,' I said. 'But he'd been dumped there by . . . whoever killed him. Presumably the killer or killers chose the venue.'

'And you think the killers were Aponius and Pettius.'

Statement, not question. Well, the attempt at disguise had been pretty thin, and Macro wouldn't be where he was if he was stupid. 'Uh . . . yeah,' I said carefully. 'Yeah. It's a strong possibility, anyway.'

He went back behind the desk again and sat down. 'Corvinus, I've got a lot of respect for you,' he said. 'You may not believe that, but it's true. I'll take it you know what you're about here, and if you're right I'll see the bastards broken. That's only for starters.' He grinned suddenly. 'Not that I've got much sympathy for Soranus, mind, I'll tell you that now. He was an out-and-out bastard, and he had it coming. You know he was a blackmailer?'

I nearly swallowed my wine cup. 'Yeah,' I said. 'I knew that. Or at least I've found it out. I didn't know it was common knowledge, though.'

'It isn't. Still, he was all the same. Not that I'm suggesting that's relevant here, of course, but it's another reason why Rome's better off without him.' There was a knock on the door. 'Yes. Come in.'

It was the orderly. He was holding a wax tablet.

'Well?' Macro said.

'I've checked with the adjutant, sir,' he said. 'Aponius and Pettius were assigned to garrison duty on Capri, starting on the kalends.'

Macro held out a hand. 'Let me see.' The orderly passed him the tablet, stepped back and saluted. 'All right, Titus, thank you. You can go.'

Shit. I waited until the guy had left. Macro was reading the tablet.

'They're in Rome,' I said. 'I've seen them myself.'

He shook his head. 'Not according to this. Here. You read it.'

I took the tablet. Sure enough, there was the entry: 'Kal Oct. Cs Sex Aponius coh 1 & Q Pettius coh 5 Capri garrison.' Bugger. 'Who authorised this?' I said.

'My camp commandant Aquillius. He handles all that sort of thing. Although naturally I would've countersigned the order.'

'And yet you didn't remember the names when I mentioned them?'

'Corvinus.' For the first time Macro's voice sounded a little tetchy. 'Do you know how many of these things appear on my desk for initialling every morning? Temporary transfers, notification of leave, defaulter punishments and so on? And do you know how much *real* work I have to get through? I said the names rang a bell. Obviously this was why.' He spread his hands. 'Now I'm very, very sorry but under the circumstances there isn't much I can do for you. Perhaps you made a mistake, perhaps the men gave false names.' I kept my lips tightly shut. 'Of course I can and will double-check with Aquillius, in your presence if you like. I'll also send to Capri to make sure the men are there, although that may take time. Apart from that I'm afraid I can't help you further.'

Shit. Well, all that was fair enough, reasonable and better than reasonable. I knew what I knew, sure, but I couldn't blame Macro for not believing me. Or rather, not *not believing* so much as wanting external confirmation. And, after all, what more *could* he do, in practical terms? If the guys were on Capri they weren't, ipso facto, Soranus's killers; while if they weren't there, he couldn't put his hands on them anyway . . .

Or maybe he could; but then that was an angle that I didn't want to dwell on. Certainly not here in the middle of the Praetorian barracks.

'Yeah. Yeah, right,' I said. 'Still, wherever they are officially I've seen that pair twice in the last five days. And I'm pretty sure they murdered Soranus.'

'In that case they're deserters and will be dealt with accordingly when we find them. Not *if*, when.' Macro stood up. 'Now I'm not rushing you along, but I do have a staff officers' meeting in half an hour and I have things to prepare. Titus will take you to Fregellanus.' He held out a hand. 'It really has been a pleasure to see you again, Corvinus. Any time I can help, please feel free to ask.'

I shook. 'Uh . . . thanks. That's . . . very kind.'

'My regards to Perilla. And I won't forget the matter of the dinner invitation.' He walked me to the door, his hand on my shoulder, and opened it. 'Titus, take Valerius Corvinus to Pontius Fregellanus's office, please. And you're to make sure that he's escorted formally to the front gate when he chooses to leave.'

'Yes, sir.' The orderly gave another snappy salute; then, as Macro's door closed, he turned to me.

'This way, sir.'

I followed.

28

Fregellanus's office was practically next door. My tame Praetorian knocked and entered without waiting for an invitation.

Fregellanus – presumably the guy behind the desk was Fregellanus – looked up in alarm and half rose. A pile of wax tablets slid sideways and he grabbed them before they fell.

'Pontius Fregellanus?' I said.

'Yes.'

Small, nondescript, balding with the hair combed over the bald patch. Also, nervous as hell.

'Valerius Corvinus. I wonder if we could have a word.'

'Ah . . . certainly. Certainly. Of course.' I'd been watching his expression carefully when I gave him my name, and it had definitely registered, which was interesting in itself. No 'What about?' either. He turned to the orderly. 'Thank you, Titus. You can go.'

'Commander says the gentleman's to be escorted to the main gate when he's finished, sir.' The guy had come to rigid attention as soon as he was over the threshold, and his eyes were fixed on the plasterwork behind Fregellanus's left ear.

'Oh, very well! But wait outside.'

'Sir.' The Praetorian threw a sketchy salute, right-about-turned and exited, closing the door behind him.

'They're so literal-minded, the military.' Fregellanus gave me a jerky smile: it was obvious that the guy was more on edge than a cat in a glove factory. 'I'm sorry, you must forgive the mess, ah, . . . Corvinus, did you say your name was?'

'Yeah.' The subterfuge wouldn't've passed with an intellectually challenged monkey; but then I suspected Fregellanus didn't do subterfuge all that well. 'Valerius Corvinus.'

'I'm especially busy at the moment, what with one thing and another, so I can't give you very long. Still' – jerky smile again – 'have a seat.' There was a chair in the corner. I pulled it out and sat. 'Now what can I do for you?'

'First off, I was wondering whether you knew a couple of centurions by the names of Sextus Aponius and Quintus Pettius.'

The hesitation was just a smidgeon too long; like he was gauging the implications of the question and deciding which way to jump.

'No,' he said. 'No, I'm afraid I don't. But then I don't have many dealings – direct dealings – with the purely military side of things. If you're looking for the men then you'd do far better asking Aquillius, the camp commandant.'

'No, that's okay, I've already asked Macro.' Now *that* was a distinct flash of . . . something-or- other. Interesting. 'According to him they're both on Capri. Only they aren't because I've seen them here in Rome, and I'm pretty certain they murdered a guy called Mucius Soranus. You know him at all?'

No doubt about that one, either: when I'd said the name Fregellanus's eyes had gone glassy, and I thought he was going to keel over, but he righted himself. 'Yes,' he said. 'I do. That is . . . Excuse me a moment, it's just . . .' He filled a cup from the jug of water on his desk and drank. The cup rattled against his teeth, and some of the water spilled on to the desktop. He set it down. 'I . . . Soranus is an acquaintance of mine, yes. A casual acquaintance. We . . . you say he's dead? *Murdered?*'

'Yeah.' Again, I'd been watching closely. He hadn't known, or if he had he was a bloody good actor. And the news had rocked him seriously. 'It happened early yesterday morning. Or maybe the day before.'

'Indeed?' He refilled the cup and took another gulp; I had the impression he'd've rather the stuff was neat wine. 'Corvinus, I've . . . I'm sorry, but I've changed my mind. I really do have a lot of work to get through this morning, and I honestly can't help you. Would you think me very rude if I asked you to leave?'

'No, I wouldn't think you were being rude at all.'

'That's . . . very understanding of you.' He reached for the top wax tablet and gave me a ghastly smile. 'Well, it's certainly been a pleasure—'

'I'd think you were mixed up in something nasty involving your girlfriend Acutia, Lucia Albucilla and Domitius Ahenobarbus and were shit-scared I might find out what it was.'

The tablet dropped from Fregellanus's fingers. If he'd been rattled before, now he was staring at me like he was on the verge of apoplexy.

'On the other hand,' I went on, 'I could just sit where I am and you could tell me all about it. After all, you could be next, right? Your decision. Take your time.'

His hand scrabbled for the water jug, dislodging the pile of tablets again. This time he ignored them and they scattered. He poured and drank.

'Get out,' he said. The voice was hardly more than a whisper.

I didn't move. 'Look, pal, you're no villain. Not a real one, anyway. Why don't you make it easy on yourself? This is your last chance. If I know part of it I'm going to find out the rest eventually. You might as well save us both trouble and spill your beans now.'

'*You* look, Corvinus.' He was making an obvious effort to pull himself together; wasted, sure, but I had to admire the guy for trying. 'I don't know what fantasies you're indulging in, but

I assure you they're totally without foundation. Now if you've finished insulting me—'

Too late, and fake as a wooden sestertius.

'Sextus Papinius,' I said. 'That name ring any bells?'

What colour there was left in Fregellanus's face drained away completely. 'You mean the consul's son who killed himself a few days ago? I know the name, certainly, but the young man himself wasn't—'

'He was the son of Domitius Ahenobarbus. And the kid was murdered. Don't spread the first bit of information around, by the way, Ahenobarbus wouldn't like it. The second you probably knew already.'

'Corvinus, I've already told you that—'

The hell with this. I stood up, and his mouth shut so fast I could hear the teeth snap together. 'Okay, have it your way,' I said. 'Let me level here. I don't exactly know what you and your girlfriend and Lucia Albucilla are into yet, but I'm getting there slowly. And when I do find out, which I will, I'll fucking nail you to the floor. Understand?'

Without giving him time to answer, I turned and left, slamming the door behind me. Titus the friendly Praetorian was standing outside, still at rigid attention, eyes blank and fixed on the wall six inches from my face. The guy must've heard, sure, certainly enough to get the gist of the interview, but there was nothing I could do about that. Nor about the fact that six got you ten Sertorius Macro would have the full details just as soon as he could trot along to the commander's office.

Ah, well.

'You're ready to go, sir?'

'Yeah, Titus. Lead on.'

He took me back to the admin block, turned me over to a couple of squaddies, flashed me a crisp salute and disappeared inside.

The litter boys and attendant trolls were waiting for me at

the gate where I'd left them scratching themselves, picking their noses and generally letting the side down. Well, that was that done, and at least I was still loose and walking out on my own two feet. The way things were going, that was a bonus.

So. Next stop the Caeliolan, and Albucilla. I thought about dumping my mantle in the litter, sending the lads back home and walking the rest of the way, but I needed a bit of thinking space here. Besides, it was clouding over again and I'd no particular wish to get soaked. I climbed aboard, stretched out on the cushions and gave the lardballs the thumbs up.

Fine; so I'd rattled Fregellanus's cage for him. Satisfying, but not very productive. So what *did* the interview tell me? That he – and so Acutia – were involved in this business to their eyeballs, sure; but that they weren't responsible for Soranus's murder. Which meant that it hadn't been Fregellanus who'd given Aponius and Pettius their instructions. Which meant . . .

I was putting this off. Oh, bugger; it had to be Macro, it *had* to be! Macro was the only other obvious Praetorian link, and as Praetorian commander it would be easy-peasy for him to falsify transfer orders. Or even give the guys other, private orders countermanding the official ones. The *how* wasn't a problem; what worried me like hell was the *why*. If Macro was behind all this for reasons of his own then we'd opened a very large and nasty can of worms indeed.

Not that that was the worst-case scenario, either. It hadn't escaped my notice that Aponius and Pettius had been assigned to Capri. Gaius was on Capri. Macro on his own was bad enough. If Gaius was involved – for some reason that I couldn't even begin to fathom – with or without Macro's knowledge then we were *really* into nightmare territory.

Ah, well; we'd cross that bridge when we came to it. And hope the fucking thing had a far end to cross to.

★   ★   ★

I found Albucilla's house, a rambling, old-fashioned property at the end of a cul-de-sac. There was a carriage and a couple of wagons waiting outside: the sort of carriage you use for long-distance travel, when you're spending the night on the road rather than putting up with friends along the way or – gods save the mark! – lodging at inns. Slaves were ferrying boxes, trunks and various small bits of furniture out from inside.

The lady was planning a trip. Obviously an extended one.

I buttonholed a couple of slaves carrying an inlaid chest that could've held anything from clothes to a body. 'Mistress around, pal?' I said.

That got me a frightened glance from both of them.

'In the study, sir,' one muttered; and they hefted the chest on to the wagon, ignoring me completely.

Well, if that was the only attention I was going to get from the staff I might as well make my own arrangements. I went through the front door, pushing past another slave with a bronze lamp-stand, crossed the lobby and carried on into the atrium. There wasn't much left of the furnishings: they'd lifted practically everything bar the floor mosaics and the pictures off the walls. The study should be straight through, then to the left or the right, depending.

It was left. I followed the smell of burning.

Albucilla had a brazier lit in the middle of the room, and she was feeding it with sheets of paper. When I came in she spun round, her eyes wide with fear.

'You going away for a few days, lady?' I said.

She'd got a hold of herself now, although I noticed she'd glanced behind me to see if I had anyone else with me. 'Yes,' she said. 'For rather longer than that, Valerius Corvinus. An extended holiday, if it's any of your business.'

I sat down on a chair she'd obviously decided not to take. 'This has something to do with Mucius Soranus's murder, right?' I said.

She didn't answer, just . . . *looked* at me. It was the equivalent of putting salt on a slug. Then she burned another sheet. It
looked like part of a letter.

'Getting rid of unwanted correspondence?' I said.

'Yes.'

Time, again, to level. Where Albucilla was concerned, it
didn't look like I was going to get another chance. 'Who are
you running from?' I asked. 'Domitius Ahenobarbus or Sertorius Macro?'

No answer. She kept her eyes on the flames and fed in
another page.

'It's one of the two. It has to be, because no one else in Rome
has that amount of clout.' Still nothing. 'Look, lady, I know
you and Soranus were working together as a team blackmailing rich young smartasses. I know you seduced Papinius
and got him to tell you about the fire commission scam he was
involved in with his father Ahenobarbus. I know—'

'*Fire commission scam?*' She'd stopped, and she was staring
at me with her mouth open. Then she laughed. 'Oh, gods! You
stupid, *stupid* . . . !' She turned back to the brazier. 'Just go
away, Corvinus! Go *away!*'

Bugger. 'What do you have cooking with Acutia and
Fregellanus?' I said. 'That's why Soranus was killed, wasn't
it? Not just for the blackmail. There's something else. And you
think – you *know!* – that you'll be next.' I stood up, moved
towards her and grabbed her shoulder. 'Why did Papinius
have to die?'

She pulled herself free without a word. Then she went over
to the desk and began opening and closing drawers. Another
sheet of – presumably – incriminating evidence went into the
brazier. The room was full of floating bits of ash.

'Albucilla! Come on!' I said. 'This is your last chance! You
never wanted any part of this from the beginning, did you?
Tell me what's going on and I swear I'll do what I can for you.'

That stopped her again. She stood staring at me like I'd grown an extra head. 'I didn't want any part in it?' she said. '*I* didn't? Corvinus, you are so . . . bloody . . . *thick*! You don't know a thing about it. Besides, there's nothing you can do for me. Nothing anyone can do. Now just go and leave me alone. Find out the truth for yourself.'

Ah, well, if that was the way she wanted it that was how it'd have to be. I couldn't force her to talk, and whoever she was running from, Ahenobarbus or Macro – I didn't dare even think about Prince Gaius – she was far more frightened of them than of me.

'Okay, lady,' I said, turning for the door. 'Have a pleasant trip.'

She didn't answer. I doubt if she'd even heard.

Thick, right? Yeah, that just about covered it.

Home, and on foot, this time: the weather had picked up again, and I didn't fancy another half-hour of lolling around on cushions. I unlimbered the heavy mantle, bundled it inside and told the litter guys with their attendant trolls to go on ahead.

Okay; if I was being thick then what was I missing? Let's start with what we'd got for sure. First of all, a definite grouping: Soranus, Albucilla, Acutia and Fregellanus. They'd been involved in some sort of scam which *wasn't* – this, just now, from Albucilla – connected with the fire commission . . .

Only that didn't make sense. The fire commission link was the one that brought in Ahenobarbus and Papinius himself, not to mention sideline characters like Carsidius and Balbus. If I scrapped that then my whole case, or virtually all of it, went down the tubes.

Hell!

Don't panic, Corvinus. If I was stymied then let's look at

things from the other angle, the group itself. What would bring them together in the first place? What did they have in common?

The answer was, Not a lot. To put it mildly. The two couples were as different as chalk and cheese. Soranus and Albucilla were a pair of fast-living out-and-out crooks; Acutia was – on the face of it, at least – a dumb but respectable Roman matron, and from all accounts her boyfriend Fregellanus's idea of a good time was cataloguing his rock collection. Hardly a compatible *ménage à quatre*. Of course, there was the Sejanus link between the two women, we'd spotted that already. Still, that couldn't be relevant, not at this late date five years down the road. Sejanus was dead, his family was dead, the Sejanan party were all dead as mutton or rotting in exile. There wasn't even so much as a single statue to the guy out of the dozens that there'd been in Rome six years ago because after he was executed they'd all been pulled down and replaced with . . .

The hairs rose on my neck. I stopped.

Oh, shit.

Oh, holy Jupiter best and greatest!

Well, at least it was something I could check up on right away; not that I'd much doubt what the result would be because in its own twisted way it would *fit*.

Bloody, *bloody* games!

I'd been walking along Caelimontan Road, heading towards the Caelian. Now I took a right at the next major junction and headed for the centre of town. Just my luck to be completely the wrong side of Rome. Still, I was rested after the litter journey.

The caretaker would know. He'd said he'd been in the job since Augustus rebuilt the place, and it wasn't something you'd miss.

Bugger!

29

It was mid-afternoon when I finally got home, but Perilla was in the dining-room and the table was still set for lunch. She came off the couch like the upholstery had just spontaneously combusted.

'Marcus! Where the *hell* have you been?' she snapped.

Bugger, I should've thought of that: when the last thing you've told your wife is that you're just popping over to the Praetorian camp to have a word with Sertorius Macro re a mysterious death probably involving two of his soldiers, unscheduled detours on the way back aren't such a bright idea. And the litter would've arrived back hours ago.

'Pompey's theatre,' I said. 'No hassles, lady. Seriously.' I lay down on the other couch and reached for the cold pork and pickles. I wasn't feeling proud of myself where making connections was concerned, not proud at all. Albucilla's *thick* had been spot-on. 'Something came up.'

'Namely?'

'You remember that statue of Diana I found Soranus propped against?'

'Of course I do! What about it?'

'It wasn't. Or rather in a way it wasn't. I had a chat with the caretaker. The thing's new, only been there for eighteen months. Prior to that the plinth was empty; but prior to *that* – three years or so prior – it had another statue on it. Care to guess whose?'

She threw herself back on the couch. 'Marcus, I have spent

the last two hours worried sick waiting for you to get home, and I am in no mood for guessing! Just tell me.'

'Aelius Sejanus's.'

She stared at me. '*What?*'

'Yeah. That can't be coincidence. If we're playing games here – which we are – then we've got the Sejanus connection again. Whether we like it or not.'

'But we've already been through all this! Anything involving Sejanus *can't* be relevant! Tiberius and Macro together stamped out—' She stopped and put a hand to her mouth. 'Oh!'

' "Oh" is right.' I tore a bread-roll in half and bit savagely into one of the pieces. 'I made that jump myself about ten seconds after I came up with the theory about the statue. Sejanus is the key to this whole business, and I've been too fucking blind to see it. Macro was responsible – directly responsible – for hunting down and killing his supporters after the guy himself was chopped. Albucilla was Sejanus's mistress, and Acutia lost a husband. Acutia just happens to take up with Pontius Fregellanus, who's on Macro's staff and therefore has direct access to him on a regular basis.' I scowled. 'Hell! Of all the stupid, myopic—'

'Marcus, stop it.' Perilla was frowning. 'Let me get this clear. What you're saying – or are about to say – is that Albucilla and Acutia are plotting to kill Sertorius Macro. The motivating factor being revenge.'

'It makes sense. And don't discount revenge as a motive, either.'

'I'm not discounting revenge at all; in fact motive is one of your strongest arguments, and I have nothing against it. But you don't think there are, well' – she hesitated – 'inconsistencies?'

Damn. When Perilla adopted that tone you learned to go careful. I laid down the bread. 'What inconsistencies would these be?' I said.

'First of all, why *now*? They've had over five years, life has moved on.'

That one I was ready for. 'Opportunity. They're women – assuming the core of the conspiracy is Albucilla and Acutia, who've got the real axes to grind – and Macro's a public figure. More, he's the Praetorian commander. He's squirrelled away in the Praetorian barracks and he's got four thousand plus of the best troops in the empire to guard his back. Before they could make their move they needed an insider like Fregellanus. And before you say anything, lady, persuading him to join the team would've taken time and delicacy. He's not the hasty type, and he's no natural killer.'

'All right. But that leads me on to my second point. It's all very amateurish, isn't it?'

'Of course it is. It had to be. However badly they hate Macro, Albucilla and Acutia are the women they are. Acutia especially. She's a mouse, but even a mouse can turn given the right circumstances. And as far as Fregellanus is concerned, poor sap though he is, he was the best they were likely to get.' I reached for the cold pork stew. 'Added to which, who else could they rope in? Macro was pretty thorough. All Sejanus's supporters – his *real* supporters, not just the fair-weather guys who licked his backside while he was in charge – are either dead or eating beets in Lusitania. And if they're not then they're keeping their heads well down in case next time Macro decides to chop them off. Which he would. Lady, I am *right!*'

'Hmm,' Perilla said. She was twisting her curl furiously, and I had to suppress a smug smile. I was winning here, and we both knew it. 'So if you are right then how do the others fit in?'

'What others?'

'Ahenobarbus. Carsidius and Balbus. Not to mention Papinius himself.'

'Jupiter, Perilla, give me a break, will you? How the fuck should I know?'

'It's your theory, dear. It has to take everything into account. And don't swear, it smacks of desperation.'

Hell. The lady was right, at least about the theory having to cover all the angles. It didn't, nowhere near, even I had to admit that.

She was right about the desperation, too.

I filled a cup from the wine jug. 'Okay. Okay, admitted, I haven't a clue. None of them fits at present, not nowhere, not directly. But the root of this business has to be a plot against Macro, it *has* to be! I can feel it in my water! And at least it explains Soranus's death.'

'Really? Then let's leave the rest aside and begin with that.'

'Okay.' I took a swig of wine. 'To a certain extent, Soranus was in the plot already from the start. He was Albucilla's long-term lover and a natural villain. He'd probably've got involved anyway just for the hell of it.'

'You're assuming that he *was* involved.'

'Gods, lady, he's the one who ended up against the statue with his throat cut! Of course he was involved!'

'I'm sorry, Marcus, but that's not good enough to substitute for a lack of motive. Soranus had nothing personal against Macro, as far as we know, and he was a pragmatist. How did he benefit? I'm perfectly willing to accept that he was part of a plot to kill him, yes, of course I am. But I still need to know *why*.'

'Because he was blackmailing Papinius.' I took another mouthful of wine. 'Yeah. Yeah, I know, that doesn't make logical sense. But there's a whole chunk of this business that we're missing. Macro knew what was going on. Sure he did, he had to: Soranus was killed by Aponius and Pettius, Aponius and Pettius are Praetorians and barring Fregellanus who'd have no reason at all to kill the guy Macro's the only person in a position to use them, as well as having a credible motive. Plus he can cover his tracks by producing a set of spurious orders proving they were nowhere near Rome when it happened.'

Perilla looked up quickly. 'Did he?' she said.

Oh. Right. I hadn't given her the details of my visit to the Praetorian barracks yet. 'Yeah. Turns out they're both on the strength, only officially they've been on Capri for the last twelve days.'

'Ah. Now that *is* odd.'

'Damn right it's odd! Another odd thing was how matey the guy was. It seemed almost as if—' I stopped.

'Marcus?'

'Almost as if,' I said slowly, 'he didn't mind whether I knew Soranus was killed on his orders or not.' I shook my head. 'No, even that's not right. It was his whole mood. The bastard seemed actually *pleased* that I might think he'd been responsible.'

'But you've just said that, in effect, he lied by claiming your two murderers were elsewhere. That hardly squares with an admission of responsibility, even a tacit one.'

'Pleased is one thing, lady; an admission is something else. He wouldn't come out in the open about admitting he'd had Soranus killed because—'

'He'd have to tell you why. Or refuse to tell you.'

'Right. And that would put him square in the frame for being involved in – or at least knowing about – whatever the hell else is going on here. That's the side of things that—'

I froze. Oh, gods. Sweet immortal gods.

'Marcus?'

I waved her down. 'Macro is involved on the Papinius side. He has to be, because Aponius and Pettius were tailing me the time I talked to Caepio at the tenement. That part of it had nothing to do with Soranus and Albucilla.'

Perilla went very quiet. Then she said, 'Ah.'

'We've got a link between the two halves of the case, lady. For what it's worth, because I for one haven't a sodding clue on that score.'

She was looking thoughtful. 'You haven't considered,' she said slowly, 'that it might've been your Aponius and Pettius who murdered Papinius as well? On Macro's orders?'

I stared at her. 'What makes you say that?'

'It has a certain neatness, doesn't it? We have two . . . call them professional murderers. Certainly men used to killing, and far from stupid; *very* professional and very efficient. Papinius's death was meticulously planned and executed; if it hadn't been for your accidental witness across the landing you'd never have known the murderers existed. Doesn't it make sense?'

'Gods, Perilla, where do I start? I told you, Macro was *pleased* that I was on the case and getting somewhere! Genuinely pleased, as far as I could tell, not just daring me to do my worst because I'd never be able to touch him! His two murderers saved my fucking life on the Old Ostia Road when they could've just sat back and watched while the muggers took me out, and the case with me. And why the hell should Macro want young Papinius dead anyway? We've been through that before. He was no threat to anyone. He was a nineteen-year-old kid still wet behind the ears in a bread-and-butter job which—'

'But he was a threat. Somehow. Surely that's where Ahenobarbus comes in.'

I skidded to a halt. Shit, she was right; I'd forgotten about Ahenobarbus. We still hadn't fitted him into the picture, and he had to be a major piece. The guy was no lightweight. He didn't have anything near Macro's clout, mind, practically speaking, nothing like it, but he was in a whole different class from Papinius. And, I remembered with a faint stirring of the hairs on the back of my neck, when I'd talked to him I'd got the distinct impression that the guy was scared on his own account . . .

Scared. That was another thread that had run through this

whole business. Soranus had been scared; so had Acutia, or she'd looked and sounded seriously worried, anyway, the one time I'd seen and heard her. I remembered Fregellanus that morning, when I'd come into his office; I'd thought he'd been scared when he saw me, but the first person he would've seen would've been Titus, the Praetorian guardsman. And Albucilla had been fucking terrified. She'd looked behind me, too; perhaps to see if I'd brought any soldiers with me.

If Ahenobarbus had been scared then only someone of the calibre of Macro could've caused it. And the fact that he *was* put him firmly on the conspirators' side of the line . . .

'Ahenobarbus was involved in the plot against Macro,' I said.

Perilla went very still. Then she said in a quiet voice, 'You're sure?'

'Yeah, I'm sure. I should've thought of it this morning, after I'd talked to Albucilla. That's another bit of information you're missing, lady: Albucilla's skipping town, possibly Italy. When I went round there she was in the middle of packing. I suggested she and Soranus had been blackmailing Papinius because of some scam involving Ahenobarbus and the fire commission, and she laughed in my face. Called me stupid. Which I am.' My fist hit the table. 'Shit! They were on the same side!'

'But—' Perilla began.

'Excuse me, sir.'

I looked round. Bathyllus had oiled in from the house, and he was carrying a small box.

'Yeah, little guy. What is it?' I said.

'This just came for you.'

'Who from?'

'The, ah, slave didn't say. He simply gave it to me and left.'

'Jupiter and all the holy gods, Bathyllus!'

'Yes, sir, yes, I know. But there was really nothing I could do.'

'No message, naturally.'

'No, sir.'

'Okay, little guy. You're hopeless. Bugger off.' I took the box and opened it.

Inside was an iron key. Nothing else. Just that.

Games.

30

We stared at it.

'It's another key to the tenement flat,' Perilla said. 'Isn't it?'

'Yeah. Or at least I'd bet good money. Still, that's one thing we can check on now. Hey, Bathyllus!'

He was on his way back through the portico. He turned round.

'Yes, sir.'

'You'll find a key in the top left-hand drawer of my study desk. Bring it out, will you?'

'Yes, sir.'

I sat back. 'You ever get the feeling you're being manipulated, lady?'

'Mmm.' She was twisting her curl. 'Where did it come from, do you think?'

'My guess is Macro. How the hell he got it I don't know.'

'But he must've had a key! After all, if Aponius and Pettius did kill Papinius they'd need one to get into the flat.'

'Yeah, but—' I stopped. Something, somewhere, was niggling. 'Hang on, this isn't right.'

'How do you mean, it isn't right?'

'Carsidius told me that there were only three keys in total. Assuming he isn't lying, what keys do we know about?'

'The one Papinius took from Caepio's key-board to get in. Then of course there was Caepio's own duplicate on the ring.'

'Okay. That's two. Add the third legit, the one Carsidius's bailiff would've kept, that we haven't seen. Now we get to the crunch. There was a fourth key, the one that Mescinius found in Caepio's bedroom that he handed over to Lippillus and Lippillus gave to me. That's the one Bathyllus is going for, right? Only now there's this one. Notice anything strange?'

Perilla was looking at me with wide eyes. She'd seen the problem, just like I had. 'There has to be one too many,' she said. 'Even if one of the extras is identical with Carsidius's bailiff's.'

'Right. So if the one in the box is the one Macro's hit-men used to get in – assuming for the moment that they *were* his hit-men and Macro sent me the key – then where did it come from? And how does it figure?'

'Couldn't it be just an ordinary spare?' She shook her head. 'No, I'm sorry, that's nonsense. Why a spare for only one flat? And if Caepio had an extra key to that particular flat in his possession then it's suspicious in its own right.'

Bathyllus was coming back. I put the two keys together. They matched.

'Okay,' I said. 'Check. Always best to be sure. Thanks, Bathyllus, off you go and buttle.' I turned to Perilla. 'Fine, so we're playing games again. We're being told to think about keys. You want my theory?'

'Yes, of course.'

'Listen carefully, lady. I may not know where Macro's key came from, but six gets you ten the key Mescinius found in Caepio's bedroom was the one on the board.'

'But Papinius had that one with him when he died!'

'Yeah? Who says? Who says it was *that* particular key?'

'But—' She stopped. 'Ah.'

'Right. Caepio lied. He took the key from the board himself after the Watch found the one with the kid, so he could claim to me or anyone else asking awkward questions that Papinius had filched it. The key Papinius had on him when he was killed was one he'd brought with him.'

'But that would mean . . . Marcus, are you saying that Papinius had his *own* key to the flat? Why on earth should he?'

'Because he was a member of the conspiracy against Macro.'

'*What?*'

'Come on, Perilla! It all fits together. Take everything we said about the Ahenobarbus scam and apply it here, only for some racket involving the fire commission substitute killing Macro.'

'Marcus, I'm sorry, but we're back to the fact that Papinius was an ordinary nineteen-year-old young man with no particular talents. Now I'm perfectly willing to believe that his father Ahenobarbus might recruit him for some sort of skulduggery in the fire commission, but why should the boy be part of a plot against Sertorius Macro? Leaving motive aside, what possible use would he be?'

Yeah; that was worrying me too. The simple answer was, None whatsoever. The trouble was that I was *right*. I had to be.

'Okay,' I said, 'so we're still missing something. Let's run through the scenario, see if everything squares and where the rough areas are. Then we'll have another think.'

'Very well. Go ahead.'

I topped up my wine cup and took a swig. 'Fine. First of all, we've got the conspiracy itself. My bet is that it started as an idea with Albucilla and Acutia, just the two of them. Motive simple hatred and revenge: Albucilla was always a big supporter of Sejanus as well as being his mistress, while Macro was responsible for Acutia's husband committing suicide. Fair enough?'

'Yes.'

'So if they want to kill Macro then how can they do it? Not alone: what they need is an insider on the team, someone close to him who can plant the dagger or poison his porridge or otherwise stiff the bastard.'

'Pontius Fregellanus.'

'Right. Fregellanus isn't perfect, by any means – I'd say the dagger in the ribs'd be out for a start – but like I said he's the best they're likely to get. Now they have to hook him, and they're women, remember, so that means sex.'

'Marcus—'

I grinned. 'Yeah, well, take it or leave it, lady. We're talking the real, practical world here, and if sex isn't the only way possible it's the quickest and easiest. So. Albucilla's no use, she's not his type: she's fast, she's brash, she's too in-your-face. Fregellanus is the staid retiring sort with no experience of women, and if she makes a play for him he'll probably run a mile. Acutia's different: he'd go for Acutia in a big way, given time and care. In any case she's the one who makes the running, and besides, maybe she genuinely likes him. She bats her respectable matron's eyelashes at him, they talk about literature and rocks, and eventually she seduces him. You're frowning.'

'Not at the seduction,' Perilla said. 'That's reasonable, and I do take your point about it being the best way to recruit him. But seducing someone like Fregellanus is a completely different thing from persuading him to assassinate one of the top men in Rome. You said it yourself, Marcus: Fregellanus is staid and respectable. Also, according to Sergia Plauta he's never been interested in politics. Surely he'd need a bigger incentive than just infatuation with Acutia. If that's what you see as his motive.'

I rubbed my jaw. 'Yeah. Yeah, okay. Mark that as the first rough spot.'

'Fine. Duly marked. Go on.'

'So. We've got three conspirators. The fourth to come on board has to be Ahenobarbus, because . . .' I paused. 'Shit, *why*? On the conspirators' side, why do they need him? And on his side why should he join? Not hatred or revenge: he's got nothing against Macro personally that we know of, and he wouldn't benefit from his death. Added to which, he's well out of their league, socially and in every other way. There's no fucking *reason* for him to be involved!'

'Rough spot number two, then. Never mind. Carry on.'

'Right.' I took another swallow of wine. 'Ahenobarbus recruits young Papinius – rough spot three, again *why*? – and lets him into the secret. This is where Mucius Soranus comes in . . .'

'Wait a moment. Why should it be Ahenobarbus doing the recruiting? Why not Albucilla?'

'It's possible, sure. Not that it matters, because it comes to the same thing in the end and it doesn't explain the *why* any better. Still, if Ahenobarbus was responsible it'd fit with getting the kid his fire commission job, because that provides the in for Papinius as far as the conspiracy goes. Also, it'd fit with the timing: three months ago Papinius and his girlfriend Cluvia were still an item. Albucilla didn't come on the scene until later.'

'All right. Accepted. Go ahead; Mucius Soranus.'

'Yeah. I was wrong about him. Soranus wasn't involved in the actual conspiracy to kill Macro at all, not then, not ever: Albucilla told me that herself, or as good as. When I suggested that she hadn't wanted any part in the business from the beginning but had gone along with Soranus she just looked at me like I was mad. As far as she and the rest were concerned, Soranus was the spanner in the works. How he found out what was going on I don't know, and it isn't important; maybe Papinius said a word out of turn, maybe he overheard something and got suspicious, maybe he just guessed. The bastard was smart, whatever else he was, and he had a nose for secrets. One thing that's certain, though: Albucilla wasn't part of the blackmail scam, quite the reverse; she must've been spitting blood. That was why the pair split up.'

'So Soranus decided to blackmail Papinius on his own account.'

'Yeah. Hence the loan, hence – after he found out – Ahenobarbus stepping in. Damage limitation, plug the leak.'

'But why didn't Ahenobarbus simply have Soranus killed?' Perilla tugged at her curl. 'Oh, yes, I know we discussed that, but it would make perfect sense now. As you say, Soranus was a spanner in the works, an outsider, isolated: not even Albucilla would defend him. And someone like Domitius Ahenobarbus wouldn't have any scruples.'

'I don't know, lady. Rough spot four.' I sipped my wine. 'Now we come to the fifth conspirator.'

'The *fifth*?'

'Carsidius.'

'Oh, Marcus, I'm sorry! Ahenobarbus is bad enough, but at least he's morally questionable. Carsidius is a respected senator. Why on earth should he be involved?'

'Call that rough spot five, lady, but he has to be because that's where the keys come in, plus the whole Caepio business. Whatever else his job was, Carsidius supplied the safe house, the place where the conspirators could meet if they had to. Caepio was in on the secret. Again, he had to be because that's the only possible explanation for the cover-up with the keyboard. Also, for why he was so scared to open his mouth the second time I talked to him but insistent that Carsidius couldn't've been behind the kid's death. Not that it did the poor bastard any good in the end.'

'You think Macro's men killed him? Aponius and Pettius?'

'It's possible; but my money's on Ahenobarbus. Damage limitation again, this time in-house. And Ahenobarbus wouldn't have any problems finding a hit-man.'

Perilla frowned. 'Wait a moment,' she said. 'You've explained Caepio but not Carsidius. Why not stop with the factor? Ahenobarbus or one of the others could easily have paid Caepio to allow them use of the flat and turn a blind eye. Why should Carsidius necessarily know anything about the conspiracy at all, even if he was the building's owner?'

'Because he lied to me over the bribery business. The only reason he'd do that is if he had a personal interest: he wanted to cover the conspirators' backs, stop that line of the investigation. Damage limitation again.' I stopped. 'Shit!'

'Marcus?'

'We've got a sixth conspirator. Laelius Balbus.' Sweet gods! This thing was sprouting more heads than a hydra. 'Remember, the fake bribery story was a closed circle: me, Papinius's boss Laelius Balbus and Carsidius. Balbus claimed he'd talked to the kid in private, so if the guy was genuinely on the level Ahenobarbus'd know nothing about it. The tip-off to Carsidius had to come from him.'

'Oh, *Marcus!*' Perilla put her head in her hands. 'Listen to me, dear. I'm sorry, but this is getting more and more improbable. Ahenobarbus I'll grant you, he's the type, although as you say there's no reason for him being involved. But we've now got three perfectly respectable, law-abiding senators caught up in this plot of yours, Fregellanus, Carsidius and Balbus. Don't you think you're straining credibility just a little too far? Especially since we started with the motive being simple revenge?'

Bugger. The lady was right; I wouldn't go for it, and it was my theory. There were too many holes, and so many things just didn't . . . fucking . . . *fit!* I took an irritated swig of wine and reached for the jug.

'So we're still missing something on the motive side,' I said. 'Something big. Oh, yeah, sure, I can see Macro being seriously persona non grata with some of the more poker-arsed members of the Senate, maybe even unpopular enough and dangerous enough for them to want him in an urn. Given time and rope he could even turn out another Sejanus. But wishing and doing aren't the same thing. These guys aren't stupid, Perilla, and they know which side their bread is buttered. Macro's Prince Gaius's blue-eyed boy, Tiberius is on the skids and in a matter of months at most he'll be dead and Gaius'll be emperor. A conspiracy that took out Macro and left Gaius alive would be—' I froze as it hit me. 'Oh, Jupiter,' I whispered. 'Oh, sweet Jupiter best and greatest!'

And then something went *click* in what I had for a brain. Fool! Bloody, bloody *fool*!

Games . . .

Pastry-sellers . . .

'Marcus?' Perilla was staring. 'Marcus, are you all right?'

I reached out a shaking hand for the wine cup and took a big swallow. I'd never needed it more. 'Pompey's theatre,' I said. '*Pompey*'s theatre.'

'What on earth does—'

'*Pompey*, lady. The man himself. And a corpse – a murdered corpse – at the base of a statue. Put all of them together. They make you think of anything?'

And then Perilla had it too. The colour left her face. 'Caesar,' she said. 'Pompey was the enemy of Julius Caesar, and Caesar was assassinated at the foot of his statue.'

'Right.' Sweet gods alive! 'We're still playing games. The bastard who sent us the message wanted us to think of a dead Caesar. That's who the conspiracy's target was. Not Macro, or not just him: Gaius. The plan was to assassinate Prince Gaius.'

There was a long silence. Then Perilla said, very quietly, 'Marcus, what are we going to do?'

I shook my head. 'I don't think we're supposed to do anything. That isn't the point. Macro's already done it.'

'But—'

'I said *was*. Past tense. The conspiracy's busted. Papinius is dead, the rest of them, Ahenobarbus included, are running scared. Fregellanus isn't going nowhere, not from the middle of the Praetorian camp with Macro's eye on him. Six gets you ten Albucilla didn't make it past the city gate. Carsidius and Balbus – well, it's up to Macro what happens to them, isn't it?' There was an itch at the back of my mind. I reached for it, but it was gone. 'Apropos of which, Carsidius is someone I have to talk to soon. Just for confirmation, sure, but the guy has serious beans to spill and I may as well fill in the corners.'

'You said getting you to do something wasn't the point. So what was?'

'Fuck knows, lady. That's the first question I'm going to ask the devious bugger when I see him. After I let go of his throat and stop bashing his head against the nearest wall, that is.'

Perilla's brow wrinkled. '*What* devious bugger?' she said.

'Oh, come on, Perilla! If we're talking Prince Gaius then that clever sod will be in it up to his greasy little neck. Plus the games are him all over. No wonder I kept thinking of pastry-sellers.'

'*Pastry-sellers?* Marcus, have you gone completely—'

'I was trying to tell myself something and I wouldn't bloody listen. The woman – the pastry-seller – that Placida and me crashed into on Head of Africa. Her brother had a boarhound once called Lucky.' I could see the penny drop; yeah, well, once we'd made the Gaius connection the next jump was pretty obvious. 'Right. Him. Q E fucking D. *Shit!*' I put my hands either side of my mouth and yelled: '*Bathyllus!*'

'Marcus. Wait. One thing, the most important. How does Papinius fit in?'

The answer to that was obvious, too; at least, now it was. And it'd been staring me in the face right from the start. Fool!

I told her . . .

At which point Bathyllus soft-shoed up.

'Message to Sertorius Macro personal at the Praetorian barracks, little guy,' I said. '*Strictly* personal, remember: no one else to be involved, right, or you're cat's-meat. Use your fastest runner.'

To give him his due, Bathyllus didn't blink. 'Yes, sir.'

'Tell him I know why he had to kill Sextus Papinius. And tell him I want to speak to that slimy bastard Felix as soon as he can get his duplicitous arse over here. Exact words, please.'

'Yes, sir. Although the messenger may have problems with "duplicitous".'

'My heart bleeds. Do it, sunshine.'

He left.

Meanwhile I'd go on up to the Esquiline to talk to Carsidius. If Felix arrived before I'd got back then tough cheese. Let the bastard twiddle his thumbs and sweat.

31

By the time I'd reached Carsidius's I'd realised what the itch in my brain had been trying to tell me, and the last bit of the mosaic was in place.

Carsidius wasn't going to like it. I didn't much like it myself.

He was at home. Mind you, I'd spotted three or four unconvincing loungers across the street who looked hard and mean enough to've filled the same number of sets of Praetorian armour no problem, so maybe he didn't have much option. If Macro – and my old pal Felix – were anything, they were thorough. Carsidius, like Fregellanus, wasn't going nowhere.

A scared-faced slave showed me through to the guy's study, where we'd talked first time round. He was lying on the reading-couch with an open book-roll in his hands, and he looked like death warmed up.

'Ah, Valerius Corvinus.' He grinned like a skull. 'I won't say "welcome", because you're not, or not particularly. But you don't come entirely unexpected, and in a way I'm glad of the chance to talk to you again. Our last conversation left a bad taste in my mouth. Sit down, please. Flavius' – to the slave – 'some wine. We may as well be civilised about this.' The slave bowed nervously and left. Carsidius held up the book-roll, then laid it aside. 'Cicero, *On the Nature of the Gods*. A great man, a true Roman and a fine writer. I find he has a steadying effect. Now. Would you like to start, or shall I?'

'You were involved in a plot to assassinate Gaius Caesar and Sertorius Macro,' I said. 'The other conspirators were

Lucia Albucilla, Acutia, Pontius Fregellanus, Laelius Balbus, Domitius Ahenobarbus and Sextus Papinius. Fregellanus's job was to assassinate Macro, Papinius was to kill Gaius the next time he visited the Greens' stables. How am I doing?'

Carsidius had heard me out impassively. He nodded. 'All quite correct,' he said. 'I'm impressed. Incidentally, that latter opportunity would have occurred within the month. Gaius is in a very difficult position, you see: he has to be at the emperor's bedside on Capri in case Tiberius dies, and yet he can't leave Rome – and Sertorius Macro – unsupervised for too long. So he has to shuttle back and forth.'

'Gaius would've had a bodyguard. Papinius was just a kid. How would he do it?'

'You mean there's something you *don't* know?' I waited. 'Very well. You remember the story of Pelops and Oenomaeus, of course?'

'Ah . . .' Shit. 'Remind me.'

Carsidius chuckled: coming from that mouth, the sound was like a death rattle. 'Really, Corvinus, I'm shocked. Didn't you learn anything at school? To win King Oenomaeus's daughter Hippodameia, any prospective suitor had to beat him in a chariot race. Hippodameia fell in love with Pelops and persuaded her father's groom to substitute linchpins made of wax for the real ones. The wheels came off Oenomaeus's chariot at full gallop and he was killed.'

Right. Clever. A good classical education is never wasted. 'So Papinius was going to sabotage one of the cars,' I said. 'How would he know Gaius would play ball?'

'Oh, Gaius always takes a turn round the practice course when he visits the Greens, and he always uses the lead driver's team and chariot. It wouldn't have been difficult for the young man to arrange things in advance. He was trusted completely, and he'd had the run of the stables unsupervised since he was a child. That was why he was so essential to the plan. Papinius was unique, perfect. If he hadn't existed, or if he had not been the true, patriotic Roman that he was, our task would have been much more difficult. That's what I meant by the bad taste. To protect myself – or rather others far more important than me – I had to slander him to you, and I found it repugnant in the extreme. I ask his soul's forgiveness.'

'You couldn't be sure that Gaius would actually be killed.'

'No. But the way the prince drives . . . Well, let's just say that it would have been a miracle if he'd survived. Gaius has never lost the child's ambition to be a racing driver, and indulges it to the full whenever he can. Besides, as you'll appreciate, a staged accident gave us a far better chance of success than a more direct approach would have done.'

Yeah, well, that was true enough. As a common-or-garden assassin an inexperienced kid like Papinius wouldn't've had a hope in hell of killing Gaius. Still: 'Even if you did succeed you'd never have got away with it. There'd still be an enquiry.'

'Would there? Who would authorise it? Who would care? By that time Macro would be dead too. The assassinations were to be simultaneous, or as near so as possible.'

'Tiberius would still be alive. The Wart may be on his last legs, but he wouldn't ignore the killing of his heir, and he's no one's fool. He'd find out it was murder, and you and your pals would be up shit creek without a paddle before you could whistle.'

Carsidius got off the couch. Like I said, he was an impressive guy, tall, silver-haired, straight as a ramrod, and he was looking down at me like I'd just scuttled out of his salad.

'You think, then,' he said, 'that Tiberius didn't *know*?'

It was like being slugged in the brain with an iron bar. I gaped at him, and the silence lengthened. He moved over to stand beside the shelf of portrait busts, and I could see the physical resemblance: strong jaw, firm mouth, straight aristocratic nose.

Oh, Jupiter! Oh, sweet holy Jupiter!

'You're telling me he did?' I said at last.

'Not just that. The plan was Tiberius's own, right from the start. I told you when we talked before: I'm no traitor and I've always been a faithful servant of the emperor. The same goes for the others, the men, anyway.' He frowned. 'Do you think I, or Fregellanus, or Balbus, or even Ahenobarbus for all his moral shortcomings, would ever dare consider killing the legitimate heir except on explicit orders from Tiberius himself? Let alone Sextus Papinius, who was one of the bravest and most honourable young men I have ever known.'

Gods, this made no sense! Or maybe it did, and I didn't want it to. 'Tiberius wanted Gaius dead?' I said. 'His own fucking *successor*?'

'Tiberius hated Gaius and dreaded his becoming emperor. You know that yourself from your own conversation with him five years ago.' Carsidius smiled; again the effect was ghastly. 'Oh, yes. He told me about that, when we discussed things and I put that very question to him. "Ask Valerius Corvinus," he said. "When it's all over, naturally. Remind him of Thrasyllus's forecast and what I said to him about the consequences to Rome of destroying Sejanus." Well, it is all over, bar the shouting, although not as the emperor hoped, and I am asking you.'

Shit. I felt sick. If I'd thought the guy was lying, or been hoodwinked somehow – and the thought had crossed my mind – then I'd no doubts now. That part of it he couldn't've known except from the Wart himself, because I'd never, ever spoken to anyone about what had been said in that loggia on Capri. Not even to Perilla.

Still, you don't buck a direct order from the emperor. That was the whole point of this business.

'He told me,' I said, 'that Thrasyllus had predicted that Gaius would be the next emperor. And what kind of emperor he would be. He said that if the choice had been his, even knowing what kind of man Sejanus was and what crimes he'd committed, he would've chosen him over his grandson, or let his plots go unhindered. For the good of Rome.'

Carsidius was staring at me. 'Tiberius wanted Aelius Sejanus to *succeed*?'

'Yeah. In both senses of the word.'

'Then why did he destroy him?'

I looked away. What could it matter now? And Carsidius, by his lights, was a good man; I owed the guy that much honesty, at least. Let him have the whole boiling. 'Because Sejanus had murdered his son, who would've made a far better emperor than either of them,' I said. 'Also because – I'm quoting old Thrasyllus here – you can't cheat the stars.' I brought my eyes back to his. 'Only evidently, from what you're saying, he changed his mind about that.'

Carsidius went back to the couch and lay down. He moved like a man ten years older than his years; I could almost hear his bones creak as he settled. 'No,' he said quietly. 'No, I don't think he did. At least, not in the sense you mean. The good of Rome. That always was Tiberius's yardstick, wasn't it? Perhaps he simply thought it was worth a try, and now Thrasyllus is dead there was no one to dissuade him. But Thrasyllus was right all the same: you can't cheat the stars. Not even an emperor can do that.'

Yeah; I remembered that Thrasyllus had said that, too.

There was a knock, and the door opened: the slave Flavius with the wine tray. He set it down on the table, poured and left without a word. Without even a look.

'So,' I said when the door had closed again. 'What was the plan? After Gaius and Macro were dead?'

'Tiberius gave me a letter, a will, really, appointing his other grandson Gemellus as emperor. Or that's what it amounted to.' Carsidius picked up one of the wine cups but didn't drink. 'Useless now; if I tried to produce it I'd only hasten the young man's death. He *is* young, of course, only just eighteen, and not experienced enough to rule.' He tried a smile, and produced a rictus grin. 'That, incidentally, was the inducement we used to bring Domitius Ahenobarbus on to our side, or one of them. If you were wondering.'

'Yeah,' I said. 'Yeah, I was.'

'It's natural enough.' Carsidius's voice was dry. 'Ahenobarbus would not have been my choice as a colleague – I've never liked or trusted the man – but the emperor insisted. He has the ruthlessness, Tiberius said, which the rest of us lack, and that is certainly true.' I thought of Caepio, and my Aventine muggers, but I said nothing. 'Tiberius pointed out that Gemellus would need a strong . . . let's call him a regent. For a year or two, at least. As a member of the imperial family himself, Ahenobarbus was the perfect candidate. Besides, as you know, he was Sextus Papinius's real father, he had influence over him, and we needed Papinius. Perhaps the fact that when Tiberius ordered him to kill Gaius he was doing so as the young man's grand-uncle as well as his emperor helped too.'

Yeah; Cluvia had said the kid was proud of his family, and you don't get higher than the imperials. Stars in his eyes must've been right. 'You said *one inducement*,' I said. 'There were others?'

Carsidius hesitated. 'One other. Just one.'

'And that was?'

'A . . . something the emperor had from Thrasyllus. Just before he died.' Carsidius was frowning into his wine cup. 'You understand, Corvinus, this is not for repetition. I tell you because Tiberius said you could keep a secret, and perhaps it's better that someone else knows. One day Ahenobarbus's son will be emperor.'

A chill touched the back of my neck. 'Ahenobarbus doesn't have a son,' I said.

'Not yet. But he will.'

Sweet gods! 'Doesn't that, uh, make it even more dangerous to trust the guy? I mean, if he knows his *son* will be emperor then—'

'Why choose him as regent? Perhaps the temptation to seize power himself might be too strong?' Another rictus grin. 'Corvinus, we're not fools, nor is Tiberius. First of all – although of course we didn't tell Ahenobarbus this – Thrasyllus was completely certain that Ahenobarbus himself would never wear the purple. Second, Gemellus would have other advisers whom he likes and trusts far more than Domitius Ahenobarbus, and Gemellus, although he's young, is far from stupid. Third . . . well, it was a way to use the man's own greed and ambition for our own purposes. As I say, we – and the emperor – needed him on our side.' Finally, he took a sip of his wine: I hadn't touched mine, but for once I didn't feel like drinking. 'And now, if you have no more questions, and if I can't help you further—'

'You know Laelius Balbus betrayed you?' I said.

The cup slipped from Carsidius's fingers, spilling wine across the couch. '*What?*' he whispered.

'Yeah. It had to be someone, otherwise how did Macro manage to decoy Papinius to the flat and get hold of a key so his lads could be there waiting? How would he know about the flat – or the conspiracy itself – in the first place?'

'That's impossible!' Carsidius's face was grey.

'I'm sorry.' I was, too, but the guy deserved to know, and I couldn't leave without telling him. 'Oh, sure, I might be wrong, but I don't think so. It was Balbus who set up Papinius's death. Besides, he was the only one of you who didn't give the impression, when I talked to him, that he was nervous or afraid. He'd no reason to be, because he was working with Gaius.'

'How could he be?' Carsidius was staring. 'He's an honourable man, an old and trusted friend, as loyal to the emperor as I am.'

Yeah, right; still, it was a sign of the times. Or what would be the times, shortly. And loyal to which emperor? – the de iure Tiberius or the de facto Gaius? In another few months at most the question would be pointless, anyway. Me, I couldn't bring myself to sympathise with the bastard, let alone excuse him, but at least I could understand his motives. Maybe the distinction is the reason I stay out of politics.

Or try to. Sometimes – like now – politics sneaked up on you and slugged you from behind. Not a particularly pleasant experience.

'I'm sorry,' I said again, and turned to go.

'Corvinus!'

I looked back. 'Yeah?'

Carsidius had himself under control again, and he was sitting up on the couch. Even with his wine-soaked mantle, he looked impressive as hell, and not out of place among the busts of his ancestors at all.

'Perhaps I'd better say this in case no one else does. He may never have come to the proof, but Sextus Papinius was a hero to be ranked with any of the Greek tyrant-killers or our own famous names. Certainly he was more of one than any of his Domitii Ahenobarbi forebears of whom latterly he was so proud. He deserves far more than the footnote to history that he is going to get, if he is lucky, because it is very difficult for a good man to kill, even in the best of causes, especially if he is disinterested. And Papinius was a good man, in every sense of the phrase. He knew the risks if he failed and the benefits for Rome if he succeeded, and he chose accordingly, consciously and deliberately as a true Roman would. Young as he was, I honour him, and I grieve over his death, as will the emperor. Balbus has blood on his hands, as does Macro, and if there is any justice then they will both suffer for it.'

Yeah. Well, as a formal eulogy I reckoned it was the only one the kid would ever get; but at least it was sincere and from all I knew he deserved it. I raised my hand – there wasn't anything I could say, now, to the old guy, and he wouldn't want my sympathy – and left.

Felix.

32

He was waiting in my study when I got back, with Perilla sitting opposite and Bathyllus hovering like an anxious mother hen. He stood up as I came in.

'Valerius Corvinus, sir!' he said. 'You're looking extremely well. A real pleasure to see you again.'

'Yeah.' I turned to Bathyllus. 'Wine, little guy. Make it the Special. Oh, and a fruit juice. Bring them and then bugger off. This isn't for your sensitive ears.'

'Presumably my sensitive ears don't count,' Perilla said as Bathyllus exited and Felix sat back down again.

'Your ears are fireproof, lady. Or if they aren't and you want to stay you can go selectively deaf. Your choice.' I lay down on the couch. 'Right, you bastard: *why*? You had the whole thing stitched up from the start, you, Gaius and Macro. Why involve me?'

'We didn't involve you, sir, you involved yourself. Or rather, Minicius Natalis involved you.' Felix was looking fetching in his natty yellow tunic and green belt; but then for a slave – if he still was a slave – he'd always been a sharp dresser. No doubt he felt he owed it to his boss Prince Gaius.

'You know what I mean! The case was closed before it opened. Balbus had blown the conspiracy all over the shop, Macro's tame Praetorians had thrown Papinius out of the window as an oh-so-subtle hint to the rest of the conspirators that they were rumbled and you had the whole business laced up tighter than a vestal's corsets. End of story, roll up the book. So why the hell let me faff around solving a mystery that was no mystery at all?'

'But you got so much *pleasure* out of it, sir!'

'Felix, you bastard!'

'Sir, if you'd just calm down for a moment and think. What else could we have done? Once Natalis had called you in, trying to stop you would have been counter-productive; you know that yourself. Telling you the truth, that a pleasant-natured, inoffensive nineteen-year-old from a relatively minor family was intending to assassinate Rome's next emperor: well, would you have believed us?'

'I might have.'

'Oh, Marcus!' Perilla murmured.

I scowled. He had a point, at that: I wouldn't've believed *anything* the twisted, devious little bugger told me on principle, not even if Jupiter himself had come down specially to confirm it in a haze of ambrosia and backed by the whole bloody pantheon. And as for his loopy, amoral boss and Sertorius Macro . . .

'Yeah, well,' I said.

'Besides.' Felix smiled. 'Very shortly our conspirator friends are all going to be arraigned before the Senate on a blanket charge of treason or similar. Certainly something suitably bland: no details given, no explanations, just the charge and a resulting conviction nem con. You'll understand why yourself.' Yeah, I did: with the guy behind the treason being the current emperor *sensitive* isn't the word. 'Papinius is already dead; he won't be implicated or even mentioned. But the others . . . well, they include some of the most respectable names in Rome. Where men such as Ahenobarbus, Arruntius and Marsus are concerned—'

'Hang on, pal!' I was staring at him. '*Arruntius and Marsus?*'

'Oh, yes, indeed. Very much so. They were two you missed, sir. Not your fault: they had no role to play until the prince and

Sertorius Macro were dead, at which point they would facil-
itate the Senate's acceptance of Prince Gemellus as emperor.
But they were the first people the . . . old gentleman on Capri
approached.'

I sat back. Shit, Arruntius and Marsus! Still, it made sense;
more, it confirmed – if I needed the confirmation – that
Tiberius actually had been involved. Arruntius and Marsus
were gold-chip respectable: the long-term leaders of what Dad
would've called the responsible element in the Senate,
straight-down-the-government-liners who would've spat in
the eye of anyone who even hinted they might contemplate
or condone treason against the state. I'd met both of them in
the past, and whatever my opinion of them – Arruntius
especially – I could vouch for that. Where poker-arsed rectitude and good old-fashioned moral principles were concerned, you could bend iron bars around them. If the Wart
had needed a strong counterbalance to Ahenobarbus – which
he must've done – he couldn't've picked a better pair. And
with them on the team to establish the plot's moral bona fides,
persuading Carsidius and young Papinius to join would've
been all that much simpler.

'So you see,' Felix went on, 'allowing you to continue was a
sort of PR exercise. Prince Gaius will be emperor in a very short
time, and Macro will be his right-hand man. To begin a new
principate with a series of treason trials that would recall the
worst days of Aelius Sejanus . . . well, you can imagine, sir, what
impression that would have created. As it is, there will be at least
one disinterested person we can call on if necessary to confirm
that everything was quite above board and to provide hard
impartial evidence to that effect.' He smiled. 'Think of yourself,
Valerius Corvinus, as Gaius and Macro's insurance policy.'

Fuck.

Bathyllus came in with the drinks. I took a cup of the
Special, sank it in a oner and held the cup out for a refill.

'So they'll all be chopped,' I said.

'Oh, no. Most certainly not.' Felix waved away the cup Bathyllus offered him: the guy probably felt he was on duty, but there again he'd never been much of a wine drinker. 'For the same reasons I gave, Prince Gaius will be . . . magnanimous. We don't want any deaths, or even enforced suicides. Exile will be quite sufficient.'

'Papinius died. That doesn't say much for the bastard's magnanimity.'

Felix froze. 'Valerius Corvinus,' he said quietly. 'I have to remind you again. Prince Gaius thinks very highly of you; very highly indeed: the very fact that he took the trouble to assign our military friends Aponius and Pettius to protect you from any . . . excess that Domitius Ahenobarbus chose to perpetrate is ample proof of his genuine regard. He is now also . . . obligated. Very much so. Shortly, as I said, he will be emperor, and keeping his good opinion will be valuable. Do not, sir, push your luck, now or ever in the future. I'm warning you seriously as a friend.'

I took another swig of wine. The guy was right, of course: things had been bad enough when Gaius was a not-so-humble Prince of the Blood; now he was practically emperor the stakes had been upped with a vengeance. With that weathercock-brained egotistical bastard in charge, like it or not we were at the start of a whole new ball-game. And I wondered just how long the *magnanimity* would last.

'Okay,' I said. 'Point taken. One final thing, though. Why the games? The business with Soranus's body?'

'Oh, dear.' Felix smiled again. 'I'm afraid, sir, that was just a little naughty, but I couldn't resist it. Not that they were totally unjustified, because we needed you to solve the problem reasonably quickly. A few judicious hints were quite within the rules, so long as they were cryptic enough not to spoil your enjoyment. I hoped and believed, indeed, that the process of working them out might even add to it. And I did so want you to enjoy yourself, Valerius Corvinus. After all, where was the harm?' Bastard! 'You understood the implications of the statue, of course: the link with Sejanus and Papinius's intended victim being Prince Gaius Caesar?'

'Yeah. Yeah, I got that.'

'How about the place itself? Pompey's theatre?'

'Uh . .'

'In the light of the solution, sir. Gaius's planned assassination. Come on, you can do it; the answer really is very simple.'

Shit; this was like one of these examinations at school where the teacher asks you who Hecabe's maternal grandfather was. I found myself beginning to sweat.

Then it came. Bugger!

'The theatre's right next door to the Greens' stables,' I said. 'You could practically hit the door-guard with a rock from the top tiers. Felix, you utter bastard!'

'Oh, well done, sir! Well done indeed! Now the coin.'

I was on firmer ground there. 'That's easy, pál, we got it straight off. Soranus was taking bribes.'

The smile faded. 'Ah. *Not* the coin, then. A pity; I thought you'd really appreciate that one.'

I sat up straight. 'What the hell do you mean, *Not the coin*? Soranus was a bloody blackmailer! That's why he was killed in the first place!'

'Gently, sir, gently. You're partly right, of course, but there is more. A lot more. Do you happen to have it to hand?'

'Yeah. Yeah, sure I do.' I got up, went over to the desk and took it out from the drawer where I'd put it away with the two keys.

'You didn't notice anything unusual about it? *Special?*'

'Uh-uh. It's just an ordinary silver piece.' I looked at Perilla, who shrugged.

Felix sighed. 'Oh, dear. Now I really *am* disappointed. I'd hoped for better from you, sir. And from you, madam.'

Shit. This was getting more like a school test than ever. I half expected the guy to produce a birch-twig from somewhere and start tapping it against his palm.

I turned the thing over in my hand. 'It's an old one. Augustan,' I said. 'But so what? There're thousands of—'

'Look at the reverse.'

I did. It showed a figure standing next to a horse, and the legend *Germanicus Caesar Leader of the Youth*, so worn away that I could hardly make out the letters. Not surprising: the thing had to be almost forty years old. 'So what again, pal? Unless it's another cryptic allusion to the Greens' stables, but we've had that already.'

'Hmm. Ah, well, perhaps I was being a little too obscure there. Let me say, though, that it was the best I could get in the short time available because it was *not* an easy coin to find. I had to look through several bags at the mint.' He waited. 'No? Still nothing?'

'Felix—'

'Think of our conspirators, sir. Who was it who idolised Germanicus when he was young? You learned that in the course of the investigation, I'm sure.'

. . . and then I had it. Jupiter and all the bloody gods! I'd never have got that one, never in a million years! The twisted, devious, *clever* . . . !

'Carsidius,' I said. 'Felix, you *bastard*!'

'Quite, sir. We haven't finished yet, though. Look on this as a piece of extra information, completely outwith the case but possibly of academic interest. To you especially. Did you happen to find out about the only previous occasion when Carsidius found himself . . . well, at odds with the authorities?'

'Uh . . .' Shit, Crispus had *told* me that! Now what was it? Something about . . .

Oh, gods! 'He was acquitted of supplying army grain to the rebels in the North African war.' Bugger, the Germanicus scam, when he and Agrippina were engaged in stitching up the frontier provinces! The only gap I'd been left with, when I was putting that scenario together, had been in the south-west, the Africa-Numidia stretch; but then that'd been the least important area, and I'd ignored it. Now it seemed that Germanicus – or maybe Agrippina, rather, because she had been the real brains of the partnership – had had that part covered as well. 'You mean Carsidius was guilty? He was a traitor, part of the Germanicus plot?'

Felix was beaming. 'Of course he was. Although naturally he would not have thought of himself in these terms. Carsidius always was a fervent Julian supporter, which was why he hated . . . Well, we won't go into that.' Yeah, right: why he hated Gaius, who might be a Julian himself but who'd been responsible for shelving the remaining members of his family. I couldn't agree with Felix about that angle not being relevant – far from it – but the guy had his own loyalties, and up to a point I respected them. Still, it was yet another proof – if I needed one – that politicians like Carsidius could bend the truth when it suited. Even be blind to it themselves. 'It's ancient history now, and it doesn't really matter, but I thought you might like to know. Well done again, sir, you've redeemed yourself admirably.' He stood up. 'I think that's everything now. Unless you have any more questions.'

I looked at Perilla. She shook her head. 'No,' I said. 'That just about covers it.'

'Then I'll be—'

'Wait. There is one more thing. Not a question as such. Or not exactly.'

'Yes, sir?'

'What do I tell Natalis? And the boy's mother?'

'Tell them what you like. As far as we're concerned, barring any mention of Tiberius's involvement, naturally, you can even tell them the truth; although personally I wouldn't so advise. They may not want to hear it.'

Yeah, that was fair enough, although it would be for different reasons: Rupilia, because her son had turned out a crypto-potential killer, Natalis – his feelings for the boy aside – because the bugger would have a heart attack if he knew how close his faction stables had come to hosting the assassination of Rome's crown prince. Still, I'd think of something. I always did.

Felix beamed at us both. 'So that's that,' he said. 'Again – as always – my congratulations and respect, Valerius Corvinus. And I'm sure my master and Sertorius Macro would wish me to add theirs as well. No doubt our paths will cross again.'

Not if I could help it. But I didn't say that to Felix: the times were changing, and a comment like that could be dangerous.

He left.

Perilla was very quiet after he'd gone, nursing her cup of fruit juice.

'Well, Marcus?' she said at last. 'It's over. Are you pleased?'

I sank a quarter-pint of the Special. Powerful stuff or not, it wasn't having much effect. 'What do you think, lady?' I said.

Long pause. Then, quietly: 'Would you rather they'd succeeded? Assassinated Prince Gaius and Macro?'

I didn't answer. That was the question I was trying not to ask myself. Mercifully, it was academic: the conspiracy had been a dead duck before Natalis had even sent me his letter, and Carsidius and his pals were already living on borrowed time. I hadn't made a pennyworth of difference; I certainly hadn't been responsible for the whole thing going down the tubes. Still . . .

I'd slagged the Wart off practically all my life, not to mention career politicians like my father and Papinius Allenius. Oh, they weren't paragons, no, and at times they could be real out-and-out five-star bastards; times like when Lucius Arruntius and his broad-striper mates had been responsible for the violation and strangling of Sejanus's twelve-year-old daughter. I'd never forgive Arruntius for that, never, not even when hell froze over. But at least they were *predictable* and they *cared*; they had their code and they stuck to it, whatever the cost to them personally. The Wart especially. He'd been a good emperor by his lights, even if he'd got little credit for it and hated the job; and whatever he'd done, he'd done it because he thought it was for the good of Rome . . .

The good of Rome.

Livia had used that phrase to me, too, a long, long time ago. She was out of the same mould, a real, hard-nosed, first-class bitch, a murderess a dozen times over, no argument; but again she'd done what she'd done because she'd genuinely *cared*. Maybe, now, with the principate of Gaius looming, I could even sympathise with Livia. Gaius didn't care about anything, except himself.

Like I said, we were into a whole new ball-game. Yeah, in retrospect maybe I would've preferred it if Gaius and Macro had died. I suspected that, in a few months' time, a couple of years at most, Rome in general would agree with me.

Still, like the man said, you can't cheat the stars, and there ain't no point in trying.

I picked up the wine jug . . .

'Marcus?'

'Hmm?'

'Perhaps this isn't the time to mention it, but I was talking to Alexis earlier. Did you know that Placida was pregnant?'

The wine splashed on the table. '*What?*'

'There are certain signs, apparently. Besides the obvious one, or prior to it rather. Eating the cucumber frame could be one of them, but Alexis wasn't sure about that, he thought it might just be normal behaviour for Gallic boarhounds.'

I was goggling. 'Eating the—'

'Cucumber frame. Yes. Or most of it, anyway. In any case, he's quite certain she's pupping.' Perilla looked down. 'So I was wondering if . . .'

Shit; I knew what was coming, I just knew it! 'Lady, read my lips: we are *not* having a dog, okay? Especially not a Mark Two Placida. With that thing's predilections the father was probably star billing at the Games. Not necessarily canine, either.'

'Don't be silly, dear. And I'm sure Sestia Calvina wouldn't mind parting with one of the litter if I asked her.'

'Damn right she wouldn't! In fact she probably . . .' I stopped. Hell!

'She probably what?'

Probably planned it from the start, that was what. Bugger! Felix hadn't been the only one pulling strings in this case: we'd been manipulated *again*, right down the line! If Sestia bloody smart-as-paint Calvina hadn't known the brute was pregnant when she stuck us with her then I was a blue-rinsed Briton. Yeah, well. You can't cheat the stars, especially when they've got Perilla fighting their corner. And if the lady had decided we needed a dog – loosely speaking – then that was that. No point arguing, I'd only lose in the end anyway.

'Calvina probably what?' Perilla asked again. 'Marcus!'

I grinned and finished pouring the wine. 'Nothing,' I said. 'It doesn't matter.'

Besides, I couldn't *wait* to tell Bathyllus.

AUTHOR'S NOTE

*I*n at the Death is my usual mixture, in the 'political' books, of fact and fiction; so to keep the record straight perhaps I should distinguish between the two here.

Sextus Papinius and his death – at least in essence – are real. The young man committed suicide by 'throwing himself from a height' (*iacto in praeceps corpore*). Tacitus (*Annals* 6.49) gives no more circumstantial detail than that, so the tenement is my own invention, but he does go on to give a little of the boy's background and family circumstances (mother – unnamed – long divorced, over-indulgent up-bringing, suicide for financial reasons) which I've integrated into the story as and where possible. The link between Ahenobarbus and Papinius as father and son is, of course, completely fictitious.

The plot against Gaius and Macro isn't real – at least, not in terms of hard historical fact. What is true is that the people I chose for my conspirators – they are all real people, with the backgrounds I've given them – were prosecuted together in the final months of the year, at the instigation of Macro, for either treason (*maiestas*) or disrespect towards the emperor (*impietas in principem*), both blanket charges, with no particulars of their actual crimes being offered. Ahenobarbus, Arruntius and Marsus are all brought in on the frequently used charge, under these circumstances, of complicity and adultery with Albucilla; scarcely credible, as far as the latter two are concerned, given their advanced age and extreme respectability. In Acutia's case, the prosecutor is named: Decimus Laelius Balbus. It is interesting, in view of the nature of the charges, that Tiberius himself did not intervene or comment by letter to the Senate at any point; as is the information provided by Tacitus that he was having very serious last-minute doubts about the succession and about Gaius's suitability in particular. So, fiction or not, a conspiracy against Gaius and Macro is at least plausible, especially given the timing and with so many high-rankers coming to grief at once; while the emperor's involvement is *just* defensible, in fiction terms anyway.

What, though, was especially interesting for me is how many of the conspirators I'd used in previous books and made to act out of largely hypothetical motives which meshed perfectly with their roles in the present plot: see *Germanicus* and *Sejanus*. Apropos of this, I didn't know myself, until I found it out in the course of my research, that the 'real' Carsidius Sacerdos had been unsuccessfully prosecuted for supplying corn to the enemy in the North African war. *That,* again given the timing and the fact that he was a supporter of Germanicus and the Julian family from childhood, was truly fascinating. For me, as for Corvinus, it plugged a very significant information-gap and provided yet another of these eerie blurrings of fiction and genuine history, this time in retrospect. But, as I've said before, coincidences happen. If they are coincidences.

The Aventine fire commission is also real. The fire, earlier in the year, had destroyed a large part of the Aventine and neighbouring Racetrack district, and Tiberius had appointed Ahenobarbus together with the other three husbands of Augustus's granddaughters to head it. Neither Papinius nor Balbus have any historical connections with the commission whatsoever, but given their respective ranks their involvement

– and at the levels I've allocated them – is well within the bounds of plausibility.

On the other hand, Soranus's coin was a complete invention, and one I feel very guilty about. I'm not at all sure that Germanicus ever *was* appointed *princeps iuventutis* (Leader of the Youth), as Augustus's grandsons Gaius and Lucius were on different occasions; probably he wasn't, since the semi-military title was given by the *equites* (narrow-stripers, but the word actually means 'cavalry' or 'knights', and that is the context here) as a sort of recognition of the emperor's current tacitly designated successor. However, I did need all the associations, so once again purists will have to forgive me: I'm only a writer, after all, not a genuine historian. And Felix did say it was difficult to find . . .

Lastly, also real – perhaps surprisingly so, but there you are – is the contemporary prediction that a son of Ahenobarbus would be emperor; although of course this could have been backdated from hindsight by the Roman authors themselves. The future Emperor Nero was born to Ahenobarbus and Agrippina on 15 December AD 37.

Tiberius died on 16 March that year, five months after the story closes; helped on his way, so contemporary rumour had it, by Gaius, who then succeeded him.

I should say that at this point the surviving manuscript of Tacitus's *Annals* breaks off until it resumes ten years later with the downfall of Claudius's wife Messalina, who would, incidentally, have been a relative of the 'real' Marcus Corvinus. I will miss Tacitus enormously. My grateful, heartfelt thanks to the ascerbic old bugger's shade, wherever it may be. He has had his tributary glass of wine poured out, although it was not, unfortunately, Setinian.

My thanks also, as always, to my wife Rona for her patience; to Roy Pinkerton for the occasional fielded question; and

especially to our second dog Annie, whom we found aban-
doned in the Vosges two summers ago and who turned out a
complete – if highly likeable – barbarian, for supplying me
with Placida.

In her case I hardly had to invent anything at all.